Cole knew what Paige was capable of. Still, he was shocked to see that weapon come toward his chest.

There was no hesitation in Paige's movement.

There was no trace of anything clouding her judgment.

There was no pity in her eyes.

Sorrow, but no pity as she was about to plunge the crude weapon to the spot that would pierce Cole's body, destroy his heart and kill the thing currently attached to it.

"I've seen it happen, Cole," she said quietly "And I won't see it happen to you."

Without another word or even another breath, Paige dropped the hammer toward his chest . . .

MARCUS PELEGRIMAS's SKINNERS

"An amazing talent!"

—Robert J. Randisi

"Peels you right down to the nerve. A must-read."

—E. E. Knight, author of the Vampire Earth series

"A hell of a lot of fun. . . . Fans of Jim Butcher and Laurell K. Hamilton will definitely want a bite of this!"

—Jonathan Maberry, Bram Stoker Award-winning author of *Patient Zero*

By Marcus Pelegrimas

Skinners
BLOOD BLADE
HOWLING LEGION
TEETH OF BEASTS
VAMPIRE UPRISING

Vampire Uprising

SHINNERS

MARCUS PELEGRIMAS

An Imprint of HarperCollinsPublishers

This is a work of fiction. Names, characters, places, and incidents are products of the author's imagination or are used fictitiously and are not to be construed as real. Any resemblance to actual events, locales, organizations, or persons, living or dead, is entirely coincidental.

EOS
An Imprint of HarperCollins*Publishers*
10 East 53rd Street
New York, New York 10022-5299

Copyright © 2010 by Marcus Pelegrimas
Cover art by Larry Rostant
ISBN 978-0-06-198633-8
www.eosbooks.com

First Eos paperback printing: November 2010

HarperCollins® and Eos® are registered trademarks of HarperCollins Publishers.

Printed in the U.S.A.

10 9 8 7 6 5 4 3 2 1

Vampire Uprising

Prologue

Things had gotten crazy over the last few months. Wild dogs prowled city streets. People were infected with exotic diseases. Armed psychos killed other armed psychos. Freaks were spotted in Chicago and on top of buildings in Kansas City. Detective Kilmer shook his head when he thought about witnesses that came forward to tell stories about vampire attacks in his own city. At least some things had been taking a change for the better. He'd been getting real tired of those doe-eyed pretty boys staring longingly at him from every magazine cover on the newsstand at the convenience store where he got his daily Almond Hazelnut Cappuccino. But those were the stars of movies and television shows. From what he'd been hearing lately, the real bloodsuckers weren't so kid-friendly. Kilmer chuckled and sighed at the fact that he was wasting his time buying in to the bullshit he'd been seeing online and on the tabloid news shows.

"Strange days have found us," he muttered, quoting some of the classic rock he'd been listening to for the last hour. "You said it, Jim."

The industrial district was quiet at this time of night, populated mostly by homeless guys looking for a corner they could claim long enough to catch some sleep or a jacket that had been left behind by a driver of one of the many trucks parked in the lots outside of the warehouses lining 50th and Oneida Streets. Kilmer was in his late forties and had allowed a formerly athletic build to spread around the middle after he'd traded his uniform for a Detective's shield. He hated to buy in to those "cops and donuts" stereotypes, but he'd hit a Hostess Discount Store on his way to the station the day before and had picked up a good selection of treats for under ten bucks. The pure chocolate-covered bliss of Ho-Hos contrasted perfectly with a variety of frosted pies. An apple a day and all that. "Close enough for me," he said while picking up an apple fruit pie.

Thanks to his rearview mirror, he caught sight of a guy staggering up to his car who matched a description he'd been given earlier that night. Kilmer stuck his hand into the plastic bag on the seat next to him. When he saw he'd randomly pulled out a two-pack of raspberry Zingers, he put them back and replaced them with some chocolate mini donuts. He was grateful for his informant, but not raspberry Zingers grateful.

"Here you go, buddy," Kilmer said as he rolled his window down and tossed the donuts.

Catching the snack in one hand, the man squatted down outside the unmarked police car's window. He had a lean, muscular build and tanned skin. Bushy eyebrows formed a border across the top of a set of cheap sunglasses with light brown lenses. A thermal undershirt was stuck to his torso by a film of sweat beneath a layer of rumpled denim. "I better be getting more than this for delivering these assholes to you."

"How about the satisfaction of a job well done?" Seeing the almost disgusted look on the other man's face, Kilmer added, "Free tickets to the Policemen's Ball?"

"There really is a Policemen's Ball?"

"Hell, I don't know. You'll get the standard snitch fee. Actually, Informant's Incentive is the official name."

"I don't care what you call it," the man outside the car said while pulling open the pack of donuts and stuffing one sugary circle into his mouth. "Long as I get it."

"So you're the one that made the call? Larsen?"

"Yeah."

"What happened to Michael?"

"He's inside. I know he's the one that usually talks to you, but he couldn't get away and told me to make sure you came along before things got too out of hand."

Kilmer looked down at a little spiral notepad that lay open on his knee. On it, he'd scribbled notes regarding the principals he could expect to encounter on the bust at the warehouse. Michael's name was at the top of the list, followed by Larsen's. "All right," he said while opening the door and rolling up the window. "Let's see what you got going on in there."

Watching Kilmer exit and lock his car, Larsen asked, "Don't you have a partner with you?"

"Not for peeking in on a suspected fencing operation. If things go bad, backup's just a call away. Are you expecting them to go bad?"

"We've been telling you they would for weeks now. All that got us was a few squad cars driving by now and then before they found somewhere else to be."

"The uniforms didn't see anything and there wasn't one call made to us while they were here," Kilmer groused. "There's other shit happening in Denver, you know. We don't have the resources or manpower to lock down a bunch of empty warehouses just because you and your buddies say so."

"What about those meth dealers Michael told you about? Wasn't that worth something?"

"Yeah. It was worth diverting some squad cars to patrol Oneida for a few weeks. What the hell else do you want? Now what's so damn important that you called for me to watch this place all night long? I thought there was supposed to be some big bunch of stolen goods brought in here."

"Something like that."

They'd walked about half a block and had yet to cross paths with anything larger than a cat. Stopping to turn on his heels, Kilmer butted his chest against Larsen's shoulder to knock him off his balance. In a series of swift movements, the Detective had the other man pinned against a wall.

"Handing over those meth dealers bought you some clout, but it's all used up. You want to jerk us around to make it look like you got some cops on a string? That's a real good way to land you in jail right beside those shit-stain dealers you set up."

Larsen didn't get a word out of his mouth before something thumped against the window of the large, single-story building farther down the street. Placing one hand flat against Larsen's chest, Kilmer put his other upon the grip of the gun holstered at his waist. "Stay put," he said.

The warehouse was one of several in the neighborhood and was flanked by parking lots filled with semis that formed a wall between the building and the street. Skirting the closest lot, Kilmer headed for the building's main entrance, which was marked by half a sign sporting three faded letters. The numbers over the door were the same as the ones he'd written on the pad he'd left in his car and committed to memory in the time he'd been waiting for his informant to arrive. One window was covered by a set of old blinds yellowed by the sun. The pane directly beside it was cracked from the impact of a body that still had its back pressed up against the glass from the inside.

"Son of a bitch," Kilmer said as he reached for the radio clipped to his belt. As soon as his hand found the device, the person on display in the window was pulled back and slammed forward again with enough force to shatter the glass. The moment the body fell outside and flopped over the bottom of the frame, Kilmer saw the piece of sharpened wood protruding from its chest.

After drawing his pistol, Kilmer gripped his radio in his free hand and tensed his finger upon the key that would connect him to his precinct. Before he could bring the radio up to his mouth, a woman appeared among the shadows within the building and leapt outside to dash around behind him. When he turned around to face her, the radio was slapped from his hand.

"Stop where you are!" Kilmer bellowed while widening his legs and putting himself into a stiff-armed firing stance.

The woman who'd jumped through the broken window

crouched down like a coiled spring. Sweat plastered her hair to her face and formed a glistening sheen upon her narrow features. When she curled her lips back, it was as much a grin as it was a display of the long, sharp teeth extending from her upper and lower jaws.

Kilmer fired out of instinct, but hit nothing. The woman was no longer standing in front of him, but had sailed back through the window. A sharp pain made him look down to see that both of his wrists had been opened deeply enough to expose veins as well as jagged ends of bone that had been broken by whatever had torn him apart in less than half a second.

A cold sweat broke upon his brow.

He started to lose his balance and would have fallen if not for the young men that swarmed out from the building to catch him.

As he was being carried in through the window, Kilmer's head lolled to one side and the edges of his vision started to blur. The body that had broken the glass belonged to a young man somewhere in his late twenties. He convulsed with haggard breaths that were forced out in spastic coughs before sitting up and letting out a pained groan as the sharpened stake in his chest shifted. When he grabbed the stake to pull it from his chest, he was attacked by others dressed in ragged clothes that emerged from the shadows on all sides. Locking eyes with Kilmer while swinging the stake to defend himself, the man said, "You . . . can't be here."

Hands grasped at Kilmer. Some of them dragged him farther into the building while others tore at his flesh. Wet things slapped against him, most of which were tongues protruding from parched lips. He tried pushing the licking horde away, but that only angered the ones closest to him and caused even more fangs to sprout from slits in their gums.

"Put him down!" the man near the window said. "He's not part of this!"

More figures entered the room. There was no furniture to get in their way so they flowed in like a tidal wave. Trained to figure his odds upon entering any hostile environment, Kilmer counted ten of them before the assholes shoved him against a wall and went to work. Their knuckles cracked against his jaw like frozen iron and thumped into his gut. He struggled, but was weakened by the blood that had sprayed out from his torn wrists and continued to leak down his hands and drip off the ends of his fingers.

The woman who'd brought him inside was crouching down over another prone body that looked to be a male of average height with a slender build. As she loomed over him, the fallen man stretched out one arm to grab some kind of sword that was made of wood. He would have gotten to it if the woman didn't sink her fangs into his throat.

Everything Kilmer saw was blurred and only got worse as the blows hailed down relentlessly upon him. Years of training and experience on the streets of three different cities helped him slam his knee into the groin of one of his attackers and grab the face of another. If he'd had any strength at all, he would have gouged out the bastard's eyes. Instead, he could only watch as the son of a bitch pulled his head away from Kilmer's fingers and snarled to show a set of curved teeth that slid down along the inner edge of fangs that were already sticking out of his upper jaw. After those curved fangs were sunken into his shoulder, something was pumped into Kilmer's system that sapped the rest of his will and caused his mind to wander in several directions.

The man who'd been impaled in the window straightened up as best he could and raised the stake over his head. All of the figures around him retreated, allowing the woman to dash over to him and use the wooden sword to chop off his arm and kick him into the crowd lurking within the nearby shadows. Meeting Kilmer's clouded eyes as the amputated limb hit the floor, she asked, "Is this one a cop?"

Larsen told her he was.

"Bring that one with us so we can keep an eye on him," she said while nodding toward the sword's former owner. "We're almost done here."

Kilmer had never thought he'd consider begging for his life until he felt the points of both the sword and the stake against his midsection. By the time the woman pushed the weapons into his stomach, it was too late to do anything at all.

Chapter One

Ours is not a world of subtlety.

The wounds given to him by the man who called himself Jonah Lancroft were still wreaking havoc throughout Cole's body as the same man's words echoed through his brain. All the reporters, headlines, and websites lamenting the damage caused by the Mud Flu weren't nearly as interested in its cure. In the weeks following the epidemic, the number of cases had dwindled. Hospitals shifted their focus to more common tragedies and the story was eventually dropped.

Cole scooped some dirt from the pile beside him and tossed it into the hole he'd helped dig. He and Paige had been two of many who spent the last several weeks sifting through the remains of what was left behind. Whether Lancroft was truly as old as he'd claimed was no longer an issue. The man knew his stuff. He'd been a Skinner through and through, which meant he had taken meticulous notes about everything he'd ever done.

Cole felt guilty for keeping all those scribbled pages to himself so he could be the first to read them. But with the last panicky echoes of Mud Flu fervor sulking in the lower portions of news websites, and werewolf photos still coming out of Kansas City, it was Lancroft's thoughts on dealing with public scrutiny that remained at the front of his mind like the chorus of a bad song that had snuck in through a set of unwary ears and refused to leave.

Lancroft had written:

> Ours is not a world of subtlety. The common man will see what we fight just as they will undoubtedly bear witness to the war we wage. Skinners are human, which means we cannot control all that is seen or whispered about while we go about our tasks. We are mortal, which means we have no time to waste in educating the masses on what it is that stalks them.
>
> The uninitiated, either through choice or necessity, are ignorant.
>
> Too sheltered to know.
>
> Too stubborn to learn.
>
> That is how they must remain.

According to the journal, those words had been written in 1851. Cole didn't know whether he should be amazed or disappointed with how well that sentiment held up.

"Not a world of subtlety, huh?" he grumbled as he scooped the last of the dirt onto the pile and slapped the ground with the blade of his shovel.

"What was that?"

He'd been so wrapped up in his thoughts and his shoveling that he had all but forgotten he wasn't alone. "Nothing," he said. "Just thinking about something I read."

Walter Nash pressed one of his steel-toed boots down onto the pile of freshly turned earth and stuck his own shovel's blade into it. "You talking about Lancroft's journals?"

Furrowing his brow, Cole looked at the other man carefully. Although Walter's wide face was friendly enough, Cole wasn't quick to return his smile. "What makes you think that, Prophet? Another dream?"

While there was definitely an edge to Cole's voice, the reference made perfect sense when directed at a man who frequently saw the future in his sleep. At least, that was his claim. In the time that Cole had been among the Skinners' ranks, Prophet's occasional warnings were hit and miss, and his lottery picks hadn't panned out well enough for early retirement. For anyone who hadn't gotten used to chasing down shapeshifters or holding conversations with nymphs, that might have been impressive. In the mind of a Skinner, there was always room for improvement.

"Don't need dreams to figure that out," Prophet said. It was a cool night, but the sweat he'd worked up while digging and subsequently filling the hole added a sheen to his coffee-colored skin. Wiping away some of the perspiration trickling into his eye, he explained, "The only thing any of you Skinners have been talking about since you put the old man out of business is those journals." He picked up his shovel to smooth over some of the rougher spots on the dirt pile and nodded solemnly. "Too late to deny it now."

Cole sighed. Even though Paige wasn't with him, he half expected to feel the swat of her hand against the back of his head. He hadn't forgotten the other man was a professional bounty hunter, but he did allow Prophet's more unusual talent to overshadow ones that had been honed through years of tracking people down the old-fashioned way.

They stood in a field ten miles south of Salem, New Jersey, and about an hour's drive from Philadelphia. It was a calm stretch of flat land that was close enough to the Delaware River for them to catch a whiff of briny mist if the wind blew just right. Cole had picked the spot after riding in the passenger seat of a pickup truck that bottomed out with every bump it hit along County Highway 624. Since they'd stopped digging, the only sounds were the two men's voices, the rustle of wind against tall grass, and the occasional rumble of engines from the highway. Despite their relative solitude, Cole lowered his voice when he said, "The journals are supposed to be a secret."

"Then why mention them?" Prophet asked in a matching whisper. Straightening up, he motioned toward the pile of dirt under his boots and asked, "Why mention any of this to me? I'm not even a Skinner!"

"That's why."

Prophet's dark brown eyes narrowed intently as he said,

"Just because I help you guys every now and then doesn't mean I come when I'm called."

"You got here pretty quickly when I called."

"Because you said it was important. I believe the exact words were 'really, really' important. You call burying some dead animal important?"

"You know Henry was more than just some animal."

"Sure, I was there when he tore apart that little town in Wisconsin. You told me what he did since then. Hell, I think some of that Mind Singer garbage may have interfered with my dreams. They've been coming a lot easier since you two finally put Henry down for good. That doesn't explain why you need my help burying him."

"Fine," Cole said. "What's the standard Helping Me Move fee? Pizza and beer? I'll buy."

"Jesus. I wish I was taping this conversation. That way I'd have something to give to anyone who wonders why I refuse to join up with you guys. Hope you brought that useless touch-screen phone of yours because you'll need it to call yourself a cab."

Before Prophet could take more than a few steps away from the earthen mound, Cole said, "I made a promise to Henry that I would give him a proper burial. I couldn't drag him out of that basement on my own and you're the only one I trusted to help me."

"And that's because I'm not a Skinner?"

"Yeah. Another Skinner wouldn't let that body out of their sight. They also wouldn't have helped me distract all the out-of-towners who've come along to grab what they could after Paige, Rico, Daniels, and I did the hard work."

Prophet couldn't take his eyes away from the patch of overturned soil. "What the hell would they want that mess for? It's damn near stripped of parts as is. We had to carry it out in pieces." Just thinking about it caused something to rise at the back of his throat, but he pushed it back down again with a few well-timed swallows.

"Henry's still a Full Blood," Cole said. "There's more that can be done to him. Trust me."

"What about Paige? Can't you trust her with a job like this?"

Cole knew that he and Paige had pulled each other through too much hell for him to say the first words that flew through his mind. Instead, he opted for others that were just as true. "She's got her own problems right now."

"And the vultures that have been coming and going through that basement?" Prophet asked. "What about them?"

"They're Skinners too, but I've never met them and I doubt they'd be willing to part with the mother lode of all dead werewolves. I promised Henry a burial. That's what I'm giving him. I can't afford to lose what little sleep I get by being haunted by him."

Prophet let out a wary sigh. "From what I heard of the Mind Singer's voice, I don't blame you one bit for not wanting any more of that shit. So that covers this job. What about the journals?"

"I didn't distract you enough to forget about them, huh?"

"Nope. I also didn't forget how you said they were supposed to be a secret. If Paige is your partner, maybe you should tell her."

"I did. She's the one who wanted me to read through them before anyone else. I've already transferred as many of his computer files as I could to my laptop. Took the whole hard drive."

"And?"

"And," Cole grumbled, "for a man who's supposed to be old school in every sense of the phrase, Lancroft knew a whole lot about encrypting files. The journals were the first things I found, but there were other things too. Formulas for chemical compounds, techniques behind rune writing that verge on black magic—"

"Oooh," Prophet hissed. "Don't use the M word around Paige."

Cole smiled as he shifted his eyes toward the general direction of Philadelphia. "She still insists those runes are a set of 'complex rituals that tap into natural energies,'" he said while using the appropriately placed finger quotes. "Not magic in the slightest."

"Guess I see what she's saying there. When someone calls me a fortune-teller, I damn near wanna rip their head off. Cheapens the craft, you know?"

"Call it whatever you want, there's some scary stuff in that computer, and there's got to be more I haven't found yet."

"Not to mention whatever's squirreled away in that house," Prophet said.

"Exactly. Ever since we put the word out that Lancroft was killed, the other Skinners have been coming out of the woodwork to loot that place."

"Why'd you mention anything about it if you're so worried about them?"

When Cole removed the shovel from where it had been stuck, he started walking toward a ridge that overlooked a stretch of peaceful terrain to the south. "Between the nymphs and all the folks who were infected by that flu, there's too many out there who already knew something was going on. Someone would have done some digging and found out about the house in Philly eventually. As long as there's an Internet, there'll always be someone out there using it to dig stuff up that shouldn't be found."

"Kind of like those specs for *Hammer Strike 2*?"

Hearing someone from his new life make a reference back to his old one was jarring. It took a moment for it to sink in, and when it did, Cole still had to wonder if he'd heard the other man correctly.

Obviously enjoying the jolt he'd given Cole, Prophet laughed and swung his shovel over his shoulder. "I heard about it on a forum. Ever since you claimed to leave Digital Dreamers, I been keeping an eye on what comes out of there."

"I didn't just claim to leave. I was fired."

"I saw your name attached to some smaller projects that are supposed to be in the works. Or was that more Internet bullshit?"

"Damn, you really have done your research."

"Part of my day job is knowing what phone calls to make and which names to run searches on."

Since the alternative was to try to deceive a man who was not only experienced at dealing with liars, but legitimately psychic to boot, Cole said, "It's not bullshit. I've been knocked down to a minor consultant. Every now and then Jason will farm out some work to me. Jason's my boss."

"I figured."

"Compared to what I used to do over there, I might as well be fired from Digital Dreamers. *Hammer Strike* and some of my other stuff is still doing well enough to earn royalties, so that sends a check my way every now and then."

"What's with that wistful tone in your voice? Don't tell me you seriously wanna go back to designing video games!"

"And give up the glamorous life of a monster hunter?" Cole said while holding up a dirty shovel and gazing out at a deserted portion of the New Jersey landscape. "Why would I ever want to do that?"

"You ask me, the work's been doing you some good. You're in better shape than you were in Wisconsin."

Patting a stomach that had been somewhere between "a little soft" and "very soft" his entire life, Cole was happy to find a more solid surface beneath his black T-shirt. The belt on his faded jeans was new, as was the noticeably slimmer waistline encircled by it. Inevitably, his hand drifted up to a jaw covered by coarse stubble that was still too scattered to form a real beard. Scars from recent fights made it even tougher to grow decent facial hair, and even though his lineage blessed him with an unwavering hairline, he didn't have time to do much grooming. Whenever it was thick enough to be visibly flattened by a pillow, his hair was buzzed off using a set of cheap shears. At the moment, he found it to be more mossy than bristly. "Yeah," he chuckled. "No gym membership would have whipped my sorry ass into this kind of shape. There'd be fewer things trying to tear my head off, though."

"I don't know about that. I had one personal trainer who threatened to break my fingers if I touched another plate of goulash. That bitch was scary."

Cole had to take another look at the man in front of him. As always, Prophet was about an inch taller than him, had a good amount of muscle under his tattered sweatshirt, and a beard that seemed tailor-made to hide a scowl. Hearing someone like that admit to fearing a gym employee was just plain wrong. "I appreciate the help with this, Walter. And I'd appreciate it even more if you kept it between us."

"I know a few of the Skinners on this side of the country, but not a lot. They all seem to think they know every damn thing."

"They also think your dreams are bullshit, right?" Cole guessed.

"Yep, but they're more than willing to cash in their tickets when I give 'em the right lotto numbers. Arrogant pricks. You know some of them got Nymar working for them?"

"Have you ever met Daniels?" Cole asked.

"I'm not talking about a science geek consultant. I mean Nymar actually being called Skinners. Sticks and everything."

That one hit home. In the time that had passed since Cole's introduction to a werewolf, he'd become accustomed to the weight of his weapon either in his hands or in the harness strapped to his back. It wasn't often he was far from the specially treated wooden spear, and the scars its thorns had made were part of him. Creating it had been his first rite of passage. Learning to use it had been his introduction to the life of hunter. Killing with it forged him into a Skinner. "They're teaching Nymar how to fight with our weapons?"

"I seen a few vampires carrying them," Prophet replied. "Haven't seen them fight with 'em yet. Never seen the sticks change shape like yours or Paige's either."

"Then it's even more important we keep this to ourselves. Daniels has proven himself, and I don't even want him to know where Henry is buried. I'll leave it up to Paige to decide how much we tell him about everything else. There's something else I wanted to ask."

"You want me to keep another secret from Paige?" Prophet asked. He gritted his teeth and pulled in a hissing breath while shaking his head. "I don't know about that, Cole. Me and her go a ways back."

"This isn't a secret. It's from Paige directly."

Cole wasn't lying about that, which Prophet could tell after staring him down for less than three seconds. Even so, he was reluctant when he nodded and said, "All right. Let's hear it."

"She wants you to follow anyone that comes and goes from that house in Philly. Everyone but me and her, that is."

"That could be rough. You guys have struck a deal with the nymphs, right? From what I heard, you've all been coming and going through that temple Lancroft slapped together in his basement."

"She's more interested in the locals for now. Can we count on you to start your surveillance soon?"

"Soon as you do that job Stanley's been bugging you about." When Cole started to groan in protest, Prophet added, "He's my boss and he did bail you and Rico out of jail in St. Louis. Paige said she'd track down those fugitives in Denver that got turned into Nymar, and Stanley wants to collect before they disappear."

"We'll get on it."

"How soon?" Prophet asked.

"As soon as you start that surveillance."

"I got expenses, you know."

"And we'll pay them," Cole was quick to reply. "You can take a chunk of money now or wait for a bigger chunk later."

"I'm still not interested in becoming a Skinner."

"And that's the way, uh-huh uh-huh, we like it."

Prophet's stern exterior cracked into a friendly smile. "There's the cornball Cole I knew from the Wisconsin days. But KC & the Sunshine Band? Ain't that a bit before your time?"

"Not really. And Wisconsin wasn't that long ago."

"The hell it wasn't," Prophet said as he turned around to look back at the final resting place of a full-blooded were-wolf. Both men gave the grave a wide berth as they headed for the truck. "I got cop friends in Wisconsin that still talk about that supposed gang fight in Janesville. You sure the local PD hasn't figured out what's going on down in that basement?"

Cole shrugged. "There was plenty of commotion for a week or two after the Mud Flu thing cleared up. After that, the police have had the same ol' crimes to keep them busy. A fresh batch of witnesses stepped forward about Kansas City, which I'm sure Paige and I will have to deal with."

"You two are silencing civilians now?"

"No, but we need to find a way to keep things from getting out of hand. If we didn't have some friends of our own in the KC Police Department, I'm sure Paige and I would have been dragged in already. I've been back and forth from there and Chicago so much that the mixture of barbecue sauce and pizza grease are starting to form a new kind of toxin in my bloodstream."

Having arrived at the truck, Cole tossed his shovel onto the pile of tarps and garbage bags they'd used to carry Henry out of the basement. Without giving it a second thought, he'd reached into his jacket pocket for a small case designed for nail files, tweezers, or other toiletries that now contained little syringes filled with Nymar antidote and a healing serum brewed from an ever-changing Skinner recipe.

"Sauce and grease," Prophet mused. "That's why you need that stuff?"

The syringes were about the size of a crayon, and held one dose of their prospective contents. The one Cole held over the meaty section of his upper arm went in with a quick jab. "Lancroft busted me up pretty good," he said. "I'm still feeling it."

"I bet you are. So what do you wanna hear from me where this job is concerned?"

"That you'll do it." Reaching into another pocket, Cole found a flat blue envelope that was about half the size of a comic book and tossed it over.

After snatching the envelope from the air, Prophet opened it and pulled out a greeting card with a dog's face on it. It contained five hundred dollars and the words, *Sorry I forgot, but it's been seven of my years since your last party. Happy Belated Birthday.*

Cole put everything away and climbed in through the truck's passenger door. "They were out of the ones that said 'Congrats on being psychic.'"

"This'll buy you two days of surveillance."

"With a man like you on the job, that should be plenty."

Prophet tucked the money away and walked around to the other side of the truck. Despite the dented frame, the interior was in pristine condition. He sat behind the wheel with his keys poised in front of the ignition and asked, "Will I need to worry about some pissed-off Skinner coming after me for this?"

"If you're sloppy enough to get caught, you deserve to get your ass kicked."

"You guys ain't exactly normal, you know. Do you have any spray or some other concoction that allows you to see when someone's following you?"

"No, but if one of the others uses something like that, be sure to save some for us."

Prophet turned the key and pumped his foot on the gas pedal. "Listen to that engine. It's sweet enough to make me forget about working with difficult, foul-smelling, violent assholes like yourself."

"Foul-smelling?"

"You think you can work around that much dead shit and not get any on you?"

Rolling down his window, Cole looked out toward the spot where he'd buried Henry. It was a pleasant night in the latter portion of a hard summer, and the wind carried the river's scent along with it. Although he hadn't known Henry as much more than a crazy, rampaging freak, he thought the Full Blood would have approved.

"You think this is a good spot for a bunch of houses?" Prophet asked while looking at the same spot that had captured Cole's attention.

"Why? You planning on sinking some roots next to a dead werewolf?"

"No, but some construction company might find that thing. I doubt they'll make any sense of it, but still . . ."

"It'll be just one more weird discovery that gets lost in the shuffle of all the other weird shit that's been cropping up. We've seen people shrug off stranger stuff than that."

"What's this *we* crap? I'm the closest thing to a normal person you deal with on a regular basis, and we don't stumble upon the kind of thing I just helped plant in a hole back there."

Cole wanted to dispute that, but a psychic bounty hunter truly was the closest thing to a normal person that he dealt with anymore. Just as he was about to get dragged down by that particular revelation, something else sprang to mind. "What about the MEG guys? Stu's more normal than you by a mile."

"Okay," Prophet said. "Call them up and tell them about the possibility of Henry's spirit tearing the hell out of who- ever might disturb this spot. Wait for their happy squealing to die down and then tell me how normal they are."

"Check and mate."

Chapter Two

When Cole was dropped off at the house formerly owned by Jonah Lancroft, he was greeted by a small party of neighbors and a few vaguely familiar faces. He only recognized the neighbors because the large men wearing football jerseys and polo shirts under denim jackets and flannel shirts had been camped out on their porch across the street and halfway down the block for the last several days. It was a cool night, but not enough to warrant the amount of layers they were sporting. So far the neighbors had been content to watch the Lancroft house with what they surely thought were intimidating scowls etched onto their faces. Now they strutted across the street and climbed the curb as if storming the beaches at Normandy.

When he'd been a video game designer, those men might have put a fright into him. After what he'd seen in the last several months, however, it would take a lot more than that. Judging by the impatient expressions on the faces of the Skinners gathered on Lancroft's front step, they were equally unimpressed.

"What's going on here?" Cole asked the neighbors as he climbed down from Prophet's truck. "Block party?"

The man at the front of the group had a shaved head, clean face, and a gut that marked him as the source of a good portion of the empty beer bottles scattered along his side of the street. He wore an Eagles jersey. It was a custom order, unless the NFL had drafted someone named Madman and given him the number 69. "Yeah," he said as he shifted a cocky eye toward Cole. "Welcome to the fucking neighborhood. Maybe you should have a word with your bitches over there. They're not too friendly."

If Paige was within earshot, there was about to be one hell of a block party indeed. Fortunately for everyone involved, she wasn't. The Skinners in attendance were some of the local crew. Jory was a big guy who looked to be somewhere in his fifties. He was solidly built and hadn't spoken more than half a dozen words to Cole since introducing himself. His face looked as if it had been molded from too much clay behind a curtain of gray whiskers sprouting from his chin.

Abel was a skinny kid in his mid-twenties with a Mohawk long enough to cover half his scalp.

At the head of the Skinner group was a short blond woman whose face was too tanned for its own good. Her eyes were always bright, but were practically flaring after hearing herself referred to as one of the "bitches." Before she could say anything about it, though, she was shoved aside by another woman.

If the blonde's eyes were flaring, Maddy's were about to explode in their sockets. "What did you call us?" she demanded. Her dark brown hair formed a single braid that hung down past her shoulder blades. The structure of her face struck Cole as Asian, but her accent and complexion could have been Cuban or maybe Puerto Rican. When she was through laying into Madman 69, her hand was drifting toward the leather harness wrapped around her waist that kept her weapon pressed against the small of her back.

One of the other neighbors wore a sweatshirt with the collar and sleeves torn off in a fashion that might have been trying to fool people into thinking he was a beast. All it really did was put him at the top of the list of suspects who'd thrown all the little skinny cans of energy drink next to the empty beer bottles on the lawn. "Just chill, bro," he said while ambling over to pull Madman back, as if he was sparing the Skinners a grisly fate. "Let 'em think it over."

And just when it seemed the storm was about to pass, the dude in the sweatshirt looked over to the dark-haired woman and said, "These ladies know where to find us when they get lonely."

The blonde knew better than to get in Maddy's way, so she stepped aside. Cole was barely fast enough to put himself between her and the neighbors. "Come on, now," he said. "We don't really want to make a big deal out of this, do we?"

Maddy glared at him as if she still had every intention of drawing her weapon. Her dark green eyes narrowed and she grit her teeth when she told him, "Step aside before you get the same thing I'm about to give them."

"Ooooh," Madman sighed. "Sounds great. Come on. Let's get the fuck out of here." With that, he led the rest of his boys across the street and down the block.

Once the neighbors' laughing had sufficiently faded, Cole asked, "What the hell was this about?"

Maddy moved her hand from behind her back and shoved Cole back with it. "Those pricks came by to see what's going on in our house."

"Hey, Cole!" Prophet shouted from the curb. "Everything all right?"

"Yeah, we're fine. You can take off."

Like any other man with a functioning brain and any experience with the opposite sex, Prophet knew when to clear out of a bad situation. If that meant abandoning a friend, so be it. He pulled away and drove down the street.

When she leaned to look past Cole, Maddy's braid swung behind her. If not for the fact that she seemed ready to strangle him with it, he would have found it very appealing. She and the rest of the Skinners were covered in several layers of sweat that had soaked through dirty clothes. Maddy wore a dark gray wife beater that clung to her gritty skin like a coat of paint. Even though Cole was able to keep his eyes from wandering, she looked disgusted with him all the same. "You take that Full Blood meat out of here?" she asked.

"Did you see me take anything out of here?"

Without any proof to use as ammunition, Maddy stormed into the house.

Cole shifted his focus to the remaining three Skinners standing outside the front door. "You guys are from around here, right?"

Jory nodded.

"So do you know those meatheads across the street?"

Abel turned his back on him before grunting, "Do you know everyone in your territory? I'd guess probably not, since you and Paige were supposed to be watching KC when it fell."

Cole stepped up to the guy with the Mohawk. Since he'd never gone toe-to-toe with him, he hadn't realized how much taller he was than Abel. "Right, but you're the ones who had Lancroft living in your own damn city. Couldn't you have kept a closer eye on things before they went *this* far into the shitter?"

"This is a big city, not some stretch of prairie like you're used to."

"Chicago's a stretch of prairie? What the hell's wrong with you? Take your hands off me, Selina!"

The blonde had grabbed Cole by the arm and pulled him back. After letting him go, she turned to Abel and said, "This isn't the place to talk about our business."

Following her line of sight, Cole saw that Madman 69 and his other buddies had plopped into lawn chairs on their porch and were cracking open a fresh round of drinks. All of the Skinners stomped inside and slammed the door shut. The house was protected and cloaked by a series of runes etched into the walls, but Cole only knew three men who could use them with any degree of accuracy. Lancroft was at the top of the list, but he was dead. Ned Post used similar runes to protect his home in St. Louis, but he was also dead. That left Rico. Unfortunately, he'd gone his own way soon after Lancroft had been dealt with. Before leaving, he'd shown several of the remaining Skinners how to activate or deactivate the runes cloaking the door to the basement. Since the rest of the angular markings were more complicated than glorified switches, everyone just left them alone.

For the moment, the door to the basement was just as visible as any other. Beyond it, a cement stairwell led down to a workshop filled with benches and several sets of tools. The grisly works in progress Lancroft had left behind were all gone, leaving only the scent of rotten meat and burnt leather to mark their passing. Skinners from across the country had been coming to look at Lancroft's place over the last several days and were taking as much of the old man's belongings as they could carry. Supplies it took months or years to find in the field could be found in neat stacks of old mason jars and tool boxes. Lancroft even had racks of handcrafted weapons, some of which still bore bloodstains from their previous owners upon the handles' thorns. Cole didn't even know there were so many Skinners to be found, and with a pulse of green light from the next room accented by the scent of freshly cut trees, more arrived from parts unknown.

Stepping into the next room, he was always happy to watch the Dryads at work. Based in clubs around the country, the nymphs had been sticking to their word and allowing Skinners to use their temples as a means of transportation. They resisted parting with the knowledge of exactly how the process worked, but that was fine by him. Sometimes it was nice to just sit back and enjoy the show.

The man who emerged from the enchanted room's glowing beaded curtain didn't seem at all concerned with the miracle of being teleported by mythological strippers. Somehow, even the faint whiff of expensive body spray following him through his end of the bridge wasn't enough to brighten the man's mood. "What the fuck is this that I hear about the Full Blood going missing?"

He was a bulky man in shredded jeans, scuffed boots, and a simple black work shirt that looked as if it had been stolen from a mechanic. The hand he raised was so scarred that it could very well have been sewn onto his wrist after Frankenstein's monster was through with it. "You," he said, while aiming a callused finger at Cole. "Are you one of them from Chicago?"

"Yeah," Paige said as she stepped out of a small, brightly

lit room where Lancroft had cut Henry into the chunks Cole so recently buried. "And I'm the other one."

Paige hadn't stepped foot out of the basement for more than an hour or two over the last several days, and it showed. Her skin was pale. Dark circles ringed her eyes and her newly sheared hair hung limply around her face. "What are you doing here, Jessup? Didn't I just tell you there's nothing to see that your little trainees hadn't already seen?"

The phone still clutched in Jessup's other fist looked like a toy that was about to be broken into pieces. Stuffing it into his pocket, he stepped away from the curtain of shimmering beads and glanced over both of his shoulders. What he saw was a large room with walls covered in flowing Dryad script. Behind him were the women whose song had created the bridge connecting one temple to another. Now that they were done singing, the ridiculously beautiful nymphs strutted out of the basement for some fresh air. Having already encountered the loudmouth neighbors, they knew well enough to head to the poorly tended backyard.

"Where the hell are those broads going?" Jessup asked.

All of the people in the temple were riveted by the sight of the Dryads. Even though they normally wore something much more provocative than the sweats and baby doll shirts these two had on, they exuded raw femininity that reached down through every human sensory organ to caress the recipient from the inside out. Paige and Cole weren't immune to the effect, but they'd felt it enough to know how to brace themselves.

Closing the distance between herself and Jessup with a few powerful strides, she reminded him, "The deal was for them to help us with transport when we needed it. Not act as a subway system with flights leaving every hour. They're pushing it as it is to run everyone through their temples for as long as they have."

"I had to go to some shithole club an hour's drive from Helena."

"And you won't be able to return for another three hours."

"Maybe I'll stay. Looks like this place could use some real

leadership." Gritting his teeth, Jessup stalked toward Cole and growled, "What's so goddamn funny?"

"You've had quite a day," Cole said. "To Helena and back."

Jessup gazed at him like Roosevelt looking down from Mount Rushmore.

In too deep to back out now, Cole asked, "You got any flying rodents in Montana or did they all fly away like bats out of—"

"Am I supposed to believe *the* Jonah Lancroft was taken down by you two?"

Paige nodded confidently to Jessup as she replied, "Yep. You can also believe that Boise was one of the cities hit hardest by Lancroft's Mud Flu. According to his records, he was there to plant the virus himself." She scratched her head, feeling one of the spots that had recently gotten a major trim. "Isn't Idaho your territory?"

"And what about Wyoming?" Cole asked. "I've seen some videos on the net of some pretty bad Mongrel activity."

Jessup stomped past Cole and Paige, waving them off like a cranky old fart dismissing the bells and whistles of modern technology. "Stuff that Web garbage up your asses where it came from. Let me get a look at this place."

After he passed her, Paige was all smiles. She was still smiling when she wrapped an arm around Cole and led him to the far side of the room where there was a better chance of speaking in what would have to pass for privacy.

Cole ran his hand along the back of her head, feeling the hair cut drastically short to match the clump she'd been forced to hack off during her fight with Lancroft. From the back of her neck and up to the bump on the back of her skull, her black hair had been clipped to a soft bristle. The front and sides were still long, but in a long bob that swooped down to frame her cheeks like a set of wispy, inverted horns. Keeping his fingertips on the clipped portion in back, Cole said, "I like the new look. Feels goo— *Ow!*"

Interrupted by a lock applied to his hand that turned it against his wrist in a very uncomfortable way, Cole was quickly reminded of one thing: the hair might have been different, but the woman beneath it was very much the same.

"Where's that frickin' body?" she snapped. Before Cole could give so much as a peep in his defense, she tightened the lock and added, "And you should think verrrry carefully before you ask me 'What body?'"

"Do we really want to discuss this now?" he whispered.

"Yes." Paige let him go and marched back to the room with the workbenches. Jessup and several others shouted for her, but she ignored those tersely worded requests and went all the way up to the main floor of the house.

Cole followed behind her, doing his best not to return the stern glares coming from any number of Skinners sifting through the creations and unfinished projects that Lancroft had left behind. Upstairs, only one of the locals remained. As soon as they saw Paige and Cole emerge from the basement, Abel promptly turned his back on them and joined the rest of his crew outside.

Apart from the runes etched into the walls, there wasn't much of anything to see on the main floor of the house. Furnishings were limited to a few folding chairs that had only recently been brought in and several coolers strewn around the kitchen.

"Told you we should've kept this place a secret," Cole grumbled.

"We did for the first few days," Paige replied. "After that, it was only a matter of time before Jory and those other two showed up."

"Where the hell were they when Lancroft was here? If they're supposed to be locals, how come we didn't know about them until they came to grab this stuff?"

"Abel, Selina, and Jory broke contact with MEG about the same time that Gerald and Brad took their trip into Canada."

No matter what Cole was thinking about, it was always wiped away when those names were mentioned. Gerald and Brad were the first Skinners he'd ever met, and they were ripped to shreds in front of him by a Full Blood he'd come to know as Mr. Burkis. Nothing had been the same after that.

Nothing.

"A lot of things could have happened between these Philly guys and MEG," she continued. "Not all of us are as fond of the ghost guys as you are." When she saw the look in Cole's eyes, Paige sighed and admitted, "Fine. As *we* are. The point is, this bunch isn't the first to go off the grid. Selina says they were forced to go into hiding when some cops were getting close to putting them away."

"What'd they do to get in trouble with the cops?"

"Their job, Cole. See, that's the problem with being the only ones who know about things like Nymar. We see vampires while everyone else sees a bunch of strutting dickheads with smooth skin and black tattoos. Knocking around assholes like that isn't exactly legal. Shooting them or injecting poison into their veins is most definitely frowned upon. The good news is that Selina claims to have made some friends in the Philadelphia PD after resolving their little problem. And speaking of a little problem, where's that frickin' body?"

Over the past few months, Cole had been acquiring many new skills. He was getting better with his weapon. He'd picked up on methods used to track creatures of the night. He could even fix mac and cheese in five exotic ways. Lying to Paige, on the other hand, wasn't exactly a skill. It was a risk to life and limb.

"I buried it," he said.

"You what?"

"Buried it."

As one question piled on top of another, Paige's face went through a series of contortions. The expression he'd least expected for her to settle on was calmness. As a surprise bonus, she actually smirked. "How the hell did you manage to get that thing out of here when everyone else was rummaging around?"

"I asked Prophet to help me wrap it up and carry it out after the last batch of looters were teleported out of here," he admitted. "The nymphs only zap us around twice a day, so I waited for one of those times when most of the house was cleared out. Even the Philly crew drove away to get something to eat. When all the planets aligned, Prophet and I carried Henry out of here and drove him somewhere to be buried."

"Why didn't you tell me?"

"Because you've had enough on your mind." When he said that, Cole glanced down at her right arm. After a particularly unsuccessful field test of the tattoo ink that still itched under his skin, Paige's arm had been rendered close to useless. Her skin was still soft, but several discolorations that might have been internalized scars had begun appearing on the surface. Through a lot of hard work and base-level stubbornness, she'd moved beyond the need for a sling. Her arm was still stiff and gave her the occasional twitch of pain, which meant a lot if someone as hard-headed as Paige was doing the twitching.

Balling her right hand into a fist, she said, "Don't give me that bullshit. You knew I'd tell you what a stupid fucking idea that was."

"Yeah. Pretty much."

"So where did you take him?"

"Aren't you going to ask me why I took him?"

"No," she snapped. "First tell me where."

After a few seconds of deliberation Cole replied, "Nah. Everyone else seems to be able to do whatever they feel like no matter what, so now's my turn. Some get to come in here and demand or just steal anything we fought and bled for. Fine. Others spend their time looking through every last bit of work that Lancroft did without so much as a thank-you to the ones who kept the old man from killing more people to spread his plague. I guess that's supposed to be fine too. Those assholes across the street decide to come over and start their shit? Whatever. They might as well, right?"

"Cole, things are just crazy right now."

"They haven't been any other way since I can remember!" Lowering his voice and stepping closer to her, he placed a hand on Paige's arm and rubbed the smooth lines of muscle beneath her skin. "When can we get some time for just . . . you and me?"

"Seriously?" she asked. "With everything happening, all these people driving in, some of them *teleporting* in from all over the place, and all you can think about is getting quality time with me?"

"Is that so bad? Seems like we could both use something to loosen the tension."

Once again Paige's expression took a turn that Cole hadn't been expecting. "You're right. We could use a stress reliever."

"Really?" Cole gasped. "I bet nobody would even miss us if we—"

"No, not that," she said, casually dashing his highest hope.

"What, then?"

Instead of answering his question, she walked out the front door and toward the street. Cole stayed close to her, noticing how the group of local Skinners halted their conversation and glared defiantly at them.

"What are you doing, Paige?"

"Tell me what we've been doing since the whole Lancroft thing," she replied.

"It hasn't been that long, but seems like a bunch of cataloguing and—"

"Nothing," she snapped. "Just going through a dead man's house and squabbling over his leftovers. Meanwhile, Jory and those other two waltz back in from wherever the hell they've been and all these other jackoffs come here after finding out from Lord knows who that there's a shitload of buried treasure here. And how do they get here?"

"Through a magical teleportation system that we opened up," Cole said.

Stopping at the curb on the opposite side of the street, Paige spun around fast enough for the bobbed ends of her hair to whip against her cheek. "It's not magic. There is no magic. You know I hate it when you write something off like that."

Cole grinned and showed her a quick upward nod. "Yeah, I know. Isn't it nice just being away from everyone?"

Although reluctant to cave in all the way, she did give him a few quick pats on the face that verged on slaps. "And here I thought you were getting sick of me."

"Not when you play rough."

"Very nice. Can you hand me that empty bottle?"

Looking down at the plethora of dead soldiers scattered on the strip of grass between the curb and sidewalk, he asked, "Which one?"

"Doesn't matter."

Opting for one of the bottles that contained a minimum of backwash, he grabbed it by the neck and handed it up to her. "Cleaning up the neighborhood?"

"Something like that." Wearing one of the widest grins she'd had in a while, Paige wrapped her hand over the bottle's soggy label and whipped it at the front porch that was currently infested with goateed guys who took their fashion advice from Super Bowl commercials. It sailed past their heads and straight into the window behind them. "Since you don't seem to have a job," she screamed at them, "spend a few minutes picking up your goddamn trash!"

The porch dudes were too stunned to respond.

"Better?" Cole asked.

"Getting there."

Chapter Three

Alcova, Wyoming

The pickup was covered in a yellow paint that had been faded by decades of punishment from a relentless sun. Even after the sky's glare faded to a soft, burnt orange, the truck still looked like something that had been flipped out of the proverbial frying pan. Its frame rattled around a powerful engine humming with a dull roar as it slowed to a stop on the shoulder of County Road 407. The passenger side window came down, allowing the driver's voice to be heard as he leaned over and asked, "You need a ride, buddy?"

The man who'd been walking along the shoulder of the road kept his hands in the pockets of a Salvation Army overcoat. A mane of tangled dark brown hair flapped against his face when he turned to fix blue-gray eyes upon the driver. "No, thanks," he said.

"You sure? It's a few miles until the next gas station."

"I'm sure. Thanks, anyway."

The driver grumbled under his breath and raised the window.

Having heard the man's snippy comment just fine, Mr. Burkis turned away from the truck and let it move along.

"Funny," said a voice from the hills amid a rush of bounding footsteps and the skid of heels in rocky sand. "After all the death that has been brought to them from strangers, they can still justify stopping to ask for more from a monster walking along the side of the highway."

The county road cut through a section of exposed rock that made the area seem like something closer to a desert than a place within range of so many rivers and dams. No running water could be seen from this stretch of road, although both of the men who now faced each other could smell moisture in the air as easily as they could feel the fading sunlight upon their faces.

"Hitchhiking, Randolph?" the vaguely amused voice asked in a guttural cockney accent. "You've never been one to indulge in the finer things, but surely you don't need to travel on human roads."

The man in the overcoat wasn't impressed by the display of speed that had brought the other fellow to his side. He merely stuck his hands deeper into his pockets, turned away from the road and started walking at a normal pace into the surrounding wilderness. The new arrival fell into step beside him, wearing a set of rags that wrapped around his waist and hung over his chest thanks to the good graces of a few stubborn strips of leather and canvas. He wore no shoes. The hair sprouting from the top of his head hung in strands like greasy wires. A jagged scar traced the side of his nose, but that was the least of his injuries. His right eye socket was filled with a mass of hardened flesh resembling wax that had been stirred to the point of hardening.

"I stuck to the roads because I knew that's where I would find you, Liam."

"Have I become so predictable?"

"Only since you've become famous." Stopping after cresting a small rise, Burkis removed his hands from his pockets so he could cross his arms sternly over a chest that was thicker now than it had been a few moments ago. "Didn't you get enough camera time in Kansas City?"

Liam smiled wider than any human could. The corners of his mouth stretched back to his ears, and a few of his teeth flowed into fangs as if melting down to points. "I made a damn fine run of it there, didn't I?"

"You made a mess and you stirred up the Skinners, just like I said you would."

"Always know best, eh, Randolph? Remember when you were the one listening to what I had to say?"

"That was a long time ago."

"And in that time, you've become the one with all the answers?"

"This is my territory," Burkis snarled. "You don't get to come here and sully it by terrorizing humans for no reason. Feeding is one thing, but you're—"

"Sending a message," Liam snapped, in a way that sent his last syllables rolling along the tops of the hills. Immediately aware of the impact he'd made upon his environment, the man in rags lowered his chin as well as his voice. "So you found me. What do you want?"

Burkis pulled in half a breath and grimaced. "You reek of Mongrels."

"Of course. The filthy buggers took me out of Kansas City."

"Before the Skinners could finish you off?"

"To be honest, I think they got closer to putting an end to my days than that group who cornered me in Whitechapel. I always knew the Mongrels were opportunistic little shits, but I never banked on them working with the Skinners."

"That has yet to be determined," Burkis said. "How did you get them to take your side?"

"A wild stab on my part. Common greed on theirs." Casually shifting his gaze to the east, he squinted at the darkest horizon as if he could make out what was happening two states away. "I told the lot of them that Full Bloods are created when one of us bites one of them."

"And they believed you?"

"One of them did. That's all it took to get me out of there before I was damaged any further. After that, I suppose the one with the ambition had a convincing couple of words with some of his fellows, because getting bitten by me was all they could talk about when I woke up."

"Please tell me you didn't."

"I did. Of course," Liam added sheepishly, "some of them

didn't make it. Seems those Mongrels aren't put together as well as they like to think they are. They had me at a disadvantage so I nipped a few more. Only took some fingers and half an arm. Had to get down to the bone, after all."

"I know that. What happened then?"

"What do you think happened? They changed."

"Into what?"

"Into something that's close enough to a Full Blood to fool the likes of them." Seeing the other man's glare, Liam explained, "They're stronger and bigger than what they started as, but they're also a little slower. I'd say I did us a favor to that end. Takes away some of their speed advantage. Whether or not those Mongrels truly think they're becoming Full Bloods, they trust me. I may possibly get more on my side. That's why you're here, isn't it?"

Letting out a cynical huff from flared nostrils, Burkis asked, "You honestly believe they'd trust you after the history of blood spilled between our kinds? They took you away from the Skinners to use you, and they'll keep using until they figure out a way to be rid of you."

When Burkis started walking even farther from the road, Liam dashed around to get in front of him. "I know what I'm doing, Randolph! If you tracked me down to preach about the error of my ways yet again, you can stuff it up your self-righteous arse."

"What I want is for you to help me find someone that can give us the answers we've all been after for longer than these cities have been scattered across this continent. We'll need his help before one of the several that may have gotten your message pays us a visit."

Not only did that cause Liam to straighten his posture, but it put a curious tilt into the angle of his head. "Go on."

"I want to meet the Mongrels you changed. I've seen you in those videos that the humans have been passing around."

"Ah yes. That motorist with the cameras. They all have cameras these days, don't they?"

"And they spread their pictures like rumors over a campfire," Burkis said.

"Have the Skinners seen my movies?"

"I'd wager so. But right now that's not your concern. You were seen traveling with Mongrels, so I'm assuming those are the ones you altered. Any others wouldn't split from their pack, and they sure as hell wouldn't defer to you the way those did."

"Wouldn't be so sure about that." Filling up the massive lungs within his chest, Liam expelled his breath and said, "But I could hardly ever slip one past you, Randolph. They're not far from here. Maybe ten or twenty miles up in the mountains."

"Take me to them."

When he backed away from Burkis, Liam hunched over and pulled his shoulders back while lowering his head. A ripple passed through his body that started from his ribs and flowed out in every direction, to stretch his skin and align his bones into a new pattern. His upper body became too heavy to maintain an upright stance, so he dropped down to all fours. Newly formed claws scraped at the dry earth, digging ruts into the ground as his legs became the hindquarters of an animal. His mouth extended into a snout, and the scar on his nose was soon covered by a patch of white fur that stood out from the rest of his coal black coat.

Randolph shrugged off his outermost layers of clothing before gripping the rocky surface beneath him. His body grew thick with layer upon layer of added muscle beneath dark brown fur. His shoulders and chest were accented by deep scars that looked more like scratches dug into the side of a mountain. The final moments of his transformation forced him to arch his back and hang his head as his face was bent into the fearsome visage of a Full Blood. Teeth stretched from his jaws, quickly becoming long enough to tear through his cheeks. When he opened his mouth and lifted his chin, the daggerlike protrusions shredded the sides of his face before his unnatural healing mended the ugly wounds.

Randolph's howl was a long, steady cry. Liam added a harsher tone to the song that was more scream than melody. Together, they created a sound that scattered wildlife for miles around. The rodents, birds, and other animals in the vicinity may not have encountered a werewolf before, but they knew when to clear a path for a predator that was superior to them in every possible way.

The first thing Randolph did after settling into his new form was to use his hind legs to kick some dirt over his clothes, the way a common dog would attempt to bury its scat. He then turned around, pulled in a lungful of air next to that section of ground and committed the scent to memory. When he turned to face Liam again, the other Full Blood was gone. Following the trail as if it had been painted onto the air in front of him, Randolph leapt toward the highway and landed several yards past it on the other side. He didn't need the swirling motes of dirt to tell him something big had raced in that direction a short time ago. His nose was giving him enough information to find Liam, the driver of the truck that had offered him a ride a while ago, the previous ten other drivers that had passed through the area, and several dozen animals that would make a good snack along the way. Focusing only on what he needed, Randolph angled his head forward and started to run.

The wind caressed his face lovingly at first, but as he picked up speed, it rushed along his back and roared in his ears, pressing them flat against his wide head. His lips curled back to allow his tongue to loll out just enough to moisten his lips. When his paws touched the ground, Randolph gripped it tightly and sprang forward. Each leap sent him into the air long enough to stretch out his entire ten-foot frame from the tips of one set of claws all the way down to the opposite ones. He pulled his legs in, touched down and grabbed on tighter, as if the world itself was a beast he intended on mounting and taming.

Liam was in sight. The black Full Blood stayed low to better navigate the increasingly rocky terrain, while shooting a challenging glance over his shoulder. Curling his upper lip into a responding snarl, Randolph churned his legs in a powerful rhythm that covered miles upon miles with the ease of a loping stride. The sky stretched above them, presenting itself as the only thing able to cover more ground than the creatures below.

Mountains rose ahead of them. The werewolves' paws scratched at the ground as they pressed forward and climbed upward without breaking their powerful strides. Even if their weight caused the rocks to give way beneath them, the creatures simply jumped over the shifting boulders with the ease of a dog hopping over a puddle. By the time they reached an oval basin surrounded by craggy peaks amid the Seminoe Mountains, civilization was a distant memory.

Randolph couldn't see the Mongrels, but he could smell them well enough to set his sights upon a pile of rocks at the other end of the basin. After skidding to a stop, he paced in front of those rocks and issued a warning growl to let the others know he wouldn't hold himself back for long.

Three Mongrels poked their heads out from behind or beneath the rocks. At least one of them had maintained his affinity for digging.

Having perched upon the edge of the basin, Liam slid down into the rough clearing awkwardly at first, while shifting his body into an upright form. By the time his feet touched the basin's floor, they were large enough to support his towering, nightmarish frame. He stood on thick hind legs and hunched forward so his shaggy fists nearly scraped the ground. "This 'ere's Randolph," he said in a thick cockney accent that was stronger when emerging through all those teeth. "An old friend of mine from way back."

Two Mongrels emerged from behind the fallen rocks, walking unsteadily upon thickly muscled legs. The first had the build of a wolf but the extended limbs of a burrower. This one's digging days were over, however, since its normally wide feet and long fingers had shrunken down into paws. Judging by its awkward, shuffling steps, the Mongrel was still getting used to being aboveground. The second creature looked like a bobcat that had become a twisted version of its prehistoric ancestors. Thick fangs curled down from its upper jaw. Her light brown coat was uneven and grew in clumps, as if there simply wasn't enough fur to go around. "Another Full Blood?" she asked through oversized teeth.

"Whhhhyyyy?" asked a third Mongrel as it slithered up from the ground beneath a pile of rocks. Only the front section of its body could be seen, but it looked somewhat similar to the other digger. Unlike the other, however, this one was more than equipped for tunneling. His coat was slick with a waxy grease that allowed it to wriggle easily within whatever opening it found or made. Even as he steadied himself upon the lip of the hole, his claws loosened chips from the stone as easily as a careless hand obliterated a cobweb. What struck Randolph the most was its eyes: yellow pupils of a wolf surrounded by pools of black.

Crouching down to rest his elbows upon his knees, Liam studied all three Mongrels. "Like I said. He's a friend of mine."

While Liam's form allowed him to speak clearly, Randolph was content to communicate with low, rumbling growls issued from the back of his throat.

The burrower-wolf crossbreed scampered around the back side of the rocks. It seemed ready to approach Liam, but was hesitant to glance in Randolph's direction.

When Randolph stepped back, his body flowed into an upright form and settled somewhere in the middle ground inhabited by creatures whose appearance was just human enough to bring its prey in a little closer. "You are the ones who delivered Liam from the Skinners?" he asked.

The burrower with the greasy fur pulled himself from the hole he'd dug and trembled as his body attempted to mimic the Full Blood's transformation. With a great amount of effort, his limbs became shorter and thicker. His teeth were sucked up into his gums, leaving thick rounded points, and his fur retreated under his flesh to leave a coarse layer of stubble. With a bit of clothing and the right lighting, he might have passed for a man with a skin condition and an aversion to showering. "I'm the one who took him from Kansas City. My name's Max. The Skinners were gonna finish him off when Liam told us about how Full Bloods are made. The deal was for him to change us in return for his life."

"But we ain't Full Bloods," the bobcat said.

"Who are you?" Randolph asked.

Deferring to him out of instinct, the Mongrel removed the

edgy tone from her voice and said, "Lyssa," in a way that made it sound close to *listen*.

"Liam passed the gift to you," Randolph said. "I've heard others of your kind weren't strong enough to endure as much."

Lyssa glanced down at one forepaw that looked as if it had been nearly halved by an axe. "We're different, but not like you. We think Liam was lying just to save his own skin."

"Lying?" Liam asked as he reared up and showed the full glory of his one multifaceted eye. Subsiding like a tide after laying waste to a beachside community, he growled, "Maybe a little."

"Kayla warned us of that," Max explained, curling his lips and tongue around every word, as if still getting used to his new mouth. "But I knew there was a chance of something happening. At the very least, his meat would have been shared by our entire pack instead of handed over to those Skinner ghouls."

"Shared," Liam beamed, "and most definitely enjoyed. Just ask some of my old lady friends from London."

After silencing Liam with a growl, Randolph shifted his focus to the burrower wolf. "Your name?"

As the Mongrel bared his teeth, its eyes showed equal parts fear and longing.

"He don't speak," Liam explained. "Either that or the poor fella's shy."

"What about the rest of your pack?" Randolph asked. "Have they been changed?"

Even on a face as twisted as Max's, the contempt was clear to see. His eyes narrowed into yellow lines as he replied, "Kayla wouldn't allow it. She and Ben are content to grow fat in Kansas City, scrounging for whatever human scraps they can find. When she saw what we became, she wanted to be rid of Liam forever."

"Some of us volunteered for the change anyway," Lyssa said. "It's not perfect, but it's more than we were before."

"You think so?" Randolph growled. Even after he stood up straight, his body continued to rise. His ankles stretched into reversed knees as his legs stretched to new lengths.

Claws snaked out of his toes and fingers. When his snout emerged from his face amid a series of loud, wet cracks, the true Full Blood stood before them.

Liam looked on with an eye that darted back and forth between the Mongrels. "Oh, see I was afraid of this. Randolph don't exactly like to share his territory with anyone."

"You brought us here to be slaughtered?" Max asked. Reflexively changing into his squat burrower form, he sprouted claws that curved around like scythes to dig trenches into the rock. Whiskers sprouted from a nose that extended from his face to make way for the uniformly rounded teeth in his mouth. "You said we'd look for others like you," he snarled.

"And it looks like we found one. Sorry, Max. Nothin' I could do, you see."

There was no more talking after that. When Randolph sprang forward, he reached out with both hands. A bellowing breath came from his mouth, and if not for the deadly arsenal of fangs and claws, he might have been just another rush of wind.

Lyssa and the digger-wolf hybrid scattered in opposite directions. Their speed was impressive, in that it was enough to get them out of the way before Randolph tore them into bloody ribbons. Max, on the other hand, dove straight into the hole from which he'd appeared.

As soon as Randolph hit the pile of rocks, he slashed at the hybrid with his claws. One bony talon snagged in the Mongrel's flesh, but the creature was so panicked that it tore itself loose without seeming to realize the damage that had been done. Since that one was temporarily out of reach, Randolph moved his hungry gaze to the female. Lyssa bared her fangs, which were even longer now than when she'd been speaking to him a minute ago. Although she'd shifted into a more bestial form, her body retained the lithe silhouette that defined her species. As blood pumped through her veins, muscles grew beneath her flesh until she was large enough to pose a challenge.

Randolph sized her up in a fraction of a second and twisted his upper body around to snap at her. Impossibly fast, and strong enough to turn one unlucky rock into powder with a wild swipe, the Full Blood would have sunk his fangs deep into her neck if not for the hole that opened up directly beneath his left forepaw.

Thick, rounded paws reached from the hole, sank curved nails into Randolph's leg and began shredding. Instead of simply flaying skin from flesh, Max used the werewolf's limb to pull himself up from the ground. As soon as he snagged a tendon, he hooked a claw around the sinewy fiber and pulled until the ropy strand snapped. A bellowing roar flowed from the depths of Randolph's massive frame and filled the sky above him. Perhaps spurred by the sound of his fellow Full Blood, Liam pounced at Max. If his claws had found their mark, they would have easily torn the Mongrel into uneven chunks. Instead, they scraped along rock and even grazed Randolph himself when Max ducked back down into his hole.

When he'd dug his first tunnel through the mountain, Max was able to take his time and slither through the narrow passages he'd made. Now, the Mongrel scraped frantically beneath the surface, knocking flat sections of the basin's floor askew as he carved his escape route.

Randolph left a trail of blood in the air as he sprang forward to get ahead of the burrowing creature. Skidding upon his wounded leg, he brought a fist down like a hammer to crush through the rocky crust. Before he could pull Max from the ground, the wolflike Mongrel circled around from another angle to dig into the Full Blood with every tooth and claw at his disposal. Reaching over his shoulder, Randolph grabbed the hybrid by the scruff of its neck and pulled him free the same way he might rip out an arrow lodged between his shoulder blades. The hybrid tore open a large flap of skin from Randolph's back, but the Full Blood still maintained his grip and slammed him to the basin floor.

As this one went, Liam had to contend with Lyssa. He'd been blindsided by the feline Mongrel as she ran along the edge of the rock wall like a race car cruising on the steepest slope of a track. She pushed away from the wall and flew at him with the intention of sinking her claws into his side, but was stopped in midair when Liam snapped his head around to clamp his jaws around her neck.

The muscles beneath Lyssa's skin were more solid than any other Mongrel he'd faced. They shifted around his teeth to add another layer of padding before anything vital was pierced. Liam savored the moment while curling his lips back and pressing his jaws in tighter around her. His fangs sank in another quarter of an inch before Lyssa began scraping madly at his eyes and throat.

Unlike the Skinners who needed charmed weapons and trickery to hurt a Full Blood, Mongrels had a natural weapon at their disposal. Even Nymar fangs could wound a werewolf, but the leeches simply didn't have the raw power needed to get the job done. Normally, a single Mongrel didn't possess that kind of strength either. Lyssa, on the other hand, was proving that her uniqueness ran deeper than Liam had previously expected.

He pondered this while she shredded half of his face and further ravaged the callused pit where his right eye had been. Considering how bad that wound had itched since he regained consciousness, the Mongrel's claws weren't entirely unwelcome. Once the scratching dug a little too deep, he ended it by clenching his jaws shut tight enough for the Mongrel to shift her priorities from attack to defense. He swatted away one of her paws as if disciplining a child and then absorbed a few painful gouges along his forearm before grabbing the front portion of her chest. From there, he tore her off and pinned her to the ground. "There you go, sweetness," he growled. "Just lay down and let me take care of you."

"You said you'd lead us somewhere safe," Lyssa growled. "Somewhere away from the packs and Skinners."

"I don't see neither of them around here, luv."

"You changed us. Made us better. There's no reason for this."

Leaning in so he could be heard over the commotion of the other Full Blood's struggle with Max and the hybrid, Liam said, "Randolph ain't the sort who plays well with others. Never was."

Since she was no match for the werewolf in a one-on-one

fight, and her pleading was falling upon deaf ears, Lyssa only had one remaining option. She clenched her eyes shut, relaxed in Liam's grip, and bared her neck to him.

Recognizing the gesture that would bring an end to a great number of disputes between wolves, Liam seethed with an anger that showed even within the ravaged pit of his right eye socket. "What are you doing?" he snarled as he tightened his grip on her. "You wanted to be one of us? A Full Blood defers to no one. Not ever! You make me sick, you pathetic little bitch. Killing you is too damn easy."

"Liam."

If the ebon werewolf heard his name, he didn't acknowledge it. He was taking too much pleasure in slowly grinding his claws within Lyssa's flesh. "You know how long I made humans suffer when I led the charge against their city? I had to keep them alive so they'd survive long enough to turn into a Half Breed. But you, luv," he said in a voice that was less intense but twice as chilling. "You can take so much more punishment than one of them."

"You'll be taking some punishment yourself if you don't back up."

Blinking as if he'd been awoken from a dream, Liam turned toward the source of the voice. Randolph stood behind him in his human form. His fur had receded all the way under his skin, leaving him naked but still less vulnerable than any of the other Mongrels in the vicinity. Liam sought them out next. He spotted the hybrid curled against the far side of the basin licking one of several wounds. Max emerged from another hole and stretched his neck out toward Liam's belly. All of the Mongrel's teeth were bared and poised to eviscerate the Full Blood. Even if Max couldn't get the job done, he was bound to make a hell of a mess.

"You really think you can put me down before I get to you?" Liam growled.

"That doesn't matter," Randolph said. "I wanted to find out what these Mongrels were made of, and they've shown me plenty."

"We're not Mongrels anymore," Lyssa said. "Kayla was very specific about that."

"Well you're sure as hell not Full Bloods," Liam pointed out. "And if this little bugger doesn't crawl back into his hole pretty damn quickly, he won't even be a resident of this plane of existence."

Reluctantly, Max eased back into his tunnel. As he retraced the path he'd dug beneath the surface, dislodged earthen plates rattled over his squirming back. The motion stopped and one of the plates was shoved aside so he could poke his head up several paces away from either of the werewolves. "He's right," Max said to the other Mongrels. "We shouldn't follow someone like Kayla if she's not willing to accept us. But we won't follow the likes of you, Liam. Not anymore."

"I've never seen anything like you," Randolph admitted. "Our two kinds have fought many times, but there have never been survivors to go through this sort of change."

"That's not true," Max said. "The survivors of those battles were always killed after the fight was over. Put down for their own good, we were told."

"It's in our history," Lyssa told him. "Most of it's known only to the pack leaders, but it's there. I saw it for myself in Kansas City. Some of the Mongrels that were wounded while fighting you were killed by Kayla herself. I was tending to my husband after he was wounded by Liam when she came and told me to rest. She thought I was gone, but I watched from a distance and saw her slash his throat. After it was done, she told me he'd died and that we should burn his body immediately."

Randolph's brow lifted slightly above his crystalline eyes. "So she knows about the change?"

"She knows the rumor," Max said. "I spoke to her when the humans in KC were still cleaning up the mess Liam made. She knew something would happen, but not what. I think she was hoping to find some missing element that would make a difference between us changing into whatever she feared and changing into a Full Blood." Looking to Randolph, he asked, "Is there?"

"Honestly, I don't know. Most of the times I've encountered Mongrels, I've been forced to fight back a swarm of them intent on killing me." Holding up a thick hand before the inevitable argument came, he added, "Whatever the reason for our past conflict, it's behind us for now." The wounds on that hand were closing like clay being reshaped by an unseen sculptor. His leg was in much worse condition, but not as bad as it had been a short while ago. "Things are different. Do you know of a Skinner named Jonah Lancroft?"

"The Mind Singer spoke of him," Lyssa said. "For a while I thought I'd only dreamt that name. Is he real?"

"He was, but I lost track of him over sixty years ago. Lancroft was a creator. He made things to help the Skinner cause, and it's possible he came up with a way to hide his scent from us. There are groups of Skinners meeting in Philadelphia right now. Loose talk among them mentions Lancroft's name and that he was the one behind the Mud Flu. It's also said that he was killed by his own kind."

"Does Lancroft have a way to complete our conversion into Full Bloods?" Lyssa asked.

Always quick to pounce on an opportunity, Liam jumped in with, "If anyone would have such a thing, it would have been him."

"Their intent is to kill us, not help us become more powerful. The reason I asked about Lancroft is that he was rumored to have created a way to inhibit our ability to heal. The Skinners must rely on antiquated methods of harming us, but we've still been able to heal after surviving a fight with them."

"Well," Liam said as he turned the right side of his face toward the others, "more or less."

"Liam's eye may well heal if given enough time," Randolph said. "Anyone who has seen the Mind Singer knows that some of his wounds never did."

"Got his neck snapped somewhere along the line," Liam said. "Something like that should have either killed poor Henry before he became one of us or cleared up after his first change."

"He was a Full Blood, wasn't he?" Max asked. "Wasn't that enough to sustain him?"

Randolph sighed and turned his back on the others as if he'd either become fascinated by the rugged landscape or bored with the company he was forced to keep. "I've had my neck broken a few times. It's not pleasant but it's also not fatal for us."

"I been hung," Liam said with the same tone he might use if comparing his story to the ones told by a bunch of drunken fishermen. "Rope burns are just as bad as the bone gettin' snapped."

Continuing as though Liam hadn't opened his mouth, Randolph said, "Henry's neck was broken while he was held in Lancroft Reformatory. I've been through the ruins of that place and found nothing but a single intriguing scent. Years later I'd assumed whatever advances Lancroft had made were either lost after the place became a Half Breed den or taken when it was cleaned out by the Skinners. This new discovery in Philadelphia has unearthed more than Lancroft's research. Much more. The place is swarming with Skinners. They're anxious and expecting to be attacked. Fortunately, all five of us have advantages that go beyond brute strength or speed."

"Perhaps we could talk to them," Max said. "Some of them are more open to reason than others. After working with them in KC, they may still trust us."

"Talk will come later." Shifting his eyes to the other Full Blood, Randolph said, "They think Liam's dead. Or, they would have if he hadn't been intent on sending childish taunts to them."

Liam curled his lip into something between a snarl and a disgusted sneer.

"And I've had words with them myself," Randolph continued.

"Right," Liam grunted. "We both know how well that turned out."

Randolph's face twitched. More specifically, the muscles that ran beneath the jagged scar tissue on his cheek flinched as if he could still feel the Blood Blade sliver that had put it there. "You Mongrels have proven to be an asset. You fight well and can prove valuable in the times that are to come.

We cannot allow Lancroft's creations to be freely distrib-
uted. When this current turmoil among them settles, we
can cripple their efforts before they even know they're in
danger."

"They're always in danger," Liam said. "Even the dumb-
est animals would know that by now."

Focusing on a point to the east, Randolph said, "Yes, but
some dangers cut deeper than others."

Chapter Four

"Who the hell are these guys?" Cole asked as yet another batch of new arrivals walked into the basement through the glowing curtain of beads. The Dryads called the room a Skipping Temple because it could be used as a waypoint to shuttle someone to a further spot like a stone skipping across the top of a lake. Ever since Lancroft had been killed, nobody was skipping much farther than his basement.

Since the Skinners didn't have membership cards, they identified themselves by holding out their hands to show the distinctive scars on their palms made by the thorns in their weapons. Those scars were more than just conversation pieces. Elements from the varnish that made the weapons powerful enough to combat supernatural creatures mingled with a Skinner's blood, tainting it with traces of the Nymar and shapeshifter components within the mixture. Cole learned firsthand that the scars itched in the presence of Nymar, burned when shapeshifters were in the vicinity, and made his hands cramp when a heavy rain was on the way. That last part could have been a product of his age but he preferred to blame the scars.

Paige sifted through a pile of weapons stored in an old locker that looked as if it had been pulled out of a bus stop. Holding a wooden stake in one hand and a rusted cleaver in the other, she only glanced up long enough to take a quick look and reply, "I dunno who they are. Why don't you ask them?"

"It's three in the morning. How much longer do I have to meet and greet these people?"

"Stop whining, Cole. We were here when all the Lancroft shit hit the fan, so we're the ones everyone'll want to talk to."

"Rico and Daniels were here too," Cole whined. "How'd they get out of this?"

"Daniels is tweaking that ink. Ever since you put it through a successful field test, he's been all giddy about it. As far as Rico goes, if you want to drag him back here by the ear, be my guest."

The new arrivals almost got past Cole before he realized he hadn't seen all of their hands. When he tried to get a look to confirm the other ones, he felt the itch in his palms grow into a bone-deep irritation. With so many Nymar and shapeshifter spare parts rattling around in that basement, his scars had been acting up since he arrived. But there was no mistaking when he was that close to a live vampire.

"Son of a bitch!" Cole shouted as he instinctively reached for the spear strapped to his back. "Nymar!"

Two of the four new arrivals sighed and nodded while holding their unscathed hands out to show they were empty. One was a tall man with a scalp that was shaved clean. A long brushy beard hung well past his chin and split in two separate directions toward the bottom. Now that Cole was closer, he could see the black markings of Nymar tendrils just under the man's skin that led all the way to a spore attached to his heart, which caused his bloodsucking tendencies. The tendrils formed different patterns within each Nymar, and his were collected in thick clumps around the base of his neck like a collar that stretched up toward his ears in a dark, slowly swaying wave. He was almost Cole's height but shrank a little as his shoulders slumped with tired resignation.

"Well, Bobby?" the other Nymar snapped. She was an inch taller than the bald one, but wasn't talking to him. Staring daggers at the Skinner directly in front of her, she asked, "Aren't you going to say something?"

The Skinner on the receiving end of her glare was slightly taller than average and thin as a rail. Simple rumpled clothes hung off a lean frame, and impatience filled his reddened eyes. Scratching burnt orange hair with callused hands, he wheeled around and replied, "I will if you give me a chance!" Turning around to face front again, he asked, "Is this the Lancroft house? In Philly?"

"No," Cole replied. "It's some other stop along the Spirit Bead Expressway. Of course it's the Lancroft house!"

"No need to get lippy. That's Paul," he said while pointing to the bald Nymar. Nodding to the woman, he said, "And that's Trudy."

Dropping her angry grimace, Trudy extended a hand marked by dark tendrils on her wrists that tapered out and became lighter while maintaining a visible presence all the way to her fingertips. "Call me Tru."

"Great," Cole said. "You saved me a syllable when I ask my next question. Why are you here, Tru?"

"They're with us," Bobby replied.

"What about him?"

Until Cole nodded in his direction, the fourth member of the mixed party seemed content to blend with the background. Considering the background was a curtain of beads crackling with mystic natural force, blending in there was quite a feat. The only distinguishing characteristic the guy had was the web of scars on his hands. Other than that, he was the shortest of the bunch, had light hair and three knives strapped to his belt. It was yet another sign of Cole's new outlook on life that three blades worn in plain sight wasn't enough to make someone stand out anymore.

"That's M," Bobby said.

"M? Like the boss in the James Bond movies?"

Hearing that brought a bland smile to the man's lips. "Yeah," M said to Cole. "I like that. Like in the Bond flicks."

"It's short for Mathias," Paul announced.

Cole smirked. "Oh, like Johnny Mathias?" It wasn't the first time he was the only one laughing at his own jokes. Normally, he only had to tolerate dry stares from Paige, but now there was an entire room full of unimpressed people to make him squirm. " 'Chances Are'? What about the Christmas album? That's the good stuff, right?"

Without a hint of emotion, Bobby asked, "Don't you mean Johnny Mathis?"

"Yeah," Cole said, officially giving up on the attempt at humor. "That's what I meant. What can I do for you guys?"

"We came to see if there's anything left for us to take from the Lancroft haul. Ain't that why everyone's here?"

Someone bolted down the stairs from the main floor. Cole couldn't see through the people milling around in the workroom, but he recognized Abel's voice when it screeched, "One of you might wanna get up here!"

All of the eyes in the workshop turned to Paige. The ones in the Skipping Temple and the room where Henry had been dissected found Cole.

"It's those assholes from down the street," Abel continued. "They just trashed Jory's car."

Paige hopped off her stool, claiming the wooden stake by sticking it into the vacant holster strapped to her boot next to a baton that she'd crafted personally and carried all through the Lancroft incident. Her face was brighter than it had been for a while when she said, "Took them long enough!"

Cole hurried to catch up as she and Abel climbed the stairs to the main floor. The pale glow from the streetlights coming through the front windows seemed colder at that time of night. Across the street the dudes in the jerseys and T-shirts were laughing to each other and filling the air with obnoxious music and the slap of enthusiastic high fives.

In its prime, Jory's car had been an '08 Sonata with a decent sound system. When it had been driven to the Lancroft house, it was a better-than-average vehicle with a refurbished sound system. Now it was a dirty sedan with a broken front window, a dented hood, and a few words scratched into the passenger door by a key. One of those words wasn't even spelled correctly.

"F-U-K yourselves?" Cole recited.

"Yeah!" Madman 69 shouted as he strutted toward the house with two of his buddies backing him up. "And if you don't want us messing up anything worse than this, you'll tell us what the hell you pricks are doing in the old man's house."

Paige stepped forward to mark herself as the spokesperson of the group and also to test to see if any of the idiot neighbors would back down. So far they were either too drunk or too stupid to do so. "First you threaten us and then you're concerned about your neighbor? Make up your mind."

"That," Madman said as he jabbed a finger at the car, "is for throwing the bottle at our house. You broke one'a our windows, so we break one'a yours." Stepping even closer, he added, "C'mon. You can tell me. What's goin' on in there? You got some kind of tunnels under that place?"

"What makes you say that?"

"There's only one car parked outside, but there's shitloads of different people walkin' in and out so you gotta be comin' and goin' some other way. We heard there were some tunnels runnin' under this whole city and that the old man had a way in. If you can get us in, maybe we can work something out. I'll forget about our little argument, nobody else will know what you got goin' on in that house . . ."

"You don't even know what's going on in that house," Cole said.

"Sure, but maybe I'm a concerned citizen who'll call the cops. You want that?"

Now it was Abel's turn to step up. "You won't call the cops and we both know why."

That put a dent in Madman's facade. He tried to scowl at the Skinners but couldn't quite pull it off. "Let us get a look at them tunnels or clear out. You do one of those real quick or we'll clear you out ourselves."

Paige allowed Madman one moment of glory. She even granted him the chance to strut away amid the hoots and hollers of his cronies before gritting her teeth and saying, "Let's go turn that place upside down."

"What?" Cole asked. "I thought we were trying to keep a low profile."

"And we can't do that if some mutated frat house is watching us." Turning to him, she patted Cole's chest and said,

"This is another part of the job. We're in new territory here. These assholes are testing us. We need to squash this kind of shit before anyone worse than these guys gets any ideas."

"This isn't Tombstone and those guys aren't a real threat to us."

"Onc's a Nymar." When Abel saw the perplexed look on Cole's face, he asked, "Didn't you see the markings on the dude waiting at the curb? Didn't you feel the itch?"

"This whole place gives me an itch," Cole grumbled.

"He's right," Paige said. Shifting to the kung fu master voice, she told him, "One must feel the subtle differences in the breeze before one may appreciate the wind."

Abel shot a quick glance across the street, where Madman, a guy in an Anthrax concert shirt, and the shifty fellow who hadn't left the curb were all gathered. If he squinted hard enough, Cole could just make out the thick black markings snaking up one side of the shifty one's face. At first glance the tendrils had looked like just another stray piece of shadow cast from the nearby trees.

"Selina drove Jory down to meet with a friend of ours in the Philly PD," Abel explained. "They're checking up on those idiots across the street and we're not going to do anything until they get back. We can't risk—"

"I'll tell you what we can't risk," Paige said as she grabbed Abel's shirt with her right hand. Although that entire arm was still stiff after nearly being petrified by a concoction of tattoo ink mixed with melted fragments of the Blood Blade bonded to shapeshifter plasma, she'd been working to bring it back into full use. Her skin was soft to the touch, but stiff as hardened leather underneath newly risen scars. "We can't risk being made to look weak in front of anyone, especially a Nymar."

Cole put his back to the house across the street. "She's right."

"Oh, big surprise," Abel snickered. "You agree with her."

"Paige. Let him go."

Reluctantly, she did.

The moment Abel caught his breath, it was stolen from him as Cole picked up right where she'd left off. Grabbing two handfuls of the other man's shirt, he shoved him up the steps and through Lancroft's front door. "I know this isn't exactly Thanksgiving dinner, but we're all here to take advantage of a major win, right?"

"Yeah," Abel replied.

"Seems pretty rare that so many of us are all in one place, but there's no reason anyone else should know that. All we need is one Nymar spreading the word that we're a bunch of petty little kids snipping at each other before they'll all get it in their heads that maybe Skinners aren't anything to worry about after all. I've seen how Nymar jump on any sort of weakness, and that won't go well for anyone."

Abel shrugged and agreed halfheartedly under his breath.

Touching his shoulder was all Paige needed to do for Cole to let him go. "Aren't all of you bored with looking through this crap?" she asked anyone within earshot. "How about we cross the street and remind those assholes why they should think before shooting their big mouths off. Give the Nymar a good story to pass around to his buddies." Turning toward the door to the basement, she found no fewer than three Skinners huddled there and several more watching from the kitchen and bedrooms like a bunch of schoolkids trying to get a good view of a fight. "How many sets of armor have we found?"

One of the Skinners at the top of the basement stairs told her, "Five. There were more, but they've already been taken. Three of those are spoken for, though."

"Fine. Five," Paige said. "That's enough for me, Cole and Abel here plus a few more. Who else wants to go tell the neighbors they're making too much noise?"

Volunteers were not in short supply.

Chapter Five

It was a time of night that was starting to acquire the feel of day. Just shy of 3:30 A.M., every obscene comment from Madman and his bros echoed down the street. Every clink of empty bottles hitting the sidewalk rattled through the air accompanied by the perpetual thump of a cheap radio set up somewhere within the messy house.

The Skinners didn't try to sneak up on them. Cole, Paige, and Abel led a group of seven more that fanned out to form a wall in front of Madman's water-damaged front porch. The house's owner, along with most of the guys from the party, came outside to meet them. Drunken insults and threats were spat at them, but the Skinners weren't there to talk. Cole and Abel wore military surplus jackets that came down past their waists and had tanned werewolf hides stitched into the lining. Paige wore her own black harness, which covered her torso and was strapped in place like a bulletproof vest. She'd had no trouble finding Half Breed skins to zip into the harness for padding that could stop anything the drunken idiots had to offer.

"What the fuck do you want?" Madman asked.

Spotting the Nymar instantly, Cole extended a hand to point at his target. "Him first."

The guy had pockmarked skin, spiked brown hair, and wore a shirt with the collar torn out to show his markings, as if the tendrils were expensive tattoos. With so many Skinners in front of him, he no longer seemed anxious to display his ink.

"What do you want with Finn?" Madman asked.

"I just want to make sure he gets a good look at what's about to happen." With that, Cole stepped forward with the aggression that had been building inside of him since the first guy in a football jersey knocked him aside in the tenth grade. The fact that he now had armed killers to back him up was simply glorious.

The inside of the house was exactly what had been advertised on the outside. Couches with stuffing flowing from tears in the upholstery formed a pit around a big TV showing the final table of a poker tournament. Crushed beer and pop cans were strewn on the floor along with enough empty pizza boxes to build a very flimsy and greasy fort. Cole had barely taken four steps inside before all hell broke loose.

Madman rushed up behind him, but was immediately overpowered by the Skinners. Cole walked all the way back to the bedrooms, following the itch in his palms that had brought him this far. There were more Nymar inside. Having them this close to the Lancroft house was not a good sign.

The first door he encountered was closed, so Cole opened it. Inside that room, a Nymar wearing nothing but dark blue boxers climbed out from under the sheets of a twin bed. The tendrils marking his skin were fat and dark, meaning he'd recently fed on the one substance that the spore attached to his heart would crave. Judging by the state of the other man, slumped in a corner with blood running from slashed wrists, Cole was certain he'd found the vampire's snack.

"This isn't exactly feeding in public," Cole said, "but we're doing a surprise insp—"

He was cut short when the Nymar used a portion of his enhanced speed to reach beneath the mattress to grab a .44 that had been stashed there. The gunshot exploded within the room, spitting a round that hit Cole in the upper chest a few inches from his collar. Part of his brain was still trying to come up with a funny way to insult the Nymar who'd just killed him. That thought rattled in his brain as he lost his footing, bounced off a wall and dropped to the floor. He couldn't breathe. A blurred jumble of dark shapes was smeared across his eyes. His ears were filled with muffled, thumping movement inside the house and a piercing ringing left by the .44.

The Nymar landed on top of Cole as if he'd been dropped from a helicopter hovering above the house. As the vampire pressed down on him with more weight than his scrawny body should have had, the coppery stink on the Nymar's breath washed over him. Eyeing him hungrily, the Nymar peeled Cole's jacket open.

His jacket.

Cole was dazed and battered, but the jacket's lining had kept the bullet from breaking through. Unfortunately, the Nymar had already found a way in.

"She said you'd come running," the Nymar hissed while looking down at him. "Just didn't think it'd be this quick."

When the Nymar settled, pinning him to the floor, there was nothing Cole could do about it. Seeing the top set of feeding fangs slip out from beneath his gums, however, sent a jolt of adrenaline through his body. He rolled onto his side, reached over one shoulder, grabbed the spear from its harness and drove it straight down into the base of the Nymar's neck.

The spear was in its compact form, so it was almost as thick as a baseball bat. Thorns sprouting from the handle punctured Cole's palm, allowing him to tap into the shape-shifting powers imbued into the weapon.

The Nymar stretched his head back and opened his mouth wide. Thinner, curved fangs slid down along the inner edge of the feeding fangs, and a thick, stout set on his lower jaw snapped out like a trap that had been sprung. Before Cole could will the spear to change its shape, the Nymar grabbed to pull it out from where it had been lodged.

"Wha . . . what's going on?" the man with the slit wrists groaned.

More gunshots blasted through the house, but Cole focused on the voices in the next room. One of them was Paige, and she was quickly drowned out by the blast of a shotgun.

Just as Cole was getting the spear to extend deeper into the Nymar's torso, the .44 was angled to point at his head. He stared up at the pistol while both of the Nymar's eyes widened in anticipation.

The Nymar was pinning all but one of his arms to the floor, so Cole flipped the spear around with a snap of his wrist, bringing around the end that was carved into a set of forked points. From there he willed the weapon to extend to its full length with a voice that filled the inside of his skull with a frantic scream. The spear responded by almost doubling in length, as if loaded with a spring. The forked end caught the Nymar's wrist, shoving the gun away from Cole's face a fraction of a second before it went off with a blast that sent a piercing shriek through Cole's ears. When the forked end of the spear snapped shut around the Nymar's arm, it did so with enough power to slice down to bone.

The Nymar couldn't jump away from Cole fast enough. He dropped the .44 and scampered toward the bed like his boxers had been put to a torch. His hand was still stuck, however, and Cole wasn't about to let go.

After pulling in a few cautious breaths, he was certain the Skinner-crafted armor had held up under the second shot. Trying to get up was enough to throw him into a world of hurt, but the Nymar's flailing efforts to escape actually helped pull him to his feet. As soon as his legs were under him, Cole tightened his grip on the spear and swung the Nymar into a wall.

"Please!" someone shouted from the living room. "Just get out of here! I'm sorry about the car!"

The Nymar turned toward Cole and opened his mouth to show the murky venom dripping from curved upper fangs. Cole twisted away so the paralytic substance was spat onto his borrowed jacket instead of his face. Before the Nymar could come up with another trick to tip the scales back in his favor, Cole reeled him in. When the Nymar stumbled toward him, Cole drove one leg straight out to bury his foot in the vampire's midsection, dropping him to his knees with a huffing grunt.

"Cole? Where'd you go?"

Standing over the Nymar with his spear in a bloody grip, he responded, "In here, Paige."

She hurried into the bedroom wielding her baton. "You found another one?"

"Yeah. I think he's got something to say." Giving the spear a little twist, Cole bent the Nymar's hand in the wrong direction and said, "Isn't that right?"

The young man with the slashed wrists rushed forward. Even though Paige held him back, he still reached for the Nymar and pleaded, "Let him go. He didn't hurt me, I swear!"

Pushing the man back, Paige bought herself enough time to drop her baton into the holster on her boot. She grabbed one of the man's hands and inspected his bloody wrists. "He didn't? Than what's this?"

"It's a game we play, that's all."

The cuts made across his veins and had been partially wrapped by shreds of thin material. Studying his eyes, she asked, "Are you on something?"

"Just some weed and pills. They grow it here. In the basement. I only took it for our games. That's all. We weren't hurting anyone!"

"He shot me!" Cole said.

"Because you stormed in here!"

"Cops!" one of the Skinners shouted from the living room.

"Okay, Cole," she said calmly. "Let him go. It's all over."

Even though he wanted to rid himself of the Nymar currently attached to his spear, the weapon didn't seem ready to let him go. Part of the reason might have been the large portion of Cole's brain that wanted to take the Nymar's gun hand for a souvenir.

"It's all over," Paige repeated. Raising her voice to shout in the direction of the living room, she asked, "Are we through here?"

"We're through, we're through!" someone squealed loud enough to fill the next room.

"Cops are coming," Abel calmly announced.

Cole still couldn't get the spear to open, so he did the next

best thing and glared down at the Nymar as if trapping him
there was his only purpose in life. "If the cops want to see
something," he shouted, "tell them to look in the basement
and forget about our visit tonight!"

"Sure! Look, sorry about the car. It's just that we got a
reputation to maintain. We're the hook-up around here."

From the front room, Madman squealed and begged for
leniency from the other Skinners surrounding him.

Cole lowered himself to one knee so he was the only thing
the Nymar could see. "Who said we'd come running?"

"Wh-What?"

"When you had the drop on me before, you said she knew
we'd come running. Who's 'she'?"

"I wanna see Finn."

"Paige, bring the other Nymar in here."

Now that things had died down, the man with the cut
wrists had collected himself enough to formulate a plan. His
main course of action was to wait for Cole to look away and
then run straight at him. When that happened, Cole merely
snapped his fist into the bloody man's face to stop him cold.

Paige left the room, only to reappear while dragging the
other Nymar along by the back of his neck. After dumping
him off, she stomped away to assist the others in the living
room.

"You all right, Finn?" the Nymar in boxers asked.

Finn ran a tongue along his split bottom lip. "Yeah.
Madman and the rest of these stupid shits started swingin'
when I told 'em to stay put."

"Are there any more of you around?" Cole asked.

"Not anymore," Finn replied. "What the hell are you
doing to him?"

Thanks to a clearing head and a bit of luck, Cole was finally able to get his spear to loosen up. The forked ends split
apart, but were snagged by the threadlike tendrils that had
emerged from the Nymar's wrist to stitch up the wound. He
kept the spear close to his chest in a horizontal grip as he
positioned himself so his back was to a wall. "Who put you
two up to this?"

"It's too late to worry about that," Finn said. "She's already gone."

"Gone where? Who are you talking about?"

"The one who told us about the old man in the house across the street."

"How long did you know about Lancroft?"

"A year or so," the Nymar replied. "Not like it did us any good. He knew about us too. Waved at us sometimes when he left to go wherever the hell he went."

Outside, the sirens were getting closer. From what he knew of the street, Cole figured the cops would be pulling to a stop in front of the house in less than a minute. Stabbing a finger toward the man with the cut wrists, he said, "You're coming with us. We can get you fixed up."

"No! I'm staying here."

"If he wants to stay, let him," Paige said with a resigned sigh from the doorway. "Unless Selina or any of the other locals have some good cop connections, we've already got enough to worry about."

"He's on drugs," Cole told her.

Looking over to a bong shaped like half of a Viking's helmet, she said, "I kind of guessed that."

"He said there were pills too. He could be messed up."

"Let me guess," she said to Finn. "The usual float and flow?"

"Yeah," the Nymar replied.

Cole looked around at the bong and several other colorful bits of paraphernalia lying around. If not for the scent of burnt cordite after the gunfire, he would have smelled the weed a lot sooner. But that didn't answer the main question on his mind. "What the hell is a float and flow?"

"It's a way people like to get fed on," Paige told him as she led him from the bedroom so she could get a good look at what was going on in the rest of the little house. "They get a little high, sometimes a lot high, and then pop a whole bunch of aspirin to thin their blood. The Nymar can feed slower since the blood doesn't clot as quickly and they both get a buzz. Float and flow. Thing is, it's not really what we would consider a terrible offense. Weird? Sure. Worth maiming someone over? Not so much."

In the living room, Skinners were letting themselves out through the front door as several of Madman's buddies skulked back to their own respective corners. Between the TV and a few lamps whose shades had been knocked off, it was difficult to tell if the oddly angled light came from there or from cops closing in on them. The squawk of a radio outside put that little quandary to rest.

"There's no time to finish this up properly," Paige said as she shut the door to the bedroom. "We're going to walk out of here calmly without looking any more suspicious than we already do."

"Don't you think these guys will say something about the way we busted in?"

Opening the door again and looking into the bedroom, Paige said, "I don't know. Do you think these pot-smoking vampires will say anything to make the cops stay here any longer than necessary?"

"No," Finn said through gritted teeth, "but I'd better make sure." He shoved past the Skinners and into the living room. Thanks to the people clustered in the living room and on the porch, he made it all the way to the front door before he was noticed.

"Stay where you are, sir!" one of the cops said from the street directly in front of the house.

"I'm the owner of this place. We just had a fight after a big party," Finn said while shooting a loaded glance over to Madman. Judging by the way the big dude in the Eagles jersey looked over at the Nymar, he wasn't anxious to step on Finn's toes.

Although nobody came forward to dispute the story, the cop was still wary. "Someone said they heard gunfire."

"It's all right, Nate," Selina said as she crossed the street from Lancroft's side. "We were just having a party. Remember the one I told you about?"

The cop wasn't much older than Madman's crowd. His clean-shaven face was cut from hard lines and marred by a few small scars, but it softened a bit when Selina came along. "I thought that party wasn't supposed to be for a while and that it was going to be at the place across the street."

"It got changed," she said with a shrug.

"Great. Can we go?" Paige asked.

The front door remained open and a breeze was blowing through the little structure thanks to some other open windows. When the stench of burnt cordite drifted outside, Cole swore he could smell pot as well. If the cop with Selina or the other one directly behind him had functional noses, they wouldn't be able to miss those scents.

"Things look all right here," the cop said. "Everyone go on home and keep the noise down."

Chapter Six

Paige walked calmly across the street, and it was all Cole could do to keep his voice down to a whisper when he said, "Those cops had to know there was more going on in there."

"I know. Keep walking." When Cole took a quick glance over his shoulder, she snapped, "Don't look. Just keep walking. Selina and Jory know some cops around here, but it looks like they've got a better arrangement than I thought."

It felt like miles before they were finally on the other side of the street. "I think they're working with the Nymar," he said in an overly deliberate whisper.

Paige stopped just after stepping onto the curb in front of Lancroft's house and went against the order she'd just given. "Who?" she asked while looking back at Madman's house. "The cops or Jory's crew?"

"Maybe both. The Nymar doing the float and flow mentioned something about a woman telling him we'd be coming."

"You mean Selina?"

"I don't know," Cole replied quickly. "He just said 'she' told them we'd come running and that she also told the Nymar about Lancroft being in that house. I tried to get more out of him but didn't have time. Then that cop made it sound like he knew something was going to happen as well."

"Why would they expect us to go over there, unless . . ." Paige spun on her heels so she was once again facing the Lancroft house. "Unless we were being pulled away from the only thing in this neighborhood valuable enough to convene a Skinner summit meeting."

She strode into the house, pushed open the door and shoved past the Skinners waiting in the living room. Her mouth was pressed into a tight line and her eyes burned with an intensity Cole knew all too well. Rather than try to get in her way, he did his best to watch her back as she climbed down the stairs to the basement.

"You think the locals were trying to draw us away from here?" Cole asked once they hit the small brick-walled room at the bottom of the stairs. A doorway led into the workshop where half a dozen Skinners from almost as many places were going through boxes of weapons collected or made by Lancroft himself.

"There's some good stuff in those files," she said quietly. "And then there's the basement below this one. The creatures in some of those cages downstairs may be more valuable than anything else. Even the dead things have their uses to Skinners who know their craft. Since the only thing that's been preventing anyone from carting away too much for themselves is the agreement we made when we opened this place up, there's plenty of reasons for someone to want some time alone in here."

"Plus," Cole chuckled, "there's the stuff we stashed before everyone started arriving."

"Yeah," she said with a comfortable smile. "That too." As easily as it had come when she looked at him, her smile disappeared when she looked back into the workroom. "I thought the right thing to do would be to take what we needed and let everyone else pick from the rest. Some of the others were bound to get snippy and squabble over some stuff, but I wasn't interested in being the mommy around this house. Maybe I'm the dumb one for thinking this could go smoothly at all."

Cole held her face in his hands, slipping his fingers beneath the newly clipped slopes of hair framing her cheeks. "We've been here the whole time," he told her. "There's no way to catalogue this crap, and even if there were, these are the people we would have called to do the cataloguing, right?"

"Yeah." Suddenly, Paige's face lit up and she pulled away from him so she could get another look into the next room. "Cataloguing! Did you ever print that sign-out sheet you were talking about?"

"The one you said was a stupid idea because it was treating Skinner weaponry and artifacts like rental movies?"

"That's the one."

"Yes I did."

"Has anyone been using it?"

"They'd better!"

"Or there'll be a late fee?" she chided while jogging through the workroom, stopping a few paces shy of the Skipping Temple. "Do you smell that?"

Compared to the smells that had filled Madman's place, the scent of freshly cut timber was a blessing. Cole nodded quickly.

Taking a quick look at her watch, Paige cursed under her breath and ran into the room covered in wall-to-wall Dryad script. Although the ancient markings were as beautiful as they were mysterious, the nymph sitting in the corner poking out a text message on her phone was the only thing Paige wanted to see. "When did you get here, Jordan?"

Dressed in a baggy shirt and cutoff sweat shorts, Jordan looked up from her phone and smiled. The hair she flipped over one ear was chestnut brown with amber highlights. By anyone's standards, she was a knockout. Because she was a lower level Dryad more commonly known as a nymph, even the curves of her ear were sexy enough to hold a human's attention once she fixed her eyes upon them. Cole had met her before, while rescuing Jordan from being worked to death by Jonah Lancroft, but he still had to brace himself to keep from being mesmerized by the sight of her perfection. When the nymph straightened her back and shifted to the edge of her seat, it became clear that she was gloriously unsupported beneath her shirt. He cleared his throat and tried to do the same for his mind.

"My shift just started," Jordan said. "Will you be needing us much longer? Every hour I'm away from the club means less money in my pocket."

"Shouldn't be much longer," Paige replied. "Did someone just come through here?"

"Sure. It was off the usual schedule, but I just got here. My pipes are in good shape, so I bent the rules a little. Seemed like the ones who went through were in a hurry."

"Who was it?"

"I don't know. The only Skinners I know by name are you and Cole. Hi, Cole. I see you squirming over there."

"Hi, Jordan."

Uninterested in the nymph's attempts to make Cole even more uncomfortable, Paige said, "I need to know who came through."

"All I can tell you is where they went."

Paige's eyes lit up and she leaned forward expectantly. "Where?"

"Florida. They got here in a rush and needed to leave quickly. The only club that had enough juice stored up to transport them on short notice was in Miami. Always plenty of juice in Miami."

The Dryads used spiritual energy gleaned from the emotions or excitement within living things. Humans were the richest source of that energy, and the oldest, most reliable way to get a human excited was to appeal to their baser instincts. The nymphs had been doing the same act for years, tempting mankind through everything from belly dancing to songs sung in forest clearings on summer nights. More recently they'd been making a killing at strip bars scattered throughout the country. Money was the least of what they harvested from their customers, but no harm was done.

Cole had already picked up the clipboard resting against the wall and was scanning the front page. When he shook his head and put the board down, Paige shifted from one foot to another as if getting ready to bolt and just needed to be pointed in the right direction. "Did they take anything out of here?" she asked.

"Sure," Jordan said. "Everyone's taking stuff out of here. Isn't that the point of all this?"

"Can you send me to where they went?"

Smirking while blowing a few strands of auburn hair away from a mouth that glistened with the color of ripe raspberries, she replied, "You know I can."

"Then do it. Cole, stay here and see if you can find out what was taken."

"I'm coming with you."

When Jordan stood up and started to hum, the melody of her voice carried throughout the entire room. It rustled beneath Cole's skin like a passing ghost that brushed its fingers along his spine as it went looking for another attic to haunt. In a matter of seconds the symbols on the walls thrummed with latent power.

"I want to go with you, Paige," Cole insisted. "We can figure out the rest later."

She placed a hand on him, and this time there was nothing close to a smack tagged onto the gesture. "If the locals or any other Skinners are involved in something dirty, they'll be quick to cover it up."

"Then stay here so we can both do a search. After that, we can—"

"No. The search needs to be done now. If someone told those Nymar across the street to rile up the neighbors to draw us away from here, then it was probably to clear a path for whoever came and went in between the scheduled songs or jumps or whatever the hell we're supposed to call this stripper subway."

"Good one. I think I just decided what I'm calling it from now on."

Jordan poked the keys on her phone and stuck it into one of the microscopic pockets in her sweat shorts. "They're ready for you on the other side."

All Paige had to do was tilt her face upward to get Cole to come closer to her. The crooked line of her nose cast a funny shadow on her face when the glow from the wall hit her. Despite the recent escalation in their partnership, he still hadn't noticed all the little scars she'd collected throughout her tenure as a Skinner. And even though her hair had been cut within the last week, it was already getting unruly around the edges.

"Most of these guys are good enough," she said, "but that doesn't mean we'll assume they're above stealing some better gear. You're smart. Come up with a way to figure out what was taken from here that was so important to the people who broke the schedule that they couldn't take a number like everyone else."

"And you've got to hang back when you find them," Cole said. "If you need backup, call and let me know."

"So you're keeping tabs on me?"

"No, I'm your partner. Even when you decide to shoot your mouth off to the wrong people."

"Fair enough."

He couldn't hear Jordan's voice, but he could feel the energy building within the beads like a static charge that rippled ahead of a thunderstorm. As Paige backed up, she nodded at something behind him. He turned and saw Abel standing in the doorway leading to the workshop. There was more crackling before Jordan let out a string of ethereal notes and Paige was gone. Paige didn't emerge on the other side of the curtain. All that was left was the scent of the Dryad energy and the clatter of the beads knocking against each other like any other outdated decorative room divider. Jordan sat back down, crossed her legs and resumed texting.

The Dryads assured him that walking through the beads when they weren't active was perfectly safe. Even so, Cole maneuvered around them cautiously, placing one shoulder against the wall and stepping past as quickly as possible. He went to Jordan and asked, "What did the people look like?"

"The ones who were in such a hurry to leave?"

"Yeah."

"There were four of them. Two were Nymar. I thought that was strange and tried telling someone about it, but they said it was okay."

"Was one of the Nymar a woman and the other some bald guy with a long beard?"

Jordan nodded immediately. "You got it. One of the guys was tall with red hair."

"And the other one carried a bunch of knives."

Relaxing into her corner again, Jordan shifted her attention back to the little keyboard on her phone. "That's them."

"Where'd they go once they got here?"

"They split up. The woman and the redhead went into . . ." Rather than acknowledge the dissection room by name, she waved as if the room where Henry's remains had been kept was a festering sore growing in one corner. "The other two headed that way with the rest," she explained while pointing toward the workroom.

"That's great, Jordan," Cole said. "Thanks."

"Anytime, sweetie."

"What's going on here?" Abel asked him. "Who broke the transport schedule?"

"Oh, now you notice, huh?"

"What do you mean? I can smell the pine, so I know someone went through. Was it Paige? Where is she?"

"Why don't you ask your cop buddies outside?"

Abel smirked and started picking something from between his teeth. "We told you we had some friends on the force."

"But there's plenty more you didn't tell us, right?"

When Cole walked to the smaller doorway in the other corner, his path was quickly blocked by the lankier Skinner. "What's up your ass?" Abel asked. "If you got some kinda problem, just spill it."

"Those cops were expecting something to happen," he said. "The Nymar inside that house across the street were expecting something too. For that matter, how is it that you didn't know there were Nymar camped out across the street?"

"In case you haven't had a look around, there's mason jars full of Nymar blood, venom, spit, and probably a few goddamn stool samples in the next room. My palms haven't itched this bad since I hit puberty. How the hell are we supposed to feel when a few more Nymar sneak in across the street?"

"This is your town, Abel. None of you guys have let anyone forget it since you got here. And, I might add, you got here way after me and Paige arrived."

"If you must know, Jory needed all of us to deal with a bunch of Half Breeds tearing through Lima, Ohio. We don't need to check in with you, those geeks at MEG, or any other goddamn body before we make a move to defend our territory. You got something to say about that?"

"Not really. I've got more important things to do." Cole shoved past him and walked into the starkly lit room that was dominated by a large table and several racks of equipment suited for jobs ranging from surgery to welding. There was a computer set up along the far wall, which was his first stop.

"You gotta understand where I'm coming from, man," Abel said while tagging along behind him. "I'm tight with my partners. Skinners gotta be that way since we don't exactly work well in big teams. Plus, you gotta expect to catch some flak from the rest of us."

Cole's fingers flew over the computer's keyboard to access a set of hidden files that he'd placed after the house was turned into Grand Central Station. "Really? Why's that?"

"You, Paige, and Rico all got first dibs on this stuff. While we all appreciate what you've done, we should've all gotten a chance to carve off a piece of that freak before Rico came in to take him away."

Cole's fingers paused momentarily. He'd known that Paige must have said something to the others about the empty space on the examination table where Lancroft's prize catch had been. Since Rico hadn't wanted to participate in what he knew was going to be a mess, he went back to his own business and left the infighting to the rest of what he called the "more sociable" Skinners. Pinning the disappearance of Henry's body on him seemed the best way to shut the others up about it. Even when he was in another state, Rico wasn't someone people wanted to question.

"Be honest," Abel said once Cole resumed typing, "Rico split some of that Full Blood meat up with you and Paige, right? If you got some of it stashed, it's only fair to at least let us know. I mean, coming in and taking that carcass away when the rest of us were followin' the rules laid down from you Chicago folks just ain't sporting."

"Well, that's Rico for ya."

"What the hell are you doing?"

The computer's display was split into two sections. One of them was a small window in the corner where Cole's interface was located and an image of the examination room as seen from the top of the computer's table filled the rest of the screen. A time stamp at the bottom rolled backward as Cole held down a button. "This computer's got a camera attached to it."

"It does?"

"Yes," he said, since he'd been the one to attach it. "That way, we can see who comes and goes through here to get to the valuable stuff."

"You didn't go back far enough. That freak was dragged out of here at least—"

"I'm not looking for that."

"So what are you looking for?"

Rolling backward through the video until he found the image of someone walking directly past the computer, Cole played it at normal speed. "That'd be it."

Abel leaned in to see. "That's the dude from Toronto. Bobby."

"Right, but that's not the same Nymar he had with him the last time."

"Sure it is."

The image on the screen wasn't perfect, but it was good enough for him to pick out the differences between Tru and the Nymar who was with Bobby in the video. The one captured by the webcam had similar hair to Trudy's, but was definitely shorter and skinnier. Even the way she walked was different, in that the one on the video had a definite stride while Tru walked more like someone waiting to step out of someone else's way. Aside from that, the tendril markings were all wrong.

"You seriously think that's Tru?" Cole asked.

"Sure. As far as I can tell, or at least as far I can see on this piece of shit monitor."

"When all else fails, blame the equipment." Before taking one step away from the computer, Cole put that section of video into a separate file and e-mailed it to himself. After that he secured the computer and headed for a narrow trapdoor in the corner. Although the entrance to the dissection room had been hidden by Skinner runes placed by Lancroft, the smaller door was hidden by every means possible. Apart from more runes, there were subtle techniques to hide the markings, which ranged from painting over them to arranging the equipment racks to make it seem like a door didn't even belong in that corner. All of those techniques would have been enough to keep the door a secret if Lancroft himself weren't forced into revealing it during the battle that ended his life. When Cole walked toward it, he was grabbed by Abel.

"Where are you going?"

Cole shook loose of the grip, walked through the door and down the stairs to a brick hallway that looked to have been charred by a flamethrower. "Checking to see what those other two were after."

Tagging along like an anxious puppy, Abel said, "I'm surprised you and Paige didn't already comb through all of this good enough to know what's here."

"We've been busy."

"Yeah, I just bet you have."

The snide tone in Abel's voice was easier to pick up than the markings on the mysterious Nymar woman's face. Cole let it slide, however, since he'd already spotted something out of place farther down the hall. He jogged past bulbs fit into sockets every fifteen to twenty feet along the wall. Alcoves on either side widened into anything from storage spaces to small cells sealed off by thick, rune-encrusted bars. Some of the cells had doors built in that forced anything bigger than a child to crawl on all fours to pass through, while others were simply one-way storage units. The things imprisoned there had died there. As of yet, the Skinners that claimed the Lancroft house hadn't figured out how to cut through to those remains.

Cole's sights were set on one of the smaller cages. Its little square gate was open, so he reached over his shoulder and grabbed his spear to prepare himself for what might be loose. He tried to remember what was in that cell but couldn't pick it out amid all the other things he'd discovered underneath that single, empty shell of a house.

"Shit, is one of those cages open?" Abel asked.

"Looks like it."

Gripping the spear in both hands, Cole felt the familiar pinch of its thorns piercing his flesh as he extended the weapon to its full length. The main spearhead had been treated with one of the innovations recently created by Daniels, which used melted fragments of the Blood Blade to form a new type of metallic coating. Apart from making the spearhead nice and shiny, it gave it more of a bite, to do serious damage to any shapeshifter. He only hoped that extra punch would be enough to put down whatever was in that cage.

When he arrived at the bars, Cole angled the spear down to point at the little door. Abel stepped up beside him, holding a wooden version of a short scimitar at the ready. Blood welled between his fingers, showing that his thorns cut just as deep as anyone else's. "Is it still in there?" Abel asked.

"Can't tell."

Digging into his pocket, Abel removed a small flashlight attached to a keychain. With a click of a button, a pale blue light filled the brick alcove. The cramped interior of the cage had feces crusted on the walls, dozens of small animal carcasses on the floor, and the body of what looked to be a short man laid out on his back. One leg was propped up and the other was skewed to one side. Both arms were splayed out in a cruciform position, and his head was angled in such a way that his wide, clouded eyes caught the light being shone into the cage. Despite having all the basic parts, the thing wasn't human. Black, uneven claws extended from his fingers. His musculature was swollen well out of proportion to his stature, and thick black veins ran beneath almost every inch of his skin.

"This thing was cut open recently," Cole said. "I would have remembered seeing this before."

"Looks like a Nymar. See the markings?"

"Yeah, but there's something different about it."

"You sure?"

It was a simple question, but sparked a whole lot of uneasiness in Cole's gut. He was rarely sure about anything anymore. All he could rely on was a motivational tool that had taken him from a desk job at a mid-range video game company to the basement of a monster hunter who might have been alive since before the nineteenth century. He'd come this far, he told himself, so he might as well keep going.

"Give me that light," Cole said as he reached back to Abel.

The other Skinner slapped the key chain into Cole's hand without taking his eyes from the body lying in the squalid little cell.

Cole crouched down and shone the beam on the Nymar carcass. Its chest was pulled open, but not in the same way as Henry's victims back when the crazed Full Blood still had his taste for vampire spores. Before he crawled in there with the dead thing, Cole used the spear to reach between the bars and jab the carcass. Having been coated with the new varnish, the spearhead was sharp enough to puncture its flesh with little effort.

"Is that the new Blood Blade treatment for the weapons?" Abel asked.

"Yes."

"When the hell do we get some of that stuff?"

"Just shut up, okay?"

While Abel grumbled about having last year's weapon model in his hand, Cole dropped to all fours and crawled into the cell. He scraped through the opening, thinking about how much he didn't like Abel and how little he trusted him. Then he thought about how stupid he'd been to turn his back on that guy while entering a cell designed to keep things trapped for extremely long stretches of time.

Once inside, Cole was instantly struck with how much smaller the room felt. Its floors were rough and soggy due to layers upon layers of filth and decay left behind by its inhabitants, wandering rodents, or whatever slop might have been tossed in for food. Considering the looks of the thing on the floor, however, the rodents could very well have been the food.

"What is it?" Abel asked.

Holding the light closer to the thing's exposed arms, Cole picked out gray tendrils beneath the flesh. Thinking back to some of the lessons Paige had taught him, he eased the flap of skin on its chest open using the tip of his collapsed spear. It came open with a wet sucking sound. He was no surgeon, but the heart was easy enough to spot. It was at the center of the hole dug into the thing's chest, like a Valentine's gift dropped there for safekeeping. He leaned in as close as his nose would allow. The smells rising up from the exposed cavity were like a living entity that reached down to tug at the back of his throat. "Looks like a Nymar, all right," he said. After finding the telltale puncture marks on the sides of the heart as well as the scratches put there when the spore hung on during the removal process, he added, "Yeah. Nymar."

"Wait a second. Do that again."

"What?"

"The light. Move it again."

Cole had only turned his head so he could give two of his senses a break at the same time. To appease the other Skinner, he waved the light back and forth across the dead Nymar's upper body.

"That's it!" Abel said. "Did you see it?"

Although his movements gave the corpse's exposed, ravaged heart a cool strobe effect, Cole found one major difference with the tendrils shooting through the vampire's arms and legs. At first glance they just seemed thinner than normal. What differentiated them from tendrils on any other Nymar he'd seen was the way they reacted to the light. When the flashlight's beam was shining directly on them, they shriveled into crooked, almost imperceptible lines. When the beam moved away, the tendrils fattened and spread out until they were almost touching one another.

Cole moved the beam back and forth a few more times, but the effect was less noticeable with every pass.

"I wonder if it could do that when it was alive," Abel said.

"The tendrils only become gray when they're drying out. If all the plumbing was still connected, it may cover this thing in some sort of black . . . cloak?"

Abel pressed his head against the bars to get as close a look as possible without crawling through the muck. "Pretty smart. I see why Paige kept you around. Well, apart from the obvious reasons. A living Nymar may even be able to control when those tendrils spread out like that. He could damn near go invisible if he was in the shadows."

"That's pushing it, but it might help him stay hidden. There's something else that's strange. This thing isn't tripping much of anything in my scars. What about you?"

"It's dead, Cole. Just like damn near everything else down here. That's why everyone's upstairs. I bet Lancroft just set this place aside as a dumping ground."

Something at the far end of the hall growled at them. More than a simple animal's snarl, it directed itself at Cole and Abel as surely as if it had known their names.

"Let's get the fuck outta here," Abel grunted.

Cole dug his phone from his pocket and took a few pictures of the dead Nymar. The tendrils still had some flex to them as he passed the light back and forth, so he got some shots of that as well. "Check the rest of the hall, Abel."

"You check it."

"Just go!"

Cole didn't care if Abel did the job or not. All he really wanted was to get the other Skinner to move away from that little door when he crawled through. There wasn't a way for him to exit without making himself vulnerable to a quick downward stab, and more than likely, Lancroft had constructed the doors with that very purpose in mind. Either that, he thought, or he was getting too paranoid for his own good.

Once he was outside, Cole checked on Abel. Nothing else struck him as more peculiar than it had been the last time he was down there. Whatever was caged at the farthest end kept its back against the wall and stared at the Skinners with glittering eyes. It was a shapeshifter. He could tell that much from the way it swelled or contracted, as if its entire skeletal structure was an illusion. Finding out any more than that would have required getting much too close to the thing, and despite their differences, all the Skinners agreed that the creature at the end of the hall was best left alone where it was.

On their way back up the stairs, Cole asked, "What's the word with the cops? Is there going to be a problem?"

"Nah. Selina straightened it out. A few of the officers know about Nymar, and they're glad to let us take care of 'em. Since there were two feeding on someone in that house, we got a pass. Still, tell Paige to rein it in when she gets back."

"Tell her yourself."

Abel chuckled all the way up the stairs. Although Cole tried ignoring him when he asked some of the others in the workshop about where Paul and M had gone, the greasy smile plastered on Abel's face made that task next to impossible.

"I remember Paul coming through," a Skinner from the West Coast said. "He was a quiet guy who'd come alone to poke through the house."

"Where did they go?" Cole asked.

Pointing to a stack of crates filled with old baby food jars containing a multitude of fluids that most definitely should not be fed to babies, he replied, "M went straight for that pile there and left with half a milk crate full of stuff."

"What stuff?"

"Don't know. Without Lancroft's journals, a lot of this is being filed in the unknown category."

"And they just walked out with it?"

"M's supposed to be with Paul, and Paul is a Skinner," the guy pointed out. "Why would I stop him? Is there some sort of pecking order I don't know about?"

"No," Cole grunted. Of all the things that were bugging him, not one of them had to do with the guy from the West

Coast. In fact, most of the Skinners who'd drifted in had been content to take a few supplies or one of the old weapons and be on their way. The ones that grated on Cole's nerves the most were the ones that refused to leave.

As if picking up on his chance to grate some more, Abel asked, "Where's Paige?"

"Not sure," he lied.

"You're not sure? You don't keep track of your partner?"

"No," Cole snapped. "Do you?"

When Cole walked over to the crates of jars along the opposite wall, Abel stuck with him. "Jory and Selina are pretty close," Abel said, "but not like you and Paige."

The words didn't bug Cole so much as the creepy way Abel said them. Crouching down to pull some of the crates away from the wall so he could get to the back stacks, he found a few that weren't quite in line with the rest.

Either Abel was used to being ignored or he took Cole's silence as an invitation to continue. "From what I seen, you two are *real* close."

"And what have you seen?"

"You know. The way you look at her. That sappy shit when you touched her hair."

Cole gnashed his teeth. He'd forgotten about the hair thing. His phone rang, saving him the trouble of continuing the conversation. When he saw who was calling, it was even easier to pretend the other man didn't exist. "Hey, Paige," he said into the phone. "Where are you?"

Screaming over the thumping tones of a remixed version of Duran Duran's "Rio," she replied, "Some club in Miami. Did you find anything?"

"I think so. There's some kind of—"

"I can barely hear you. Are you finished with everything over there?"

Abel grinned and nodded as if he'd paid five bucks to sit on a sticky chair and watch the show.

"Yeah," Cole grunted. "I'm through here."

"Then head to Chicago."

"Actually, there are a few loose ends I should wrap up here."

"Fine," she said. "I'm headed home now. When you're about to leave, give me a call and I'll pick you up at the subway station."

"Will do. 'Bye." He hung up, put the phone in his pocket, and found Abel still looking at him with that same grin. There was a renewed speed in Cole's movements when he picked a sample jar from each of the crates that looked as if they'd recently been moved.

"So," Abel sneered, "you're hittin' that, right?"

"Shut the hell up."

Abel smirked as if his clumsy attempt at slang was too cool for the room. "You two aren't just close. You're like, *close*. You screwing her or what?"

Once again Cole's silence didn't deter the other man in the slightest.

"Not that I blame you," Abel continued. "She's got a sweet little ass. Kind of a butter face, but—"

"Wait," Cole said as he straightened up and turned to face the other Skinner. "What the hell did you just say?"

"Butter face. You know, like she's got a nice body, but her—"

His fist slammed into Abel's jaw as if it had a mind of its own. After taking a moment to think, he did the right thing and hit Abel again, this time with enough force to knock the little prick onto his ass.

Chapter Seven

Watching the Dryad temples work was somehow more impressive than actually stepping through the beads. A crackle of energy washed over Cole's body. He caught a strong whiff of clean woods. There was a rush of sound and that was it. He'd only been teleported a handful of times, but it was already getting old. Of course, some receptions were better than others.

The beads were still rattling behind him when he was lassoed by a tall blonde wearing fishnets and a suit jacket that was cut to frame her bare breasts despite all three buttons being buttoned. With her hair up in a bun and plastic-framed glasses perched upon the bridge of her nose, she looked like a naughty secretary pulled straight out of a porno from 1958. "Just try to look frazzled, honey," she said while dragging him away from the beads.

Staring out at a large room partially filled with men in business suits, Cole replied, "No problem there."

The place was a typical strip club, but with the distinction of having most of its neon on the inside instead of out. Replicas of vintage Las Vegas casino signs, complete with the old-school cowboy leaning against a post, lit up two large stages. Only one stage was being used at the moment, but considering it was early afternoon, that still seemed like a lot. His entrance was made even more peculiar due to the fact that he was still carrying a banker's box filled with the samples he'd taken from Lancroft's basement.

"How was it, partner?" one of the businessmen asked.

Cole's fumbling attempt at a response brought a round of hollers from the sparse crowd.

"Find out for yourself, honey," the blonde said. To Cole, she added, "Your date's right over there."

Paige sat at a bar that was another throwback to Sin City's golden age. When she waved at Cole and hopped down from her stool, the businessmen broke into another round of applause before being distracted by a nurse named Florence Naughtygale.

"Where the hell did I land?"

Although it was tired, Paige's smile went all the way down to the bone. "The nymphs just set up shop here after Tristan spread the word that Lancroft wasn't hunting them anymore. They don't have the temple portion sectioned off yet, so they just made it a part of the scenery."

Cole looked back to find the beads strung across an alcove bearing the large flowing script. It was supported by an arch inscribed with more symbols and a sign that read: VIP ROOM.

"When I called, you could have warned me I'd be on display," he said.

"And miss your grand entrance?" she asked while leading him to the front door. "Not a chance. Besides, I arrived at the tail end of last night's party crowd. The hoopla you got was nothing in comparison to me being escorted through that curtain by some leggy broad in a kitty cat outfit. Wipe that grin off your face. Save the image for when you're alone."

"Oh, you know I will."

Once he stepped outside, Cole was hit by the sun blazing down at him through a thin layer of fog. So far, most of the other nymph-run strip bars had been on lonely stretches of highway with a minimum of neighbors. West Chicago wasn't exactly urban, but there were several small businesses, convenience stores, and gas stations within sight of the place. Farther down the road the scenery was taken over by small houses.

"So," Cole mused as he turned to get a look at the sign above the purple A-frame. "Pinups, huh?"

"Yep. This'll be our local stop on the Stripper Subway."

"I like it. Hell, I like just being away from that damn Lancroft house."

Paige crossed the narrow parking lot that wrapped all the way around the club. "I got a few things that I wanted from there, so let the rest of those assholes fight over the rest. I see you found something else."

"Just some samples that look like Nymar blood," he said as he spotted the beat-up white Chevy Cavalier parked between a Dumpster and the cluster of businessmen's cars. The single piece of metal on it that wasn't dented was the front bumper, and that's only because it had been replaced after its most recent accident. The front window was new but had picked up several chips already, thanks to gravel kicked up on the interstate. "Aw, man! Can't we get a new car?"

"What for? We won't be needing to take any long road trips anymore."

"Yeah, but still!"

Paige tuned out his whining with the same efficiency that she ignored the grinding of the motor as she started up the Cav. Cole set the box on the floor next to his feet as he dropped into the passenger seat. Every spring poking him in the back or butt through the minimal padding felt like the touch of a familiar hand. Even the smells of exhaust, dried blood, and stale fast food struck a nostalgic chord. The car might have seen some rough times, but he'd been there for them as well. Settling into the seat as the Cav lurched into motion, he was more relaxed than he'd been in weeks.

"This is nice," he said.

"What? Pinups or the fact that we're just in time to get stuck in rush hour on our way back to Raza Hill?"

"Just . . . this. No more sitting around some basement from a serial killer movie. No more listening to a bunch of were-wolf hunters bicker over mayo jars filled with old teeth. No more putting up with assholes like Abel or . . . well . . . Abel. Just you and me. Back to the normal routine."

"Don't get used to it. The way things are going, we'll be dealing with those others for quite a while. Tell me what you found after I left."

Cole gave her the rundown of his investigation as Paige drove up North Avenue. When he was done, she asked, "So what did Abel do that was so bad?"

"Apart from getting on my nerves, not much."

"Sounds like something happened while I was away."

"No, Ma, I swear," Cole said in a slow drawl. "We was good."

"Maddy said you punched him."

"Maddy saw that?"

"Yep."

Cole fiddled with the radio until he found something other than talk or a commercial. "Well, okay. I punched him. Now how about you tell me what you did in Miami while I was crawling around a basement?"

"First of all, the club in Miami had some of the most im-pressive asses I've ever seen. And I'm not just talking about the dancers."

"And?"

"And one of the ladies attached to one of those asses pointed me in the right direction to catch up with the Skin-ners that arrived just before I did. It took some fast footwork and a taxi ride that damn near required a change of pants before it was done, but I caught up to them."

"Did you recognize them?"

Paige focused her attention on the traffic in front of her. Although it was bad at that time of day, it was unusual for her to focus that much on driving. The Chicago blood running through her veins allowed her to control a motor vehicle without being restricted by fear of losing life or limb. "Yeah," she said after cutting off a black Toyota. "I did. Bobby was one of them."

"And the other?"

"The other wasn't Tru. I followed them for as long as I could and broke off before I was spotted. It didn't take long for them to disappear among all the other bloodsuckers."

"Miami's a big Nymar town?"

"Are you kidding me? All those half-dressed hotties looking to dance, hook up, or party? I wouldn't be surprised if a Nymar founded that city. It's bad enough those Canadians are working with Nymar so closely, but having Bobby smuggle in a new one after making sure our backs were turned makes this a whole new game."

"We work with Daniels pretty closely," Cole reminded her. "He's Nymar."

"I know Daniels. I don't know Bobby well enough to cut him that kind of slack. So what am I supposed to make of those pictures you sent me?"

"They're pictures of that dead Nymar I found in the basement. Last time you were down there, were any of the cells open?"

"No," she replied without hesitation.

"This one was about halfway down the row."

Paige didn't have to think long before saying, "The only cells that had much of anything in them were toward the end of the hall. Nobody touched the thing at the far end, did they?"

"No. This Nymar had a lot more tendrils in it even after the spore had been taken out. Tendrils that reacted to light. They'd swell up and turn the skin black. Also, I didn't feel anything in my scars. I know it was dead, but I was right there and should have felt something, right?"

"Yes. That part could be bad."

"Also, I think Bobby and M went through some of those jars that were piled up in all those milk crates. I took samples to see if we could figure out what they wanted."

They drove in silence for a while. A triple play of Aerosmith was on the radio, so both of them relaxed during their stop-and-go journey across town. Cole knew he hadn't heard everything that had happened in Miami. Paige was in too good a mood for there to have been a fight, but she was holding something back. Since he was holding back a few details of his own, he figured he'd let the matter drop. The silence was comfortable and easy. After the final swaying notes of "Dream On" had faded away, Paige reached out to shut them off with a twist of the radio knob.

"I'm going back, Cole."

"Back to Philly? It'll just be more of the same. If those locals are setting something up with the Nymar, we shouldn't go back alone. Let's bring Rico. We can say he's just taking his turn claiming some of that Lancroft crap. We'll have to warn him about Henry, though."

"No. Rico's not coming with me, and neither are you. I'll probably head back to Philly sooner or later, but I meant I'm going back to Miami. There's something I need to double-check. You're going back to Raza Hill and staying in Chicago. We've been gone for too long. Steph was just getting the Nymar organized here when we left for KC, and kept organizing while we were in St. Louis. Who knows what she's got going on by now. She and the rest of her girls need to see a Skinner presence around here again. Make the rounds. Show yourself around town. Bust some heads if anyone's stepping out of line. Let's face it, with Steph and Ace in the area, someone's bound to be stepping out of line."

"If you're not taking me along, then at least tell me you're taking someone." Cole's eyes drifted to her arm. Since her injury in Kansas City, Paige had been able to move it a lot better and even found some creative uses for the hardened tissue impeding her movement. The sling was long gone, but the scars made it clear she wasn't functioning at one hundred percent. "You really shouldn't be on your own, Paige."

Despite flying down a rare stretch of open road, she shifted her focus away from the windshield and to her passenger. "You don't even know what I'm doing. Why the hell should you tell me how I should go about doing it?"

He had plenty to say to that, but held it back. At the moment he was so pissed off that he no longer even wanted to hear her voice.

Chapter Eight

"They're back in town."

Steph had plenty of smiles in her repertoire. Most of them were sincere, but in a way that most smiles weren't supposed to be. She had the grin that she put on for her customers at the Blood Parlor, which was prospering in its location on Rush Street. That was always a crowd pleaser since it was accompanied by one or more of her girls coming in to take customers off to a room to enjoy the pleasures of feeling Nymar teeth ease into their necks or wrists. There was the hungry smile that allowed all three sets of her fangs to slide out from beneath her gums. That was her favorite, since it was the predatory equivalent of stripping naked and showing yourself to a lover before the much anticipated next act. And then there was the one that came to her now.

Her smooth face was illuminated by an earnest display of joy when she asked, "Are you talking about the Skinners?"

Standing in the doorway to her office, Ace nodded. He was a skinny guy who looked to have been somewhere in his late twenties when he'd been turned. Although he still looked youthful, there was too much experience in his eyes for him to properly carry the baggy jeans and netted shirt he insisted on wearing. The narrow patch of hair sprouting from his chin, and the heart shaved into the side of his head, didn't help his case much. "Come on," he said. "You can hear them now if you want."

Steph hopped up and practically skipped around her desk to follow him down a hallway that led to the back rooms of her parlor. Little stone gargoyles lined the walls, each of them holding electric candles in clawed hands. The walls were painted dark red. Newly purchased black carpeting rubbed her bare feet. Muted, moody music played from hidden speakers to complete the parlor's effect. So far the people who paid to have the Nymar feed on them loved every last one of the clichéd gothic touches. They especially liked seeing Steph in a good mood. One of the men, a stockbroker in his early forties, scooted all the way to the edge of an overstuffed couch in the waiting room just to get a look at her as she left her office. Fully aware that she was on display in a lavender nightie that stopped just short of covering the ruffles of her cream-white panties, she looked back at him and kissed the air. That was enough to convince him to spring for the deluxe package.

Most of the rooms branching off the hallway were small, luxurious bed chambers that came complete with closed-circuit video cameras hidden behind sculptures and wall sconces. They were all wired into the room full of monitors that the Blood Parlor's managers were now entering. The security room was all sharp edges and glowing reminders of what century it truly was. Ignoring the assorted depravities being displayed on the screens, Steph and Ace went immediately to a laptop set up on one metal desk in the corner of the room. On that screen was a display mapping the time and pitch of scratchy sounds being played through the computer's speakers. Ace selected a time stamp he'd already highlighted and pressed the button for it to play.

When she heard Cole and Paige having their conversation on the way back from Pinups, Steph pressed her hands to her mouth to hold back a giggle. "So this is from their car?" she asked through her fingers.

"Sid rigged it while they were gone the last time."

After pausing the recorded conversation, Steph asked, "Where did they go?"

"Hell if I know. We've been following them like you wanted for a while. They were out of town for that shit in Kansas City and then again awhile after that."

"See? I told you it was a good idea to keep track of them! Especially since that skank with the billy clubs started cracking down on my girls."

"Yeah, yeah," Ace droned. "I wanted to clean them out way before then, but you said it would be too much trouble."

"Well forget that," she said after crossing her arms over her proudly displayed cleavage. "Word's being spread on CP that the Skinners won't be such a threat for much longer."

"Did that come from Toronto?"

"Oh yeah. Cobb wrote the post himself." Steph's painted lips curled into half a grin as she looked down at the laptop and stroked the right mouse button as if teasing a customer's anatomy. "This is priceless. I still don't know how Paige got access to our security feeds, but she always knew when the good stuff was happening in this place. Let's see how she likes it."

"Probably did it when she and that other guy stormed in here after we opened." Ace tapped the Internet browser on his cell phone and hit the link to ChatterPages.net. Ninety-nine percent of the population used the social networking site to post family pictures and play games, between writing updates about what they had for dinner. Although veiled as a fetish fan group, the ChatterPage used by the Nymar was run like a science and alerted its nationwide members about things ranging from Skinner movements and Full Blood sightings to the juiciest, most poorly guarded feeding spots in most major cities. Ace didn't have to scroll down very far before finding the most recent postings from Cobb38, the page's founding member. "Holy shit! Someone found the Shadow Spore?"

"Took it right out from under the Skinners' noses. On top of that, most of the Skinners in the country are either in

Philadelphia for some reason or going back and forth from there right now. That means all of them are distracted."

"It's not all of them we need to worry about. Cobb never knew exactly what the Chicago Skinners were doing."

"No, but we do." Tapping the mouse button again, Steph allowed the conversation stolen from the Cav to roll for another minute before sighing, "Just listen to them. Sounds like two crazy kids who just climbed out of bed long enough to realize the other one's not perfect. So cute."

"That was just recorded about twenty minutes ago," Ace said. "It should still be a while before they make it back to that shithole restaurant they live in."

"Are Sid and Rita down there?"

Smirking in a way that allowed the tips of his feeding fangs to poke out from their sheaths, Ace said, "They never left."

"Good. Give them the go-ahead."

It was late morning on a weekday, which meant the section of West Twenty-fifth and Laramie was mostly deserted. People drove by, and a few walked along the dirty sidewalk, but none of them cast more than half a glance at the boarded windows and locked door of the old restaurant marked only by a broken sign with enough remaining letters to spell RAZA HILL. Anyone from that section of town hardly noticed it was there anymore. The place was too shabby to rob and just clean enough to escape official notice.

Although there was plenty of space inside, the Skinners used only a few rooms at the building's core. The basement was their private gym and sparring area. What had once been offices were now used for storage and Paige's bedroom. The kitchen was self-explanatory. A few of the ovens still worked, along with the large stainless steel fridge. The walk-in freezers were shut down, however. One was full of broken furniture and the other was sealed for sanitary reasons. Cole slept in the one with the broken furniture.

"Yeah, Jason," he said into the phone he kept trapped between his shoulder and the side of his face. "I'm working on it right now."

The voice that came through the digital connection to Seattle was patient and only slightly distracted. "What happened to those concepts you were going to e-mail me? The ones with the shapeshifting death-match players. You were supposed to be working on those all month."

What Cole wanted to say was that he'd been distracted with things like a mind-controlling Full Blood and a Skinner from a hundred years ago making the entire country sick with Mud Flu. The best he could come up with was, "I'm still working on that too."

"You've got some great ideas, Cole. I know I've asked you this before, but—"

"No," Cole snapped. "I'm not planning on moving back to Seattle."

"Then what I'd like to do is offer to buy you out."

"Buy what out? The only thing I do for Digital Dreamers anymore is consultant work and some private contracting."

"The ideas for the shapeshifting stuff," Jason said with a sigh that Cole knew went along with a slow hand gliding over a scalp covered by thinning hair. "All the guys around here have been watching the stuff online about those werewolf sightings in Kansas City and the more recent ones in Indiana."

Cole stopped his typing and sat bolt upright. "Indiana? What happened in Indiana?"

"Just more of the same crap that's been coming in from all over the place after the riots in KC. There's been a few local news specials, but now the cable networks are getting in on it. Everyone from CNN to Animal Planet have some sort of wild dog or werewolf feature coming up. The point is that we want to strike while the iron is hot and get a major werewolf project in the works before people lose interest."

Cole had plenty of werewolf projects rolling around in his head, but only a few of them were the sort of thing he might discuss with Jason. Just as he was about to use one of them to try and salvage some of his old career, the phone beeped to let him know someone else was calling. He looked at the screen to find the word PROPHET blinking back at him. Poking the Ignore button, he went back to his old friend from another life. "Maybe I can come back to Seattle," he said.

"Seriously? When?"

"The way things may be working out here . . ."

Prophet beeped in again with a text message that Cole didn't bother to read.

"We have an opening for a designer that could carry over into a lead position," Jason said.

Not only did Cole forget about the text, but he almost dropped the phone. "Why tell me this?" he asked hopefully.

"Because word's gotten around that the next *Hammer Strike* will be without the guy who made the first one and the fans aren't happy."

"That many fans know about me?"

"Well, they did after someone let it slip just how much you did for this company while you were here."

"Jason, that's a hell of a nice thing you did. I knew you'd—"

"Wasn't me," Jason said. "It was Nora."

"Nora?"

The phone beeped again, but Cole didn't even hear it. "Nora?" he asked. "As in, the girlfriend who I thought was my ex a few times already Nora?"

"That's the one," Jason replied in a tone that was the closest thing to a grin his voice could convey. "I don't know how much luck you'll have with the whole girlfriend thing, but she's been doing a hell of a good job in paving the way for your return. The fact that you're still responsible for a ton of royalties ain't hurting your cause either."

Hearing the executive of Digital Dreamers, Inc. try to purposely use incorrect grammar was almost as bad as hearing his drunken attempt to rap during the infamous Christmas Party Karaoke Incident of '02. When the phone beeped again, he turned it over as if expecting to see photos from that December night all those years ago. Instead, what he got was a text message that read: GET OUT OF THERE IDIOT!!!!!!!

Cole glanced toward the next room but couldn't see much more than a sliver of the kitchen through the freezer door. Rays of light coming in from the front half of the restaurant were given form by the smoke rolling in toward his living quarters. That's when the smell hit him. Something was burning. If he and Paige hadn't been so concerned with more unnatural threats, they might have replaced the batteries in the smoke detectors instead of yanking them off the ceiling and throwing them into a corner when they'd started chirping.

The first thing Cole grabbed was the harness containing his spear. That went onto his back, freeing up his hands to stuff a few essentials into a satchel that he slid over his head and one arm. Keys and wallet joined a shoe polish tin filled with the newly refined varnish containing the Blood Blade fragment in his pockets. Lastly, he snapped his laptop shut, jerked it from the power strip he'd installed in the freezer wall, and left the rest behind. Smoke rolled through the front of the restaurant, but he still couldn't see any flames. After walking through the swinging doors leading to the dining room, he heard the crackling rush of a fire.

Cole rushed back through the kitchen and into the storeroom to get to the rear entrance. Ramming into the metal door with his shoulder, he bounced off before grabbing the bar that released the lock. A second later the piercing cry of the security buzzer went off. Naturally, Paige remembered to keep *those* alarms in working order. The shattering of glass and the rolling crackle of a fire was almost enough to drown out the electric shriek as he stumbled out to the back lot. Breathless and confused, he wheeled around to take a look at the restaurant. There wasn't much to see other than dirty brick and trash cans. From the front of the structure, however, black smoke drifted on the wind and tongues of flame peeled along the edges of the old building.

"What the hell happened?" he asked a man who stood in the parking lot waving a phone at someone.

The man whipped around and snarled at Cole, baring two upper sets of fangs. "You overstayed your welcome in this city," Sid growled. "That's what happened."

Two cars were parked in the front lot, angled to make sure nobody else could approach Raza Hill without jumping a curb and damaging the underside of their vehicle on one of many cement barriers. Another pulled up, and before it came to a stop, Steph jumped out and clapped her hands with giddy delight. She wore large retro sunglasses and a long coat that had been hastily thrown on over her nightie, which made her look like someone roused from bed and forced outside due to the fire instead of someone who'd arrived to watch it burn.

"What did I miss?" she asked.

The girl who jogged over to greet her looked to be somewhere in her late teens. The tendrils under her skin snaked along her arms to collect at her wrists, marking her as a Nymar that had been drinking blood for a good long time. Her dark hair was pulled into pigtails, which further marked her as one of the girls under Steph's employ. A denim skirt laced up the side was short enough to display a whole lot of leg with tendrils running up the backs like a seam in nonexistent stockings. "Jason and some of the others are shooting up a diner and some gas stations about a mile from here, so that should keep the cops busy. Once that gas station goes up, the fire department will have their hands full too."

"Nice," Ace said as he stepped out from the driver's side of the car. "How long's this been burning?"

"I told him to wait until you got here, but he got antsy."

"That's fine," Steph snapped. "How long?"

"Only a minute or two. It's really starting to kick in now, though. Should be a good one."

"Are they both in there?"

"That junker Chevy wasn't in the lot, so probably not," Rita said. "I know at least one of them's inside, though."

Steph leaned against the hood of her car and beamed as if watching her youngest child in its first school play.

There wasn't much of an alley on the left side of the building. A tall chain fence studded with unevenly spaced boards encircled all but the front of the lot and got to within eight feet of the structure. Weeds had reclaimed the bottom of the fence, and the rest of the ground was covered with gravel, garbage, or broken glass. The flames made a steady roar that wasn't quite loud enough to cover the crunch of footsteps made by a Nymar who shuffled toward the back corner of the building.

He was dressed in an old army surplus jacket that was too big to fit him properly but perfectly concealed all of the instruments of chaos stuffed into the inner pockets. In one hand was a beer bottle with a wet rag sticking out of the top. With his other hand, he flicked open a Zippo lighter, waved it under his nose so he could savor the scent of its fluid, and then rolled his thumb against the rough little wheel to make a spark. He never took his eyes off the triangular flame as he brought it close enough to the rag to set it alight.

The Nymar pulled in another breath, held it, then pivoted on the balls of his feet to face the man that had crept up to within ten feet of him.

Coming down the alley, Prophet cursed under his breath and broke into a dead run to charge at the Nymar. His intention had been to get to the arsonist before the next cocktail hit the side of the restaurant. In that respect, he succeeded. He wasn't feeling too good about the victory, however, since the lit firebomb was tossed at him instead.

The bottle hit Prophet's shoulder and bounced off to sail so close to his face that he could hear the crackle of the flame on its rag. There was another *whoosh* as the bottle hit the ground behind him to create a large, burning puddle that sent a blast of heat washing over the back portion of his body. As Prophet rammed into him, the arsonist raised both arms to absorb the impact and then slapped both hands onto Prophet's back and shoulder to divert him into a brick wall. Prophet hit solidly and skidded along the side of the restaurant. Rolling around so his back was pressed against solid cover, he reached for the shoulder holster under his jacket. The .38 was an older model that was light in his hand and came out quickly. He aimed at the Nymar's center of mass as the arsonist rushed straight at him.

The gunshot cracked through the air, drawing the eyes of all three Nymar in the front parking lot. "Who fired that?" Ace asked.

Rita dropped into a low stance that made her look as if she was in a set of starting blocks. "Someone else must have been around when the torch was being lit."

Suddenly, an inhuman howl arose from the opposite end of the building. "That's Sid!" Rita said.

Steph grinned and rubbed her hands together. "Looks like we caught both of them in there after all. You two see if anyone needs a hand and I'll do crowd control."

Several cars were clogging Laramie Avenue and groups of pedestrians either stopped to watch the fire or were taking pictures of it with their phones. A few of the less voyeuristic of the bunch actually approached the cars blocking the entrance to Raza Hill.

"Could you help us?" Steph asked the people who were close enough.

Her strained voice and thrown-together outfit brought one man in his late forties rushing toward her to ask if there was anything he could do. The question was still fresh on his lips when Steph grabbed him and threw him toward Ace, who sank his feeding fangs along with the lower set of teeth into the man's neck. When the Good Samaritan tried to pull away, he only widened the gash in his veins and hastened the flow of blood into Ace's mouth. Rita latched onto the other side and helped drain the guy in a matter of seconds.

"Make this quick," Steph said. "Our distraction won't hold up much longer."

Strengthened by the blood covering the lower portion of her face, Rita dashed across the parking lot in a flicker of movement that took her to the last known location of her partner. Ace was flushed with color and swelling with newly awakened muscles. He darted halfway across the parking lot before springing up to a section of the roof that had yet to be touched by the fire.

Of the people who were close enough to see the fangs in Steph's mouth, all but one ran away. That man shuffled backward while holding his camera phone in front of him to take a video of the Nymar. The last thing he filmed was Steph lunging forward to clamp her jaws around his jugular and then crush the phone in a powerful grip.

People screamed.

A gun was fired.

Cars screeched on Laramie Avenue and Twenty-fifth Place.

Cole's home was burning.

And yet, all he wanted was to keep his laptop from being smashed. There simply was no accounting for the priorities of a frantic mind. When Sid came at him, his first impulse was to turn so the Nymar didn't smash the computer. The Lancroft files were there, along with everything he'd done for Digital Dreamers. All of the new stuff he hadn't sent in or backed up to another system was on that drive. If he was to have any chance at getting back to a normal life again, it was in that machine.

And then, in the time it took for Sid to reach for him and extend his upper set of fangs, Cole was forced to admit something vital to his continued existence: this *was* his normal life. After that, it was a simple matter of holding the laptop in front of him to shield himself from Sid's attack. Once that was deflected, he gripped the laptop in both hands and pounded the metal case against Sid's temple. It wasn't enough to drop the Nymar, but it gave him some breathing space.

Sid's jaw opened to the point of hyperextending, and his fangs stretched out as if they'd developed a hungry mind of their own. He lashed out with one hand to nearly crack the laptop in half. Cole jumped away and ducked under a follow-up swipe of claws that had sprouted from beneath the Nymar's fingernails. Sid's other hand came around to shred the front of Cole's shirt along with a portion of underlying skin.

The claws stung, but Cole's system had been producing the Skinner healing serum on its own for long enough to deal with it. Rather than worry about blood loss, he used the pain to fuel his movements. "You've been working out," he said while dropping the laptop's remains so he could draw the spear from its harness.

Sid wasn't interested in talking. He surged forward amid a flurry of claws, leaving Cole no option but to try and block as many of them as he could. Sid's foot swept out and across in a quick motion that hit his ankle like a cement post and dropped him to the ground with an impact that emptied his lungs and turned his surroundings into a blurred mess of sight and sound. Light from above was eclipsed as Sid loomed over him and slashed at his face. Cole rolled to one side, allowing the claws to clip the back of his head and carve a set of grooves into the concrete. Better prepared for the next swing, he held the spear diagonally in front of him. When he twisted to block, however, the wooden shaft wound up clamped in the Nymar's grip.

As Sid leaned down, the overpowering stench of blood rolled from his mouth in a coppery wave. His tongue emerged from between crusted lips, catching the venom that dripped from his curved set of snakelike fangs. Cole closed his eyes, turned his head and drove a foot straight up toward Sid's groin. The kick landed a bit lower than he'd hoped, but was still enough to knock the Nymar off balance and force him to spit most of his venom onto the ground.

The venom was meant to be injected into a victim through the curved fangs, to slow them down for easier feeding. If spit into the eyes, it made a human sluggish and open to suggestion. In the hands of a particularly talented Nymar, it could get worse than that. Cole knew as much firsthand. What he felt on his arm was something more than the normal venom. It burned like a piece of supercooled metal before soaking in and numbing his skin.

"So you're hopped up in more ways than one, huh?" Cole

mused as he pushed away from Sid and rolled to his feet. "I'd like to hear all about that."

Sid's mouth hung open as he swayed from side to side. Rather than watch the Nymar's eyes, Cole watched his shoulders. That way he didn't fall for the head fake Sid attempted before rushing him. Holding the spear in front of him like a bar, he pressed it lengthwise against Sid's chest and diverted the Nymar's momentum to send him flying into a collection of trash cans. From there, Cole raised the compact weapon and was about to lunge when a pair of strong little hands grabbed him from behind and pulled him down to his knees. A bony arm snaked around his throat and grabbed the forked end of the spear with the other hand. It was Rita. Pressing her mouth against his ear, she hissed, "You're done in this town, Skinner."

Cole pulled as hard as he could but was unable to get the spear away from her.

Having leapt to his feet after recovering from his involuntary flight, Sid grinned at the sight of Cole being wrapped up by the spindly girl in pigtails. "Skinners are done everywhere," he said.

"Actually, this isn't the first time I've heard that sort of thing," Cole replied.

"The funniest thing is that you brought all of this on yourselves," Rita said. "You're the ones who wouldn't work with us, and now you're the ones who gave us a way to wipe all of you pricks off the map."

Cole struggled against the arms holding him, but she wasn't budging. She even knew just how hard to press against his throat without killing him or knocking him out. The edges of his vision were clouding, but it didn't look like he'd miss the evisceration that Sid obviously had in mind.

More shots were fired.

Flames were claiming Raza Hill.

In the parking lot, people were shouting.

"Why not stop fighting it?" Rita whispered. Her lips brushed against his ear and her soft bangs tickled Cole's skin. "Just say the word and I'll give you a freebie before Sid guts you. There are guys all over town who would love me to pay such special attention to them."

Sid stood his ground, waiting for the signal to proceed.

When Cole tried to reclaim his spear, Rita pulled it back. "Poor baby. Last time you laid down the law, you were so tough. Now look at you. About to die carrying a broken stick."

"That's right. The last time I kicked your ass, the varnish was still fresh on this thing," Cole mused. Focusing all of his will into a single purpose, he twisted the spear and extended it to its full length until the gleaming spearhead drove directly into Sid's chest. He then collapsed the other end of the weapon so it could be pulled from Rita's grasp. After finally pulling out of Rita's stranglehold, he twisted the spear even more to pry a loud scream from the back of Sid's bloodstained throat.

During one of their sparring sessions, Paige told him that the inside of a Nymar was a lot like an insect; a fluid mass of simple organs designed to process one food source, all wrapped up in a strong exoskeleton. The core of any Nymar's being was the spore attached to their heart. Because the weapon was bonded to him at a blood level through the thorns in its handle, Cole could feel the spore inside Sid's chest rubbing frantically against the spearhead. As Sid dropped to his knees, Cole pulled the weapon out of him and pivoted around to take a swing at Rita. From then on he only needed to rely on his training, experience, and the rush of adrenaline pumping through his system.

After backing away from or ducking under the first series of Cole's attacks, Rita hopped over him and grabbed onto the overhang of Raza Hill's roof. Hot tongues of flame had heated that section of the building, forcing her to drop down again and hurry to her fallen comrade. Instead of comforting or helping Sid in any way, she dug under his shirt to remove the 9mm pistol tucked there. Sid might have been overconfident in his unearthly abilities, but Rita wasn't too proud to fall back on the basics. She fired a quick shot at Cole that hissed several feet wide of its target. Before she could pull the trigger again, he was snapping the forked end of the spear around to slice through a good section of meat along her arm. If not for the black tendrils that spewed from the wound to pull it shut, she might have been forced to drop the gun. Even with the spore's self-preservation reflex, she wasn't able to fire accurately before her arm was pinned to the wall between the tines of Cole's weapon.

"Who sent you?" he demanded. "Steph?"

Unable to use the gun, Rita dropped it and ripped herself from where she'd been trapped, without a thought to all the skin shredded along the way. Her entire forearm was almost peeled to the bone, but she was free.

"You'd better run far away, Skinner," she said. "Tell that to your skank partner too! Time for Nymar to hunt you again!" With that, she jumped above the spear's range and ran away as soon as her feet made contact with the ground.

Cole grabbed the 9mm and followed Rita toward the alley. Before he rounded the next corner, a figure in a battered army surplus coat was herded into his view.

"This son of a bitch won't stay down!" Prophet said while firing another couple rounds at the arsonist.

Rita was nowhere to be found. Rather than take a chance on upsetting the Nymar by just shooting it, Cole tucked the 9mm under his belt, and holding the spear in both hands, rushed the son of a bitch who'd lit the fire that had all but consumed Raza Hill.

From the ground it looked as if the entire roof was on fire. Standing up there amid the flames, however, Ace could see that most of them rose up from broken windows or spots where the arsonist's mixture had seeped into the structure. It wouldn't be long before the job was done, however. The roof sagged and buckled under his feet as he gazed down at the Nymar caught between Prophet and Cole. It was time for the boss man to step in and make things right.

As soon as he landed in a spot that gave him a clear view of his targets, Ace pulled a thin, perfectly balanced throwing knife from his custom-made Italian boot. After that, all that remained was for him to pick the spot where he would stick it between Cole's shoulder blades. Ace cocked his hand back, only to have the knife plucked from it and his wrist twisted at a very uncomfortable angle.

"Lights out, dipshit," Paige said as she jammed a syringe into one of the thicker tendrils in his arm and pressed the plunger.

The Skinners called the stuff now flowing through Ace's body an antidote. To him or any Nymar, it was liquid pain that flowed to the vampire spore and dried it up on contact. Ace's knees shattered into dried bone and flakes of dead skin, and by the time he dropped onto his side, the only thing holding him together was his fancy silk shirt.

Chapter Nine

Cole stood with Paige and Prophet, watching Raza Hill burn from a distance. The police scanner in Prophet's van wasn't the best, but it was good enough to pick up the chatter going back and forth between the dozens of units that had been sent to put out other fires throughout the city. Robberies were in progress. Shootings had taken place. A gas station had been put to a torch and threatened to blow up part of a city block. Almost twenty minutes after getting away from the burning ruins of a once mediocre eatery, the wail of an approaching fire truck reached Cole's ears.

"About damn time," he said while squinting at a rising column of black smoke.

The three of them sat in the parking lot of a nearby White Castle on Cicero Avenue. It seemed fitting since Cole had been on his way home from that same burger joint months ago when he first spotted Rita and Sid in a part of town the Nymar had been warned to leave alone. Now, that warning seemed almost as silly as an old lady wagging an angry finger at an invading army.

Paige sat on the hood of the Cav, eating fries from a rectangular cardboard box. "They should let it burn," she said.

"That's our home! How can you want to see it burn?"

"I don't *want* to see it burn, but that's what it should do.

There's bigger things for the cops and fire department to worry about."

"Yeah. Bigger things like tearing down that Blood Parlor over on Rush Street."

Prophet sat behind the wheel of his van, tapping the police scanner as if he could somehow coax it into telling him more. Although he wouldn't say it out loud, out of risk of offending his vehicle, he obviously missed the truck he'd rented after being ferried to Philadelphia. "Sounds like the cops are shifting into clean-up mode," he said. "That means any bad guys out there either took off or were brought in. This other stuff that's going on may have been a distraction. Makes sense, if those Nymar wanted as much time as possible to take a crack at you."

Wheeling around to look at Prophet, Cole said, "Let me guess. You dreamed this would happen so that's why you're here?"

"I did have a dream about fire!" he said. "It could have been this one too." The enthusiasm died down when he paid more attention to the looks he was getting from both Skinners. "But Paige got ahold of me while you were still in Philly. I got zapped back over here and was keeping an eye on your place."

"You mean the place that's burning to the ground?" Cole snarled. "Great fucking job!"

The bounty hunter put the scanner down and got out of the van so he could stand toe-to-toe with Cole. "Those assholes just rolled in and lit a match. I called you the second the fire started, but you wouldn't answer the goddamn phone!"

Unable to dispute that without losing the angry roll he'd gotten onto, Cole snapped his eyes over to Paige. "So what's your excuse? You called Prophet. You came back after telling me you were leaving. Think you could have let me in on whatever was going on before I might have been cooked alive in that shitty freezer of mine?"

"If I'd have told you, that would have ruined the surprise."

Her joke didn't go over well, even with her. Despite the steady stream of junk food going into her mouth, Paige simply didn't have the energy to feign a smile. Setting her sights on something in the general direction of Raza Hill, she said, "Daniels called while I was in Miami. He's doing some minor work for one of the Nymar running Steph's newest Blood Parlor. Apparently, she's expanding even further than we thought."

Tossing a quick wave at the smoky horizon, Cole grunted, "No shit."

"Seems Steph was keeping tabs on us through some sort of surveillance. Daniels said he'd heard about it a while ago but wanted to find out more before calling us." When Cole dug his phone from his pocket, she added, "Those Nymar must talk a lot of shit about us, Cole. Daniels can't tell us every little claim they make. He got ahold of me as soon as he heard something more concrete, like the fact that they had the car bugged."

Cole looked at the car. Then he looked at Paige. He looked toward the smoke and then looked at Prophet. After all of that head turning, he needed to get off his feet, so he sat down beside Paige. "That's why you said you were leaving? To make them think you were out of the picture?"

"Yeah."

"Couldn't you have written me a note or something? Maybe a hand gesture?"

"I haven't picked out a suitable gesture for, 'Look out. The car's bugged and I'm pretending to leave.'"

"You know what I mean!"

"Yeah, I know. It's just that, if I was going to force Steph's hand, whatever I said needed to be convincing. You've got some real promise as a Skinner, but I'm not sure about your acting skills. That's why I wanted Prophet here to back you up until I made it back. And before you ask, I already found the bug and got rid of it. It was tucked behind one of the loose door panels."

"That's not to say there aren't more," Prophet said. "I got some equipment that'll sniff out anything transmitting from your car."

"Don't bother," Paige said through a mouthful of fries. "If they were still listening in or tracking me, I don't think I could have caught Ace by surprise like that. We're getting the hell out of this city anyway, and we'll notice if anyone follows us that far."

Cole watched her for a few seconds until he was certain she wasn't going to take back what she'd said. "Hold on now. We can't just leave! That's probably all Steph wanted."

"No," Paige replied. "She's after something more than just putting us in our place. They all are."

"All the Nymar in Chicago?"

"All the Nymar in the country. Maybe more."

"Aw, hell," Prophet sighed. "Last time I tried to lend a hand to you two, I was pulled into a massacre in the boonies of Wisconsin. Now this?"

"Janesville isn't exactly the boonies," Paige said. "More like the Edge of Nowhere."

"Why the hell did you even get me involved in this?"

Showing enough intensity to send a chill down the bounty hunter's spine, Paige said, "Because you owed me after going behind my back to bury Henry when you knew damn well I'd come looking for him."

"Oh yeah," Prophet muttered. "I suppose there's that."

"Plus," she added, "we should only deal with people we trust after what happened in Philly. I don't want to speak to anyone unless I know whose side they're on."

"I can see why Cole wanted to fly under the radar to bury that body," Prophet said, "but are you tellin' me you've got something against those others too?"

Cole looked over to Paige and got a reluctant nod from her. "Something's going on with the rest of those guys in Philly," he said. "I don't think it's all of them, but there are some Skinners who are up to something on their own. We think they may even be working with Nymar."

"How the hell could that happen?"

"Some of us work with Nymar," Paige explained, "but Daniels isn't a Skinner. Some of the other groups have been bringing Nymar in even further to make them official. There's no ruling body or anything like that among us, so we run on tradition. It's how we've always done things. It's who we are. We work independently, but together, you know?"

"It's a lot like that in the bail bonds business," Prophet

said. "We're our own companies with our own ways of doing the job, but there's always been an understanding of how that job should be done."

"Sounds about right," Paige said as she hopped off the hood of the car, then brushed off her hands and tossed her fry box into the Cav. "We've always spoken to the others, helped each other out, shared information. Well . . . most of the information. The Toronto Skinners started working with a few Nymar who weren't on board with the Canadian bloodsuckers when they started getting into slavery rings. Feeding's one thing, but I guess they weren't ready to work hand in hand with the kind of scum that steals babies from hospitals or ships girls around to appear in underground porn before disappearing to be sucked dry."

"So what the hell do we do now?" When the Skinners looked at him, Prophet said, "Hell yes it's 'we.' I may not know your secret handshake or whatever, but I'm in on this. Or did you wipe out every one of those Nymar that may have seen me shooting that asshole with the Molotov cocktail in his hand?"

"I'm going back to Miami to follow up on a lead," Paige said.

Cole couldn't look at the smoke coming from Raza Hill anymore. For now it was easier to just turn his back on it and think about anything else. "I thought that Miami stuff was just to convince Steph you were leaving town."

"It was, but I still need to go. It's not about Steph. I doubt she's got any connections that far away from Chicago that we need to worry about."

"And what if she does?"

"Then worrying won't do us any good. I need to get back to Miami and that's all there is to it. Whatever is happening with the Nymar is connected to the ones I followed out of Philly. They're getting bolder. Not just here, but all over the place. Reports are coming in from across the country that Nymar are running wild and hitting Skinners left and right."

"Sounds like they're marking their territory," Prophet said. "Just like any other goddamn bunch of criminals. When they've been locked up or held down for too long, they come back like a nightmare. It builds up in their systems. I've seen it too many times with regular fugitives. They just ain't wired to sit still, otherwise they'd be able to keep an office job. They get anxious and when they finally do cut loose it's an event. I've nabbed a whole lot of fugitives during parties like that. They're dangerous, but careless. After being away from their home turf for too long, they need to remind everybody that they're still around. If they don't, they either lose their contacts or settle at the bottom of the pool where they can get swallowed up."

"There," Paige said to Cole. "See why I insist on keeping him around?"

"What else have you heard about the Nymar that you haven't been telling me?" Cole asked.

"The last I heard from Rico, he was still in Toronto. He meant to check in on those guys before he got sidetracked to St. Louis when all that Lancroft business hit. He's already heard about what happened and wants in. After we get out of Chicago, you'll meet up with him."

"I'm not letting you go to Miami on your own, Paige."

She took out her phone, pressed a few buttons and then put it away again. "When you find Rico, show him the picture I just sent."

Before Cole could ask, he felt a rattle from the phone in his pocket. "No matter what's going on, you can still send a hum through my pants," he said with a tired smirk.

She wasn't laughing, but her expression did get warmer around the edges.

Cole dug out the vibrating phone and saw the picture Paige had sent him. It was a hastily taken shot of Bobby and the Nymar woman that had snuck into the Lancroft house.

"Tell him where I went and to tell you about shampoo banana."

Cole squinted as if that would somehow make things clearer. When he looked over to Prophet, the bounty hunter seemed just as confused as he was. "Did she say shampoo banana?"

"Yes she did," Paige told him. "And tell him I know he's

got the hound dog notebook and that you should have it now. He'll know what that means. Do you still have the Lancroft journals?"

"I e-mailed what I could to myself but . . . shit! My hard drive! It's back at Raza Hill! Damn it, I *knew* I should've brought that along no matter what!"

"Calm down," Paige said. "What about the paper copies?"

Patting the satchel he'd thrown over his shoulder on his way out of his freezer, he said, "Right here."

"See if you can get all of that to Ned's house. We need to keep them somewhere safe and that's the safest place I know."

"Aren't you gonna check in with the other Skinners?" Prophet asked. "What if this kind of shit's happened to them? Maybe you can get some help."

"Our main priority is to keep things from getting any worse." With a sigh, Paige admitted, "If we give the Nymar a chance to hit us this badly again, they'll gain too much momentum. This is exactly why we stay in small groups and as mobile as possible, Cole. It was a mistake for me to get too comfortable in this city."

"Great," he said. "Living in a gutted restaurant and sleeping on a cot was your version of getting comfortable."

She walked up to him and held his face in her hands. After pulling him down so they were close enough to bump foreheads, Paige said, "Walter, give us a minute."

Prophet moved away to join the people who were watching the thinning cloud of smoke filling the air to the southwest.

"Something big is happening," she whispered. "It may be something that's been brewing for a while."

"Why do I get the feeling that there's a lot more you're not telling me?"

"Because there is. I don't have the time to get into it right now but you need to know the whole story. You deserve to know." Lowering her eyes, she said, "After you hear all of it, if you want to get away from me and all of this shit I'll understand."

"Paige, with everything that's already—"

Her hands clamped around him harder and her eyes bored right through him. The voice she used had an edge that was sharper than any weapon in the Skinner arsenal. "You can still get away if you want. You may have to lay low for a while, but you know enough now to have a chance on your own."

"And what if that's not what I want to do?"

"Then you can stand with me. I just want you to know who you're standing with. What's happened between us has been worth all the shit we've had to go through to get to it. If anything happens to me, just know that I had a hell of a good time with you."

"We could still fit in another good time, you know. Just a quick one."

When she pulled his face a little closer, Cole swore she was coming in for a kiss. Instead, she gave him a gentle, tapping head butt. "That's just what I needed to hear," she said with an easy laugh. "At least everything hasn't gone to hell in the last hour. Go find Rico. Show him that picture. You remember what to tell him?"

"Yeah, yeah. Shampoo banana. Hound dog notebook."

Paige pulled him in and kissed him on the mouth. It was a hard, lingering kiss that was over way too soon. Walking around to the Cav's driver side, she climbed in and fished around inside the glove compartment. "Here," she said while tossing him the .44 revolver she kept in the car.

Between wanting to keep the gun hidden and not wanting it to go off accidentally, Cole nearly tripped over himself twice in his haste to catch it. By the time the .44 was in his possession, Paige had the Cav's motor running.

"Get your hard drive and anything else you can scavenge from Raza Hill. But don't stay too long," she said while pulling away.

Prophet ambled over to him as Cole was doing his best to casually stuff a gun under his belt along with the .38 he'd taken from Sid. "You need a ride?"

"Sure. There's a bar down the street that always looked pretty interesting. First round's on me."

"Isn't there something more important to do? Like something about the vampires that burned your house down?"

"Screw it. If things are just going to get worse anyway, I might as well cushion my system for it."

Slapping Cole on the shoulder, Prophet said, "Makes sense to me."

Chapter Ten

The Lancroft house was quiet. Most of the Skinners had come and gone, taking whatever they could find and leaving before being challenged by locals or anyone else. Selina and Jory were taking their turn in the basement, overseeing the flow of traffic and cataloguing whatever they could.

Bobby and M were in the dissection room, removing each tool from its tray so they could look behind every surface and tear down as much of the desk and equipment racks as humanly possible in case there were any more trapdoors or switches to be found. M sighed. "Those Chicago assholes must've taken the journals. That's all there is to it."

"Given enough time, we should be able to piece together what we need with the journals we already have," Bobby said. "Lancroft sent plenty of the technical stuff to those of us he trusted, but what's missing is his personal notes and experimental procedures. There may have been lists of what was here, but he could also have just kept an inventory in his head."

"Or stashed it somewhere else."

"That's why we keep looking. If we don't find it soon,

we'll recruit more help from the ones Lancroft mentioned in those lists."

After pulling out a drawer from a steel rack of trays next to the empty examination table, M stuck his arm into the space and felt along the interior of the metal structure. "What about that bullshit they handed us about the freak's body going missing? You think Rico really got it?"

"If he did, we would've heard about it a long time ago."

Suddenly, both Skinners perked up like a pair of dogs that had heard the same high-pitched whistle. A fraction of a second later the entire house filled with the sounds of movement as everyone with scars on their palms mobilized at the same time.

Bobby raced into the Skipping Temple. "Did anyone deactivate those protection runes?"

"We had to," Selina replied as she entered from the workshop doorway. "So your Nymar buddies wouldn't get fried the moment they stepped through that curtain."

"Tell Paul to brace himself. The runes are going back up whether he gets fried or not."

Of the flowing symbols etched into the temple walls, a small percentage were blocky and sharper than the rest. While most of the Skinners couldn't read them, they knew they'd been put there by Lancroft as opposed to the more artistic hands of a Dryad. Bobby went to some of the symbols near the doorway to the workshop and began tracing them with his finger. Doing so in the proper order and direction activated the ritualistic energies stored within the runes. Before he could complete the process, he knew it was too late.

Upstairs, several Skinners rushed toward the back door, which opened to a small yard that wasn't even big enough for a decent swing set. They shouted among themselves before the door was smashed in with the force of a runaway car.

"God damn it," Bobby said as he finished tracing the last rune. A crackle of energy rippled through the wall but didn't make it much farther than the stairs leading to the main floor. "The circuit's broken. Something busted the runes upstairs. Go see what it is."

M pulled two of the knives hanging from his belt. The varnished wooden blades became razor sharp as the small thorns in the handle punctured his palm. Even with the weapons in hand, he wasn't anxious to get up the stairs. "We know what's up there. Didn't you feel it?"

"Yes, I felt it! Go up and help the others. I'll try to get as much as I can out of here before that thing finds its way down here. Whatever you do, make sure nothing gets down those stairs!"

"How do you suppose I keep a Full Blood from going down some stairs?"

Bobby grabbed him by the shirt and threw him into the workshop. "We're Skinners, for Christ's sake! This is what we do. Get up there and fucking *do it*!"

With those words ringing through his ears, there wasn't much else for M to do. He gripped the knives so the blades ran down along the inside of his forearms and followed the last few Skinners to the first floor. With the crashing of bodies hitting the walls and floors, followed by screams of pain and cries of battle, he might as well have been charging into a war.

At the top of the stairs three Skinners huddled with their weapons in hand. One was Jory, Maddy was another, and the last was one of the new arrivals that M didn't recognize. "What the hell's going on?" he asked.

"That thing found us," Jessup said as he waved one of his weapons toward the kitchen. They were carved into large wooden hooks, and blood seeped between his fingers as one of them shortened into a thick machete. The other straightened and split at the end to form a barbed, narrow V. "There's more of 'em too. I can feel it." With that, he charged into the fray.

The kitchen was a tiny room with barely enough room to maneuver, thanks to the outdated, broken appliances protruding from beneath grease-spattered counters. Not only had the back door been pulled from its frame, but several chunks of the wall around it were missing as well. Framed in that jagged opening, Liam stood in his upright form. Even while hunkering down upon thickly muscled haunches, he was just shy of seven feet tall. Powerful arms hanging from massive shoulders swung at the Skinners who slashed him with their weapons. His right eye socket was a tangle of scar tissue, but the left one blazed even brighter to make up for it. After digging a bloody trench through Abel's chest, he bared a mouthful of daggerlike fangs and roared into the house.

Jessup shoved past one Skinner from southern California who'd lost an arm upon Liam's arrival and leapt over another who was curled up on the floor. Swinging with the wooden machete, he clipped Liam's elbow and caught the answering slash between the V of his other weapon. Rather than try to hold onto the werewolf, Jessup dug in and drove the V-shaped weapon all the way down to Liam's elbow.

Blood flowed from Liam's arm and a flap of skin came loose when he pulled away. He crouched down and cradled the flayed limb against his chest while snapping at the Skinner with a set of jaws more powerful than a hydraulic press.

Seeing the callused mass in Liam's right eye socket, M circled around to the blind side and attacked the Full Blood's rib cage in a series of quick stabs using both of his wooden knives. They made it through the wiry mesh of fur but didn't penetrate more than a quarter of an inch of flesh. M was familiar enough with his weapons to expect as much and made up for the quality of strikes with sheer quantity. Very soon he'd chopped deeper and blood sprayed from the werewolf's side in a fine mist.

"Close in on the bastard!" Jessup shouted.

Some of the Skinners that were on the floor a few moments ago had healed enough to answer his call. Abel was one of them. He pressed a hand against the wound in his chest that had already stopped bleeding thanks to the serum in his bloodstream. As he climbed to his feet and gritted his teeth against the pain of nerve endings being plugged back into his nervous system, the window to his left shattered inward. Lyssa's long feline body flowed through the broken frame in a graceful jump that sent her flying straight at him. Abel managed to raise his curved weapon up to block the leaping attack and open a long gash along the Mongrel's underbelly. Too late to get away from the Skinner, Lyssa clamped on to him with both front paws and snapped her head forward in an attempt to peel his face from his skull.

A gunshot blasted through the kitchen, sending a bullet past Abel's ear and thumping into Lyssa's chin. Her teeth had come so close to their target that Abel felt them take a chunk away from the tip of his nose. As soon as the Mongrel flopped onto her side, she shifted into her human form and crawled away.

More gunshots followed as the West Coast Skinners took aim at the biggest clay pigeon in the room.

"No!" Jessup shouted. "You'll just—"

"Yes!" Liam growled as he rose up to his full height and bumped the back of his head against the ceiling. "Yes, yes, *yes*!"

The bullets pounded against his chest, only to become entangled within his fur and glance off the near impenetrable hull of his flesh. Rage burned in his eye and thick ropes of saliva hung from his chin when he stretched out both arms as if to embrace his attackers. The wounded patch on his arm was still messy, but the flap of skin was held in place by a thick paste of blood. When one bullet dug into that wound, it caused Liam's eye to glaze over and his claws to move in a series of horrific, blindingly fast swings.

Jessup and most of the Skinners that had rushed up the stairs in the first wave did their best to slash at the Full Blood while keeping their heads and limbs connected to their torsos. Abel, Selina, and Maddy dealt with the Mongrel that struck in hit-and-run attacks that brought her from one end of the house to the other.

"This is our chance!" Jessup shouted over the chaos that had become his entire world. "All of us together can take this Full Blood down!"

"That's the spirit!" Liam roared as he sent one of the West Coast Skinners into the ceiling with a powerful upward swipe of his arm.

The next wave to surge up from the basement were clad in leather armor from Lancroft's personal collection and brought extra pieces of armor ranging from vests to cloaks along with them. Whenever they had a chance, the more vulnerable Skinners took turns falling back to pull on the first bit of protection they could find. Some of them were saved by Lancroft's handiwork and others were quickly ripped into pieces and thrown against several walls.

"Ready?" Jessup shouted as he prodded Liam with the twin points of his V-shaped weapon.

A few of the Skinners moved with him, but the rest were too busy just trying to stay alive. After deflecting a few incoming swipes and ducking under a snapping set of hellish jaws, Jessup again shouted, "Ready?" The other Skinners near Liam backed up while taking a few swings to provide some cover, so Jessup shouted, *"Go!"*

Everyone in the kitchen closed in around Liam, gripping their weapons in bloody fists. They screamed like barbarians storming a castle gate, and Liam responded in kind. Instead of trying to defend against all of the incoming attackers, he grabbed the closest one's head in his hands, crushed his skull with enough force to drive his claws into her brain, and swung the twitching body at the others. Having cleared a partial path, Liam moved toward the front half of the house.

In the front bedroom, Abel and Selina traded blows with Lyssa. The feline Mongrel kept her center of gravity low and gripped the floor with talonlike claws. Her wide, triangular head bobbed and snapped from side to side to avoid Abel's blades and Selina's wooden pike. As soon as Maddy entered the room, the Mongrel put her down with a savage blow that severed the hamstring in her right leg. Between that and the pain of the wound, Maddy was out cold when she hit the floor. When both remaining Skinners came at her at once, Lyssa jumped to the side, grabbed onto the wall and sprung at them from another angle. Her claws ripped through half of Selina's face and her body knocked Abel to the floor.

"Down," Abel said calmly as he took a blind horizontal swing.

Ignoring the pain from the shallow tears running all the way down her cheek, Selina pressed herself to the cheap tan carpet as her partner's knife whistled through the air above her. Although the blade didn't hit anything, the one in Abel's other hand raked across Lyssa's side and sent the Mongrel scampering into the farthest corner.

Abel sidled along his wall, keeping the Mongrel in front of him and his partner to his right. He eased a hand to his belt, touched the hilt of the third knife sheathed there, drew it and tossed it in a snapping motion. The blade turned once in the air and stuck into the wall after missing the Mongrel by less than an inch.

"We gotta keep this thing in here with us," Selina said. "It sounds like everyone else has enough on their plate without something else to worry about."

"Always did like to set your sights high," Abel mused.

The basement echoed with sounds of battle filtering down from the upper level. Jory scrambled to collect weapons while piling on as many layers of armor as he could. "Shit," he grunted as Liam's bellowing roar shook the entire house over his head. When that was followed by the heavy impacts of bodies hitting the floor, he snarled, "Shit, shit, shit! You two get up there!"

Paul and Tru were in the workshop as well. He carried a shotgun and she had a varnished sword that had runes etched into one side of the blade.

"Is that thing loaded with them new rounds Paige brought from Chicago?" Jory asked.

"They're special rounds," Paul replied, "but not that special. They'll probably just piss a Full Blood off."

"Too late for that. Take this, get the hell up there and help."

Although Paul caught the wooden weapon that was tossed to him, he didn't seem anxious to use it. "What the hell is this? A pool cue?"

"It's all that's left. It's been treated, so it'll damage that thing."

"Damage it like all the others are damaging it?" Tru asked.

Even for a Nymar, Paul looked pale. "Yeah. Screw that. We're supposed to stay down here and protect this stuff, so that's what we're doing."

Jory drew a long cleaver from a scabbard hanging from his belt. As soon as the thorns in the handle cut into his palms, a spike protruded from the handle to curve into a thick hook. "Suit yourself. If that thing gets down here, you two are the only ones left. You guys are braver than I thought."

"Wait," Tru said. "There's something under us."

"Yeah!" Paul replied hopefully. "The other basement! We can get down there!"

Jory held his ground as a rumble passed by the wall at the base of the stairs and crackled through the floor. "Was that a tremor?"

Pointing toward the Skipping Temple, Paul said, "It's moving that way." Even as he raced in that direction, the tremor died down.

"It's still moving," Jory said. "It must have started in the yard and is going deeper. Aw shit! The subbasement! You two, come with me!"

There was no allowance in Jory's tone for back talk. It was a command that the two Nymar obeyed immediately. Also, with gunshots blasting through the upper portion of the house amid Liam's roar, any reason to get farther away from the stairs leading to the kitchen was a good one.

As they went through the temple, Jordan slipped between the beads and asked, "What's going on? Why all the shooting?"

Jory turned as if he was going to shoot the nymph where she stood. "Never mind about the shooting," he told her. "Just warm that curtain up or start singing or do whatever the hell you need to do because we're gonna have to get out of here quick."

"Why? What's wrong? Tell me!"

"The big bad wolf's blowing our house down, that's what. Now figure a way out of here before we're all dead!"

Jory and the two Nymar ran into the dissection room,

through the secret door, and down the stairs that led to the subbasement.

Jordan started to hum.

As the Skinners hurried down into the brick hallway at the lowest level of the house, Jory, Tru, and Paul were surrounded by the scraping of claws against the other side of the subterranean walls. It veered away from them and traveled in another direction, but the Skinners didn't have the means to follow it. There was only one way down the hall, so that's where they went. Before long the scraping returned.

"Sounds like it's all around us," Tru said.

Jory's eyes were almost shut in concentration. "No," he breathed. "It's coming from there." He used the cleaver to point at one of the cells about a quarter of the way down on the left side of the hall, where a gritty cloud of dirt rolled out from between the bars like smoke.

All three of them broke into a run so they could get to the cell before something had the chance to dig its way out. It wasn't until they were within ten feet of the smoke that they realized it had been loosened from the ground beneath the bars as well as the wall around them. Suddenly, the wolf-digger hybrid Mongrel darted from the hole it had created in an awkward, waddling run. Its thick bony paws were capped with wide claws. Pure black eyes glared out from beneath heavily ridged brows that shifted into a more canine alignment before its rear end had emerged from the broken floor. The Mongrel charged directly at the Skinners, unmindful or simply unconcerned with the weapons they bore.

Jory, Tru, and Paul squared off against it as the fight two floors above them raged on. With all that noise filling the house and basement, the rumble of continued digging was easy to miss.

At the farthest end of the brick hallway, something else churned beneath the floor. Unlike the wild scraping that had announced the hybrid's entrance, this was quicker and more systematic as it buckled the floor beneath the last darkened cell. After several attempts to dislodge the bricks, the digging moved one cell over, where the bricks were pushed aside by a set of strong, flat hands emerging from the dirt. Max poked his narrow snout up from the shadows, blinked a set of vertical eyelids and wriggled out of the hole he'd dug. Randolph emerged soon after, pulling himself out with powerful if drastically constricted paws. He couldn't get out of the hole fast enough before shaking the pebbles and grit from his coat like a dog sloughing off the rain.

The cell was the size of a closet and reeked of excrement from more than one species. Iron bars were fitted into a frame with a door so narrow that a normal man would have to turn sideways in order to pass. Randolph shifted into a form that was compact and upright. His fur became a thick mat over flesh that looked dense as tire rubber, his movements stiff and his features becoming blocky and indistinct. The only thing that remained of the man known as Mr. Burkis were the crystalline gray-blue eyes staring out from the primitive face.

His compact form moved easily through the narrow opening. In the darkness his thick, dark brown fur made it easy for him to remain unseen by the Skinners who were already distracted at the other end of the hall. He approached the neighboring cell, placed one hand upon the bars and immediately pulled it back with a pained hiss. One quick glance at the rusted iron allowed him to pick out the Skinner runes etched into the iron that had scorched his fingers.

"Are you Kawosa?" Randolph asked in a voice that sounded as if it had been strained and compacted along with the rest of his body's mass.

The creature in the cell kept its back pressed against a wall. At first its large unblinking eyes were simple reflective surfaces in the shadows. Then they became darker, redder, and finally took the same blue gray color as Randolph's. "You are Full Blood," the creature said in a voice that was smooth as milky honey.

"When did the Skinner capture you?"

"Since I cannot see the moon or sun, I do not know how many days have passed."

"Answer me. Are you Kawosa?"

The creature took no notice of the battle raging in the hall. He was too enthralled with the sight in front of him to care about rumblings in the distance. "There have been a people who called me by that name," it replied.

"How did the Skinners catch one like you? If you are Kawosa, such a thing shouldn't be possible."

"Do you think I am a god?"

Randolph had to think about that. He blinked heavily, as if the weight of his answer pressed upon his brow. He considered lying to the creature but gave up on that almost immediately. "I have heard stories. Legends. Some say you are a god or maybe a demon. But some say the same about our kind. All I know is that we need something to tip the scales back in our favor."

"Or," Kawosa mused while narrowing keen eyes, which had now become violet, and slinking forward upon bony legs, "do you just want to keep me away from the Skinners? It simply wouldn't do for them to sink their hooks and knives into me, now would it? That is, after they found a way to kill me or simply waited long enough for me to die. Just like they did with poor Henry. Do you even know what horrors Lancroft had to inflict to kill him?"

With every word, Kawosa's voice took a new tone; a concoction that changed as new ingredients were sprinkled into the mix.

"Can you break these bars, Full Blood?" For the first time since he'd stepped forward, Kawosa's eyes disappeared as he closed them and drew a long breath. They snapped open, green and vibrant, as an incomplete set of crooked fangs were displayed beneath raised lips. "You're the one they called Standing Bear. Could it be you're working for the Skinners now too?"

"You know better than that. I've been trying to find you for years, and all I discovered was that your trail ended when it crossed with Jonah Lancroft's. Only recently has he been found and dealt with."

"Yes," the creature sighed. "I nearly got a taste of the woman who did the dealing. So sweet."

"If we stay here much longer, we will be forced to fight

these Skinners as well as any more that come to help them. And then there are the humans."

"You fear them?"

Randolph took a moment to gauge his response. "They have numbers and technology at their advantage. I don't know how much of that you know about."

"They've always had their toys. How do you plan on getting me past these bars?" Kawosa asked.

"Tell me you want to leave and we should be able to clear a path."

"I want to leave."

"Then stand back."

Shifting into his four-legged form, Randolph swatted at the floor with a massive paw. A few seconds later the rumbling beneath him commenced. Bricks trembled as Max passed under them, but the ones anchoring the bars hardly moved. At the other end of the hall the hybrid Mongrel yelped as both Nymar descended upon him. Jory waited for the other two to clear a path before delivering a finishing blow that sent a wet crunch down the hall.

Kawosa backed into the darkness from which he'd come. He shifted his blank reflective eyes toward the floor as the bricks started to buckle and split. Dirt and subterranean filth spewed up like pus from an old wound once Max concentrated his efforts on the section of floor beneath the bars. Those bricks, either strengthened by the warding runes or powered by some other force, held firm. They did, however, need a solid foundation. Once that was removed, they shifted and slid within the churning ground until the bars were the only thing holding them in place.

Randolph looked at Kawosa again, finding the creature's eyes closer to the top of the cell and encased in a lean shape that bristled with coarse fur.

"Can you break the plane of the bars?" Kawosa asked.

"With the bricks of your cell disrupted, the runes should be weakened enough for you to—"

"That's not what I asked. Can you break the plane of the bars?"

Hunkering down on all fours, Randolph leaned so his

snout was almost touching the old iron. "We don't have time for this."

"All this world has for me are its curiosities. Meeting you this way is a surprise. I like surprises. I want more of them."

"If I were to start performing tricks for your amusement, then that would be a very big surprise indeed. You can stay here until the Skinners figure out a way to cut you apart, but if you want to leave, let's bloody well leave."

The smile Kawosa showed was crooked and verging on childish, which made it a disturbing addition to a face such as his. Rather than test his luck with the bars, he sank his claws into the earth beneath the broken floor and pulled himself under the upturned dirt. It was a short crawl through decades-old filth before his lean frame emerged inside the cell next to his old residence. By the time he pulled himself completely out of the hole, Kawosa was a wiry man with skin the color of scorched desert rock. He wore a tattered leather loincloth and a collar around his neck that might have once been attached to a shirt or some sort of tunic. Long stringy hair hung in front of his face but wasn't enough to obscure his rich, chocolate-brown eyes.

"The tunnel continues from there," Randolph said as he eased back into his dense, shaggy human form. "Once we're outside we run. Can you run?"

"We'll soon see."

"Yes we will. Max, lead the way."

The tunneling Mongrel had watched silently for this long, and was more than happy to dive back into the earth to leave the brick prison behind.

Randolph stared down the hall and locked eyes with the Skinners who were recovering from their fight with the canine hybrid. When one of them sounded the charge, the Full Blood followed in Kawosa's wake.

"Come on!" Paul said. The few stray drops of shapeshifter blood that he hadn't drank were quickly lapped up by a wildly flopping tongue. He'd never tasted the blood of a Mongrel and it flowed through him like raw volcanic energy.

Tru had drunk from the Mongrel as well and was so affected by it that she couldn't form words. All she did was race to join her partner, since he was running to what might be another of the newly discovered delicacies.

Jory wasn't so eager. He took a moment to fish a small syringe from a compartment stitched into the side of his weapon's scabbard and injected a dose of serum into his arm. Even as the healing began, he jogged while the other two threw themselves into a dead run. "Hold up!" he shouted. "Did anything get loose down there?"

The chaos upstairs subsided so quickly that the ensuing silence seemed more shocking than an explosion.

"We don't know yet," Tru replied. "What the hell was just standing there?"

"I thought it was a Full Blood," Paul said. "Looked like one, but then it changed into something different."

Jory's fingers curled in to brush against the scars on his palm. "That was a Full Blood. Just never seen it in that form before. It's gone now. Let's get out of here." He led the way back upstairs and through the dissection room. Even before he made it out of the Skipping Temple, he could tell there was more trouble on its way. Without looking back, he grunted, "Cops."

"I think those lights are just from the walls," Tru said.

"Yeah, the green ones. Not those," Jory replied as he pointed to one of the small windows along the top of the workshop wall. The windows were rectangular and barely large enough for a child to fit through, but the metal basins outside them caught more than dead leaves and small animals. It also reflected some of the red and blue lights from the street.

"Tell the nymph to be ready," Jory shouted while running up the stairs that led to the kitchen.

"The nymph can hear you," Jordan shouted back. "And it's ready. The only bridge I could get right now was to . . . are you listening to me?"

"Just keep it open," Paul said. "So long as it leads away from this place we should be fine."

Before either of the Nymar got concerned enough to venture into the part of the house that had become a war zone, Skinners began filing into the basement. Bobby was first down the stairs, helping someone who was too wounded to move on his own. The rest came down in a stream of bloody bodies and a few limp corpses. Abel was last to step upon the top stair, and quickly traced some of the runes near the door.

"Is that going to keep the cops from seeing what's up there?" Jessup asked from the landing at the bottom of the steps.

"Doesn't even matter," Abel replied in a haggard wheeze. "Half the neighborhood must've heard the shots, and Lord only knows what anyone saw if they looked over the back fence. Just get the hell out of here before we're all dragged away."

By then the first Skinners were marching through the curtain. Jessup went into the dissection room and picked up the thing that had literally been pried from Jonah Lancroft's dying hand. It was a small box with a simple control on it that was linked to explosives set up throughout the basement.

"Everyone's out," he said to Jordan. "Your turn."

"What about the Full Blood? Are you going to let the cops find it?"

"It took off and so did the Mongrel. Just move."

She didn't need to hear any more than that before approaching the curtain and placing one foot through. "Are you coming?"

"Hell yes," Jessup said as he pressed the button that triggered the first muffled thump of C4 from the bottom of the stairs. "Ain't nowhere else for me to go now."

Chapter Eleven

Chicago, Illinois

After all that had happened, Cole was amazed to find Raza Hill so quiet. The building was a blackened husk spattered by foam and water that glistened with reflected streetlights and the glare from passing cars. The parking lot was empty, but there was plenty of evidence that it had been full not too long ago. Everything from fresh tire marks to candy wrappers marked the most activity at the old restaurant since its final dinner rush. Sections of the perimeter were cordoned off by police tape, but nobody was around to enforce the stern words written in large, blocky font upon a yellow background.

"What did you expect?" Prophet asked as he stuck his hands in his pockets and shifted on his feet to get a look down the alley. "An armed guard posted at some run-down, burned-up hole in the ground?"

"Considering all that happened? I thought we might have more trouble than this getting so close," Cole replied. "Just keep your eyes open and let me know if anyone's coming."

"Sure. After the fire, the shooting, the stabbing, the dead vampires, and everything else, I'm sure folks'll be flocking to this place."

"Are the Nymar bodies still out there?"

"Just the clothes. I think one of the fire trucks ran them

over. Looks like some poor bastard who got crushed by a steamroller in one of them cartoons. How come it's so hard to find those good cartoons anymore?"

"Too violent," Cole said as he fished the hard drive from the wreckage of his old computer. From there he went to the restaurant's side entrance and pulled it open with an expectant wince. When no alarms sounded and nobody shouted through a bullhorn for him to freeze, he opened the door the rest of the way and went inside.

Prophet, on the other hand, followed along as if strolling through a store that didn't carry anything in his size. "Violent? You know what you see on every damn channel anymore? Anime. That Japanese stuff is some violent shit."

"You're thinking of hentai."

"No, that's the sexy shit."

"You think big-eyed girls with purple hair getting worked over by sea creatures is sexy?"

At that moment Prophet had the big eyes going but not the purple hair. "What in the name of hell are you watching? I'm talking about *Dragonball Z* or *Pokémon*. That kind of anime, you sick bastard."

The interior of the restaurant was charred and stank from the combined odors of what had been scorched in the fire and the chemicals used to put it out. After using Raza Hill as a home base since the beginning of his days as a Skinner, it now felt as if he was creeping around inside someone else's house after sneaking in through a carelessly unlocked door. Although the dining room and kitchen were trashed, his walk-in freezer was in fairly good shape. There just wasn't a lot in there for him to waste his time collecting.

"You could probably go back to living here before too long, you know," Prophet said.

"I don't think so."

"Nobody thought this place was anything but some condemned rat trap anyway. Hell, that's why there wasn't such a fuss when it went up. Those Nymar melted or ran away, so with all the other fires that were set around town tonight, I doubt most of the cops or firemen even remember responding to a call here."

Having already moved to Paige's room, Cole glanced around at the clothes scattered on the floor and hanging from furniture. He had a tough time figuring out what part of the mess had been made during the fire or the partially collapsed roof and what had been there before the first whiff of smoke drifted through the air. Skipping the clothes completely, Cole shifted his focus to equipment, weapons, and supplies.

"So did you catch any flak from running away with that freak's body?" Prophet asked.

"A little, but I'm sure more's on the way."

"How much longer are you gonna be in here?"

"Why? Is someone coming?"

"No. I'm getting sick of breathing ash into my lungs."

Cole wanted to insist on staying longer but couldn't come up with a good enough reason to justify it. Before long he realized he was just trying to hang onto one more home that needed to drift away. His phone chirped. He was carrying barely enough things to keep one of his arms occupied when he glanced at the caller ID and said, "Yeah, Rico. What's up?"

"Please tell me you're not in Philly."

"No, I'm in Chicago. Things aren't too great here, though."

"You didn't hear about Philly?"

Cole had spent enough time with the other Skinner to differentiate between the edge in Rico's voice now and the one that was usually there. Stopping before crossing the threshold out of the building, he asked, "What happened?"

"A pack of Full Bloods tore through the Lancroft place about half an hour ago."

"A pack?"

"Full Bloods and Mongrels," Rico said. "That's what Jessup told me. They killed three Skinners, wounded damn near everyone else, and forced him to level the place."

"Holy shit? They pushed the button?"

"Sounded like it wasn't as big a boom as we thought it would be, but it must have sealed off the basement. If you're near a computer, you can see it for yourself."

Pressing his elbow against the pocket where his hard drive resided, Cole said, "That might take a while."

"Where's Paige?"

"Not here, and she's not in Philly either. She took off after someone in Miami. Didn't she tell you about it?"

"Last I heard she was putting Prophet back to work. How'd that pan out?"

"So far so good. I'm supposed to meet up with you. Paige had some things I needed to tell you. Or . . . you needed to tell me. Everything's kind of a blur."

"Not even in your section of the country and still giving orders." Rico chuckled. "That's our Bloodhound. You taking the Stripper Subway?"

"She's got you calling it that too?"

"I was gonna call it the Pussy Pipeline."

"Wow. The Subway sounds a lot better now. You back in St. Louis?"

"Should be in a few hours. That enough time for you to get here?"

"Yeah," Cole said. "Is it all right if I bring a guest?"

"Long as it's not Prophet."

"I'll keep that in mind. See you in a bit." Cole hung up and tucked the phone away. Since Prophet was staring expectantly at him, he said, "Rico says hi."

Sirens wailed from down the street. When the cruisers flew past Raza Hill, Prophet let out a relieved sigh and asked, "We done here?"

"I guess so."

They went to Prophet's van. During the drive to Pinups, Cole scrolled through some websites using his phone. By the time they arrived, he'd gotten his fill of news reports regarding the happenings in Philadelphia. The press seemed to be split as to whether the violence at the Lancroft house was the result of a gang fight or some sort of "fiery dispute between neighbors."

Normally, trips to strip bars were exciting, magical affairs where all the women smelled like candy and were more than willing to fulfill the degenerate thoughts that drifted through every man's head. With all the trips he'd been making lately, however, Cole had come to think of them merely as destinations to be reached. This one had some nice scenery, but there were still other matters that needed his attention. Some men's minds, however, drifted in other directions.

"This place have a buffet?" Prophet asked.

"No time for that. Just head for the VIP section."

Before he could set the parking brake, Prophet was waved around the building to park in the employee lot next to Paige's Cav. A bouncer held the door open for them, grinning anxiously and focusing his attention on the bounty hunter.

"So where are you guys from?" the young burly kid asked.

Cole's reply was only, "Cicero."

"What about you, sir? Are you with the Bears? Maybe the Bulls?"

Although Walter wasn't a small man, he still had to lift his chin in order to look into the bouncer's eyes. "Do I look like a basketball player to you?"

"I guess not. It's usually the athletes that get the special treatment, though. Are you a rapper?"

Shaking his head, Walter strode past the bouncer and caught up to Cole. "I don't know if that boy's racist or just stupid."

"The smile seemed genuine," Cole replied, "so I'd go with stupid."

They were greeted by a skinny blonde wearing short shorts, high heels, no shirt, and suspenders that were just wide enough to cover the nipples of her pert little breasts. Her smile was a bit forced and crinkled her face just enough to create a few breaks in her sparkly makeup. "You're Cole?" she asked.

"Yeah. Where's Miss Naughtygale?"

"She's seeing another patient right now."

"What about the other blonde?"

"You'll have to be a little more specific."

"The one with the magic fingers," Cole said.

That caused the dancer to look at him with renewed interest. "So you're here for the *other* VIP room?"

"Now you got it. My friend and I are headed to St. Louis."

Pausing at a metal door that practically rattled from all the bass thumping from the next room, the blonde said, "Come on in and have a seat. I'll send someone right over."

Once inside the main room, the music was too loud for Cole to hear himself think. The blonde didn't even try to talk as she strutted to a little round table away from the stage, pointed to a pair of chairs and waved toward a group of drooling beer drinkers who sat closer to the stage.

"Think I've got enough time for some food?"

"Sure, Prophet. Knock yourself out."

For the next two hours Cole sat at his table, sifting through various news sites and scanning their coverage of the Philadelphia incident as well as reports of the fire at Raza Hill. When the blonde in suspenders walked by again, Prophet said, "I think she's sizing us up for the rest of the nymphs."

"We've already been sized up and she's not a nymph."

"How can you tell?"

"She's wearing makeup."

As if to show the comparison firsthand, another blonde approached the table. She was the one who'd greeted Cole when he stepped into Pinups the first time and she radiated a subtle glow even though not one of the club's many lights were pointed at her. "I just got finished with a marathon session in the back," she said. "Should have enough fuel in my tanks to send both of you through now."

Prophet looked toward a section of the club that was roped off from the main room. It was a collection of couches on a raised platform, surrounded by a veil just thick enough to provide a bit of privacy without sacrificing security. Two young men helped an older one down the three steps leading to the main floor. Judging by the sweat on his brow and the constant heaving of his chest, he was the lucky customer with the deep pockets.

"This'll tap us out for a while," she added, "so you might not be able to come back through here right away."

"Cool," Cole said without looking up from his phone. "Are we ready to go?"

"Sure thing, sweetie. Come this way."

Cole stuffed his phone into his pocket, adjusted the flannel shirt he wore over his T-shirt to cover the spear's harness, and followed the Dryad. At first her footsteps were barely hard enough to tap against the tiles. By the time she'd put on her game face and climbed up to the side stage, however, they knocked like battering rams against the floor. The crowd roared and all three of the Dryads in attendance announced their presence by letting out a chorus of sublime tones from voices that entwined around one another much like the flowing symbols on the arch near the beaded entrance to the VIP section. Crisp green energy crackled. A whiff of fresh air drifted through the room, and Cole waved to the jealous onlookers as he stepped through. Prophet went next and emerged to find himself in another part of the country.

The bounty hunter blinked, looked around, pulled in a breath and let it out.

"Thought there'd be more, right?" Cole asked.

Nodding like a kid who just realized the toy he'd been longing for was nothing but a set of molded plastic pieces, Prophet asked, "So where to now?"

The temple was located in a small room inside a club that wasn't quite as large as Pinups. A large green sign on one wall spelled out the words THE EMERALD in neon handwriting over the bar. Since Rico was nowhere to be found, Cole took his phone from his pocket and headed for another table. "We wait for our ride. There's another buffet over there."

"Don't mind if I do."

Twenty minutes after making his call, a dark-haired woman drifted toward them in a swirl of purple silk and a scent that reached down to stroke the core of a mortal's libido. "If there's anywhere else you need to go, I'm sure I can arrange to have you sent there."

"Hey, Tristan."

Prophet shot up from his chair so quickly that he nearly

dumped his plate of tuna casserole and crab Rangoon onto the floor. "Tristan! You're working here? What happened to Wisconsin?"

"Hello, Walter," she said while touching his cheek. "Wisconsin's fine. I move around a lot, especially now that we don't have to lay quite as low. Off to St. Louis with Cole?"

"Yeah, Stanley wants to hear about what's going on with the Nymar."

Cole took his eyes completely away from the phone in his hand for the first time since he'd picked up the Wi-Fi signal. "What?"

Wincing as though he'd temporarily lost custody of his mouth, Walter replied, "You remember my boss. Stanley Velasco? Paige still owes him for springing you out of that jail in St. Lou."

"Sure you can't stay here with me?" Tristan purred.

Walter's temptation was so great that the conflicting gears grinding within his head almost started smoking. Finally he said, "No, I really need to see what these guys are up to. Unlike Cole and the rest of the dudes with sticks, I got a real job that needs to be looked after."

"Every man's got a stick that needs looking after," she said.

Cole laughed and rubbed her shoulder as he stood up. "You're usually a little classier than that, Tristan."

"Water seeks its own level. Looks like your friend is here. You two be good."

Rico stood in the doorway leading to the small room where cover charges were collected. The big man gave them a quick upward nod and waited impatiently as Prophet and Cole met him at the exit.

Once outside, Cole got a cool and damp welcome to East St. Louis. A light mist spattered across his face, but there was still an underlying heat that he'd come to believe was permanently soaked into the Missouri air. Rico climbed into an SUV and had the engine going by the time Cole and Prophet joined him. His bristly, graying hair was flattened on one side and slightly bloodied on the other. The dark circles under his eyes and the rumpled state of his clothes made it even tougher for Cole to tell whether Rico had just gotten out of a fight or climbed out of bed.

"What's the good word?" the big man asked as he pulled on a heavy leather jacket made from patchwork sections of tanned shapeshifter hide interspersed with narrow strips of thick canvas. The jacket was laced up both sides, sported more than a few shallow battle scars, and smelled like cigarette smoke.

"Shampoo," Cole replied.

Rico looked over at him and then to Prophet. "Hey there, Walter. You got something to say that ain't frickin' crazy?"

After a small amount of consideration, Prophet replied, "Nah."

"Make that two words," Cole added. "Shampoo banana."

Rico's face barely changed. "What the hell's that supposed to mean?"

"Paige told me to tell you that. Actually," Cole said, "she told me to tell you to tell me about shampoo banana."

"Give him some time, big man," Prophet told Rico. "There was a fire. He inhaled a lot of smoke. There was a fight. You know, the usual shit. He's rattled."

Rico's hardened expression remained, but he shifted his face toward the road ahead. "Lots of fires popping up lately. Lots of fighting going on. Plenty of dying too. The usual shit. That don't give us permission to slip into bouts of nostalgia."

"Nostalgia?" Cole grunted. "Try psychobabble! I have no idea what's going on anymore. Just when I think I'm getting a handle on this Skinner crap, everything gets tossed out the window! Paige takes off, insists on me coming here and passing off some kind of goddamn fruity hair care product as a password."

"Did she also tell you about the notebook?"

"Yeah. A hound dog notebook."

Rico nodded and turned onto the highway that led out of Sauget, Illinois, and into St. Louis. "Tell me about what happened in Chicago, and when we get back to Ned's house I'll fill you in on shampoo banana."

"Could you two please stop saying that?" Walter pleaded. "It makes me feel like I'm stuck in some kind of shitty kid's show."

For the first time since they'd left the Emerald, Rico grinned. It was an ugly display of large, blocky teeth, but went a long way in easing the confused tension that had filled the SUV. Cole and Prophet told him about the fire and ensuing fight while Rico drove down Interstate 40 and into the Central West End.

The driveway they pulled into was a short walk from Dressel's Pub, a place that served a plethora of beers and some of the best homemade potato chips Cole had ever tasted. The house connected to that driveway was a charming, if slightly run-down old home filled with crooked shelves piled high with obscure books and pieces of junk that could very well have been collected from some of the most twisted garage sales in the world. The walls were marked with runes meant to protect the inhabitants from harm. Too bad they hadn't been able to stretch their influence far enough to keep the house's previous owner alive.

When Rico walked in, he peeled off his jacket and tossed it across the room, where it landed on a slump-backed couch in front of a good-sized TV. Despite all the additional shelves, jars of bits and pieces collected from creatures thought to be extinct or impossible, and weapons belonging to the Skinners who'd come and gone through that building, Cole's eyes were drawn to one thing: a chipped cement frog sitting on the edge of one shelf, dangling its skinny crossed legs over the side. The paint was faded to a sea-foam green and the eyes were obviously cheap marbles. Cole patted the frog's knee and thought back to the grizzled old Skinner that had paid good money for the ugly knickknack. "I miss Ned."

"Yeah, me too," Rico said as he pounded up the stairs to one of the equally cluttered bedrooms.

A set of pans were on the dining room table. They were the kind used for paint rollers and had been in the same spot the last time Cole was there. As before, they contained a small amount of silvery liquid that looked as if it was just on the verge of hardening into a solid. All he had to do was step up close enough to smell the stuff to know it was the new varnish Daniels had created using melted chips from the Blood Blade. On the other side of the pans, previously hidden from his view, were a few .45 caliber rounds with the same metallic sheen worked into four veins that ran along the lead tip. Cole picked up the bullet, held it up to the light and muttered, "I'll be damned. Took all this time for one of us to make a silver bullet. Does it work?"

"You're damn right it works," Rico said as he stormed back into the room.

"Daniels said the Blood Blade fragments wouldn't bond with the lead," Cole pointed out.

"It ain't bonded with the lead. I injected it into hollow point rounds. Some of it leaks through enough to coat the bullet to let it punch through a shapeshifter's hide. Once it's in, the rest should be released into its body when the bullet cracks to pieces. Haven't had a chance to test it for real yet. I'm working on something else right now."

"Take it with you," Cole said. "We're going to Miami to look in on Paige."

"No we're not."

"She went after the Nymar that walked off with God knows what from Lancroft's place. Considering the stuff that was identified in there, I hate to think of what could be done with the goodies that nobody knew about. They may even be responsible for what happened after we left. Having that pack tear through so soon after the Nymar left is too much of a coincidence."

"They could've just come because the defenses were dropped," Rico explained. "Those runes are what kept Lancroft hidden from everyone, including the Full Bloods. I been tellin' Paige and plenty of others that leaving those things down was a bad idea, but nobody listened."

Cole grabbed a box of modified bullets and headed for the kitchen. "I'm taking some of this new varnish to give my weapon another treatment while I head back to the Emerald. I thought you were gonna help out, but if you'd rather putz around with your Home Ec projects, I'll bring Prophet. He can handle himself."

"You ain't going anywhere," Rico snapped. "Either one of ya."

"Why not?"

The big man threw something onto the table that glanced against one of the paint pans and almost slid off the edge. "Because Paige sent you here for a reason, that's why not. You got some reading to do."

Cole approached the table again, looked down and found a set of standard, 8½ by 11, spiral-bound notebooks held together by a thick rubber band. The covers were creased and tattered on the edges. He couldn't make out what was on the other covers, but the top one bore a picture of a large, droopy-eared hound dog. "What the hell is this?" he asked.

"It's what Paige wanted you to see. She must really think a lot of you. Either that or she's . . . just read it while I work. After that we'll see what comes next."

Cole pulled the rubber band from around the notebooks and opened the first one. The first words were, *I don't know what's happening and that scares me.* He'd seen enough of Paige's hastily scribbled notes to recognize her handwriting, even though this seemed to be a slightly neater version.

That's not it, the writing continued. *I do know what's happening. That scares me even more.*

The notebook was full of her writing. All of them were.

They were Paige's first journals as a Skinner, and the hound dog one was dated eleven and a half years ago.

Chapter Twelve

University of Illinois
Eleven and a half years ago

The girls moved like a pack of wolves skirting the east side of Memorial Stadium, on their way to the residence halls on the other side of Peabody Drive. It was early spring but there was enough of a chill in the air for most of them to don university sweatshirts or layers of fashionably weathered flannel T-shirts bearing faded Pink Floyd album covers or the faces of members of more current bands. The campus was well lit, but none of the girls were concerned with dashing from one pool of yellowed light to another. There were five of them in all. The girl at the front turned around so she was backing onto the street without casting a glance toward the oncoming traffic.

"Holy shit, Paige, look out!" squealed one of the Pink Floyd fans as she grabbed her by the front of her sweatshirt and pulled.

Even with the approaching car's horn blaring at her, Paige was more amused by the earnest attempt of the other girl's attempt to save her. "Take it easy, Jenny. You'll rumple the banana!"

Now that they were on the curb instead of in the street, Jenny looked down at the front of Paige's sweatshirt. It was baggy and one size too big for her, but had been snug a few years ago when she'd put on her Freshman 15. After losing that weight, Paige kept the shirt and wore it like a second skin. Her tendency to refer to the University of Illinois at Champaign-Urbana as Shampoo Banana always made her roommate giggle and this was no exception.

"You're going to get yourself killed before we get to the party," Jenny said.

"Whose party is this anyway?" asked a short girl with straw-colored hair and glasses that seemed more like a pair of windows perched upon her nose. It was a chilly day, so she wrapped her zip-up sweatshirt so tightly around herself that it almost completely hid the picture of Ted Nugent during his Damn Yankees days that was plastered across the front of her T-shirt.

Another one of the girls came up behind her. "You know Wes."

"The one with all the tattoos?"

"Oh yeah."

"Tara's still in the bad boy phase," Paige explained while strolling across the street during a lull in traffic.

"Like you're so much better?" the Damn Yankees fan scolded.

"At least I can keep my mouth shut when screwing someone at three in the morning."

Taking that as their cue, all of the girls except for Tara chanted, "Wes, Wes, oh God! *Yes!*" as if it was a cheerleader's cadence.

Tara winced and pulled the collar of her navy blue sweater up high enough to cover most of her face. "I accidentally rhyme in the middle of a late night quickie and never hear the end of it."

"You're in the room right next door to us," Paige said. "We'd like to hear the end of it so we can get some studying done."

Rushing up to bump Paige with her shoulder, Tara said sarcastically, "Right. All Margarita Girl here wants to do is study."

"Finals are coming up soon," Jenny offered.

"You guys need to lighten up." Pivoting around to walk backward across a small field of grass on the perimeter of a set of residence halls, Tara added, "Especially Karen. I bet you could be the one screaming by the end of tonight."

Although the face behind her wide glasses was made to smile, the one she showed the other girls was forced at best. "Sure. Maybe." That got the others off her back long enough for the rest of the pack to get distracted.

Now that they were close enough to hear music rolling out of one of the smaller halls, they set their eyes on the prize and fell into a strut that made them look like a small girl gang taking over a bar in a campy fifties sexploitation flick. Playing the role to the hilt, Paige swatted the face of the second-string football player guarding the door as she announced, "You can stop wishing for it, boy. The party's here."

"About damn time," the jock said. "Bar's right down that hall and the food's upstairs. Just follow the music."

It wound up being just another loud night in a string of similarly loud college nights. Even though she was taking part in festivities that so many of her peers found enthralling, Paige soon got bored. She drank a few of the margaritas for which she'd become famous, joked around with some guys, deftly avoided their clumsy advances and promised to call the number that had been given to her on a scrap of paper that became a receptacle for her gum.

Wes made an appearance every so often. He was a tall guy who stood out from the rest thanks to a series of intricate tribal tattoos on his neck and forearms. Every so often Paige thought she could see those tattoos shift, but chalked that up to the light in the room or the alcohol in her system.

Finding the rest of her pack was more of a chore than she'd expected. The second floor of the dorm was jammed to capacity with students and townies alike who'd clustered around the free booze and boiled hot dogs like a school of piranha. Jenny was in the upstairs common area on a ripped plastic couch while getting three bottles of Michelob poured down her throat via a length of plastic tubing. Amy was one of the pack's tagalongs, having been added a few weeks after the start of spring semester. The bright red Huskers jersey given to her by her boyfriend at the University of Nebraska was impossible to miss, but Paige still couldn't spot her. Amy wasn't the type to leave a party before being given permission by her friends, so that meant she must have been holed up somewhere out of sight, ditched the sweatshirt, or both. Good for her, Paige thought. Amy's boyfriend was a self-centered jackass. The rest of the group had been swallowed up by a crowd that became one sweaty, rattling mass. Time for a breather.

Even though the bar downstairs had been stripped of its goods by a bunch of lower classmen, it seemed the best place to go to clear her head. The door to the room at the end of the hall swung open so Tara could stagger outside. Her clothes had been hastily pulled on after what looked to be one hell of a tumbling session, and her hair was a telltale mess. Before Paige could be spotted, she bolted down the stairs.

Tara was a smoker. She was the kind of smoker who rolled her eyes at any talk of cancer, coughed up phlegm because she was an adult, and had every right to do what she pleased. Anyone who approached her with concerns about secondhand smoke were quickly made to wish they'd just shut their mouth and taken their chances with the carcinogens. Tara was also a screamer. Not in the way that Wes had surely just experienced, but in the way that almost shattered glass if she looked up to find someone standing there when she hadn't been expecting them. It was all Paige could do to keep from giggling as she circled around the bar to the perfect hiding spot and hunkered down in the darkness to wait for the ideal time to jump out and scare the living shit out of a good friend.

She could hear Tara's uneven footsteps coming down the stairs and could picture the bleary, dazed expression on her face. Once she got down the stairs to step outside for her smoke, she would be focused on the door and not expecting to get jumped from someone lurking behind the bar.

This was going to be great.

Something rustled in another part of the room. That was either Tara approaching the bottom step or someone else trying to find a quiet corner in the noisy building. Paige wasn't familiar with all the little noises in the structure, so for all she knew, some of the abundant noise from above was just filtering down.

Then again, Tara might have found a window to puff her smoke through. She might have even broken her routine and lit her cigarette upstairs. The creaking could be anything, and the feet coming down the stairs might belong to anyone. Suddenly, the joy Paige felt at the prospect of scaring Tara out of her mind was dimmed by the possibility of being discovered crouched behind the bar like an idiot. Holding her breath, she placed her hands on the edge of the bar and eased herself up past a row of dusty empty bottles that had probably been sitting there since the last Super Bowl.

Her eyes drew level with the warped top of the bar, making all the broken peanut shells and dried chunks of pizza crust seem like boulders on a miniature alien landscape. A shadow wobbled within the enclosed stairwell, followed by a long sigh and, "Wes, aren't you coming out here with me?"

Paige ducked under the bar, feeling every bit of dumb giddiness returning. The mood was heightened by the drinks she'd had in her, but was completely obliterated by the sight of the man chewing on Amy's face.

He was a skinny collection of bones and saggy skin wrapped up in paint-spattered jeans and a sleeveless T-shirt. The only reason she hadn't seen him before was because he and Amy were completely under the bar where it formed a corner that pointed toward the front door of the building. Nestled in there, they might have gone undiscovered for hours. His arms were covered in thick tribal tattoos, and for a moment Paige thought he was Amy's impromptu date for the evening. His mouth was wide open and pressed against the lower section of Amy's jaw. Wide dark eyes glared out from the shadows, waiting to see if he'd truly been discovered.

Nervous fear flooded through her, starting off as something she might feel when walking in on someone else's intimate moment and gradually turning into the mild dread of discovering a deranged homeless person following her down the block.

Then she saw the blood trickle from the man's mouth.

Amy twitched, snapped her eyes open and tried to look over at Paige. When she reached out for her, Paige immediately grabbed her hand. The instant Amy's leg scraped against the floor, she was pulled back by a bony arm that wrapped around her waist. Amy's cry didn't make it past her lips before the man tightened his grip on her.

For a moment Paige thought she'd gotten a hold on the other girl. Amy struggled to get away from the man under the bar, squirming in his grasp to expose the three sets of fangs buried in the side of her neck. Blood sprayed from the openings in her flesh, dimming the last bit of light in her eyes. The man holding her took it in with a wet sucking sound before adjusting his bite so the blood sprayed into his mouth.

Although it seemed she was forced to watch that for hours, only a few seconds had passed. Footsteps crossed in front of the bar, so Paige jumped up to catch Tara's attention. She found herself looking into the face of yet another man with thick tribal tattoos.

"Who's this?" asked a man who looked to be somewhere in his thirties. He had hair that lay flat against his scalp as if every strand had been glued into place. While most of his tattoos were concentrated at the front of his neck, some thinner strands crept up along a large pointed chin before tapering off just before reaching his lower lip.

Tara stood a few paces away from the bar. Judging by the look on her face, she was all but frozen there. Her skin had paled and was clammy. She kept her arms wrapped around her body as though covering herself after being caught in the shower. One man approached her from the left as Wes came in from the right,

The man with the pointed chin wore an expression that could hardly be called a grin. It was more of a curl of the lip to reveal two sets of fangs sprouting from his upper jaw when he asked, "Have you been holding out on us?"

Wes placed a hand on Tara's shoulder to hold her in place. "There's plenty of people on this campus, Evan. You don't need me to tell you that."

"The least you could have done was invite us to the party." Closing his eyes and concentrating on something that slithered past human senses, Evan hissed, "But it seems Hector has already found a party of his own."

The man under the bar sank his teeth deeper into Amy's neck. Paige knew if there had been any prayer of her helping Amy, it was gone now. She didn't know what she could have done, but it made her feel just as bad as if she'd killed the other girl herself. When Hector pulled Amy in tight against his chest, his fangs tore her throat open wide enough for Paige to see the bloody fibers within her. Hector even squeezed Amy's limp figure to force the last bit of fluid from her veins before the possibility of sharing her was broached.

"You've brought them into your confidence," Evan said in words that built in intensity like a train car that had been cut loose and was rolling toward a house at the bottom of a hill. "You've got them coming to you, getting drunk, getting laid, getting unconscious. How the *fuck* could you not tell us about this party?"

Paige's back was pressed against the wall. She didn't want to be near Hector and Amy, but she also didn't want to make herself any more visible to the others. The men's tattoos were definitely moving now. The more Hector slurped from the dead husk in his grasp, the more the black markings fluttered beneath his skin. The sight of it hit her on the same nerve as watching a thousand newborn spiders flowing from the cracked thorax of their mother.

"Look," Wes said. "I told you I'd stake this place out and I did."

"All you've fed us is scraps. The choice cuts are here." When a group of jocks came down the stairs, they sounded like a herd of elephants. Evan's eyebrow rose and he watched the bottom of the staircase as if he wasn't quite sure what he was about to see. Then he shifted his gaze ever so slightly to stare directly at Paige. "Friends of yours?"

Hector let Amy's body hit the floor so he could wipe the blood from his chin and then lick it off the top of his sleeve.

The jocks were taking their time in getting down the last few stairs while arguing about who would carry the cooler up from their car. Within those few seconds, Tara spotted Paige and showed her an urgent, pleading stare.

She might have been too late or too slow to help Amy, but Paige couldn't watch another friend get ripped apart. Standing up to her full height, she placed her hands flat on the top of the bar where her left palm brushed against a corkscrew. As soon as she had a firm grip on the narrow plastic handle, she started to vault over the top of the dented surface. Hector was more than quick enough to stop her by lunging out from his corner to grab her ankle.

As Paige's chest hit the edge of the bar and her feet were forced down less than an inch from where they'd started, the jocks made it down the stairs. They only had enough time to notice Paige standing behind the bar before another woman lunged all the way from the front door, across the room, and straight at them with her hands outstretched to sink her fingernails into their upper chests.

Shirts were shredded like wet newspaper, right along with several layers of underlying flesh. The woman slammed her weight against the largest of the young men and regained her footing a fraction of a second before she would have dropped to the floor. Once standing, she bared a set of curved fangs that slid from her upper jaw and drove them into the shoulder of the smaller of the two jocks. He opened his mouth to speak but dropped before making a sound. Milky venom still dripped from his wound as she pulled the slender fangs out and pressed her mouth against the other jock's lips.

Paige's heart slammed against the inside of her ribs. Her breath felt like it was solidifying in her throat, but she still tried to get to Tara. The grip around her ankle was too strong to shake, so she stabbed Hector's arm with the corkscrew to loosen it. The curved steel dug straight through the upper layers of skin, only to hit a surface that was solid enough to prevent the tip from going any deeper.

Hector's strength was incredible. His fingers felt like steel bands that didn't even twitch when she stabbed him repeatedly with the corkscrew. Even when she dug in as far as she could and twisted, Hector's only response was a labored snarl. Near the stairs there was a slight rush of movement but no voices calling for help. No grunts, no punches being thrown, and no athletic young men asserting themselves against the invaders. No help for Tara.

Paige's next blow landed on the side of Hector's neck in the middle of one of the thick tribal tattoos. This time there was no mistaking it. The tattoo wriggled away when the corkscrew punctured the skin. He responded by tightening his grip even further and pulling her leg out from under her body. She hopped in an attempt to remain upright, but that wasn't enough to keep her from hitting the wall on her side.

"Hide these two somewhere," the woman said before both of the jocks' limp bodies landed on the bar.

"What are you doing?" Tara asked in a voice that was so weak it could hardly be heard over the music filtering down through the floor. Wes threw her over the bar and then jumped it himself, barely scraping his shoes against the warped countertop before landing in a crouch between Paige and Tara.

Evan walked around, pulling the two unconscious jocks behind him.

Since Paige couldn't free herself from Hector's grip, she shifted her attention to Wes. He looked at her and shook his head before sternly whispering, "Don't."

Her scream came like an explosion from her lungs and would have easily torn through the Snoop Dogg chart-topper everyone was singing on the second floor if Wes hadn't cut it off by pounding his fist into her face. No matter how much the punch hurt, Paige wasn't about to submit.

She had been in her share of confrontations. Although she would never have admitted as much, most of the physical ones had been classic girl fights. Lots of flailing arms and wild slaps without a lot of damage being done. She'd been in a schoolyard scuffle with a boy, but she could tell he was holding back on account of her smoother features and pink clothes. When Wes leaned down and hit her again, he didn't hold back. He didn't glare at her with an abuser's contempt or a rapist's ferocity. He simply smashed her face because that's what he needed to do. It was harsh. It was clinical. It was painful.

Apart from the heavy thump of knuckles against her head, Paige heard a crunch that filled her ears and sent a jolt of pain through her entire upper body. Because she didn't have the good sense to crumple, he hit her once more. Instead of a crunch, Paige heard the snap of cartilage in her nose giving way. Blood flowed down her face and her next breath set off a firestorm of pain that filled every bit of real estate in her skull.

The bodies of the jocks hit the floor behind it like sacks that had been dropped from the roof. Paige tried to get out from under them but was unable to move quickly enough due to the grip that was still around her ankle. It tightened and jerked her closer to the shadows as something sharp raked against her hip. The jocks lay on the floor with their limbs akimbo, dead weight pinning her to the floor.

"Hey, where are those beers?" someone called from upstairs.

When Paige attempted to respond, the woman leapt on top of her to straddle her chest and slap a firm hand over the lower portion of her face. The pain from having her broken nose mashed that way nearly knocked Paige out, but the sight of the woman above her was something to hold on to.

"Right down here," the woman said calmly. Her face was slender and attractive, despite the sets of black markings that ran up along both sides of it. Clear green eyes locked upon

Paige and widened as if to specifically display the black veins extending toward her pupils.

Whoever had made the inquiry about the beer stomped halfway downstairs and was met by Evan. "What's up there is all that's left," he said. "But check in the bottom of the footlocker in my room. I got a stash in there that should make up for it."

"Sweet!" was all the guys said before stomping upstairs again.

Approaching the bar so he could look over and down at Paige, Wes asked, "What now, Hope?"

"Now you hold your girlfriend down so we can all have a taste."

"You've got enough to feed on already."

"Maybe," she said, "but Evan's right. You've been holding out on us. You need to be reminded that we share so that we may all feed. It's just not fair for you to get your pick when poor Hector needs to scavenge in the dark."

"Hector always scavenges in the dark," Wes said with disdain.

"But not the rest of us," Hope said. "Not anymore."

Paige struggled to move but was held down. Even though Hector had let go of her ankle, he'd all but crushed it. In fact, the pain flooding from her injuries filled her like water coming in through multiple leaks. Hope's palm was cool over her mouth. Her strength, unlike Hector's wild display of force, lay just beneath her surface and asserted itself only when necessary.

A calm brush of her fingernails against Paige's throat was all it took for Hope to assure her that she could rip it clean away from her spine if the mood struck her. "I doubt we have much time here," she said. "Bring your girlfriend to me before I come for her myself. If that happens, I'll snap off pieces of her for each of us to try."

Whatever battle of wills was going on between Wes and Evan ended with those words. The pain had given Paige's skin a cold, clammy sheen, and the noises in the room were swirling into a breathy roar. She felt a sense of relief when Tara was laid down beside her, simply because the other girl blocked her view of Amy's empty body. Before she could feel too guilty about that, Paige was being held down by Evan's slender, immovable hands. Hope grabbed one of the unconscious jocks, lifted his wrist to her mouth and bit into his veins. The younger guy convulsed but was soon drifting into a more permanent sleep.

The rest of the vampires descended upon Paige and the others behind the bar in a frenzy.

Chapter Thirteen

> *Vampires. I saw them feed, watched them move, may have seen one of them fly, and I still can't stop questioning it. I was told to write all of this down as a way to preserve what happened. I hate him for making me do this. I hate them for what they did. Right now, I just hate everyone. With the shit that's in this world, it's not like a little more hate will make a difference.*

Cole closed Paige's journal and rubbed his eyes. He'd been staring at the scribbled words so intently, it seemed he might have permanently etched some of them into his brain. "Jesus Christ," he muttered.

"Not quite," Rico said as he walked up to the couch where Cole was sitting. "But you may still be glad to see me. What do you think?"

Grateful for a reason to set the journal down, Cole marked his spot with a gas receipt from his pocket and set the hound dog notebook on top of the stack. Rico stood beside the couch, holding what looked like a heavy patchwork curtain in front of him. When it was turned around, the curtain became a long leather coat. Although the stitching was similar to the jacket he usually wore, the material was obviously different. It was another kind of leather, with a darker reddish hue. The more Cole studied it, the more the red faded below a sheen of black, as if the bulky garment had been dipped into a vat of flame and charred to perfection.

Cole stood up so the shoulders of the coat were even with his own, and fell at its lowest edge a few inches below his knees. Grommets were sewn into the collar, under the arms, and irregularly spaced along the back. Along the sides, much like Rico's jacket, leather cords laced almost all the way down.

Turning it around so those could be seen better, the big man explained, "You can adjust the fit whenever you like. Makes it easier to conceal whatever you may be carrying underneath."

"So this is mine?" Cole asked.

"From what you told me about Henry's last request, it probably shouldn't go to anyone else. I don't know if clothes can be haunted, but I don't wanna be the one to test the theory."

Hearing Rico mention the Full Blood who'd lived inside the skin before it had been peeled off his bones, tanned, prepared, and eventually sewn into this coat, disconcerted Cole. The last request wasn't a joke. Henry had indeed been the one to tell him where to find the leather in Lancroft's basement. The Full Blood had to know what a Skinner would do with the material, but giving permission for it to happen reminded Cole of the talking space cow from *The Hitchhiker's Guide to the Galaxy* that was wheeled around the tables of a restaurant so he could proudly declare how delectable his own steaks were going to be.

"Well," Rico said expectantly. "Aren't you gonna try it on?"

Prophet was sitting at a desk checking his e-mails on an outdated PC. Seeing the coat, he said, "If he don't want it, I'll take it. That should be good for at least starting some conversations with the right type of woman. Unless that's real leather."

"It sure is."

"Then forget it," Walter said as he got back to his in-box. "Too good a chance of pissing another type of woman off."

Moving on as if Walter had never even opened his mouth, Rico said, "This is genuine Full Blood leather. Well, most of it. I had a few strips of some Half Breed to fill in the gaps, and the tops of the shoulders are mostly canvas, but the rest is all the good stuff. Do you know how hard it was to even get a stitch through it?" Gazing down at the coat as if the dead skin was attached to a living, breathing centerfold model, he said, "If I didn't have access to some of that Blood Blade varnish to treat my tools, I wouldn't have been able to put the damn thing together. It's a beaut."

"So this is stronger than Half Breed armor?" Cole asked.

"Paige uses the tactical harness way too much. That's good for one, maybe two nights on the town. I tan my own leather, layer by layer, like what I used for my jacket. That's formed from a Half Breed compound that can stop bullets and a whole mess of claws and fangs before needing to be repaired. This," he said while helping Cole ease into the sleeves and setting the coat onto his shoulders, "puts all of that to shame. Anything a Full Blood can take, this can take."

"Have you tested it?"

"We can test it right now. Got a rocket launcher?" Since Cole didn't share his enthusiasm, Rico shrugged and added, "I shot it a few times. Didn't leave a dent. Their fur gives them some protection, plus they can heal wounds faster than hell, but they're also just tough. This hide should protect you a hell of a lot better than that tactical stuff Paige slaps together. It's more fashionable too."

From behind the computer, Prophet let out an unmistakably skeptical grunt.

"Where are the pockets?" Cole asked.

"Inside. That way you don't lose your keys when you sit down. And if something does slip out, it'll hit your leg so you know what happened. What's that look about? There's more to making these things than just lashing shit together!"

The coat was heavy on Cole's shoulders, but conformed to him like the second skin it was. And the longer he kept it on, the less he felt it. Soon, the weight of the coat simply folded into that of his own body. "What about my spear?" he asked.

"There are loops on the inside, left and right," Rico said. "Or you could just wear the harness upside down and draw the spear downward instead of up and over the shoulder."

"You really thought this stuff through. I'm impressed."

"Hey, a mind tends to wander when you've got so much sewing to do." Sensing another comment from the computer desk, Rico jabbed a finger in that direction and said, "Save it, Walter."

"Well all right then," Cole said. "I got the long coat and spear. That only leaves one thing." After grabbing the Mossberg Tactical Model 12-gauge shotgun propped against one wall, he held the bulky weapon in both hands, put on his best scowl and asked, "Where's a mirror?"

"Just wait till you put this on," Rico said as he handed over a pistol wrapped in a holster built to clip onto a belt or harness. Opting for the first choice, he had it in place before Cole knew what hit him. "That's a .45 so it'll work with the ammo I made for the rest of us. I got plenty of Nymar rounds as well as some of those new Blood Blade points. Once we all use the same caliber, we can pull from the same ammo pool."

Cole set the shotgun down and tried to draw the pistol but had some trouble. "I think it's snagged on something."

"That's a rig used by the Spetznaz. Russian commandos. Grab the gun by the handle, slide it down then out."

Cole followed the instructions and felt the pistol's mechanism move with the motion.

"Nice, huh?" Rico beamed. "The rig draws the slide back so you don't have to. When you bring your hand up, it's good to go. Shaves a few precious seconds off the draw time and gets you ready to do some damage that much faster."

"Good. We'll need this when we go to Miami."

"No. We're headed back to Philly. Paige can handle herself for now. If she needs us, she'll call."

"If she's able to call. What if she's lying in a ditch some-where?"

"Then we don't have much of a chance of finding her," Rico replied.

"Damn," Prophet grunted. "That's cold."

Giving the bounty hunter a sideways glance, he asked, "You think you can find her in Miami just by asking around about a little brunette with an attitude problem and food stains on her shirt?"

Cole walked over to one of the shelves covered in sup-plies and books. Grabbing one eyedropper from a narrow wooden rack, he showed it to Rico and told him, "These are the drops we used before. The ones that allow us to see scents. We tracked Nymar with them and we know we can see Skinners the same way. We'll use these to find Paige."

Prophet was definitely intrigued by the drops, but knew better than to ask for a free sample.

"There was a breach at Lancroft's place," Rico said. "Two of them. We need to go back and see what the Full Bloods were after."

"Could have been they were just after Skinners," Cole pointed out. "That's why Burkis hit that cabin in Canada. He heard about Gerald and Brad being there and set an ambush."

"Gerald, Brad, and the Blood Blades were there," Rico corrected.

"So with all the crap that was in that place, you expect us to just go in and see what's missing? There were rooms, closets, cases, lockers, and boxes filled with God only knows what, and less than half of it was identified."

When Rico looked over to Prophet, the bounty hunter said, "He's got a point. I was in there. That place was piled high with Skinner shit."

"That doesn't mean we can't go back and have a look around," Rico insisted. "There had to be a good reason for the Full Bloods to go in hot like that. I've never even heard of two of them working together like this, not to mention running with Mongrels."

"And," Cole replied, "there's no reason for us to think that place isn't a pile of rubble. They set off the explosives Lancroft rigged, remember? Didn't you see what was left of the reformatory? The Dryads could send us right into a pile of rocks. Maybe we'll materialize into solid—"

"Aw, for Christ's sake, we're not talking about beaming in like some goddamn movie."

"Oh, excuse me. We're talking about riding a green wave of happy thoughts and music," Cole snapped. "Big difference."

When Prophet started laughing, both men turned to look at him. The bounty hunter sat behind the computer, shaking his head and chuckling to himself. Knowing he was the center of attention without having to look up, he said, "You two really don't know what the hell to do without Paige leading the way, do you?"

Rico and Cole both sputtered for a second as they tried to be the first to speak up in their own defense. Then, after thinking it over and taking stock of the situation, they found they were only sputtering. Finally, Cole took off the coat that was making him sweat like the proverbial working girl in church and asked, "Has there ever been this much going on with you guys? I don't just mean Philly. I mean KC, what happened at Chicago, Henry, Misonyk, all of it. If so, how the hell didn't I know about you guys before I met Paige?"

"It's been a hell of a season," Rico admitted.

"I'd like to think I'm not the new guy anymore, but I'm in over my head with this."

Without pausing, Rico said, "We're always in over our head."

"You know what your problem is?" Prophet asked. "You're used to dealing with these things like hunters and wild game. Now there's more game out there than you can pin down. You two are just runnin' around like kids in a candy store."

"Got any more analogies, Walter?" Rico grunted. "Or were you heading somewhere with this?"

Prophet tapped one last key on the clunky keyboard, stood up and announced, "You need to go about this a different way. And here's where you're gonna be glad I came along."

He circled around the desk so he could pick up Cole's new coat and run the unusual leather between his fingertips. "Shift your mind-set into my world on this one. Come at these guys like fugitives instead of animals."

"We know they're not just animals," Rico said.

"Sure, but you're tracking them that way."

Cole fidgeted with the .45 to get it back into its holster as he said, "Let me guess. When you say we should track them like fugitives, you mean we should track the Nymar that your boss wants us to track."

Doing his best to look offended, Prophet let out a few hacking breaths and glanced over to Rico. He got no support on that front, so he shifted back over to Cole and dropped the act completely. "You remember the last time you talked to my boss? You told Stanley you'd help track down those Nymar that were giving him trouble in Denver."

"I never said that."

"Paige did." Immediately sensing what was coming next, Prophet quickly added, "And if Paige was here, I'd be telling her the same thing. When wild animals start going nuts, you track them down and catch them. That's what you guys have been doing, and it's worked so far. When those animals get organized into groups and start making precision hits on places like that Lancroft house as soon as there's an opening, that means they're not wild at all. From where I stand, it seems they've got their shit together a whole lot more than you do. These guys in Denver have been an organized pain in the ass for a while. What're the odds they might also know something about what's been going on with the rest of the vampires in this country?"

Cole and Rico looked at each other but couldn't put together an argument strong enough to take Prophet out of his stride.

"Denver's a big city," Prophet continued. "What if things go to hell there the way they did in Chicago and Philly? Lots of people could get hurt. Me and Stanley already know where these guys are, and we know some folks to call that'll tell us when they're in one place. Wouldn't that help in surprising them when you kick their doors in? Once you do, you can catch one, make him talk, inject him with whatever, do what you do."

"What does your boss want with a bunch of bloodsuckers anyway?" Rico asked.

"To you, they're bloodsuckers," Prophet replied. "To Liberty Bail Bonds and the Denver PD, they're tattooed fugitives who don't like showing up for court dates. They've been recruiting from the lowlifes out there, which also happen to be Stanley's client base. The more of them disappear off the grid, the more money he loses. I'm a shareholder in the business, so I'm losing money too. More than that, they've been protecting their interests by attacking our bondsmen. That shit's gotta stop."

Reluctantly, Cole admitted, "We do owe this to Velasco for paying our bail when we were locked up."

"He's a bail bondsman," Rico grunted. "That's what he does for a living."

"Then we should just pull the money together and pay him back. You got that much on you?"

Looking over to Prophet, Rico said, "Ask Walter over there. He's the man with the lottery picks."

"We'll do it," Cole said. "First we check up on the Lancroft house to see what's left there. After that we'll head on out to Denver. The nymphs will be able to send us out that way, right?"

"I don't see why not," Rico said. "But if you think I'm gonna let you take off after Paige on yer own, you got another think comin'. If something did happen to her, the last thing I'll need is to be forced to track *both* of you down."

"You're right," Cole admitted. "Paige can handle herself, and she also wanted me to read these journals. I'll do my homework while keeping busy with this other stuff. If we don't hear from her before too long, we'll go after her. It's just a simple quest list."

"Quest list?" Prophet asked.

Rico rolled his eyes and stomped into the kitchen. "Aw, great. Here we go with this geek shit again."

"In any game where you get a bunch of things to do, you can't try to do all of them at once. You need to pick one and keep your eyes open for keys or whatever for the others along the way."

"Ohhhh," Prophet said. "That kind of geek stuff."

Cole continued as if everyone was right there on the gaming journey with him. The simple fact was that it felt good to touch base with his roots, if only for a minute or two. "When time is of the essence, you pick the quick quests first and work your way down the list. If Lancroft's temple was destroyed, the Dryads should know about it. They can feel that sort of thing when they try to open a bridge."

"You'd better hope they can," Rico warned.

"Tristan mentioned that when we went there last time, remember? If we're able to go, we should be able to figure out whatever we're able to figure out before too long. I'll tell you right now that there's no chance in hell of me sifting through all of that stuff to take a real inventory. If you're willing to accept a quick once-over, I'll do that much."

"You won't just fart around for a minute and call it quits?"

"No. I'll fart around for several minutes before calling it quits."

Rico accepted that with a shrug and headed to the kitchen.

Chapter Fourteen

Outside of Salem, New Jersey

Kawosa crouched with one knee and two hands pressed against a recently disturbed mound of earth. His long wiry hair hung straight down, unmoving in the wind that blew around him. The collection of clothes he wore had been picked up from several different contributors along their relatively short run from Philadelphia. His appetite had been mighty after being imprisoned for so long and he was quick to sate it by the meat wrapped up in those clothes. Even the other werewolves in his company were impressed with how quickly the gangly shapeshifter could strip flesh from unwilling bone.

"So this is truly the resting place of a Full Blood?" he asked.

Liam stood nearby, clad in the same rags he'd worn before finding Randolph in Wyoming. "We both have his scent well enough."

Looking up at Liam with a wolf's yellow eyes, Kawosa said, "What I need to find out is how this one was killed." Without another word, he started digging. It didn't take long for him to find Henry's body. When the savaged remains were uncovered, all of the creatures reacted.

"Mongrels," Kawosa snarled. "Go away."

Purposely avoiding the sight of Henry's body, Max separated from his feline companion and approached Kawosa in his human form. "Whatever you have to say, we can hear it too. We lost one of our own breaking you out of that Skinner dungeon."

"And you'll lose the rest of your number if you don't do as I say."

Randolph didn't feel the need to step in, and Liam seemed content to watch what would happen next.

Max lowered his head and moved away from the Full Bloods. Lyssa sniffed the wind that had brushed Kawosa's back, quickly lowered her head and followed in his footsteps.

When he spoke, Kawosa used a voice that could easily be mistaken for the whisper of wind through flailing branches. "I smell Amriany craftsmanship at work."

Both Randolph and Liam rushed forward to get a better look. Rather than force their eyes to absorb the sight of what lay in the upturned dirt, they studied the notches in Henry's bones and the stains upon what little there was of his tattered fur. Liam went so far as to lower himself to all fours and dip his lengthening snout into the grave.

"The Amriany have no presence here," Randolph said. "They would rather hand this continent over to us than work with the Skinners."

"The Blood Blades were forged by Amriany hands," Kawosa said. "And it seems those have found their way to these shores."

"This wasn't done with a Blood Blade," Liam said.

Randolph allowed himself to see the carnage for what it was, the sight clearly sickening him. "I am very familiar with the scent of a Blood Blade. I could have told you already if one had been used to bring Henry down."

After sniffing the remains intently, Liam perched upon the edge of the hole. "Not a Blood Blade, but there is something else." He looked at Randolph and added, "It's something I haven't smelled since I came to the New World. There was plenty of this in Britain, though. I can't put my finger on what, exactly, but the scent brings me right back to the days of cobblestones and dark ale."

At first it seemed as if Randolph was merely drawing a contemplative breath. But when the air was pulled through his nostrils, he rolled it around in his throat like a pungent vintage of wine. "Perhaps you're right."

"More likely," Kawosa said with half a smirk, "some of their influence has been taken and changed by the Skinners. The colonial hunters always did have a knack for stealing whatever they needed."

"What are you keeping from me?" Randolph asked.

Once again Liam held his tongue so he could watch events unfold.

Kawosa stood up to his full height, which expanded with every shifting muscle beneath his skin. Even though he didn't change into another form like those the Full Bloods traded like so many different shirts, each variance had a distinct personality. By the time he settled on one that allowed his dark blue eyes to gaze directly into Randolph's, he was exuding power like steam that seeped almost imperceptibly through imperfections within an engine. "I was in that cage for years, boy. All that time, Jonah Lancroft tried to figure out what to do with me, how to kill me, what he might harvest from my bones. He trod lightly upon the floorboards above my head, knowing that I could hear every word that fell from his stinking human mouth. As time went on, he grew confident, speaking louder, unknowing or uncaring that I may have heard.

"In that cage, I could smell the chemicals he mixed, the blood he spilled, the weapons he forged. I saw him fill the other cells and then drag out the bodies after cutting them to pieces using devices gleaned through methods unknown to anyone on this side of the Atlantic. That is why the Skinners came running to that house after the pretty little bird with the wounded wing finally disposed of Lancroft. In that cage, I heard Henry scream until his voice became nothing more than an insane whisper in the dark. I know about the Amriany methods because I was there to witness them put to use, which I assume is why you went through the trouble of setting me free."

"That's not the only reason."

"I didn't think so." Kawosa pivoted on the balls of his feet so he could start scraping dirt back onto Henry's remains. "Will your Mongrel friends disturb this site? They won't be able to smell it as well as us, but they'll find it sooner or later."

"They should know better than to do something as foolish as that," Randolph assured him. "They are many things, but stupid isn't among them."

"I want to find the Amriany."

"If those brigands are here, I want to find them too," Liam said. "I owe them for soiling my home ground. There will be others coming, you know. Other Full Bloods."

"He's right," Randolph said. "There aren't many of us, but surely they know of what's been happening here."

Having filled the hole, Kawosa stood up, tossed his head back and allowed his hair to move with the next breeze. "Ahh, yes. The riots in Kansas City. Even in my pit I heard of that. The others will indeed be coming. Maybe not all of them, but I can think of one or two that might be interested in partaking in such widespread debauchery."

Randolph's eyes snapped in the direction the Mongrels had gone. In the distance two shapes scurried to find another spot to wait. "Things here are getting out of hand. Lancroft's pestilence has had more far-reaching implications than I'd previously feared. The Half Breeds are replenishing their numbers."

Shifting into his hulking two-legged form, Liam clenched his clawed hands into fists and growled, "There ain't no Half Breeds after that pestilence had its way with this country."

"The wretches were trimmed back in number, but not culled," Randolph said. "The ones who've poked their noses out of their dens since Lancroft's plague have either been killed by it or adapted to endure it. I found a pack of them in the Badlands. They were far from the miserable creatures that were stricken down by the Mud Flu. If not for their scent, I may have mistaken them for another breed entirely."

When the light of the moon touched Kawosa's features, deep wrinkles showed upon his cheeks and beneath his eyes. His sunken chest swelled beneath the clothes that had been stolen several miles ago, and his teeth became chipped pieces of ivory wedged into his jaw. "You know, when the Half Breeds first appeared in the desert to the west, they weren't much more than wolves with eyes that belonged in the face of a man. They reverted to their human form every few weeks, cursing their lot in life. Some say the Breaking as we know it now is a blessing. The human dies as the bones are snapped, relieving them of their torment." Kawosa's tone during those last few words was biting and resentful, an effect that was heightened even more by the mocking sneer on his face. "They shifted into their quivering, infantile bodies to slink into holes they'd dug within earshot of human villages. Pathetic. As the Breaking became more intense, they became stronger. Like blades forged in hotter fires, they grew longer legs, stronger jaws, sharper claws, until they became the terrors that plague us now. And today, they have been reborn again."

"Why didn't you mention this, Randolph?" Liam asked.

"After what you did in Kansas City? You'd be more likely to take these wretches as pets."

"And what's stopping me from doing so now?"

"I am," Kawosa replied.

Liam's first impulse was to shift into something with more fur so he could stand it up on end. One subtle change in the other being's eyes was enough to show him the error in that line of thought.

After a sniffing breath, Liam grunted, "Fine. What's next, then?"

"We find the new Half Breeds," Kawosa said. "And we see what good they can do us."

Now it was Randolph's turn to be taken aback. "What?"

Kawosa smiled as if the muscles needed to perform the action were too far out of practice to do it properly. Despite its awkwardness, it was the most genuine gesture he'd made so far. "Those Amriany nomads have a recipe for everything. They have enough tricks to make the Skinners jealous and now they have a presence here. The Skinners are broadening their horizons, thanks to scum like Lancroft, but they've never seen the likes of this new breed, correct?"

Amused once again, Liam watched Randolph carefully until the answer came.

"Probably not."

"Then," Kawosa growled as he shifted into a lean, vaguely canine form, "let us introduce them."

Chapter Fifteen

Philadelphia

"I'm really getting sick of this place," Cole griped. As much as he'd been hoping to hear differently from the girls at Pinups, the Skipping Temple that Lancroft had built was still intact enough for the Dryads to send them there. Despite a layer of dust thick enough to completely obscure the symbols on the temple walls, the basement was in relatively good condition. The workshop wasn't completely collapsed, but several of the tables had been knocked over, and there wasn't one stack of the supplies Cole had left. The small windows looking up into the yard were blocked by sections of the wall that had fallen in the controlled explosion. It wouldn't pass any builder's safety code, but the house was still standing.

Standing next to one of the cracked cement walls in the workshop, Rico dragged his hand across a section marred by a road map of cracks. "This house was either built really well or Lancroft didn't want it scrapped all the way."

Prophet walked into the workshop from the landing of the stairs that went up to the kitchen. "He sure as hell didn't want to come back that way," he said while patting the dust off his dark gray jacket. "All I can see back there is about one and a half stairs before the rubble starts. If anyone's under there, they're toast. You think that's funny, Cole?"

"No."

"Then why are you laughing?"

"Because with that dust you just kicked up, you remind me of a black Pigpen."

Scowling and coughing within his gritty cloud of cement powder, Prophet waved his arms and strode into a clearer section of air. "What the hell are you talking about?"

Suddenly, Rico couldn't stop laughing. "He means that dirty kid from the Charlie Brown cartoons. Oh man, you do look like—"

"With all the shit happening around here, you're still thinking about goddamn cartoons?" Prophet griped.

Once Cole regained control of himself, he said, "It's either that or drive myself crazy thinking about everything. Small doses of what passes for reality plus a few cartoons thrown in makes it all easier to manage."

Even though Prophet obviously wanted to argue, he let it go. "Did you find whatever it was you were looking for?"

"No," Cole said. "I found a big mess, just like I thought I would. You ready to go now, Rico?"

"Grab some of those jars and we'll take them back with us."

"What about those jars I brought back the first time? I almost forgot about those."

"I had a look at a few of 'em. Nymar blood. It's not quite the stuff we see too often, but it's Nymar, all right. We'll need someone to take a closer look to know more than that. Forget that now. We still need to check out the other downstairs."

"I was already there," Cole said. "I told you about that body I found."

"We're here to look again." Rico grunted. "So that's what we'll do. We got a little while before the nymphs can do their thing to get us out of here."

"Doesn't there have to be girls on both ends of the bridge to let us go through?" Prophet asked.

Cole sounded like an old pro when he said, "The Skipping Temple was made to be activated remotely. At least, it's the nymph version of remote activation. Just don't worry about it."

"Yeah," Rico said as he headed through the temple and into the dissection room. "If something goes wrong to fry us while we're in Never Never Land or whatever else you wanna call the space in between strip clubs, we probably won't feel a thing."

"What if the beads won't even light up and we're stuck here?"

"Then we find another way out. Just stop asking so many goddamn questions so we can do what we came to do."

Every other time he'd been in the dissection room, Cole had needed a moment to let his eyes adjust to the stark lighting and immaculately cleaned, reflective metallic surfaces. Now, the only light in the room came from one very stubborn fluorescent tube, the flashlights the Skinners had brought with them and the dim glow emanating from behind the hidden doorway that led to the dank brick hallway below. The lights down there ran on a power source of their own, which probably wasn't anything more exotic than a spare generator or separate line spliced from the neighbors.

Rico was a quarter of the way down the narrow staircase when a scraping sound drifted up from below. All three men froze. Cole bypassed the harness that was rigged upside down as Rico had suggested and went for the holster beneath his coat on his hip. He drew the .45, which sent the metallic sound of his pistol slide rattling down the hallway. After that, more restless noises emanated from the musty depths.

Narrowing his eyes and shoving past Cole to get down the stairs, Rico shouted, "Someone down there?"

No voices responded, but the unmistakable shuffle of footsteps drifted up to Cole's ears.

"Cover me," Rico said as he drew his pistol, then pressed a shoulder against the wall and descended.

Cole aimed at a spot ahead of Rico, searched for any motion along the hallway and prayed he could differentiate between a threat and some innocent rat scurrying from one hiding spot to another. Prophet was right beside him with his own pistol held in a two-handed grip.

"Who's down there?" Rico called out. "You need help?"

Cole could hear at least two different voices echoing from farther down the hall. Having been down there enough times to picture the layout in his head, he guessed that the speakers were somewhere between the far end of the hall and the cell containing the body of the Nymar with the strange markings.

Continuing to the bottom, Rico struck a defensive crouch as soon as he could get a clean look down the hall. "Cole, you know these guys?"

Cole's heart thumped in his chest as he moved down the stairs. At the bottom he found a pair of figures standing in the hall. One was a man of average height with a stocky build and muscular frame. Even in the shadows his skin had a dusky hue. The other was a woman who'd sought cover in one of the many alcoves along the hallway. Her paler skin stood out against the dark blond hair that seemed to shine in the sparse light thrown off by bulbs encased in glass and wire casing. A backward baseball cap kept her hair from her eyes, allowing her to sight along the barrel of what looked to be a FAMAS assault rifle. It was an ugly weapon with an extended barrel and a structure along the top that looked like an oversized handle. The only reason Cole recognized it was because he preferred using that weapon to spray 7.5mm rounds all over any map in the Sniper Ranger death matches that had all but consumed his old life in Seattle. The man carried a small cannon in one hand, which he pointed at Rico as he thumbed back the hammer.

"Cole?" Rico said as he shifted nervously within the line of fire of the two they'd come upon.

"Never seen them before," he replied. "But there were a lot of people coming through here. They could still be—"

"They'll be dead unless they lower those weapons," Prophet barked with an edge to his voice that had been put there during years of storming through fugitives' doors and demanding full compliance with whatever warrant he was serving at the time.

Not only did his warning have an effect on Cole, but it did its job with the other two as well. Both the man and woman lowered their guns without relinquishing their grips. It might not have taken much for them to get into firing position again, but tensions had eased for the moment.

"You're Skinners?" the woman asked.

"That's right," Rico replied. "And my guess is that you ain't. You also ain't Nymar, so who the hell are you?"

The man extended a hand toward the woman. Only then did she take her left hand off the bottom of the FAMAS so the rifle was allowed to hang down at her side by the strap that kept it attached to her shoulder. The man then peeled open the front of his sandy brown jacket to reveal a double rig holster strapped beneath his arms. "I am Tobar," he said with a thick, vaguely Russian accent. "This is Adrina."

The last time he'd heard someone speak in that accent, Cole recalled, he was sitting in the office of the man who owned Bunn's Lounge. Bunn's had been the pinnacle of Dryadcentric adult entertainment in the St. Louis area, but was now a charred shell with a Condemned sign stuck to its front door. The club owner kept in touch with Cole and Paige, but only to scream unintelligible insults into their voice mail in hopes of getting some compensation for the damage done by a rampaging pack of local Mongrels.

"Do you know Christov?" Cole asked.

The other two were a ways down the hall, but Cole could see the questioning looks they shot at each other.

"They're not Christov's," Rico said as he tucked his combat model Sig Sauer .45 away. "They're Gypsies."

Even clearer than the confusion they'd displayed before, both of the strangers down the hall now showed angry resentment on their faces. "And you are ignorant Americans," Adrina said.

Tobar strode forward and displayed a set of perfectly white teeth marred by a few perfectly aligned gaps. "More like cowboys, Drina. These three probably think we all are fortune-tellers and thieves. Is that it?"

Now Cole could see through Tobar's jovial act. He was testing them and probably ready to follow up on whatever insult he'd taken from Rico's words. Stepping forward and putting on a friendly, oblivious smirk, Cole said, "I'm just trying to match accents. The only Gypsies I've ever seen are in old movies. Same with cowboys, though. I don't get out much."

Tobar studied Cole carefully. Adrina did the same. "We're called Amriany," he said. "It's no secret among you Skinners, but none of you seem to care about us unless you're stealing the weapons made by our finest craftsmen."

"Those Blood Blades weren't stolen," Rico was quick to say.

"Then you crafted them yourself?"

"No. We heard they were available and sent someone to pick them up. It's not our fault one of your people was careless enough to lose two of the damn things."

"One of our people," Adrina snapped. "You talk like you know anything about our people."

"Okay, okay," Cole said. "You guys have some sort of grudge. We get it. How about you settle it some other time? Right now, why don't you tell us how the hell you got here. Did you use the Skipping Temple?"

"The Dryad Bridge?" Adrina asked as if referring to a back road that led straight to the armpit of the universe. "Hardly. Unlike you Skinners, we don't rely on the creatures we hunt to go about our business."

"Really? Is that why you're here sneaking around the basement of one of the Skinner elders?"

Rico chuckled and gave Cole an approving nod. "He's got a point. What brings you two to this neck of the woods? Slumming?"

Just as Rico was hitting his stride, another man and woman stepped out from alcoves at the end of the hall. They were smaller in stature than the two who'd already made themselves known and kept their arms at their sides where they could be seen. "We came to take back what was stolen from our clans throughout the last several generations," the man said. He walked down the hall, entering a pool of dim yellow light to reveal an athletic frame wrapped in the same sort of simple, rough clothing worn by the others. In fact, all four of the Amriany were filthy. Their clothes were covered in dirt and their faces were smeared with it, but it wasn't a sign of neglect or even poverty. The dirt was fresh.

"Who the hell is that?" Prophet asked.

"It's all right," Rico told him. "Amriany travel in groups and never show their true numbers right away. You see one or two, and there's always more lurking around somewhere. Kind of like—"

"Watch how you finish that sentence," the man at the far end of the hall warned. "Before you call us something you regret, know our names. I am Gunari, and this," he said while motioning to the second woman to reveal herself in that hallway, "is Nadya. Were you friends of Jonah Lancroft?"

"I was with him right until the end," Cole said.

"Then perhaps you know how much he stole from us over the years. If not for Amriany knowledge, he would never have gotten the runes to protect this place or imprison the beasts he captured. I doubt he would have been able to hunt any of the demons he did without borrowing from us."

"Lancroft was a hell of a Skinner," Rico said. "You won't convince me he was a hack. Why don't we skip whatever else you were gonna say along those lines and get down to how you got here."

"Our methods are our own," Tobar replied.

"Okay. Then why the hell are you in the U.S.? Just to reclaim some property?"

It didn't take a master of human behavior to figure how the conversation would go from there. In a matter of a few syllables Rico had the other four screaming at him from the other end of the hallway. Accusations flew back and forth, but nobody reached for their weapons. On the contrary, everyone was more willing to set their guns down so they could use their bare hands. Cole had never been more grateful to hear his phone ring. The tone wasn't very loud, but the acoustics in the hall did wonders.

"Who the hell is that?" Rico asked.

Cole looked at the phone's screen and said, "It's MEG."

"I didn't even think that phone would get reception down here."

"Neither did I."

"Go ahead and take it." Glaring at the other four, Rico added, "I can handle these guys on my own."

Answering the phone while moving toward the stairs, Cole hissed, "What is it?"

"Are you all right?"

He recognized the voice immediately. Abby was a field investigator for the Midwestern Ectological Group, which meant she was normally too busy measuring electromagnetic fields and setting up video cameras to bother manning the phones. He hadn't heard from her since their awkward attempt at a date not too long ago.

"I'm kind of busy here, Abby. What's up?"

"We're checking in with everyone we can. Are you hurt? Is anyone with you?"

"Rico and Prophet are here, along with some . . ." Although Cole couldn't hear what the others were saying, he saw that both groups had closed enough distance to stop screaming at each other. There was little comfort to be taken in that since everyone was now in a standoff straight from the calmer moments of a gladiator movie. "We got some others here with us and I kind of need to get back to them. Why do you ask?"

"Haven't you seen the news?"

"Why does everyone think I've got the time to sit around watching TV?"

"Because just about everything from your mouth is a quote from a sitcom or cartoon," she replied.

"Okay, that's fair. No, I haven't been watching the news."

"There's been stuff happening all across the country. Bad stuff. Multiple murders, bodies being found, drive-by shootings, fires."

"Yeah, I know all about the fires."

"They're all Skinners, Cole."

"What?"

"We've been getting calls from Skinners everywhere and they're under attack. We even got a few calls while the attacks were happening. It's terrible." Abby's voice cracked under the strain, but she took a breath and collected herself in short order. "From what we've heard, all of these attacks have to do with Nymar. Something's gotten to them and they're all moving on you guys. I don't know what else to do but keep trying to tell everyone. If there's anything you need from us, just say so."

Since her speech was gaining momentum with every word, Cole didn't wait for an opening to cut her off. "Have you heard from Paige?"

At that moment, silence was the worst thing he could hear.

"Answer me," he demanded. "What have you heard from Paige?"

"Nothing," she said. "We've tried calling her after we got a report about a shooting in Miami."

"What shooting? Tell me!"

Cole's voice had become sharp enough to cut through everything else in the basement. All the others stopped what they were doing to watch and listen to him.

"There was some sort of shooting at a club in Miami," Abby said. "It was at a strip bar."

"Jesus."

"Three were killed, but no names were released yet. We've tried getting in touch with the Skinners down there but nobody's answering. The only reports we've got are what we can piece together using local news and what little we heard before the trouble started. What's going on, Cole? Is there something happening with the Nymar?"

"Looks that way." When Rico motioned for an update, Cole waved him off impatiently. "What was the last you heard from Paige?"

"She called to tell us she was in Miami and asked what we had on the group from Toronto. They'd been sighted in Miami as well, but we didn't hear anything directly from them. Does all of this have something to do with Toronto?"

"That's all you heard?"

Cole could recognize the frustration in Abby's voice when she said, "From Miami, yes. Paige found some dead Dryads outside of one of their clubs. She said she was checking on a temple and that was it. We're hearing plenty from all over, and if you'd check your e-mail, you'd see that we sent you updates from—"

"I can't worry about all over," he snapped. "There's too much right here."

"If we get anything about Paige, I'll forward it to you and mark it priority. The rest will still keep coming."

"Good. Thanks." He hung up and stuffed the phone in his pocket while marching past Prophet and Rico to look Tobar in the eyes. "Everything's going to shit for us, and don't try to tell me you don't know what I'm talking about. We're getting hit across the country and now you guys show up from out of nowhere." Cole reached under his coat, found the end of his spear that was angled toward his left hip and pulled the weapon free of its harness. "Either answer Rico's questions or answer to me."

Up close, Tobar's features were like those on the subject of a grainy photograph. His eyes dipped down to take stock of the weapon in Cole's hands. When the blood began to trickle between the Skinner's fingers, he nodded solemnly and said, "The one thing you Americans have is passion. We cannot deny that. What is this you've done to your spear? Have you found a way to add metal to them?"

"We can swap recipes later. Right now, tell us what the fuck is going on."

Upstairs, the floor rumbled in a way that Cole recognized as the Skipping Temple being brought to life. "Is that more of your buddies coming through?"

Tobar's eyes narrowed. "We do not accept help from the Dryad whores."

That didn't make Cole feel any better about the steps that drifted down from upstairs on their way to the secret door in the dissection room. All he had time to do was glance at Rico before the new arrivals scrambled down the steps. They moved like a force of nature, and in the last several months, Cole had become all too familiar with just how terrible nature's forces could be.

Chapter Sixteen

"Back up," Rico said from behind his Sig Sauer.

The group that descended from the temple and workshop level were all Nymar. Their markings were thick and dark, proving that they'd recently fed and were reaping the benefits through increased speed and strength. They were also armed. The vampires snarled and bared their fangs in a show of primal force while raising the shotguns and submachine guns in their grasp. A slender man at the front of the group shouted, "They're here! Clean 'em out!"

Shotguns roared, pistols barked, and the automatics chattered as hot lead blazed through the air like a tidal wave that swept down the brick hallway.

Cole grabbed Prophet's shirt and shoved him toward one of the alcoves as bullets chipped away at the bricks around him and impacted against his back, shoulders, and legs. By the time he got there, the battering his body had taken made it difficult for him to pull in a breath.

"Holy shit," Prophet said as gunfire began flying in the opposite direction. Putting his back to a wall so he could see what was happening, he asked, "Are you hit?"

"Yeah," Cole grunted. The effort of pushing that little bit of air from his lungs was enough to fill his torso with a dull pain. "Several times, but I think the coat held up."

Prophet stared at a spot near Cole's shoulder where the

tanned leather was still smoking from an impact that landed less than an inch from a section of canvas. A surprised chuckle came out of him as he slapped Cole's back gratefully. "Guess Rico's one hell of a seamstress, huh?"

Another barrage of gunfire chipped at the edge of the alcove before Cole could put together a response. The shotguns had been silenced but were replaced by automatic fire. He had some experience on shooting ranges with fine weaponry, but he wasn't nearly experienced enough to recognize the make and model of what he was up against. All he knew for certain about the guns was that too many of them were going off around him.

"Cole!" Rico shouted from across the hall and several alcoves down. "Get over here!" He then fired three quick shots at the stairs.

Taking a quick look at the Nymar, Cole spotted four of them pressing their backs to the wall and firing at everyone in their path. A few more peeked out from the stairway. One Nymar had a long face that was almost covered in thick black tendrils. His eyes locked on Cole and he leapt out from cover.

Cole wasn't anxious to wade into the gunfire no matter what kind of armor he wore. On the other hand, he also wasn't about to stay put to provide a snack for the first Nymar to reach him. Switching his spear to his left hand, he drew his .45 and turned so his shoulder and back were facing the Nymar's end of the hall. "Prophet, move!" he shouted while firing in the general direction of the stairs.

While the Nymar didn't seem to be afraid of Cole's pistol, they did take a moment to regroup when he, Rico, and most of the Amriany opened fire at the same time. Drina's FAMAS made the most impressive chatter as it spat its rounds straight past Cole and into the Nymar that had come at him. He took advantage of the opportunity and hurried to meet with Rico. The Nymar writhed on the floor, clawing at wounds that hissed in reaction to what must have been an Amriany version of the antidote used by the Skinners. The vampire dropped to one knee, clawed at the floor, struggled to move, and finally resigned himself to lifting his gun to fire at Cole. He sent one round thumping into tanned Full Blood leather before Cole impaled him with the metallic end of his spear.

Drina moved forward while firing her FAMAS in three-shot bursts. "Move into the cell!"

"Which cell?" Rico shouted.

Drina and the other three Amriany responded by rushing toward the next-to-last cell at the end of the hall.

While the Amriany fell back, the Nymar surged forward. Five of them filled the hallway. Cole knew there were more, but they must have been hanging back to form a second wave. Three of the Nymar tossed their weapons while closing the distance between them and the Skinners. A few sprouted black claws from the ends of their fingers, and the rest stayed behind to reload their guns.

Cole looked over to Rico to see if he was hurt or had any other instructions. Gripping a pistol in each hand, the big man nodded once and ran out from behind his cover as a primal howl erupted from the back of his throat. What Cole felt next was something that reached down to his toes and dragged him from the temporary safety of his alcove. The closest thing he would ever be able to relate it to was the wild look on the faces of soldiers in Civil War movies who threw themselves into a charge across open ground. Every piece of good sense should have told him to stay put. At the moment that sort of thing was simply washed away by the fight that had become all-encompassing and powerful enough to shove him away from temporary safety.

The Skinners reached the first Nymar within a few powerful strides and both groups collided amid a flurry of bullets, claws, fangs, and sharpened wood. Cole had barely felt the spear shift within his left hand, but it was almost full size by the time he drove it straight into the chest of a Nymar wearing nothing but sneakers and an old set of shorts. The gleaming metallic spearhead cut through the Nymar's ribs like butter and became wedged before he could pull it back. With his right hand, he pulled the trigger of the .45 and sent a few rounds into the cluster of tendrils within the Nymar's chest.

The flailing thing at the end of Cole's spear trapped the

wooden weapon in his side. Cursing directly into Cole's
face, he pulled the spearhead out and shoved the Skinner
with enough force to slam his back against the brick wall.
Cole fired another shot, but his target had already scrambled
along the wall using sharpened claws and frantic speed to
suspend the laws of gravity. Once there, the Nymar ducked
below a backward swing from the spear intended to separate
him from his head.

Meanwhile, Rico's breaths were more like primitive grunts
forced out of his lungs as he pumped round after round into
the Nymar that attempted to swarm him. Focusing both
guns on a tall woman with a ripped gray sweater and solid
black eyes, he fired again and again into her chest. When
she continued to rake at his eyes, he turned away and said,
"Something's wrong with them, Cole! The treated rounds
ain't working!"

Watching the Nymar in the shorts scurry into the shadows
of the alcove he'd used for cover less than a minute ago, Cole
saw the vampire's tendrils swell into thick bands that were
almost wide enough to give him a solid black color. Once the
Nymar was fully in the shadows, the tendrils allowed it to
blend almost seamlessly into the darkness. "It's like the one
I found in that other cell," he said.

Prophet stuck his head out from the spot where the Amriany had led him. "Not that cell! *This* one!"

"What?" Rico snapped.

Between the gunfire, the hissing Nymar, and the close
confines of the hallway, it was becoming impossible for
Cole to tell what the hell was going on. One of the Nymar
jumped on him from behind and raked both sets of claws
across his shoulders toward his neck. His coat had a large
enough collar to offer some protection, but he knew even
that wouldn't save him for long. The Nymar's claws were
supernatural weapons, which meant they would eventually
get through the leather just as they would if the hide were
still attached to a Full Blood.

Even with all the other noise around him, Cole could still
hear the thrum from upstairs and feel the surge of power
from the temple above. Reinforcements had arrived.

"Both of you get in here," Prophet shouted. "Now!"

The Nymar in the stairwell stepped out, raised their weapons and fired. Cole was overtaken by a rush of adrenaline as he lowered his head and hurried into the alcove, where something waited for him. He couldn't see the vampire at first, but soon caught sight of a shadow that separated itself from the rest.

Rather than try to stab it, Cole swept the weapon back and forth in arcs that went high and low. His first swing sent a shower of sparks from the metal-treated spearhead, which made a quick source of light that helped him figure out where the Nymar was. By the time he swung the forked end of the weapon, the Nymar had sprung up to grab onto the wall with both sets of claws and then launch itself down onto him.

He barely brought his spear up fast enough to catch the Nymar before its claws took his face off. The shaft thumped solidly into the Nymar's torso while it tried to slash at him with his claws. Cole angled the spear so the Nymar's weight sent it toppling from the alcove and into the hall. As soon as it was down, he drove the spearhead straight into its chest.

The source of their power and hunger for blood was an eel-like spore attached to the heart. Simply staking the heart would do some damage, but not enough to put the Nymar down for good. This time, however, the Nymar barely seemed to react to being impaled. Its body pivoted around the tip of the spear so its feet could force his body upward. Once it was standing, the Nymar grabbed the spear handle in an attempt to pull it out. Cole leaned against his weapon, scraping the vampire against the wall so its heels skidded against the floor. When the gunfire started up again, he used the Nymar as a living blockade while crossing to the other side of the hall.

"Hope you got a plan over there," Cole shouted.

Rico answered by leaning into the hall and opening up with the Sig Sauer. He wasn't alone. Both Drina and Tobar stepped out as well, adding their own gunfire to the storm raging up and down the hallway. Tobar's pistol didn't throw nearly as many rounds through the air, but the sound of them reminded Cole of a truck hitting the ground after being dropped from a third-floor parking garage. A bare-chested Nymar woman caught one of those rounds between her small breasts and the impact slammed her against the wall. When she reached a dark patch between light sources, her tendrils widened to make her more of a person-shaped blob within the shadows. Tobar's aim was good enough for the next round to carve a tunnel through her that destroyed her heart and liquefied anything attached to it.

"Hit the lights," one of the Nymar said from the stairwell. The others responded by shifting their fire upward until most of the recessed bulbs within their range had been shattered.

Cole had seen things turn invisible before, but this was something else. The Nymar's tendrils allowed them to blend into the darkness with a practical camouflage that, combined with their speed and climbing ability, made them a whole new kind of dangerous.

Some of the light from the other end of the hall made it to Cole's position, but it wasn't enough. The vampires simply became part of the darkness and crept in on the Skinners like death itself. Drina fired her assault rifle, lighting up the corridor in a fiery strobe that illuminated a Nymar for a fraction of a second while also burning the image of the others into Cole's retinas.

"This place is ours now, Skinners," one of the Nymar hissed. "*Every* place is ours."

"Rico?" Cole asked while holding his spear at the ready.

"Get over here," he called out from a cell farther down the hall.

Cole felt as if the weight of the cement floor above him, along with the little house above that, was pressing down on the back of his neck. It was completely dark at the far end of the hallway, but he could still make out a few shapes moving like wraiths through a dream. There was movement upstairs as well, as he joined Drina and Rico at the end of the hall, which was lit by a few of the dim, recessed bulbs. Behind him, claws scratched against brick and one Nymar closed to within a few yards of his back before being deterred by a few well-placed shots from Rico's Sig Sauer.

"We're getting the hell out of here!" the big man said. "The temple upstairs went off again. I don't know how the hell they're getting the nymphs to help them, but there's more on the way."

"I know," Cole gasped as he dashed into the broken cell. "I heard it too, but what then? Should we really give this place up?"

"They have better tactical positioning," Nadya said, "as well as superior numbers. Now is not the time to fight. If we stay here, it will be the time to die."

"She's right," Rico admitted. "I don't like giving this place over to the bloodsuckers, but we got caught with our pants down. They're shipping in backup and all we got is the ass end of a goddamn hallway."

"So the plan is to huddle together in a small room?" Cole asked as more lights in the hallway were taken out.

"You can huddle if you like," Gunari said as he grabbed hold of a metal spike in each hand. "We are leaving."

The Amriany spikes were slightly curved and about eighteen inches long. He gripped them by handles that fit around his wrists, dropped to his knees and stuffed both arms into a hole Cole hadn't noticed until that moment. Digging the spikes into the sides of the hole, Gunari pulled himself underground in a series of quick, wriggling movements. The other two Amriany in the cell with Rico and Prophet prepared their own spikes, and when Drina backed into the small room, she strapped her FAMAS over her head and around one shoulder so she could follow suit.

"You said you had a way out of here," Rico said to Nadya. "This is it?"

"It's how we came in," she replied. Now that Gunari's legs and feet had disappeared within the hole, she knelt down and stuck her arms into the cramped tunnel. "We will help you leave the same way or you can stay here. Your choice." With that, she pulled in a deep breath and dove into the freshly turned soil.

"This is a Mongrel tunnel," Tobar explained. Scrambling claws closed in on them, so he fired a few times to keep them at bay. "They know about Lancroft's dungeon, and so do the Nymar. This place is lost. To stay is suicide and we do not approve of suicide." Unwilling to explain himself any further, Tobar dove into the hole.

Drina was next and she didn't even flinch as more gunfire erupted at the far end of the hall. "I can take one of you now and escort the rest," she said.

"Take Prophet," Rico said. "Cole and I will follow on our own."

"But there is a proper way for following the Mongrel tunnels to make sure you come up on the other side."

Ducking out of the cell to take a glimpse down the hall, Rico grunted, "Yeah, yeah. Squirming through a hole. I think we can handle it."

"Fine." Looking at Prophet, Drina said, "When I'm almost out of sight, grab my foot and I will pull you through." Without waiting another moment, she stuck both arms into the hole and dug in using the curved spikes.

"You two ain't coming, are you?" Prophet asked.

Showing him a wide, blocky grin, Rico dropped his voice to a snarling whisper and said, "That's what I like about you, Walter. Very astute."

"So what the hell am I supposed to do?"

"Keep an eye on these guys. Stay with them for as long as you can. Tell them I said for you to go on without us. If they let you, find out where they're based or how many more Amriany are in the area. If they dump you somewhere, just try to—"

"She's waiting on me now," Prophet snapped. "I know how to track someone. I am a professional, you know."

Filling both meaty hands with .45s, Rico aimed at the hallway just outside the cell door. "Shit! Here they come!" he shouted while unleashing a fiery torrent from both barrels.

Prophet didn't need any more incentive to jump face first into the dirt. After being kicked in the face by the foot Adrina offered, he grabbed onto her ankle and was immediately pulled underground as if towed by a truck.

Cole stood with his back in a corner, angled so he could see through the door and toward the direction of the gunfire. "Damn. The temple just went off again. This place is gonna be swarming with these fuckers real soon. Sounds like we've got something working on our side, though. A lot of that shooting isn't directed at us, so they must be shooting at someone else."

"I was wondering if you'd picked up on that. Also, the Nymar aren't coming down the hall so much anymore. Whoever's upstairs is making a bigger splash than us. What're you doing?"

Leaning his head back, Cole held a recycled Visine bottle over his eyes and squeezed a single drop into each one. A rush of cold flowed through his eyeballs and sent a chill all the way to the back of his skull. "It's Ned's drops. The ones that allow us to see scents. They worked real well for tracking Nymar before and they should do fine now."

"There ain't a lot of that stuff left. Don't use it all up."

Cole blinked so the drops could soak in. When he looked into the darkened hall again, he saw the outline of a figure crouched directly in front of the door, watching in the calm security of someone who believes they're unseen. He stuffed the little plastic bottle into his coat pocket, picked up his spear and ran straight ahead. Once the sentinel knew it had been spotted, it sprung at him in a flurry of claws and teeth.

Rico followed him from the cell. "Hand that stuff over."

The Nymar had been quick enough to avoid getting impaled through the chest, but it still picked up a nasty wound along the top of its shoulder and along its neck. With most of the Nymar's body covered in inky black camouflage, it was tough for Rico to see more than a shifting blob in the shadows. Cole swung at it, scraping the metallic ends of his weapon against the brick to send a shower of sparks to the floor. The Nymar leapt backward, hissed at the Skinners and darted toward the staircase.

Cole tossed the plastic bottle to Rico. "Sounds like a war going on upstairs. What the hell is going on?"

Now that he'd put the drops in, Rico blinked and looked at him with eyes that had acquired a dim yellow glow. "How about we go and find out?"

Cole followed the trail left by a set of lingering scents

leading to the cell at the end of Lancroft's dungeon. Instead of seeing the strange, shapeshifting creature that had been there before, all he could make out was a cracked floor and an empty space with two trails drifting through the air like neon smoke. One of them was a color that shifted across the spectrum unlike anything he'd ever seen before, but the other was a distinctive burnt orange he and Paige had identified thanks to samples found in Lancroft's basement.

"A Full Blood was down here," he said to Rico. "Maybe it let out whatever was in here before."

Jogging down the hall, Rico lined up a shot and dropped another Nymar. "Great. Looks like this pit really is lost. The shooting's stopped. Let's just hope we're not walking into another ambush."

"That'd be close to impossible with these drops in," Cole pointed out.

"But there's something else workin' against us. You notice anything strange about your scars?"

"Aw, hell," Cole said as his fingertips grazed one of his palms. "They're not itching anymore."

"So it ain't just me gettin' old and numb. The only ones that're left are some of those striped bastards, and they don't even set off our early warning system. Looks like the bloodsuckers are after something more than just turning a new color."

"It was like that when I found the thing in that other cell before, but I thought that was just because it was dead. Aw, hell. This isn't good."

On their way to the stairs the only other sources of Nymar scent they found were a few piles of dried ash left behind after enough of the poisoned rounds had found their mark on the more traditional vampires. Cole tucked the spear through the loops inside his coat, scooped up an AK-47 dropped by one of the dead attackers and climbed the stairs two at a time.

The lights were on in the dissection room, which were complimented by dark red trails of Nymar scent that appeared like wisps of greasy smoke drifting through the starkly lit space and leading directly to a Nymar who leaned against the table where Henry's body had been kept. The bloodsucker that had been gravely wounded by his spear before making its retreat. Its arm hung from a few tendrils that reached from inside its body to stitch the wound shut. When the Nymar hissed part of an obscenity at Rico, he sent three quick shots into its heart. When he could tell the antidote infused in the rounds wasn't reacting to the Nymar's blood, he kept firing until the spore was obliterated.

"I don't know how much longer!" someone said from the Dryad Skipping Temple. "Just be ready to go when I say!"

Despite the urge to rush into the next room, Cole held the AK-47 at the ready and stalked toward the narrow door. The power radiating from the Dryad symbols in the floor, walls, and ceiling glowed enough on their own. The drops in his eyes gave them an additional bright green shimmer. Standing in that glow, with a phone in one hand and a smoking .45 in the other, Paige gave the other two Skinners a quick upward nod by way of greeting. "About time you got up here," she said.

"Paige!" Cole sighed. "Where the hell have you—"

She cut him off with a single upraised finger while lifting the phone to her ear and saying, "Okay. Now."

The Dryad symbols glowed brighter as a pulse of energy filled every last one of them and rippled through the swaying beaded curtain.

"I cleared this room but there's more Nymar on the way," she said while sticking the phone into the pocket of her jeans. "Let's get out of here and save the explanations for later."

"Fine by me," Rico said as he approached the beads and stepped through.

Paige waved at Cole impatiently, which was more than enough to get him moving. He felt a few of the beads knock against the side of his face, caught a whiff of pine-fresh goodness and then found himself in a room half the size of the Skipping Temple and covered with twice as many symbols. The curtain was flanked by a woman on each side. One was topless and the other wore gray slacks and a form-fitting T-shirt. Both sang in a pitch that rattled through the entire room.

The drops in Cole's eyes did not react well to the neon that assaulted him when Paige shoved him into the next room. All of the nymph clubs were starting to look alike to him, but the stage setup and position of the bar seemed familiar. Just to be certain, he glanced over to a brightly lit buffet that smelled of lasagna and overheated goulash. "We're in Shimmy's?" he asked.

"Yep. Try not to get kicked out this time."

Chapter Seventeen

Twenty miles northeast of Chattanooga, Tennessee

No Half Breed had a face capable of expressing emotion. While they may have been mistaken for large dogs or wolves when running at high speeds, they could never pass for one of those animals during an up-close meeting. That wasn't much of a problem since anyone who saw a Half Breed up close for that long was either too busy fighting or dying to worry about such things. There were only a few creatures on earth that could rise above such concerns. Three of them ran side by side over the rugged terrain of the Smokey Mountains, casually adjusting their strides to make sure the Half Breeds behind them didn't catch up too quickly.

Liam glanced over one shoulder at the pair of Half Breeds nipping at his heels. Already growing bored of a chase that had begun in a small cave fifty miles north of their current position, he allowed his momentum to slow until the closest Half Breed sank its teeth into his rear leg. Digging his claws into the ground in front of him, Liam tore up large chunks of cold dirt as he shifted his weight so his rear end swung around like the snapping end of a whip. By the time he came to a stop, the Full Blood had shifted into his two-legged form and was beset upon by all three Half Breeds.

Hearing the ravenous snarls of the smaller werewolves mixing with Liam's deep, barking roar, Randolph and Kawosa broke their formation to circle back around along a path of steep, tree-encrusted land. Randolph lowered his head and slammed into one of the Half Breeds with enough force to break every bone in a lesser animal's body. The Half Breed yelped and tumbled into a cluster of thick bushes, tearing many of them apart with flailing bony claws. The other two Half Breeds took a moment to see what had happened to their pack mate, but weren't going to waste any more time than that.

"These have spirit!" Liam bellowed as he stood up on his hind legs and grabbed one of the Half Breeds by its left foreleg. "Little stronger than the others too." As he said that, Liam smashed the Half Breed against the ground like a heavy load of ground beef wrapped in discarded fur coats.

Pacing around the Full Blood, Randolph kept his large head low to the ground. His mouth hung open just enough to allow cold air into his lungs and wispy steam to spill out. His blue-gray crystalline eyes were encased in a thick furrowed brow. Kawosa had picked a higher spot upon a pile of fallen trees, where he hunkered down and watched the spectacle with interest that drifted close to obsessive.

As Liam reached around to grab the Half Breed chewing on his back, another group of the creatures darted from the surrounding trees to converge on the Full Bloods. Randolph was ready for them and leapt forward to scatter the pack with a savage roar. Two of the Half Breeds streaked away while a third adjusted its angle of attack so it could sink its teeth into Randolph's hip. The bite stung, but only registered as a slight twitch of one eye. He clamped a hand around the Half Breed's face and pried it loose before it could find a more tender spot. The creature's jaws snapped shut loudly and it struggled to pull away.

It had spirit indeed. Most Half Breeds were wild and fast, but this one kept its eyes fixed upon the wound it had opened as its claws scraped against the ground. This wasn't the first Half Breed Randolph had fought, and he waited for a sign that it was about to swipe at him. The attack came as expected, but its long claws still scraped against his ribs and peeled away a few ribbons of his flesh.

"Watch the tusks," Liam warned.

For as long as Randolph could remember, Half Breeds had heads that were shaped like a shoddy interpretation of a wolf's. A low brow protected glinting eyes over an extended snout and wet nose. The main difference lay in a flesh and bone structure that looked more like melted wax drizzled onto a bony shell. The tusks, however, were completely new. Upper canine teeth extended down and curved back toward the hinge of its jaw while the bottom set curved up and slightly outward. When the crazed werewolf attempted to bite him in a series of powerful snaps, its tusks scraped together like a pair of scissors.

Liam swatted away one Half Breed and caught another between his teeth as it lunged at his leg. Before he could clamp down and finish it off, the Half Breed contorted in a way that would be impossible for any animal with a normal skeletal structure. Since every one of its bones had been fractured and lashed together by knots of muscle during the Breaking, the Half Breed was able to bite Liam's neck and tear at him with all four sets of claws. The Full Blood tossed it aside and swiped at the Half Breed's head, but caught only air when the smaller werewolf darted away. Liam did not pursue. Instead, he dropped to one knee and let out a savage howl while pressing a hand against the side of his neck.

Straightening up to show every bit of fury encased within his seven foot frame, Randolph let out a roar that would be heard by those dwelling in the little mountain homes over a mile away. The pair of Half Breeds in front of him scraped their chests against the ground as they backed away.

Kawosa watched with detached amusement from his perch upon higher ground as another Half Breed circled him. "Their noses are keen," he said in a voice that escaped his narrow, pointed snout like steam from a kettle. "Their forerunners wouldn't have even known I was here."

When the Half Breed charged, it came at Kawosa with

the speed of an electrical discharge snapping between two oppositely charged posts. The calm expression on his face didn't shift in the slightest as he popped his front half up, placed a hand on the Half Breed's shoulder and pushed the passing werewolf so he merely had to lift one rear leg to let it pass beneath him. Kawosa touched down again as if he'd done nothing more than step over a rock. Swiveling around to face the Half Breed, he flashed a pair of amber eyes that froze the werewolf where it stood.

Randolph and Liam had dispatched most of the other Half Breeds, and each held one down beneath their massive paws. The ground was covered in choppy waves of dirt kicked up by the creatures and soaked through with their blood. Even as Liam pressed all of his weight down upon the Half Breed beneath him, the creature bent and twisted in a frantic attempt to escape. "Their claws are longer," he said.

"I noticed as much," Randolph grunted. "And their tusks are more than just teeth." Grabbing the Half Breed around the base of its neck, he lifted it and quickly slammed it down with enough force to render it unconscious. Now that the creature was subdued, he pinned it with one of his rear paws so both hands were free to dig at the gaping wounds in his side. He let out a strained grunt while pulling out a pair of long curved shards that had been driven in deeper than a bullet could ever reach. Holding the broken tusks up to examine them, he said, "They're not very sturdy."

"A perfect defense," Kawosa said as he approached the Half Breed in front of him. The creature trembled anxiously but was unable to break whatever spell had befallen him. Slinking forward, Kawosa mused, "You've adapted to Lancroft's pestilence, haven't you? And you're just the first generation to do so."

"The Mud Flu wasn't cleared up that long ago," Liam said.

Randolph was studying his Half Breed, sniffing so intently that its fur bristled against his breath. "Their strength has always been in adapting to the changing world, and it never takes them long to do so. Still, this is extraordinary."

When the Half Breed pulled in a breath of its own, it was almost too light to make a sound. Its nose twitched, sending a ripple through its entire snout, which caused its eyes to snap open. If there were any lingering effects from being knocked out, they disappeared when it saw Randolph staring down at it. Before the wretch could make a move against him, the Full Blood cleaved its throat with a quick snap of his teeth. As the Half Breed's life came to an end, a shuddering, vaguely relieved sigh emerged from the pit of its stomach.

"Their sense of smell has improved," Kawosa said.

Curling his lips at the taste of the creature, Randolph added, "Or they're just not as easily put down as the previous breed."

Kawosa shifted into another form, one with an expanded torso, strong, wiry arms, and clawed hands. The fact that his head remained narrow and pointed at the snout threw off the entire picture of him. It seemed the rest of his body wanted to blend in with humanity but the part that did his thinking and speaking refused to comply. "Their noses are enhanced," he said with complete certainty. "Most likely, they can smell whether Lancroft's pestilence has touched any prey they might hunt down."

"Makes sense," Liam said. "Longer claws allow them to attack without getting as close as before. Even just a little more length there can make a difference in gutting someone without getting a mess on their fur. And those tusks must snap off so they can get away if the going gets too tough."

"Can they be made to suit our purposes?"

"I've gotten real good at mingling bloodlines," Liam said. "It may take a few tries, but I should be able to get a mix of us and them that'd be just strange enough to throw the Skinners for a loop. What do you think, old man?"

"You will need more than deception to deal with the Skinners," Kawosa replied. "Lancroft used flesh stripped from my bones to develop a way to keep Full Bloods from healing. Poor Henry's neck remained broken for hundreds of years as a testament to that. Full Bloods may be sturdy, but they do not change. The Half Breeds thrive by evolving to fit within their world. That is what you need to acquire. Whatever may have been found in Lancroft's dungeon, evolution is your answer to it."

"We found *you* in Lancroft's dungeon and pulled you out," Randolph growled. "Don't forget that."

"I doubt you'll ever let me forget it."

"Since you've told us what Lancroft took from you, tell us how to counteract it."

Kawosa shrugged in a way meant to seem sheepish but wasn't nearly enough to fool either of the other two. "I provided only the meat. I couldn't tell you how it was cooked. Not yet anyway. As for the Half Breeds, I can train them for the tasks you have in mind."

Annoyed with the dark-skinned shapeshifter, Randolph looked over to Liam and asked, "Will these wretches look like us when you alter them?"

Liam examined the pinned Half Breed for a second and casually shrugged. "Hard to say. You saw those Mongrels of mine. These Half Breeds already look odd enough, and they'll look even odder when I'm through with 'em. Will they look like Full Bloods? Even I'm curious about that."

When Randolph's eyes shifted toward him, Kawosa said, "As long as I am close enough to exert my influence, the Skinners may be swayed. The humans will be much easier. They will believe what we want them to believe. What do you plan on doing with the others when they arrive?"

Shifting into his human form as easily as someone might get up from a seated position, Randolph asked, "What others?"

"Your brethren from the Old World. Their scent grows stronger with every breath."

Both Full Bloods lifted their noses to the wind. Randolph's eyes wavered slightly as he sifted through the myriad scents of life, death, pollution, steel, and dirt that he found. "I don't smell them," he said.

"That doesn't mean they aren't there."

"Liam, see what you can do with these wretches."

The ebon Full Blood didn't need another bit of prompting before pressing his teeth against the Half Breed's side and easing his jaws shut until the tips of his fangs broke the creature's skin. While the Half Breed had been a vicious predator a few minutes ago, it now squirmed and writhed like any other animal being put through an excruciating amount of pain.

The creation of Half Breeds was mostly an accident that occurred when the marrow in a human's bones mingled with saliva from a shapeshifter's mouth. Attacks as brutal as that were most often fatal. To commit them with such express purpose required equal amounts of viciousness and precision. Randolph watched the process for as long as he could stomach it, fighting the impulse to put the poor wretch out of its misery. Liam, on the other hand, savored every moment.

"I know who you are," Randolph said in a barely audible growl, addressing Kawosa, and leaving Liam to his task on the wooded mountainside.

"Is that supposed to be a surprise?" Kawosa asked as he nodded in Liam's direction. That simple gesture was enough to convince the Half Breed in front of him to lower its head and trot over to the Full Blood's side where it laid down to patiently wait for its own portion of agony to be doled out. "I thought that's why you came to get me."

"You're more than a curiosity. More than the source of Lancroft's attempt to undo us. Some of the human tribes call you Ktseena. Among us you're known as the First Deceiver."

"All shapeshifters are deceivers, Birkyus."

Hearing his birth name spoken in such an offhanded manner by the being in front of him was enough to rattle the Full Blood. No matter how quickly he recovered, Randolph knew his slip hadn't gone unnoticed. "But you are the first."

"I am."

"Legends say you brought many things to the human world."

Nodding slowly, Kawosa cocked his head as if looking

for the perfect angle to view the creature before him. "They do."

"I want another of the secrets you are said to possess."

Kawosa's grin barely touched the corners of his mouth. "I was wondering how long it would take for you to come out and ask for it."

Chapter Eighteen

Rico drove down I-94 toward Chicago behind the wheel of a light blue Dodge Neon borrowed from one of the dancers at Shimmy's. That was strange enough, but the fact that Paige insisted on sharing the backseat with him instead of being up front where she could watch the road made Cole even more suspicious.

"Did you tell Rico what I asked?"

"After what just happened, you're still worried about Shampoo Banana?" Cole asked.

"He did, Paige," Rico said from the front of the car. "And I handed over the notebooks."

"Did you read them?" When she didn't get an answer right away, Paige grabbed Cole's shoulders and forced him to look directly at her. "Did you read them?"

Pulling out of her grip, he replied, "I read the first one, but I want to know what the hell happened back there! How do you disappear to Miami and then just stroll back in and expect to talk about some goddamn notebooks?"

"There wasn't much to find in Miami. The same two that came through before were there again. This time they forced the nymphs at that club to send a group to Philly and then killed them once the bridge was open. I got through before it closed, mopped up the ones that were left in Lancroft's basement and called ahead to get us out through another club."

"What about the ones who killed the nymphs?" Rico asked.

"Gone. I poked around for a while, but they knew I was there." To Cole, she explained, "You can barely walk across a street in Miami without being spotted by three or four bloodsuckers. Most of them are busy biting tourists or feeding on any number of willing freak jobs, but they've still got their eyes on the street. Skinners pretty much wrote off that whole city, and the fact that two of them strode through it without a care in the world tells me a lot."

"Bobby's switched sides?" Rico asked.

"Looks that way," she told him. "Smuggling another Nymar into Lancroft's place was a big enough giveaway, but this is worse. There's something more going on. You guys weren't the only ones hit by a Nymar firing squad tonight. Damn near anyone who came through Philly to fill up their shopping carts in that basement was targeted."

"I heard about some of that from MEG," Cole said. "I bet Stephanie's really laughing her ass off after putting Raza Hill to the torch."

"She won't be laughing for long," Paige said earnestly. "Pinups was tapped out on the power needed to bring us back straight into Chicago, but we'll be back home before long. As soon as we're there, we'll be heading straight to Rush Street and wiping the smiles off of those assholes' faces."

"About damn time," Cole said.

"As far as those notebooks go, it's important that you read them, Cole."

"Well, I didn't bring them along, if that's what you're about to ask next. And before you get upset about that—" Stopping himself as the frustration started to build, Cole took a breath and placed his hand on her knee. "I was worried about you, Paige. That's all."

"I'm fine. See?"

"Yeah, now I do. It's just that . . . you know . . . after what happened in KC, I want to make sure nothing happens to you."

Paige slumped like one of the toys on Ned's shelf. Her

head lolled forward for a moment before she straightened up again. "What happened, happened. It happened once, but that doesn't mean I need your protection or expect you to be worried whenever I'm out of your sight. Just because we had sex, I don't want you to get all protective and stupid on me."

"*Hel*-lo!" Rico said.

"Not now," she snapped.

"If I'm protective," Cole said through gritted teeth, "it's because I care about you as a partner and a friend. It's got nothing to do with . . ." As much as he wanted to continue that sentence as planned, he couldn't get the words out in one smooth line. "All right," he admitted. "The sex part may have something to do with it."

Rico snarled behind the wheel like a dad who'd caught two kids groping each other in the backseat on the way to a Homecoming dance. Much like those kids, Cole and Paige ignored him.

When she spoke again, the harsh tone in her voice was gone. Her eyes darted self-consciously toward the front seat and she shifted her back to Rico as if that would somehow prevent him from hearing what she had to say. "I may not be around all the time to—"

"I wish you'd stop saying that!" Cole snapped.

"And since I may not be around, you need to keep your head on straight so you can not only think about what to do next, but when to do it. There are things in motion that could affect us all in a big way real soon."

"You mean like the Full Bloods working with Mongrels to run away with whatever the hell was locked up at the end of the hallway in Lancroft's dungeon?"

Despite everything that was going on, Cole couldn't help but get a little bit of pleasure from the shocked look on Paige's face. "Are you sure about that?" she asked.

"I put Ned's drops in my eyes to help find the Nymar when the lights went out. I could see those other scents down there as well."

"The Amriany crawled in through some Mongrel tunnels," Rico added. "They had a nice little system using some handy equipment. We might wanna think about knocking off something like that for ourselves."

"Where'd they go from there?" she asked.

"Don't know yet. Prophet's with 'em, but I haven't heard back. I was about to give him a call."

"Well, it's another hour or so before we get to Chicago. See if you can find him. Once we get there, I doubt we'll have much time to take a breath." As if demonstrating her point, Paige pulled in a lungful of air and lowered her head. She busied her hands with the process of fishing a small tin of silver-tinted varnish from her pocket and applying it to the edge of one of her batons. Having the Blood Blade fragments melted into the varnish gave the weapon a steely texture, which meant it couldn't be shifted into as many shapes as before. The trade-off was an edge that could cut through anything from cement and iron bars to Full Blood hide and was thin enough to keep from setting off metal detectors with any more frequency than a few coins at the bottom of someone's pocket.

"What's going on with you, Paige?" Cole asked. "Did something else happen in Miami?"

Working the foul-smelling paste into her baton, she asked, "How far did you get with those notebooks?"

The only thing worse than reading about the Nymar attack Paige had experienced was seeing the pain resurface on her face as she thought about it. "I got through the party where your friends were jumped."

"Amy?"

"She was . . . I got to the part with her."

Paige took another deep breath, tightened her grip on her weapon and took some bit of solace from the familiar pinch of the handle's thorns against her palm. "I don't know how long I was out after they started feeding on us. When I think back to that night, it's all just a blur of sharp teeth, black tattoos, claws, and—"

"You don't have to do this now, Paige. I'll get to it."

"No," she insisted. When her fingers were sliced open as they grazed the edge of the wooden blade of the machete, she barely seemed to notice. Although her left hand could get the baton to shift into multiple shapes, her right could barely manage the machete's basic form. "After the attack, there wasn't much of an investigation. The cops came and asked a bunch of questions, but there wasn't a lot to find. Amy's body was gone by the time anyone knew something was going on downstairs, so nobody even thought to look for her right away. The rest of it was chalked up to drunk assholes being drunk assholes."

"I thought that whole dorm would have known you were in trouble."

"Nope," she sighed. "Wes blocked the front door, so everyone either stayed where the music was or found another way to get to the first floor. Just another loud night at the Residence Hall. I don't know. Maybe someone else did know something was happening, but it didn't matter."

"What did they do to you?" he asked. The question had come out no matter how badly he'd wanted to choke it down.

"I remember someone finding me," she said softly. "I may have walked upstairs on my own or maybe someone helped me. I'd . . . lost so much blood that I could barely see straight. Somehow, I got to a hospital. Now that I think of it, there may have been an ambulance. I remember sirens. Yeah," she said as her eyes took on a fresh intensity and her grip tightened around the handle of her weapon. "There were sirens, and they didn't come from any cops."

Chapter Nineteen

Carle Foundation Hospital
Urbana, Illinois
The past

Paige awoke several times after the attack, but this was the first instance when she had the strength or desire to keep her eyes open. The room was well lit, warm and quiet, enveloped by multiple sets of footsteps, hushed voices and a few blaring televisions in other rooms. In every aspect other than the square arrangement of its four walls and ceiling, it was the antithesis of the residence hall where Wes had thrown his party.

His name fluttered through her brain like a horsefly with hairs bristling on its body and wings cut from dirty plastic wrap. She closed her eyes, shifted in the bed, and took enough comfort from its clean sheets and sterilized pillow to give the whole waking up thing another chance.

She finally did open her eyes, and immediately wanted to close them. Then, as that desire soured into weakness, she choked it down and raised her lids, no matter how much it hurt or what was beyond them.

Someone was visiting whoever occupied the other bed in the room. The figure stood there, fussing with the sheets, straightening them until they were perfect. The back of his head was covered in coarse, salt-and-pepper hair. There were deep wrinkles along his neck, which could have been scars. When he reached for the other patient's head, he did so with such recklessness that Paige sat up to see what he intended to do with the pillow he'd just grabbed.

"Hey!" she said.

The man turned around, gripping the pillow in both hands. It might have been a more threatening image if there had been a face at the head of the bed or a person beneath the sheets. Now that she was sitting up, she could tell that the other patient she thought she'd seen was just a trick of shadows being cast by the light pouring through the window and the haziness within her own mind. A few more blinks cleared her vision enough for her to see that what she'd mistaken for feet was actually a bundle left at the foot of the bed.

"There a problem, miss?" the man asked. He wore simple blue pants that were too smooth to be jeans, too loose to be tailored, and too cheap to be anything but mandatory hospital issue.

"Do you work here?"

"Yes I do. Can I get you anything?"

"No, I don't want anything. Were the police here?"

"Were you expecting them?"

She turned away, suddenly ashamed of the disappointment that made her feel like a kid who'd just discovered the sad truth about who hid the eggs on Easter morning.

The man walked over to her bedside, tossing the pillow so it landed exactly in its place. "You look like you're doing pretty well."

"Yeah? Maybe you should look again." When he took another step toward her, she tensed and added, "Forget it, guy. If you think I'm helpless just because I'm in this bed, then you'll really be surprised when I jam that IV stand up your ass."

"That's good to hear."

"And if you say you like a little fight in your women, I'll jam another IV stand up there to keep the first one company."

"I wasn't about to say it quite that way," the man told her, "but your point's been made. My name's Ned."

"I know." Seeing the flicker of surprise on his face, Paige eased back against her pillows and told him, "It's written on your shirt."

"Oh, that's right. It sure is, isn't it? Normally someone in your condition isn't so quick on their feet. Actually, many of them don't get back onto their feet at all."

"My condition," Paige huffed. "I'm a little bruised, but I'll be out of here soon."

Ned walked over to the door, took a quick look to the hall outside and eased the door shut. "That," he said while walking over to the bundle he'd left at the foot of the other bed, "isn't exactly what I meant."

"So what did you mean?" she asked as her hand drifted toward the call button hanging from her bed frame.

Although Ned looked at her long enough to see what Paige was doing, he didn't make a move to stop her. Instead, he carefully unrolled the bundle, to lay it on the unoccupied bed, and began sifting through its contents. "You weren't attacked by just some bunch of drunken idiots. That fella, Wes, had some very unusual friends that put you and your friends through hell on earth."

"Don't try to tell me what happened."

"I know what happened to your friend with the glasses. I also know what happened to the pretty, quiet little one, and the girl who turned up missing."

"You mean Amy?"

Ned nodded and turned around to face her. In his hand was a syringe the size of a little pencil. It wasn't the cloudy liquid in the narrow plastic tube or the needle at the end of it that frightened her as much as the calm certainty in Ned's eyes regarding what was going to happen next.

"The police say Amy's missing," he said. "Everyone around this hospital caring for the patients from that party along with other kids from the university all say the same thing, but you know better. Amy's not missing, is she?"

Paige's eyes narrowed as she sat up in her bed. The muscles in her legs tensed in preparation of unleashing a flurry of kicks. Her fingers clenched around the sheets and the edge of the mattress as if she could somehow pull those things up and use them as weapons. "What's in that needle?"

"It's an antidote for what may be running through your system."

"The doctors already put enough into me. Get that crap away before I call someone."

Ned stopped, lowered the needle and looked at her with a contemplative expression. "Those Nymar left you alone for a reason. I think I see what that could be."

"Namor?"

"No. Nymar. It's what the vampires call themselves."

And there it was.

Paige had heard people talk about life-changing moments. Most of those were soldiers or survivors of catastrophes, or maybe even people who were critically ill. She might have had a moment like that during the attack, but her brain had done a pretty good job of wiping those memories away like hot breath from a cold window. Not only did Ned's words bring the memories back, but they convinced her that she hadn't simply exaggerated things to cover a more earthly violation. If she'd been beaten or raped, it was something she could comprehend. There were support groups she could visit, doctors to comfort her, others who might understand her pain. There were no support groups for victims of vampire attacks.

Or maybe there were. Somehow, she figured Ned might know about such things.

"You saw the vampires," he declared. "You saw what they did to your friends. They killed one and most likely fed on the others. More than one of them must have fed on you. That's why those wounds haven't closed yet. If just one bit you, there wouldn't be much of a trace left. When their saliva mingles, that gets messed up."

There were bandages wrapped around Paige's left forearm, a few taped to her shoulder, and a thick chunk of gauze attached to her neck. When she moved, she could feel the twitch of pain beneath the antiseptic wrappings. "I don't know for sure what they did. They knocked me out when I tried to fight back."

"See, that's the difference. You fought back. More than that, I'm guessing you fought back real well. Did you wound one of them?"

"I don't think so. Grabbed a corkscrew and tried stabbing him, but it didn't do much of anything."

"Where did you stab him?"

Tapping into her reserve strength, she lifted her chin and arched her back so she was almost standing up in the bed. "Right on those fucking moving tattoos. I mean," she added as her posture slipped, "the thick black tattoo on one of them."

Ned smiled warmly. "No, you're right," he told her while calmly patting her shoulder. "Those black markings moved. They're not tattoos."

"Is that why they came for me? Because I can see that kind of thing?"

"I can't say for certain, but I doubt they came for you. That one fella, Wes, lives on campus and has been feeding on students because they're easy pickin's. The others are friends of his, and I'm pretty sure one of them is the leader of the group."

"Was it a woman named Hope?"

For the first time since he'd made his presence known, Ned seemed shaken. "Is that really her name?"

"That's what I heard the others call her."

"You're sure about that?"

"Yes!" Paige snapped. "How the hell could I not be sure about what a bunch of freaking vampires called each other while they were tearing me and my friends apart?"

Ned sat down on the edge of her bed. "Most people in your situation would have been too frightened to remember such a thing or too affected by the Nymar to remember. Either that or they'd just keep their mouths shut, pretending to forget what happened or force their brains to push it out. This is what I'm talking about. You've got a strength that separates you from the rest."

"My name's Paige."

"I know."

"Then call me that. Don't just talk about me. Talk to me."

A trace of amusement crossed Ned's face. "All right, Paige. Since you seem capable of handling the truth, that's what I'll give to you. The serum in this syringe is poison to Nymar. If they left anything in you, this will kill it. If they infected you in any way, this should get rid of that as well."

"Infected me with what? Will I become a vampire?"

"I could examine you, but I'd want to give you the injection no matter what. Considering all the examinations you've endured, I figured I'd just skip the middleman. Hold out your arm."

Paige got as far as tensing a few muscles, but stopped well before her arm rose above the sheets. "How do I know you're doing what you say you are?"

"I'd inject myself with the syringe, but that would waste some serum and wouldn't be very sanitary."

"I got chewed on by Namor and you think I'm worried about getting an infection?"

"You should always be worried about infection," Ned replied with a face that was as straight as the plastic tube in his hand. "And it's 'Nymar.' 'Namor' is the Sub Mariner from those comic books." Before she could say anything to that, Ned added, "Lots of people make that mistake. Are you ready for this or not?"

She pulled in a deep breath, held onto it and let it out. "Guess I don't have anything else to lose." When Ned extended his hand, he almost got close enough to push the needle into her arm before she said, "What about the others? My friends? You said you knew what happened to them."

"I know Amy Crabtree is dead. We saw the Nymar drag away the body. Jennifer Walsh was discharged after being treated for blood loss. She recovered quicker than expected, which is normal for someone who's fed upon normally. The one with the glasses must've slipped away." He then held up the needle and raised his eyebrows as though asking her to proceed without forming the words.

Fixing a stern glare on him as if certain that would be enough to hold him back, Paige asked, "Who are you?"

"Ned Post. I've been working at this hospital since about a month or two after Wes and those other Nymar set up shop at the university."

"Unless the Carle Foundation has some sort of vampire ward, there's more to it than that."

Someone walked by the door to Paige's room. The footsteps stopped, but moved along once Ned nodded toward the door's little square window. Keeping the same casual, vaguely bored expression on his face, he said, "I'm a Skinner."

"A Skinner? Is that another comic book thing?"

"No. It's just what we're called. The condensed version is that we know about creatures like Nymar and hunt them down."

"So if you know about Wes, then why aren't you hunting him down?"

"There's more to it than that," Ned hissed. "We need to stay as discreet as possible. There's no telling what could happen if something is handled sloppily. All of us could be compromised. There could be other Nymar that we don't know about. If they're confronted and we don't have all our bases covered, things can get very bloody very quickly."

"You mean like what happened to Amy? Like what happened to me?" When she held up her arm to illustrate her point, Ned grabbed her wrist. She tried to pull it away but was held fast within the grip of his rough, thickly scarred hand. Even so, she continued to make it difficult for him to accomplish his task. "You've known about these assholes for a month and that's not enough time to get them?"

"Like I said before, there's a lot to it."

"Maybe you Skinners aren't good for anything but standing around and watching people get hurt."

Ned jabbed the needle into her arm and injected the serum into her. Then he turned and walked over to the bundle he'd left on the other bed. "You want to do something to the things that did this?" he asked. "You can help us get closer to Wes. Find out how many of them are in town and where they are."

"You don't even know that much? Fuck you. I'm calling the cops."

"They've already been here and filled out a missing persons report on a dead girl." He took the chart from the foot of her bed, quickly looked it over and put it back. "I'll be keeping an eye on you."

Those words slapped Paige in the face hard enough to keep her quiet.

After putting the syringe away and rolling the bundle up again, Ned tucked it under his arm and approached the door. He stood with his hand on the knob and his foot against the bottom edge in a way that would allow him to keep it from being opened if anyone else tried to join them. "We've killed three of those Nymar since we arrived," he said. "And still, whenever they show themselves again, there's three in the group other than Wes. Until now we've had the leader pegged as a man who looks to be in his thirties with slicked-back hair. He leads the charge on nights like the one you experienced, but that woman always follows. We never thought she was the leader."

"Why? Because she's a she?" Paige rubbed her arm, which now warmed as the serum passed through her system. "If you guys aren't wise to that trick by now, your Skinners might as well pack it up and go home. This stuff kinda burns. Are there any side effects or anything? What if I'm allergic?"

"The only side effect to one dose is the burning. At least, as far as we know. If the Nymar had gotten too deep into you, you would've known by now."

"How?" Paige asked.

"You'd be dead." Smirking at the way he'd knocked the attitude from her, he added, "You're fine. Get up, stretch your legs with a walk over to that bed and pick up my card. Don't bother with the address. If you want to call me, use the phone number, but dial the last four digits in reverse order."

Paige wasn't about to take her eyes off of him. She continued nursing her arm, trying not to let the discomfort from her wounds show on her face. After giving her another approving nod, Ned opened the door and left.

Once she'd lost sight of him through the door's window, she pulled her burning arm in close to her body. Her neck hurt. Her side hurt. Her back hurt where she'd been knocked against the wall. Her head hurt for the same reason. Thoughts of scooting under the covers and curling into a ball drifted through her mind, accompanied by memories of random faces, songs, or anything else that had comforted her over the years.

Suddenly, everything hit her stomach like a load of rancid meat. She hated being pushed into a spot where there was nothing left to do but cry. "Fuck that," she angrily grunted as she pulled herself up and struggled to free her legs from the snare of intricately tucked sheets and blankets. "Fuck that and fuck them."

Her legs ached but she moved them anyway.

Everything else ached, but she clenched her teeth against it and turned the pain into kindling that made the flame in the center of her body burn even hotter. The first step she took was crooked and would have become a stumble if she hadn't clenched her hand into a fist and pounded it against her upper thigh. She reached for the bandages at her neck with every intention of ripping them off, but paused before digging her nails into her skin. Instead, she left the gauze alone so she could snatch the business card from where it was lying at the foot of the other bed.

"You're up?" someone said at the same time as the door was hastily opened. "That's so great!"

The young woman who rushed through the door wasn't wearing her Damn Yankees shirt anymore, but still had the same bouncy curl in her straw-colored hair. Oversized glasses would have dominated a cute face if not for the wide, beaming smile beneath them. She clutched her purse tightly until she got close enough to toss it onto a chair and tackle Paige with a hug.

"Still a little sore, Karen," Paige grunted.

"Oh, sorry!" Backing away, she shrugged and placed a hand over her mouth as she lowered her voice and said "Sorry" again.

"It's okay. How are you?"

"I'm fine. I feel terrible about what happened. When I heard, I rushed down here as fast as I could. Did Amy really take off somewhere?"

Paige looked at Karen and saw more than a friend dressed in new jeans and a faded peasant blouse. She saw a girl who still lived in the world that might as well have stopped existing for her a few nights ago. It was a warm, friendly place where the worst things that could come after you were other human beings. Even those tended to keep their distance more often than not. There was an openness to Karen's face that looked like a childhood home as seen in the rearview mirror of a car speeding in the opposite direction.

"You just now heard about this?" Paige asked.

Karen folded her hands and nodded timidly. "I . . . I never liked those kinds of parties, but I wanted to be with you guys. I stayed for a while, but it just got to be too much so I left early." Lowering her head only lined up her eyes with more of Paige's bandages, so she turned to the side as she said, "I snuck out and had someone drive me back home. When I heard about what happened, I felt horrible. I should have been there with you."

Before Paige knew what she was doing, she had Karen wrapped up in a hug that strained several of her bandaged wounds. She couldn't remember the last time she cried, but felt the tears coming now. Clenching her eyes shut against the bitter droplets as she loosened her hold, she said, "Don't apologize for missing out on what happened. I'm just glad one of us made it out of there as . . . as the same person that went in."

"You'll be the same too, Paige," Karen replied while gently embracing her friend again. "All you need is time to heal. I'll help any way I can. You and Tara will be better."

"I don't even know where Tara is, sweetie."

"She's in a room on the second floor."

"What?"

Karen nodded. "She's being examined."

"Examined?"

"They were looking at some marks on her neck."

Holding Karen at arm's length, Paige asked, "What marks? What did they look like?"

"They were just lines. I couldn't see much, but her skin was pale. The nurses were looking at her then, so the doctors are probably with her by now."

"What room is she in?" Before Karen could answer, Paige spun her around and pushed her toward the door. "Never mind that. Just take me to her."

"Hey! Watch what you're—"

"You need to take me to her!" After nearly charging through the door before allowing it to open, Paige asked, "Did you see some other guy with her? An older man with rough skin and—"

She stopped as soon as she saw Ned at a nurse's station farther down the hall. Karen was headed in that same direction, walking toward a bank of elevators a few paces away from Ned's spot. Grabbing her once again, Paige redirected her almost hard enough to send her staggering into a wall. "Not that way."

"Should you even be out of bed?"

"I'm fine. There's the stairs. You said Tara was on the second floor?"

"Right, but take it easy!"

Paige didn't let her go until they'd gotten past the heavy metal door leading to the stairwell. They had a few flights of stairs to negotiate, and Paige descended them as quickly as she could. The first time she stumbled, she felt Karen's hands on her back and shoulder for support.

"What's the hurry? Tara's not going anywhere. You probably shouldn't either."

"Just take me to her, okay? Please?"

Karen's sigh echoed within the concrete stairwell, and Paige kept up with her. As they approached the second floor and she heard the slap of her feet hitting the floor along with the sound of Karen's flats, she realized her feet were bare. Looking down, she prayed she wouldn't find one of those terrible, backward paper gowns wrapped around her body. Instead, she saw lilac pajama pants bearing the hospital logo and a plain gray T-shirt. Someone put her in those clothes soon after she'd gotten to the hospital, and she didn't even remember it.

The door at the next landing was a heavy one that opened to a hall similar to the one they'd left behind. Rows of larger windows to her right looked in on examination rooms filled with families going through either the best or worst days of their lives.

"She was over this way," Karen said as she marched down the hall. Most of the people they encountered had enough on their minds to overlook the two young women. "But we might not be able to see her. The man outside her room said she wouldn't be able to have visitors."

"What man?" Paige asked. "Was it an older guy named Ned?"

"I don't know," Karen replied.

"His name was on his shirt. He works here. Did he try to inject you with something?"

Karen didn't know what to say to that, so she slipped into a soothing tone as she assured Paige everything was all right. That tone couldn't have had a less soothing effect as Paige stomped along beside her. The hall bent around a corner, widening into a row of doors being visited by several nurses, orderlies, and people in street clothes trying to find their relatives as quickly as they could. Karen stopped to check a few of the rooms and eventually found the one she was after. Before she could step inside, however, the door opened and Paige was confronted by Tara, although her friend's face was only vaguely familiar.

Tara's skin was pasty and had a wet sheen that glistened beneath the stark hospital lights. Thin black markings stretched up from beneath the collar of a shirt bearing the hospital logo and stopped a few inches under her ear. They weren't nearly as large as the markings on Wes, Hope, Evan, or Hector, but were just as dark and trembled excitedly beneath her flesh.

"Tara?" Paige said. "Are you okay?"

"There were doctors," Tara replied drearily. "They wanted to tell me something."

When her friend's voice faded into a strained version of

the one she knew, Paige got frustrated and anxious. "What's wrong with you? What are those markings? Talk to me!"

Karen peered over Paige's shoulder and tried to say something but was overcome by sobs that made it difficult for her to breathe.

"Not now, damn it!" Paige said as she wheeled around to deal with her. "We need to think before—"

But Karen wasn't looking at either of her friends. She stared past them both, through the doorway and into Tara's room. There were four bodies in there, stacked like bundles of soiled laundry between the two beds. Paige only saw the heads and feet at first, so she stepped farther into the room, to stand next to Karen, who had wandered in to look down at the gruesome find with both hands clasped over her mouth. Two of the bodies were dressed in white coats and the others wore baggy scrubs. All of them were covered in blood, unmoving and staring at different angles through eyes glazed over and frozen in an expression of terror.

Tara wandered past the other two girls and knelt beside the bodies. Reaching out to swipe her fingers against the coat of a woman who had a thin face and stringy blond hair, she scraped off some of the blood that had dried there and brought it to her lips. "Paige," she said as she opened her mouth to reveal a set of fangs sprouting from her upper jaw. "I think I'm in trouble."

Chapter Twenty

Paige's story had been interrupted several times with road trip necessities such as stops for gas, a pause to pick up some fast food, and the occasional phone call. Despite all of that, it seemed to Cole as if her voice never stopped. When she wasn't speaking, Paige switched between refusing to look him in the eye and showing him more emotion than he'd thought her capable of displaying. She wasn't finished when they reached Chicago but seemed to have run out of steam for the moment.

"So that woman you followed to Miami . . . ?" he asked.

She nodded. "It was Hope."

Rico shifted in the front seat after slapping the car into Park. "Enough story time, kids. We've got work to do."

Although he couldn't see the Blood Parlor from where Rico had parked, Cole knew it wasn't far away. "What's the plan?"

"We go in," Paige said as she swapped out the ammunition in her pistol with a load that consisted strictly of rounds treated with the Nymar antidote, "and burn them down."

"Just the three of us?" Cole asked. "I get it that we can't

let what happened to Raza Hill slide, but going in for pay-back now could get us killed. There's more going on than just—"

"This ain't got a damn thing to do with payback," Rico said in a roar that filled the interior of the car and rattled the deepest bones in Cole's body. "It's not vengeance and it ain't keeping the peace. This is strictly gangland shit."

When Cole looked over to Paige for some level reasoning, he got a response that was spoken in a cold, emotionless tone. "We always try to keep things from going this way, but when they do, they need to be dealt with. If too many dangerous people step too far over the line, they need to get their feet stomped as quickly as possible."

"Haven't you heard a word anyone's been saying?" Cole snapped. "MEG's been calling, there's crap all over the news. What we've seen ourselves is more than enough to tell us this situation is already way out of our control. Trying to lay down the law now is like tossing a bottle of water onto a fucking forest fire!"

"We won't be the only ones making a move like this," Rico assured him. "I've been talking to some of the others and they're all tracking down any Nymar that may have a clue about what's going on."

"Are we coordinating with any other groups for this?" Cole asked.

Paige tucked a .45 into the holster under her arm and dou-ble-checked the weapons wedged into the modified holsters on her boots. "Nope."

"They think they got us on the run," Rico said. "That gives us an advantage."

Cole nervously checked his own weapons while grunting, "They *do* have us on the run. We ran all the way to Philly and then Wisconsin."

"Right. They've probably written us off and are getting ready to roll on whatever they got planned next. We hit them hard. Make them pay for burning us and then start peeling the skin off of some bloodsucker that might know where the next batch of shit is going down. Lather, rinse, repeat, and we'll work our way to the top of this chain."

Stuffing some extra magazines into his coat pockets, Cole muttered, "What if we get killed before making it to the second floor of that Blood Parlor?"

"Then our work is done," she said calmly. "At least we won't have to worry about this crap anymore. You wanted to go after these guys when Raza Hill was burning, didn't you?"

"Yeah," Cole replied.

"Now we're doing it. If we wait any longer, they'll implant spores in more than enough humans to make up for the Nymar that have been killed already. And those won't be the kinky, voluntary seedings they normally use. These will be young, healthy people snatched off the streets or out of their cars so they can be dragged away and violated without being able to do a goddamn thing about it. That's why I wanted you to read those journals, Cole. So far you've seen the Nymar under control, and even then, they still manage to come off as sexy assholes with fangs who are into the kinky stuff.

"You know what they are? They're rapists. They control someone, tear them open and stick themselves in while someone else is forced to take it." Something glistened at the corner of Paige's eye, but was swallowed up as she narrowed her vision until she was glaring out at him and the rest of the world through slits. "When that spore gets inside someone that wants it, it makes them into something different than what they were. It makes them hungry and vile. When it wraps around the heart of someone who doesn't want it, it keeps raping them from the inside out until their soul has no choice but to give in and just let it happen."

She practically kicked her door open and joined Rico on the sidewalk. They were parked near an eight-story building on a corner where the structures were geared more toward business than pleasure. Straight lines, striated levels of color, and simple planters holding little bits of greenery were the norm. To the north, neon light spilled onto the sidewalks and loud music blended with voices that struggled to be heard over it. The hour was late, but not nearly late enough for the streets to be empty. There was a chill in the air that

Cole could barely even feel on the parts of him that weren't wrapped up in the new coat. His thoughts had been divided across too many fronts, but Paige had done a good job of narrowing them to a few cognitive avenues that were less friendly than the grittiest of Chicago's alleyways.

Since the dancer who'd loaned them the car didn't seem worried about getting it back, Rico didn't spend much time getting it situated before joining them on the sidewalk. He tucked away a sawed-off shotgun in a harness that hung under the opposite arm from his trusty Sig Sauer and draped his leather jacket over the rig. The end of the shotgun barrel hung down below the laced side of the jacket, so he let that arm hang down to cover it. "Shit," he growled as his cell phone chirped from another pocket. He grabbed it as though he meant to crush it in his callused paw of a hand, but flipped it open instead. "It's Prophet."

Paige strode up Rush Street, glaring at nearby pedestrians with a set of eyes that were sharper than any weapon at her disposal. Anyone who happened to look at the Skinners quickly looked away. "We're not going in there to bargain with anyone or make threats, Cole."

"Yeah, I kinda figured."

"Every Nymar in that place will come at us. Steph must know we weren't killed in that fire, so she'll want to finish the job."

"There were cameras around the perimeter of the Blood Parlor last time we were here," Cole pointed out. "They may have seen us already."

"Then let's get in there."

"All righty," Rico said as he snapped his phone shut and pocketed it. "Prophet's still with the Amriany. He says they're following Bobby to San Antonio."

"You think the Amriany are working with Bobby and Paul and those others?"

"Either that," Rico said, "or those Gypsies are tracking them just like we are."

Paige bent slightly at the waist and plucked the metal-edged baton from its holster. "When we're done here, if we don't find any other leads, we'll catch up with Prophet."

"You mean *if* we get done here," Cole said.

"Yeah. Whatever."

There was no way Cole was going to talk her down and no good reason to try. Stephanie's Blood Parlor was less than half a block away, located above a bar that made half-hearted attempts to cater to at least half a dozen consumer groups. Even from a distance he could make out the glow of televisions broadcasting basketball games, beer signs both foreign and domestic, video games, and the pulsing strobe lights of a tricked-out jukebox. The building's architecture had a medieval feel, with a large pointed roof and elevated rounded corners done up to look like miniature castle towers pointing toward a starry Chicago sky. In front, faded bricks loomed over a striped awning as suited to concentrating the glow of the first floor's neon as to shielding the second floor from prying eyes.

As the Skinners drew closer, people streamed out of the building. They moved in an orderly fashion at first, conversing with each other, lifting phones to their ears and hailing cabs. Cole was glad to see the customers leave, until one of them stepped away from the neon and tendrils widened on his face until they became thicker than tiger stripes.

"They're here!" he warned.

Paige broke into a run while tightening her right hand around the grip of her weapon. Ever since that arm had been injured, the best form she could manage was a sloppily crafted machete. The curved section of the wooden baton creaked as it flowed outward and flattened until it was the same width as the sharpened strip that had been treated with the new varnish. By the time she closed the gap between herself and the front door of the bar, the machete's metallic edge sliced through the air and hacked no fewer than five inches down through the shoulder of the first Nymar to present himself as a target. If not for his quick sidestep, she would have cleaved through the top of his head down to his eyebrows.

Most of the crowd panicked and scattered like a flock of birds flushed from a bush. The four that remained came at Rico and Cole with ultraquick steps or leapt to collide with them amid a flurry of scraping black claws. All four of the newly revealed Nymar were marked by the thick tendrils Cole had seen on the one in Lancroft's dungeon. Unlike the creature that had been left on that floor to die, these spore were alive and well within their hosts, and it was clear they provided more than simple camouflage on a shadowy night. As the stripes widened, the Nymar became stronger and faster. Cole could feel the impact of their fists and forearms even as he blocked them with his spear. As far as that was concerned, he'd barely been quick enough to draw the weapon before the first Nymar was upon him.

Rico's Sig Sauer thumped once, its powerful blast muffled by the body of the Nymar in front of him. A hole erupted from the vampire's back and was quickly closed by ribbonlike tendrils. Without pausing to acknowledge the slightest bit of discomfort from the gunshot wound, that Nymar pulled back one clawed hand and drove the sharp talons straight down into Rico's shoulder.

Where anyone else might have panicked, Rico wrapped his free arm around the Nymar's torso. That way, when he reached the front of the Blood Parlor, his momentum drove the Nymar through the thick glass of the front door and carried him inside.

On the street, people had divided into two camps. The first group stopped to see what was happening after retreating a safe distance, and the second group was intent on putting the Blood Parlor behind them whether they had a car or just a pair of frantic feet to make it happen. What surprised Cole most when he got a chance to notice the crowds from the corner of his eye was the fact that more of them seemed frightened by the spear in his hands than the gun in Rico's. Welcome to Chicago.

The coat held up better than expected when a Nymar scratched and scraped at it as if she didn't quite know how to use the claws that stretched out from her fingers. Having been through more than his share of ineffectual sparring sessions, Cole recognized inexperience well enough. He twisted the spear sideways and used it as a crowbar to lever the Nymar off him before she started doing any real damage. As soon as she was pried loose, he used the metallic tip to open a gash straight across the upper edge of her breastbone. When she fell, Cole swapped the spear for his .45 and fired two shots into her heart.

She was still reaching up for him when the convulsions started, but the antidote on the bullets had no reaction to her spore. She bared all three sets of fangs in a feral warning gesture as Cole descended to drive his spear into her chest. His aim was true, and soon all of her muscles strained to prolong the inevitable. Cole was getting used to the sight of it, which was the hardest thing for him to accept. Even so, he moved on.

Something tugged at his shoulder, so he twisted around with his elbow in what would have been a vicious blow if there had been anyone there to catch it. Instead, his arm became snagged in what felt like a mix of heavy rubber bands and wet silk that led back to the Nymar he'd shot. He grabbed the slick black strands and pulled them from where they'd gotten snagged in his coat by hooklike claws. The Nymar screamed in pain as her body was reduced to a dried husk.

Paige was at the front door of the bar, holding onto another Nymar by his collar. The machete was in her other hand, and from what Cole could tell, it was buried in the Nymar's gut all the way to its hilt. Inside the club, a man held a machine gun that could have fit inside a shoe box with a minimum of disassembling. Recognizing the powerful MAC-10, Cole ran straight at Paige to wrap her up within the flap of his coat in what was either going to be his last act of well-intentioned stupidity or one of the coolest superhero moments of his life.

Bullets thumped on the Full Blood hide like hail bouncing off a leather tent. The impacts hit the Skinners hard enough to raise several bruises and welts along their arms, shoulders, and backs, but none of the rounds made it through. Just as Cole was about to give voice to the excitement he felt after flicking death in the nose, one of the last rounds in the MAC-

10's clip nipped a piece from the top of his left ear.

"Thanks," Paige said as she allowed the Nymar to finally slide off the end of her machete. "Movin' on."

The man with the MAC-10 was Astin. He owned the bar beneath the Blood Parlor, and the last time Cole had checked, hadn't been seeded with the Nymar spore. He still worked his primped hair and smooth dark skin as if that was the only weapon he needed. Of course, the MAC-10 didn't hurt. Moving behind the bar so he could reload, Astin turned toward a set of stairs leading to the upper floor and shouted, "They're here! They're here!" in a Middle Eastern accent that would have sounded cultured even if he'd been calling out bingo numbers.

Paige pushed away from under Cole's coat and charged like a bull through a red cape. He followed. The bar was filled with the bright glow of house lights that even made the neon beer signs harder to see. Gaudy but similarly bright red light was cast from upstairs, giving the group of Nymar that rushed into the bar even more of a demonic appearance. None of them showed any visible markings, and so far none had sparked the slightest hint of a warning from Cole's scars.

The first one to make it to the bottom of the stairs was greeted by a storm of lead that knocked the young man completely off his feet. Black tendrils spewed up from the bullet holes amid a spray of oily Nymar blood. Rico stood up from behind an overturned table, pinning the Nymar he'd used as a battering ram to the floor with his free hand. "They all got that new shit in 'em!" he shouted. "The stuff from Lancroft's place!"

The Nymar to descend from the second floor grabbed onto the walls and tore out chunks of plaster as they pulled themselves up to drop onto the Skinners like bombs. Cole fired again and again, hitting one of the Nymar in a chest bared to expose a webbed pattern of black tendrils that shrank down to almost invisible lines once the vampire hit the brighter light of the downstairs room. Even after being hit several times with the treated rounds, the Nymar kept coming.

Cole's aim improved as his hands stopped shaking. He

no longer had to try and convince himself he was in one of his games, as he had the first few times he fired at a living thing. He'd been brought around to the line of thought that if Nymar were indeed living, it was better to remedy that situation before one of them tore his head off and drank from the stump. From then on, putting the vampires down had become a whole lot easier.

Paige buried her machete into the side of one Nymar's neck with enough force to knock it over. When it gripped the horrific wound with both hands, she fired at another Nymar. Enough of her rounds hit home to get it out of her way as she vaulted the bar and placed the blood-smeared edge of her machete against Astin's throat. "Where's Stephanie?"

Astin's skin was the color of perfectly ground cappuccino. He opened his mouth to reveal perfect white teeth and the upper two sets of Nymar fangs. "She came looking for you earlier," he replied. "Must've missed her."

Sirens blared in the distance. They were too far away for Cole to see the police cars rolling down East Superior, but he knew it wouldn't take them long to arrive. "You had a plan for getting out of here, right?" When he didn't get a response, he moved over to where Rico was huddled with his back against another overturned table. "What's the goddamn escape plan?"

"Don't need one," Rico said while slapping a fresh magazine into the Sig Sauer.

"So we just go to jail for shooting this place up? Sounds on par with everything else that's been going on."

"The bloodsuckers always have escape routes. We follow the rats into their own holes and go from there."

As if on cue, footsteps rumbled overhead and stomped down another set of stairs toward the rear of the building.

"See?" Rico said through his blocky grin. "And how much you wanna bet the head bitch herself is leading that charge?"

At the bar, Paige used her machete to force Astin to turn with her as she looked in the direction of those footsteps. "What did she do to you?"

Astin smiled as if he was talking to a sultry voice over

a $3.99 per minute phone call when he replied, "Nothing I didn't want."

"These Nymar are different. Explain now or I cut you open, pull that spore out through the hole and figure it out myself."

Astin's smile abruptly lost its confidence. "The spore's different. Stephanie got it from some other Nymar who came into town the other night."

"Where's the other Nymar?"

"Don't know. They stopped by, made their delivery, and left. The man with her was a Skinner," he added venomously. "Seemed like he had a whole list of cities he wanted to hand over to us."

Now that she was closer, Paige could just make out the thin lines creeping up from beneath Astin's collar. Light beamed across his face, so she shoved him into a narrow strip of shadow created by a tall shelf of presumably expensive liquor. The shaded section of his face was quickly marred by tendrils that widened until they were slightly fatter than typical Nymar markings.

"You'll never see us coming now," he told her.

Paige's response was to move the machete away from his throat so she could snap that elbow around in a quick chopping blow that pounded against his chin and cracked the back of his head against the shelf.

Her partners had already raced up the stairs and weren't able to get much farther than that. She shifted the machete back into the form that would fit into its holster, gripped the .45 in her right hand and drew her backup .38, which was situated in a small holster at her hip. Hoping that the layout of the Blood Parlor hadn't changed much since the last time she'd been there, she kept her back against the wall and hurried up the stairs.

At the top was a small waiting room that felt more like a velvety cave where couches and chairs were clustered like fallen logs covered in thick, dark purple moss. A few artificial candles flickered on the windowsills, and colored mood lighting was cast from recessed bulbs in the ceiling, but that was all wiped away by the harsher light coming from the halogen lights bolted to the ceiling. Three-ring binders containing pictures of Steph's employees were still displayed on tables in the waiting room where customers could pick the set of fangs that would pierce their neck that evening. Those tables had been overturned and shot full of holes. One of the binders jumped from its spot, bleeding shreds of its contents after taking a direct hit with what must have been a high caliber rifle.

"Get over here, Bloodhound!" Rico shouted from his position at the entrance to a hall that ran all the way to the back of the building.

Cole stood with his back against the wall on the other side of that opening. Instead of his spear, he carried a .45 in one hand and Sid's .38 in the other. Part of a smile drifted onto his face as he leaned out and fired both guns at once. He didn't hit anything other than wall, but at least he scratched the itch that had been plaguing him since the first time he'd seen a John Woo movie.

Taking advantage of the distraction Cole's wild gunfire created, Paige ran across the mouth of the hall to stand by his side. "Are all the Nymar like the ones downstairs?"

"So far," he replied. "They're all reacting to changes in light. Makes 'em faster and a little stronger. Something's weird with their claws too," he added while firing another short volley of bullets at a door halfway down the hall that had just been opened. "It's like the tendrils reach out through the claws or something. I'm not sure if—"

"If you're not sure, then save it for later," Paige snapped. "Where's Steph?"

"Escape route out the back!" Rico shouted. "Her and a few others just headed that way. They gotta be heading down, right? Think we can go through the bar and catch up to 'em?"

"Don't have time to risk it!" Cole shouted over a burst of gunfire being thrown at him by a set of pale hands firing a small machine gun into the hallway from the newly opened doorway. Looking to Paige, he asked, "Do we?"

"Nope. It may be too late already. We'll need to send a few more rats down that hole. Rico?"

"Already on it," the big man said as he dug into his jacket for a small plastic bottle that was a little longer than a deck of cards and just about as wide. There was a narrow red nozzle at the top, which he opened and pointed at the furniture in the lobby.

Cole could smell the lighter fluid as soon as the stream was flowing. When he angled his shoulders so his coat covered him as much as possible and headed down the hall, it was to get away from the flammable sitting room and Rico's lighter as much as to pursue the vampires that had set a match to his Chicago home.

The hall was carpeted in a thick burgundy blend that insulated sound as well as footsteps. While moving down the plush corridor, Cole drew from his previous knowledge of the place. He knew the doors on either side led to bedrooms where the Blood Parlor's customers got whatever diverse perversities they'd purchased before Steph's girls and boys got down to feeding. The Skinners had allowed the business to run because it was voluntary on the humans' part and they'd been powerless to keep too tight a rein on Nymar affairs anyway. Considering the way things had turned out, Cole couldn't help but feel his guts clench at the shortsightedness of that decision.

The more steps he took, the farther his mind wandered. Cole's thoughts drifted to past dealings with Steph and Ace, dealings with other Nymar and even a few snippets of random conversations. It wasn't until he pushed beyond those thoughts to examine their source that he realized what was going on.

"Get the fuck out of my head!" he shouted as he widened his arms to fire through the closed doors as well as the open ones.

Not all Nymar could manipulate human thought, but plenty could sneak into someone's mind far enough to gum up the works. When the fire alarms started to blare and sprinklers went off in the burning sitting room, Cole's mind snapped back into perfect focus. One of the doors at the far end of the hall burst open and a Nymar wearing a tight sweater and black leggings bolted outside. Cole fired a low shot at her, hoping to catch a leg and slow her down. His bullet hit the wall a few inches from her hip and sent a small explosion of plaster and wood chips into her flesh. It wasn't exactly what he'd wanted, but she was slowed down.

The sound of that pained cry acted as a call to arms for every other Nymar on that floor. When they rushed from their rooms, the Skinners were there to meet them. Cole, Paige, and Rico dispatched the first few with shots fired at point-blank range or smashed the guns themselves against temples and noses. None of the rooms appeared to have more than a few Nymar in them, but the hall was cramped enough to make it seem like a flood. And at the far end, standing in front of a door that led to the Blood Parlor's security office, was a tall, slender woman with long, dark brown hair. Her slightly rounded face was marked with Nymar tendrils that ran up along both cheeks. She was the same one Cole had seen on the webcam video of the theft beneath Lancroft's house. When she narrowed her eyes and glared at the Skinners, the fog once more rolled into his brain.

"No," Paige snarled as she rushed down the hall past two of the open doors. "I won't let you get away from me. Not again!"

Cole rushed to catch up to her while Rico fired into one of the more crowded rooms. As much as he shouted at her, Cole could tell he wasn't getting through. His own voice was barely audible through the mush being projected into his thoughts, but that wasn't the problem. Every bit of Paige's attention was focused on the Nymar woman. She didn't react to light like the others, but the ones who leapt at the Skinners from the side rooms all seemed to be taking silent orders from her.

A pair of Nymar tried to flank Paige but were quickly dropped by her .45. She took aim at a third, which allowed yet another Nymar to get a clear shot at her. They'd all come so quickly and in such numbers that Cole didn't even see their faces anymore. He couldn't bother looking for how some black markings differed from others, so he just kept pulling his trigger. Paige took another few steps toward the woman at the end of the hall but was met by a Nymar who appeared in the doorway out of the security office and crouched in preparation to jump at her.

That's when the lights went out.

"Fire's spreading!" Rico shouted as he stepped out of the room he'd been clearing. "Can't get out through the bar!"

The woman at the far end of the hall shifted her solid black eyes just enough to look past the Skinners and the vampires who swarmed them. As if acknowledging Rico's statement, she turned and headed back into the security office.

Because of the fire, complete darkness was unable to get a grip on the Blood Parlor. Flashes of bright orange and brilliant white chewed through a thickening wall of smoke, creating a churning roar that subtly masked the muffled sirens approaching from Rush Street. In the flickering light cast by the blaze, the remaining Nymar sprouted their tiger-stripe camouflage as if their bodies were being embraced by the acrid smoke. They all flowed toward the security office, which was exactly where Paige and Rico were headed.

"Come on!" Rico said as he turned to where Cole was stooping down to get a look at one of the figures on the floor. "We've only got one shot at getting out of here without having to wade through a whole lotta cops!"

Suddenly, a Nymar exploded from the security office. He had the wide shoulders and barrel chest of a man who drew a salary just for being huge and could have kept the friskiest of the Blood Parlor's customers in line. Less than half a second before Rico could react, Paige shot the Nymar in the chest and then sent him to the floor with a straight kick that landed at the guy's belt level.

"Cole!" she shouted. "Get over here *now*!"

Although he could feel the heat pressing in on him from the waiting room, Cole didn't let it push him from his spot. "You guys should see this!"

"See what? This whole fucking place is done!" Rico bellowed.

Overhead, a piece of metal snapped and the sprinkler system started raining rusty water onto the hall. Flames licked at the other end of the hall, and the set of bedroom doors closest to the waiting room were already beginning to smolder. Water sprayed against the back of Cole's head and poured off his shoulders as he leaned down to tug at the collar of the Nymar lying on the ground. The man's shirt was open at the neck to reveal a plain white undershirt wet enough to be plastered to his chest and bloody enough for the stains to soak almost all the way through.

"This guy's human!" Cole shouted.

Rico stood so he could see both of his two partners. The lights were still on inside the little security office, so it wasn't difficult to keep track of Paige. "What? Just come on!"

"The others show their markings in this light. Some are already drying up! This one's just bleeding and it's just red blood. He's human!"

Cole was still looking down at the sucking chest wounds when Rico grabbed him by the shoulder and hauled him to his feet. "It don't matter if he's a robot sent from the future," he said. "We gotta go."

Chapter Twenty-One

The security office was about half the size of one of the private bedrooms. It was packed to the rafters with television monitors, desks, a few cabinets, and enough computer equipment to record all the activities of Steph's girls and their clients, store it, and broadcast it to pay sites all across the Internet. If ignorance was bliss, the subscribers to those sites who were ignorant about the true nature of vampires had been spending the last few years blissfully lapping up anything connected to a sexy face with pointed teeth. Even as the Blood Parlor burned, the computers hummed and chugged to spit out their last bits of programming. All of them, that is, apart from the ones that were empty cases placed to hide the escape hatch used for a quick getaway.

Paige stood at the entrance, hesitantly peeking through the opening, which was narrower than the computer towers used to hide it. When she stuck her head into the dark, she was barely able to pull it out before it was taken off by a quick burst of gunfire. "Yep," she said. "There's still a few down there."

Rico and Cole headed to the back of the room and stood with her. While Rico watched the hall to make sure no stragglers were going to take one last shot at them, Cole took in the sight of all of the technical hardware within the office. "There could be some valuable stuff in here," he said.

As Paige looked at him, one more gunshot was fired from the bottom of whatever was on the other side of the narrow hatch. "You want to start hacking computers? Sure. Go right ahead. I'll make sure the Nymar or cops don't get us, and Rico will take care of the fire. Take your freaking time."

As she spoke, Cole moved among the computers. "Thought you'd be a little more concerned about the dead people we're leaving behind. Not Nymar. People."

"Nothing we can do about them now. We stick to the plan."

"Amen to that, sister!" Rico said as he holstered the Sig Sauer and pushed past both of them. When a few shots blasted from the first floor, Rico answered them with a suicidal yell and a blast from the shotgun he'd saved for the occasion.

"Steph may be a lot of things, but she's not stupid," Paige said. "These computers are probably already wiped out by now."

"It's not that easy to just—"

Silencing him with a wave of her hand that occupied the top of the charts for Cole's biggest pet peeves in his new life, Paige took another peek through the hatch. "Let's just get the hell out of here. Those bodies and everything else in here will burn before anyone can stop it anyway."

Behind them, from what must have been the top of the stairs leading up from the bar, a group of men shouted orders back and forth as high pressure water hoses were sprayed at the source of the fire. Sirens blared and someone on a loudspeaker urged a crowd to please step away from the fire engine.

"God damn it," Paige muttered.

Leading the way through the hatch, she had to fight to keep her footing on a ramp that led straight down to a black wall. After moving the hidden door into place behind him, Cole slid sideways down the angled surface. At the bottom of the ramp was another ramp, angled just as steeply in the opposite direction and went deeper than the first floor. Rico was already down there, using his back to prop open what looked to be a heavier sliding door. He held the shotgun at waist level to cover the space in front of him, but the sweat on his brow and the strained expression on his ugly face was enough to let Paige and Cole know they needed to hurry. After they rushed past him, Rico hopped aside and let the door slam shut with a solid thump. "I lost sight of 'em," he said, "but it ain't like there's a lot of places they could have gone."

Cole had figured that much out on his own. A musty passage of wooden beams and red brick stretched out before him that reeked of Chicago history. Dirty floorboards rattled beneath the Skinners as they hurried along a wide corridor lit by yellowed bulbs in outdated fixtures that must have been built beneath the city block over sixty years ago. On both sides of the passage were thick wooden racks that might well have held vats of mildly toxic beer for one of Al Capone's birthday parties. When he turned around to get a quick look at the door they'd just used, all he could see was a cracked brick wall.

The Skinners ran in a triangle formation. Paige took the point and wasn't about to be overtaken by the other two. Rico kept up for fifty yards or so of the straightaway but got winded a lot quicker when the corridor twisted and turned through a series of low passages and heavy doors that had to be lifted, pushed aside, or ducked under in order to proceed. After rounding a quick sequence of three turns, they came upon another straight section of tunnel that had the same wooden cave feel as the entrance. By now Cole was certain they were underground. The air smelled like mildew and damp soil. Sounds of traffic were muffled to a degree that could only be obtained by tons of concrete and packed earth.

The Nymar who'd clouded his mind upstairs stood at the farthest end of that passage. Even from a distance, Cole could see that her eyes were fixed on them. He couldn't feel a mental haze yet, but a distinctly foreign touch of another presence was reaching into his head. Paige drew her baton and willed it to turn into its bladed form as she quickened her pace to get to the Nymar.

The scars on Cole's palms started to itch. That meant

there were Nymar in the vicinity that hadn't been modified by the new spore. Since the drops in his eyes had worn off, he focused on that feeling, used it to zero in on where the vampires might be hiding, then ran to catch up to Paige.

The Nymar that gripped onto the ceiling directly above him had remained hidden thanks to the inky blackness of its camouflaged skin and the thick shadows filling the curved upper portion of the tunnel above the Skinners' heads. It reached down to grab Cole's collar and pull him off his feet. "Should have taken your chances in the fire," it hissed.

Even though he could feel the vampire's breath against his face, Cole had no idea if it was male or female. What little he could see of its body blended into the shadows and was further hidden by the dust shaken loose from all the activity above the tunnels at street level.

He pointed his gun at the Nymar, but the weapon was viciously torn from his hand. He kicked both legs but felt nothing solid beneath him, so he curled his lower body up to make it easier to reach his spear.

"No, no," the Nymar whispered as it sank its claws into his flesh.

A pair of thick arms he knew had to be Rico's wrapped around his waist to pull him down, but no matter how hard Rico pulled, he couldn't break the Nymar's grip. "He's got you by the neck!" Rico snarled. "You gotta break out of that so I can get you down."

Cole tried to respond but could barely draw enough breath to keep moving. Rico was right. The Nymar's thin bony arm had encircled his throat just beneath the chin, and its other hand was grabbing his shoulder to sink its claws in through a canvas section of his coat. As his vision became smeared by a wave of murky darkness, he saw that Paige had made it to the end of the hall.

She didn't even bother looking back.

As soon as Paige closed the distance between them, she took a swing at the Nymar woman she knew was Hope and hit nothing but empty air.

"I don't know what surprises me more," Hope said as she

leaned back to let the weapon sail by. "The fact that you've become a Skinner or the fact that it's taken this long to find you."

Rather than try to follow the Nymar's flickering movements, Paige looked directly into eyes that were green orbs peeking out from the mesh of black tendrils seeping out from the outer edges of their sockets. That sight alone was enough to bring her back to that bloody night in Urbana all those years ago.

"What's the matter?" Hope asked. "You don't want to rush back and protect him? It seems you've been hardened in the years since the last time we met."

Bringing her machete up so the treated edge caught some of the tunnel's dim light, Paige said, "You don't know the half of it."

Hope cocked her head to one side as the black mesh in her eyes peeled back to show more of their vivid green. "One word from me and he's dead."

"You did all this to bring us here. You want to say your piece? Then say it. It won't be long before the cops find the same passage we did."

"They'll find nothing apart from the officers that you killed."

"What officers?" When the Nymar would only smile, Paige drew her gun and took aim at her. "What officers, Hope? Tell me."

"I don't know all of the unnecessary details like names or ranks, but there have been police within our Blood Parlors for some time."

"Stephanie takes orders from you?"

"It's not like that. As you Skinners so gleefully point out whenever you feel the need to push us down, the notion of a national, organized Nymar structure is a lie intended to give overactive imaginations something to play with. I and several others have merely suggested a course of action that will change things for the better."

"You've sparked an uprising."

Even though Hope's features had an otherworldly factor that surpassed the typical Nymar, the flicker of satisfaction crossing her face was easy to read. "I hadn't thought of it in quite that way, but I suppose you could call it that."

Shifting only slightly so her voice would carry behind her, Paige shouted, "Is Cole down yet?"

"No!" Rico grunted. "But he's still kicking."

"If the bloodsucker on the ceiling doesn't let go in three seconds, kill it."

"You don't think I been tryin' that? Every time I get close to touching this bastard, it nearly pops Cole's head off!"

Paige squared her shoulders so she was facing Hope directly. "Let. Him. Go."

"Only if you do me a favor. You seem to have grown close to the shapeshifters. I know for a fact that the pack of Mongrels in Kansas City owes you a favor, and there's been rumors that a Full Blood in St. Louis even helped you on at least one occasion. I want to meet with them."

"Why?"

"Because one of them may know about a certain prisoner that was liberated from Lancroft's dungeon. We intended to get him out ourselves, but the measures protecting his cell were too strong. We went back after the entire structure had been weakened but he was already gone." Pausing as the activity on the street above grew louder, Hope allowed the black mesh of tendrils to close in again until they'd completely covered the green centers of her eyes. "Better make your choice quickly. The police are out in force, and I know at least three different safe passages through these tunnels. What about you?"

"I won't do a damn thing to help you."

"That's a shame. After how you kept so still and quiet the night of that party, I thought you knew how to behave when you're beaten. Sure I can't convince you to make the rational choice again?"

Paige raised both weapons. "I don't have much use for rational things anymore. You're gonna let him go and then you'll—"

Hope's eyes snapped toward the Nymar clinging to the ceiling and she hissed what could have been a code word. When Paige rushed at her, Hope grabbed the machete just beneath the treated metallic edge and stopped it in mid swing. The .45 in Paige's other hand went off, but not before Hope twisted her hand so the bullet punched into the brick wall behind the Nymar's shoulder. Now that she controlled both of Paige's arms, Hope opened her mouth to display all of her fangs except for the curved pair used to administer venom. What would come next was inevitable, and she wanted Paige to feel every second of it.

Cole didn't know how the Nymar remained attached so firmly to the ceiling. At times he swore he could feel both of its hands scraping against him as Rico tried to pull it down. Even though the big man hadn't been able to convince the Nymar to let him go, he hadn't stopped trying to get a grip around the arm that was cinched to Cole's throat. Suddenly, the Nymar reached out with a loop of fiber that was lowered over his head, to pull it back almost to the snapping point.

"Play time is over," she hissed in the most human tone she'd used so far. "Time for supper." With that, she latched onto the side of Cole's neck and drove in all three sets of fangs right down to the gum line.

"Son of a bitch!" Rico snarled.

The fangs drilled into Cole as the Nymar's tongue slid against his skin. Quick, excited breaths spilled from her nostrils, and when he tried to turn away, the upper set of feeding fangs shifted painfully against the tendons and fibers within his neck. He reached up to try and grab her anywhere he could but his hands merely slid off the slick, sweaty surface of her skin. This time, however, Rico was the one to slap his arm away.

"Move it or lose it, boy," he said. Once Cole's swinging body and flailing limbs shifted, Rico fired his Sig Sauer up into the ceiling as well as at the Nymar clinging to it. "You ain't leaving any choice, asshole," he said between shots. "You're letting go even if I gotta take my partner out along the way!"

Those words were just another layer of sound beneath the Nymar's muffled grunts filling Cole's ears. She pulled the blood from him in powerful gulps that dimmed every one of his senses. Rico's bullets forced the vampire to shift her weight, and Cole renewed his efforts to pull free. The set of lower fangs were in him as well, those thicker spikes moving within his neck felt like one of his bones being wiggled by an intrusive set of needle-nose pliers.

"Stop! Stop!" was all he could say. It wasn't much, but at the moment it was the only word in his vocabulary.

Perhaps he was dropping from the ceiling, or perhaps his body had finally seen fit to lapse into unconsciousness. All of his senses became so acute that he could hear Paige struggling at the far end of the hall. He could hear the stomp of fireman's boots in the Blood Parlor and the wail of sirens in the background. Something moved inside his neck, slid along the tender wound and pushed deeper into him.

"That's more like it," Rico growled amid the crunch of knuckles against flesh.

Cole could see every crack in the ceiling and feel every ridge of the boards beneath him. He realized he was lying on the floor and Rico was down there with him, doling out a beating to the Nymar.

"You can kill me if you like," the Nymar said.

"You're goddamn right I can," Rico said as he paused just long enough to remove the broken fang wedged into his fist. "I'll get to you in a second, Cole. Just stay awake, you hear?"

"There's something still in me," Cole said.

"That's just the pain talkin'."

"No," Cole gulped. "I can feel it. There's something moving."

"You mean like a little rock you swallowed? Working its way down?"

Cole's eyes widened and he nodded. The pain from that motion felt as if someone had stuck a hot poker into the open wound on his neck. "That's it!" he said, pushing through the agony. "What the hell is it?"

"The bitch seeded you. Let me give you a little something to boost your system." After patting his pockets, he grunted, "I'm out. You got your kit on you?"

"What kit?"

"The one with the Resurrection Vial. There should be a dose of antidote in there too."

Of course he had the kit with him, he realized. It was one of the first things he'd gotten when Paige officially agreed to train him as a Skinner. At the time, his impulse had been to crack a joke about getting a membership card and instructions for some secret handshake, but then memories of Gerald Keeley had sprung to mind. Gerald was the first Skinner he had met, the first person to save his life, and the first man to kill himself in Cole's presence.

The Resurrection Vial was a last ditch effort for Skinners to tack a few more moments onto their lives. The vial itself was a small glass tube with two sharp points designed to break the skin and deliver its contents into a warm body: enough Nymar spore to infect a person and bring them back from whatever grievous injury had put them down.

It was a Skinner's duty to use the antidote syringe as soon as they'd completed their final task. They had to let the spore take root in order for it to do any good, and if they didn't have the stones to kill themselves afterward, there were plenty of others out there who would make it their mission to track them down and do it for them. Since the Skinners couldn't afford to let their knowledge fall into any blood-sucker's hands, it became top priority for anyone using the vial to deliver themselves and the new little buddy attached to their heart right back to hell.

Life sucks and then you die. Twice.

"Stay focused, Cole," Rico said.

Until that moment, Cole hadn't known he'd been drifting away. The thoughts, voices, and memories all just curled around his brain and removed him from what was happening. When the needle jabbed into his arm, he barely felt it. As the antidote was pumped in, it rolled through his body like a wave of saltwater that had been charged by downed electrical wires. He sat up with nothing on his mind other than the desire to kill the man with the syringe in his hand.

Rico pushed him down with one thickly callused palm. "Take it easy. Just give it a minute. And don't think I forgot about you, bitch," he said to the Nymar. "Every bullet I got has your name on it."

The Nymar was being held in place somehow, but Cole wasn't worried about the details. He barely even noticed when Paige dropped to the floor a few feet from him. Seeing her reminded him what the Resurrection Vial was for. He'd been given a few more moments to hang on and didn't intend on wasting them.

"Son . . . of a . . . *bitch*!" Paige shouted as she propped herself up on all fours and punched the floor with every word.

Rico's voice was still nearby. "You all right, Blood-hound?"

"Yeah. She just . . . made a big mistake. Tried to seed me."

"Same here. Is this Cole's first time?"

Now Paige looked at him too. There was pain written across her face. Cole had seen that before, but there was something else in her eyes that spoke of a wound deeper than the ones already being closed by the healing serum her body had been conditioned to produce. "Yes," she replied while injecting herself with antidote from one of the syringes in her pocket. "It's his first time. Did you get him injected?"

"Yeah, but it's still tearing him up."

"He should be able to handle it." She turned her head quickly enough for her newly cropped hairstyle to flap against her cheek. "You wanted to see?" she yelled. "Come over here!"

"She's gone, Paige," Rico said. "She took off after tossing you over here. Was that . . . ?"

"Yeah. It was Hope. She's still somewhere close. She told me that— Oh, Christ!"

"You okay?"

Ignoring the question while pulling herself onto one knee, Paige gnashed her teeth and said, "She seeded me just to watch me squirm. Fucking bitch still gets off on pain. Don't worry, Cole. It hurts, but the serum in your blood will keep the spore from attaching, and the antidote should kill it. Stings like a mother, but it'll stop before long."

"We gotta get out of here," Rico said. "Those sirens are

way too close, and when the cops find them bodies, things will get messy."

The pain lessened, but Cole's discomfort grew. "It's still in there," he said.

"I know," Paige said through gritted teeth. Her hand rested on his chest, moved directly to the spot where it hurt most and rubbed him gently. "It'll keep fighting for a while," she said while trying to mask her own pain.

When Rico stood up, the Nymar beneath his heel grunted. He bent down and picked her up. "You're coming with us."

"You'll kill me no matter what," the Nymar spat. "Skinners can't be trusted."

"No, but we can be great listeners."

"I won't help you."

"Then you're in for one hell of a long night."

Chapter Twenty-Two

"One of the others is coming," Randolph announced.

Liam stood with the other Full Blood in a wooded area less than two miles east of a small coastal town. It was a cool, windy night. They'd covered a lot of ground at a vigorous pace but none of the shapeshifters were any worse for wear. Full Bloods were accustomed to traversing their vast territories. Half Breeds were only content when they were moving, and Kawosa had been eager to stretch his legs after being huddled in Lancroft's basement for too many years. Pointing his scarred nose toward the Atlantic, Liam drew a breath and said, "Kawosa told me about our approaching guest. You think it'll be our friend from Australia?"

"My money's on Sandoval. He's more the kind who would respond to the news you've been so good at spreading."

"You flatter me."

"No flattery intended. Your attack on Kansas City was meant to draw attention, and that's what you did. If it's not Sandoval, it could be any of the others. Not that there are many to choose from." Randolph crossed his arms over a solid chest covered in a jacket that had been hanging just inside the back door of a house in town. Breaking into the house had been a lot easier than convincing Liam to leave its owner sleeping, but he'd somehow accomplished both jobs.

A wind brushed through the trees with barely enough strength to shake the leaves in it.

"Do you smell the young one?" Liam asked.

Nodding to a trio of figures at the edge of a nearby clearing, Randolph replied, "No, but they do. Look how restless they are."

"Even with the old trickster reining them in, those wretches still look ready to break loose. They really are a piece of work."

The other three were just far enough away for Randolph to see the shapes of their bodies, but not the expressions on their faces. Two of them were Half Breeds, but hardly looked the part anymore. They'd evolved to survive in a world left behind by Lancroft's pestilence and had changed once more thanks to Liam's attentions. In Randolph's opinion, trying to infect the marrow of another shapeshifter was akin to sneezing on someone who already had a cold. The damage had been done. Liam had a knack for changing a shapeshifter even more, which made him something more than just company.

"You're thinking this was a mistake, aren't you?" Liam asked.

"Why would you say that?"

"Because you always start to think along those lines once things really start to get good. Do you doubt those wretches can get the job done?"

"They were once human," Randolph stated. "Now they're a little bit of three species. If they can't do the job, nobody can. What of your Mongrel friends? We haven't heard from them in a while."

When Liam spoke, he seemed to be both savoring and choking on his own words. "They're pariahs among their own kind, but there are plenty among them that have higher aspirations than living in the dirt and hiding beneath the humans' sewers. I haven't asked them to do anything that isn't within their best interests."

Randolph's eyes shifted within their sockets. "We both set the task in front of them."

Where Randolph was careful, Liam positioned himself

so there would be no mistaking his intent. "You try giving them an order without me approving it and see what happens. Are you so proud that you can't admit you need my help even this long after you've already begged for it?"

"I didn't beg," Randolph replied as his teeth reflexively melted into points.

Grinning with satisfaction, Liam said, "At least it's nice to know you still appreciate me."

"The wretches swarmed into a city. The humans have enough pictures of you on their computers to make you a celebrity. The Skinners are pooling resources that would have been lost if Jonah Lancroft hadn't been forced to play his hand, and now we're awaiting the arrival of a Full Blood who's probably looking to add to all of the confusion gripping this section of the world. How could I not appreciate your contributions to the state of things?"

"This had to happen. You know that, right?"

Randolph's only answer was a growl masked beneath a steam-laden exhalation.

"Change is good all 'round," Liam said in a more relaxed voice that dripped with his cockney brogue. "Our mistake was letting the Skinners get too comfortable, especially in this neck of the woods. Even the Travelers have had too much time to collect themselves and figure new ways to put a hurt on the likes of us. As for the other Full Blood coming here, perhaps that can work to our advantage." Lowering his voice as well as his head, he said, "The Amriany are expecting to find me or my new pack, and I won't disappoint. It's doubtful this generation has even met you. That is, unless you've made a trip across the pond within the last few decades?"

"I haven't."

"There you are, then. I set 'em up. You knock 'em down. We almost took over a continent that way, remember?"

Randolph did remember. His crystalline eyes narrowed as all those screams echoed through his mind. Before he tried to silence them, another sound caught his attention. Liam heard it as well because he angled his head to point his eye in that direction.

Lyssa darted between the trees, running close to the

ground with effortless grace that seemed like a dance compared to a werewolf's powerful gait. She veered to the north, circled around the spot where the other three figures were gathered, and then approached the Full Bloods to come to a stop in front of Liam. She wasn't even breathing heavily when she said, "We've spoken to packs in Florida and Louisiana. There are members from both who will join you so long as you change them the way you did with me and Max."

"How far can we trust them?"

"For what you have in mind, all the way."

Liam glanced over to Randolph and got a response that would have gone completely unnoticed by anyone who didn't know exactly what to look for. Looking back to the Mongrel, he asked, "Where's Max?"

"Trying to find a pack of wanderers not far from here. With you two so close, they're probably trying to get to safer ground, so he wants to catch up with them before they're entrenched."

"Tell me," Randolph said. "Can you pick up the scent of anything apart from the ones who are within your sight at the moment?"

"Like who?" Lyssa asked.

"Just tell me what you can find."

She humored him by taking an exaggerated sniff, but quickly snapped her nose toward the east and sniffed some more. Her breaths became almost frantic as she pulled in short gulps of air that were drawn all the way down to the back of her throat and let out through her mouth. When she looked back to Randolph, she said, "There are more Full Bloods coming. The scent is too far east to be over dry land, so it must be on a ship or . . . I don't know but they are coming."

Although Randolph was content to study her carefully, Liam wasn't so passive. "How long did you know about this? When did you pick up on the scent?"

"I've smelled nothing but Full Bloods for days!" she said while taking a step back. "Your scents are everywhere, mixed with everything and spread across the country, thanks to all the running you've been doing. Why do you think the Mongrel packs have scattered?" Three shapes huddled in the nearby darkness; Kawosa and two Half Breeds. She started to look back at them, but quickly averted her eyes. "And then there's him. Him being in the open air makes everything different. He's one of us, but not. One of you, but not. He's everything and nothing. How could you not know that?"

"I know who Kawosa is," Randolph said. "I know *what* he is."

"He is Ktseena," she hissed. "If you knew that, you should have known to leave him wherever he's been trapped all these years. I don't know how Lancroft managed to put him in a cage, but Max thinks . . ."

When she became too frightened to continue, Liam bent down to one knee and leaned forward. "Go on. Tell me what Max thinks."

"Max thinks he may not have been captured at all. Ktseena could very well have allowed Lancroft to think he'd been captured just so he could gain the Skinner's confidence."

"Why would he do that?" Randolph asked.

"If even a handful of the legends about him are true, there's no way for us to make sense of what he does or why. I've only been told a few of the stories, but they all say Ktseena would help no one but himself."

"There are legends about me," Randolph pointed out. "There are legends about Liam. There are legends about your kind as well as the wretches. The only difference between legends and frightened rumor is the amount of time that's passed since the tale was first told."

"So you don't believe the legends about him?"

"I believe what I can put together with my own senses," Randolph said. Leveling a firm glare upon the Mongrel, he added, "You do not need to deal with Kawosa. If you do the jobs you've been given, you will get the rewards you've been promised."

"And what if you cannot control him?"

"Then the situation is well out of your hands, Mongrel. Best to enjoy the scraps we throw you and live to spread more of your precious legends another day."

Liam stood up in the baggy clothes he'd stolen and told her, "Now that the Skinners have found Lancroft's weapons and the Amriany have come to these shores, we're going to need more to stand behind us. Kawosa agrees."

"He's the first of the deceivers," Lyssa replied. "Every word from his mouth has an equal chance of being the truth or a lie."

"The words he speaks to humans aren't worth the air they float on," Liam pointed out. "He is also the first shapeshifter and owes nothing to humans. Don't lose sight of that."

Lyssa cringed, but her question was important enough for her to push through her trepidation. "And why would he treat Full Bloods any differently?"

"Because," Liam said proudly and without a twitch, "we're his favorites."

She'd been around him long enough to know that was all she was going to get. When Kawosa barked at the Half Breeds and stood up on his hind legs, she hopped back and then scampered away.

"I should keep an eye on her," Liam said. "Make certain that she or the other one don't get any big ideas in those pointed little heads of theirs."

"Fine. Off with you, then. I want a word with the old one."

Liam jogged after the Mongrel, allowed his upper body to fall forward and shifted into his four-legged form before his front paws hit the dirt. After that, a few powerful leaps carried him out of sight.

Striding to the spot where Kawosa had been, Randolph almost lost sight of the solitary figure several times. The figure clad in tattered rags didn't fade away so much as blend in with everything around him. When the wind bent the trees, Kawosa swayed in the same rhythm. When light from the sky or the nearby town shifted to make the shadows lurch, he matched those movements as well. For one such as Randolph, it was unsettling to watch. "You truly do enjoy your work, don't you?" he asked.

"The Half Breeds have been set loose as you asked," Kawosa replied.

"Were they changed?"

"They are living sculptures already. I was able to make them into something that would be close enough to suit your purposes."

"You've been very helpful, Kawosa. I'm surprised."

"So far, our purposes seem to be more or less the same. And the ones I don't share, I find . . . interesting." Gazing in the direction the Half Breeds had bolted, Kawosa added, "They're up to your task and they'll remain loyal."

"Are you certain of that? The wretches aren't exactly the sort to be reasoned with."

"I didn't reason with them. They act on instinct." Shifting his mouth into something that could have been a grin or a snarl, he added, "So I rewrote their instincts."

"Will it last?"

"No, but it will hold long enough for them to complete their hunt. Your friend is plotting against you, you know."

"Liam's plots aren't complex. Something strikes his fancy and he runs after it."

"I suppose you know him better than I do."

"He's just someone who knows me well enough to keep me from killing him," Randolph mused.

"And you know him well enough to make him useful. It doesn't bother you that he thinks so little of you?"

Randolph studied the being in front of him. Not quite a man and not quite an animal, Kawosa seemed to be obscured by clouds that weren't even there. His eyes shifted from the color of a clear sky to one reflected in unfathomably deep waters. His face had narrowed and his posture became stooped. Whether that was to hide his true size or coddle some sort of ailment was anyone's guess.

Shifting his eyes once again to acquire a multifaceted quality and a color that was only slightly grayer than Randolph's, Kawosa said, "There is another reason you're so intent on finding this other Full Blood that is making its way here."

"If you truly are the one who created shapeshifters, then you know about the deficiencies we have in picking up some very particular scents. We can pinpoint a specific human from hundreds of miles away but we cannot find those that will become most vital to us. We can barely smell our own kind unless we've acquired their scent from its source. Is that your doing, Trickster?"

Kawosa smirked. "That would be a nice little way to make things difficult, wouldn't it? The almighty Full Bloods have to live with a fault." Bringing his tone down from the taunting edge it had acquired, he shook his head. "I'm not that crafty. Leave it to the higher powers to come up with torments that cut so deep. To be honest, I've always seen your few flaws as a boon to your kind."

"How so?"

"If every Full Blood had absolute power and could so easily find one another, what would prevent you from tearing through entire continents chasing each other around?" Using his hands and twitching fingers to illustrate his point, he continued, "All of your brothers and sisters, scampering over the globe, knocking down what the humans have taken so long to build. The ones like you would be forced into a life of defense and war, while the ones like Liam would be given the opportunity to consolidate his gifts into something far worse. Whether you agree or not, that is the way of things."

"You're fond of humans?"

"Why wouldn't I be?"

"One of them locked you in a box belowground. If they haven't figured out you're missing already, more of them will undoubtedly come to try and put you right back into that box or another that's even worse. Now," Randolph added as he stared out in the direction that Liam had gone, "the humans that didn't even know about us until so recently will kill us the first chance they get."

Kawosa faced in that direction as well. "Humans are a source of endless amusement. Throughout the generations, I have found them to be both devious and gullible. Optimistic, yet hardened. Musical and grating. Even when they know better than to trust, they still want to see what they could be missing if they strayed. No matter how much there is to fear, they never hesitate to walk away from the path."

"Yes," Randolph sighed. "Liam enjoys that aspect of them very much as well."

"You spend a lot of time concerning yourself with him."

"I know. That's why I want to leave this territory of mine."

"Leave? And go where?"

"Whoever is answering Liam's call to arms can have my territory, and I will stake a claim in theirs."

"Simple swap," Kawosa mused.

"Nothing simple about it and you know that."

"I also know that some very interesting times are coming. This has always been a land of strife and confusion. In recent years," Kawosa added enthusiastically, "doubly so. The Half Breeds are growing. The humans are regressing. Up is down. Fire is water. Even the Nymar have broken out of the stale shell they've inhabited for far too long."

Randolph watched the other being with a mix of caution and reverence. Even as some of Kawosa's words degraded into babble, he wasn't about to make the mistake of completely discounting their source. "You can sense a change within the leeches?"

Clamping his lips in a gnarled grimace, Kawosa lifted his chin and re-formed his face into something with nostrils that stretched back like a pair of offset, toothless mouths. "Ohhh yes. They evolve like anything else, but their spore is internal and slow to adjust. They can only taste through their host's mouth and see through clouded eyes. I don't know if it was the Skinners or the Amriany, but one of the groups figured this out, and Lancroft was one of the first to capture one of the evolved Nymar before they had a chance to spread their gift.

"The leeches haven't had as much reason to change as the Half Breeds, so they become lazy. If there's one thing I can spot, one thing I can smell, one thing I can feel, it's laziness inside someone's heart. Laziness makes the humans so easy to manipulate. Their legends are full of whining about being deceived by the likes of me, when all they needed to do was not give in to the temptations being offered."

"You sound like Liam."

"And what's so bad about that?"

"He's insane."

After considering that a moment, Kawosa replied, "We all have our quirks. If you've been able to deal with him thus far, why do you need my help with any other Full Bloods? I would think you'd be grateful to acquire another's scent."

"Whoever is coming so far to respond to Liam's call will not be the sort that is willing to hand over anything to anyone. If not for our kind's deficiency, I could have found the rest of us during all my years of searching. Instead, I must piece a picture together by looking at the voids instead of the solids. Once I have acquired their scent, I ask you to convince the new arrivals that it is best for them to stay here."

"Surely they will ask where you have gone. No doubt they won't have any trouble figuring it out. What should I say to that?"

"Say what you like," Randolph told him. "Just grease the wheels for this to happen. This is what I ask in return for breaking you out of Lancroft's prison."

"Haven't I been helpful enough to repay that debt?"

"We haven't asked you to do anything you wouldn't have freely done on your own. That is no way to repay a debt. What I ask of you is also well within the scope of your normal affairs, but it is important enough to me for it to carry more weight."

Kawosa nodded slowly. "I think I can arrange something. But don't tell me that is your only request. What of the matter you mentioned before? Was that a genuine concern or has it been replaced by your newfound wanderlust?"

"That matter stands, but now is not the time to discuss it any further. Once I have settled in my new territory, if you still feel inclined to grant me that favor, I am sure you can find me. Are you certain those wretches can pick up the scent we're after?" Randolph asked.

"Oh yes. They just need some time. As far as they're concerned, the single task I have given them is the only one there is. What happens when they find the one you're looking for?"

"Perhaps I'll have a companion when I take my journey." Randolph sighed, then the muscles in his brow tensed just enough for an internal darkness to make itself known upon his features. "Or perhaps one more death will be added to all of the others that are to come."

Chapter Twenty-Three

The tunnels beneath Rush Street branched off in several places, but it was easy to figure out the one the Nymar had used. Not all of them could walk on walls, which meant they left a trail in the gritty dust covering the floor. Paige scouted ahead and Rico helped Cole walk while carrying the ceiling-hugging Nymar over one shoulder. It was slow going but sped up once Paige doubled back to report that the rest of the Nymar had cleared out. The Skinners branched away from the beaten path, found a dead end, and holed up there for the next few hours.

Cole sat with his back against yet another dirty brick wall, pulling in breaths that felt like wet cement and letting them out in gasps. It helped to take shallower gulps of air, but his eyesight remained blurred around the edges.

"How you doin' over there?" Rico asked.

"Still hurts."

"How bad?"

"Like there's a fucking rock swimming around in my chest and nuzzling my heart! That bad enough for you, Doctor?"

The big man leaned against a wall with half an unlit cigarette clenched between his teeth. He held the Sig Sauer in his right hand, casually pointing it at the Nymar who'd hung Cole from the ceiling. All this time, Rico had been studying the Nymar's face, paying close attention to the markings that ran up along both cheeks. Whenever the Nymar moved, Rico used his boot, fist, or the side of the pistol to crack it in the head. If not for the strips of burlap and knotted trash bags he'd found to bind her ankles and wrists, the bloodsucker still might have gotten away.

"The spore's still movin'?"

Cole thought that if he had any psychic ability whatsoever, the focus in his glare would have popped Rico's head wide open. "*Yes*. I need more antidote. Maybe some serum."

"You've had enough of both to do the job. Paige is fine. You should be too." Biting down on the cigarette as if he meant to chew it as a snack, Rico squatted so he could stare into the Nymar's eyes while using the Sig Sauer to pin her head to the wall she was leaning against. "What did you do to him?"

"You know wh-what I did," she stammered.

"Why isn't the spore dying?"

"Maybe your friend is too weak to fight it."

Rico pulled in a deep breath. When he let it out, his face became colder than a mask cut into an iceberg. "You know we're Skinners, right?" he asked while jamming the barrel of his gun against one of the Nymar's eyes.

"Y-Yes."

"Then you know what we do to any bloodsuckers we find feeding in public."

Her markings fluttered beneath her skin, making her face seem like a bad television signal. When she opened her mouth to speak, the top set of fangs stretched out reflexively. "I know."

"Good," Rico said calmly. But any semblance of calm instantly drained from him when he leaned against the pistol and clamped his free hand around her throat. "You don't have any fucking idea what we do to Nymar that try to kill us. If you did, you would have never made a stupid fucking move like the one you made tonight. Were you one of the ones that burnt our place down?"

"No! I don't—"

Rico took his hand away from her throat, reached into his jacket and pulled out a knife that he snapped open with a flip of his wrist. The clattering handle fell into place to reveal a three inch blade that he stuck up under the ridge of her eyebrow to draw a trickle of oily blood. "I can go two ways from here. Down to flip your eye out or straight in to gouge your brain. That second one takes some effort, but I've got a whole lot of pent-up energy that's in need of direction."

The Nymar flailed against her bonds until she finally snapped one wrist free. Rico took the fight from her by poking the blade in a little more. She couldn't blink. She couldn't move. She could no longer even shift her weight out of fear of moving the blade inside her.

Cole watched the process silently. He wanted to protest, but a wave of pain from the living kidney stone moving within his chest erased that impulse completely. He managed to pull himself up, swallow the urge to launch himself into a coughing fit, and pull the spear from its harness. Dropping to one knee as the lump sought refuge somewhere in the vicinity of his left lung, he drove the metallic spearhead into the floor near the Nymar's leg and snarled, "Tell me what you did!"

"You'd better do what he says, honey," Paige said as she jogged around the corner and approached the dead end. "Every one of your friends is gone."

"Nobody's gonna help you," Rico said. "That means I get to help myself." He only moved the blade a fraction of a millimeter, but that was enough to get the Nymar's legs scraping against the floor.

"There'll be more coming," the Nymar said.

Cole's voice was a haggard croak when he asked, "Who'll be coming?"

"Hope and the others with her."

"Do you mean the rest of those Toronto assholes like Bobby and Tru?" Paige asked.

"They're the ones who make the rounds, but any of the Nymar who've joined the evolution will be happy to come along."

"Bunch of goddamn bloodsuckers think they're revolutionaries?" Rico scoffed.

The Nymar wasn't squirming so much anymore. Either she'd accepted her fate or the threadlike tendrils slipping out from between her eyeball and socket were comforting her in some way. The black filaments snaked out along Rico's blade, wrapping around it to try and pull it out of her. "Not revolution," she said. "Evolution. If we don't get what we want from that one, we'll get it from another one of you and add it to what we took from Lancroft."

"Get what from us?"

By now the tendrils snaking from the Nymar's eye had formed a thick coating around the tip of Rico's blade. He tried to move it again, but her eyeball was protected by the black barricade. If she felt any discomfort from the ordeal, her spore must have taken care of that too.

Paige stormed over. As her shadow was cast across the Nymar's face, the tendrils there widened to form a slender striped pattern flowing directly toward the blade in her eye socket. "Give me a good target, Rico," she said while digging an antidote syringe from a leather case in her pocket.

"Surely."

Once he'd levered the blade down a bit, Paige held the needle over the mass of tendrils. "I knew you bloodsuckers could be ruthless, but now you're turning multiseeding into common practice?" Always the teacher, she looked over to Cole and said, "She's got more than one spore."

"I don't give a shit if she's got more than one head!" Cole replied. "Get this thing out of me!"

"Hope's leading this group and she's not from around here," Paige said to the Nymar. "What's she doing?"

"You won't have any luck with that needle, you stupid bitch," the Nymar spat.

"I've been meaning to make absolutely sure of that. Where else would she and the others go?"

"You're the ones that need to find somewhere to go! The cops are working for us now and they're out for your heads. After they see what you left behind in the Blood Parlor, you pricks will be at the top of their wanted lists."

Paige shrugged casually and jabbed the skinny needle into the tendrils. Judging by the way the Nymar screamed, those were some very tender strands. It was all Rico could do to hold her down before she bucked hard enough to force his blade all the way to the back of her skull.

"Talk or I pump this shit in," Paige warned.

"Go ahead, you stupid Skinner whore!"

"I'm not kidding!"

"Neither am I!" the Nymar screamed. "Fuck yourself and your mother!"

Rico tightened his grip on her neck. "You should become real helpful real fast or we'll lose interest. We got better things to do than screw around."

"Suck your friend's dick," she snarled. "At least he'll get some fun before the spore takes root."

"Fine," Paige said as she pressed the plunger of the needle down.

The Nymar tensed and pulled in a sharp breath. Her eye lids fluttered as much as they could considering her predicament, but soon she let out a breath and started to laugh. "Told you to do better than that, bitch."

Paige pressed the plunger down even harder to drain the last drop of antidote from the syringe. When it didn't make a difference, she looked over to Rico and said, "Now we know for certain this stuff doesn't work on the new ones."

"All right," the big man grunted. "Plan B. I stick this blade all the way into your brain and then cut your heart out. Thanks to all that black spaghetti inside of you, I'm betting you'll feel every second of it." He pressed the blade in just far enough to puncture her eyeball. The flow of milky fluid was quickly stymied by black filaments, but the expression on the Nymar's face made it clear she could still feel plenty of what was happening.

"Hope and the others went to a bunch of different cities," she said so quickly that her words ran together in a barely comprehensible stream. "They made deliveries, set things up, arranged it so different Skinners could all be hit just like you were."

"What did they deliver?" Paige demanded.

"Blood stolen from Jonah Lancroft. Old Nymar spores from when we were different. From older evolutions. Nymar change and adapt. We develop immunities like humans with viruses. It changes us, and the spores change. That's why your poisons don't work on ones like me. Hope gave us samples that came before you had the shit in those needles. The older spore were different from us, so the poison doesn't work."

"What cities did Hope visit?"

"I don't know them all. Please! Take the knife out so I can think."

"Think now," Paige warned, "or forever hold your peace."

"They came here," the Nymar sputtered. "Here and . . . and . . . and Miami! They went to Miami."

"Already know about that one. What's another?"

"Sacramento."

Paige cocked her head to one side and narrowed her eyes. "You sure about that? Keep in mind, we're taking you with us to wherever we decide to go. If it turns out to be a wash, we'll make this shit look like a party."

"Okay, not Sacramento. Hope did go to San Antonio."

"Too far."

Something that may have been sweat appeared on the Nymar's face. Her nervous impulse forced her to try and blink, which only made things worse. The sensation of her eyelid scraping against the knife caused her to kick and thrash, which in turn wiggled the blade inside her skull even more. Rico held her down but wasn't able to keep her still. Cole wasted no time in flipping his spear around so the forked end trapped one of the Nymar's shoulders and kept her more or less in place.

"Just fucking kill me!" the Nymar screamed.

"Not until you—"

"Denver and Boston! Hope went to Denver and Boston and some other places but I don't know where! Philadelphia, I think. For Christ's sake, just—"

Paige jammed her machete into the Nymar's chest. Its charmed metallic edge allowed her to cut straight through the breast plate and the infected heart beneath it. A few more quick, plunging stabs caused the vampire to arch her back. Before she could blink, her skin was already starting to flake away. When Rico pulled his knife out, the tendrils that had held on to the blade fell away like glue that dried into a brittle crust.

Cole had seen plenty of Nymar killed from exposure to the antidote, but this one was something new. Paige held on to the machete's handle and twisted it violently from side to side. A few seconds later the Nymar caught a second wind. She kicked and thrashed against the ground until Paige stabbed her a few inches to the right of the first wound. The violent convulsions restarted as the other half of the Nymar's body flopped uselessly. Her screams were contorted and strained. Some of her fingernails were torn off against the floorboards, leaving bloody stains on either side of her.

Since nobody else was making a move, Cole aimed his .45 and emptied it into her chest. Antidote rounds or not, there wasn't enough left of her heart for anything to cling to after that.

"Maybe she had more than two spores," Paige said.

"You mean like Henry?" Cole asked as his gun hand started to tremble.

Paige knelt down to get a closer look at the Nymar's face. The vampire was still twitching but was now just being moved by the thing beneath her skin. All the remaining tendrils receded and the normal process of a Nymar death followed from there. "Not like Henry," she said. "He was a Full Blood. A shapeshifter has a whole different system that made it impossible for any of the spore to fully attach. This is different. This is two spores attaching to the same heart. It's rare and very, very dangerous."

"Maybe that tiger stripe shit makes it easier for 'em," Rico offered.

"Could be. She did mention evolution."

"She may have mentioned a few more things if we'd kept her alive," Cole wheezed. A simple inhalation turned into a painful gurgle as he was hit by enough pain to drop him to the floor. "Jesus! How come Paige is up and around and I'm . . . ?"

She didn't need to hear the rest of the question. Her hand wandered to the wound on her neck, which was already mostly shut. The healing serum in her system and the extra dose she'd administered to herself had seen to that. "Did you give him anything for that, Rico?"

"Of course I did! It just ain't doin' much more than slowin' it down."

"Doesn't feel very slow to me!" Cole said.

Crouching down beside him, Paige opened his coat and moved her hands under his shirt. "Even just a little antidote should have been enough to squash one of those things. How does this feel?"

The only answer Cole could give was a wailing groan as Paige's fingers touched a portion of his chest that felt as if it had rotted all the way down to his spinal column.

She sighed. "It's not as bad as I thought. Hasn't attached yet. When it stops hurting, you're in trouble. That means it's settling in."

"When the fuck does that happen?"

"Hopefully never. Once it settles in, it'll be too late to help you."

"Do you believe that evolution shit?" Rico asked. "Did Lancroft really have old spores tucked away in that basement?"

Every other noise in the brick corridor faded away.

"I don't know," Paige whispered. Suddenly, her face showed something Cole had never seen before. There was genuine fear, uncertainty, and panic in her eyes as she pulled his shirt up to check his chest. "There aren't any tendrils showing up yet. He's still got his color. It should have taken root or died by now, Rico. What the hell is happening to him?"

Rico's tone cut through the confusion that had rolled into the room like a fog. "That Nymar was too scared to lie," he said sharply. "We already know we're dealing with a new kind of spore our antidote doesn't hurt. Come to think of it, all the Nymar we killed with that striped shit on 'em was from destroying the heart with our weapons or bullets. The antidote on the rounds don't do shit, so we might as well switch to hollow points."

"That's for later," Paige said. "What about now? What about him?"

"The spore hasn't taken hold yet so that's all we care about. Did you find a way for us to get out of here or not?"

It took Paige a moment to think all the way back to what she'd been doing a few minutes ago. She nodded. "Yeah, I found a route that leads under a place that's either a laundry or clothes store on Erie. Maybe State Street."

"Were cops there?"

"I don't think so."

"Then lead the way and make sure it's clear. I'll take Cole."

"But what about—"

"Shut it, Bloodhound!" Rico barked. "Do what I told you to do. There ain't nothin' else for us right now. We gotta get out of here. That's it. When that's done, we'll see about the rest."

Although visibly upset, annoyed, and scared, Paige nodded. "You need help with him?"

"No. Just go."

She stood up, locked her eyes on Cole for a long couple of seconds, glanced at the gritty remains of the dead Nymar, and then ran down the hall.

"Come on, soldier," Rico grunted. "On your feet."

"You . . . call me Champ . . . or Tough Guy," Cole snarled as a lump the size of a golf ball moved freely within his chest cavity, "and I'll shoot you."

"Don't blame you one bit, sport."

Although the single chuckle that bubbled up from his throat hurt almost as much as getting punched by a set of brass knuckles, Cole was grateful for it.

Chapter Twenty-Four

It was hard enough for Cole to keep his feet moving. Breathing was a chore. Even shifting his weight while dangling from Rico's shoulder like an accessory wrapped up in genuine Full Blood hide strained a body that was still in the process of being ravaged from the inside. When his surroundings became a blur of light, shadow, motion, and stillness, he just let it pass.

There was a long stretch of dusty passages followed by a delightful haul up a ladder that made him want to die.

He thought he saw a bunch of suits hanging on all sides and was assaulted by the smell of industrial detergent. Some curious voices asked a few questions, which Rico deflected long enough to drag him into air that was almost fresh enough to be pleasant.

"Where . . . what?" he grumbled.

"Don't mind him," Rico said to someone outside of Cole's field of vision. "He's drunk. Sorry about that. Must've stumbled in here by mistake. Yeah, I know. He thought this was his apartment. I know! He's drunk, all right?"

Cole couldn't hear the other half of that conversation, but whoever was questioning Rico was left behind once they were both on the sidewalk.

"How you doin'?"

"Either I'm going numb," Cole replied, "or the spore's moving my legs for me. Feels kind of nice."

"Really?" Rico looped a thick arm around Cole's midsection, crushed his ribs and shook him like a giant martini. "What about now?"

"Mother fucking piece of shit stain!"

"He's drunk," Rico explained to someone who was either confused or offended by that nonsensical outburst. Lowering his voice, he added, "Keep trying to move. Remember, pain is good. Means your body's fighting it."

"This goddamn thing's already *in* me! How do I fight that?"

"I don't know. Contract your muscles. Clench. Squeeze. Just do something."

"You guys are supposed to have this long history of fighting vampires, and the best you've got for me is Kegel exercises. You . . . guys really . . ."

"Are you clenching?"

"Yes," Cole sighed grudgingly.

"Is it helping?"

"I . . . suppose."

"Then keep it up. If bitching to me helps, keep that up too."

"What are you going to . . . do?"

Hiking Cole's arm onto his shoulder, Rico got a better grip so he could drag him even faster down the sidewalk. "First I'm going to get you to the corner. And if Paige doesn't come back with the car soon enough, I'm dumping you into a cab."

"No. I mean with me." Gritting his teeth against a new wave of pain, Cole tried not to think about it coming from something that would latch onto his heart and grow to the size of an eel.

Too late.

"What are you gonna do with me?"

Rico hefted him up and over something that could have either been a curb or a sleeping wino and replied, "Honestly?"

"No. Lie to me."

"If you'd turned, one of us would've put you down already and gotten on with the rest of the shit we need to do."

"Thought I told you to lie."

Peeling back his stubble-encrusted lips to reveal uneven, blocky teeth, Rico said, "In that case, you'll be fine."

Not far away, tires screeched, horns blared. and drivers swore at the top of their lungs. One of those cars separated from the metallic blur at the edge of Cole's vision and skidded to a halt after mounting the curb in front of him.

"Taxi's here," Rico calmly said as he opened the car door before dumping Cole inside. It wasn't until Cole flopped over sideways that he realized he was in the back of the car they'd driven from Shimmy's. Before he could hoist himself up again, he was nearly thrown onto the floor as the Dodge lurched forward and thumped back down to street level.

"How is he?" Paige asked from behind the wheel.

"Same as before," Rico told her. "That's a good thing."

"Good thing, my ass."

"Your . . ." Cole groaned.

"What?" Paige looked in the rearview mirror but couldn't see what she wanted to since Cole was still not upright. "What's he saying?"

"That . . . your . . . *is* a good . . ."

"Probably something about your ass being the good thing," Rico said, hitting the nail on the head thanks to the Y chromosome he and Cole shared. "You know this city better than I do. Where can we go for some privacy? We need to take care of him before he gets worse."

"If he gets worse—"

"That's why we need to take care of him. I know what you're thinking, but let's not jump the gun."

The car swerved sharply, but Paige insisted on looking back at Cole instead of whatever it was she'd nearly hit. "Hope's setting me up for something. Maybe setting us all up."

"If she's found a way around tripping the itch in our scars as well as a block for the antidote, I'd hate to think what the hell else she's got going on."

"Cole was right about some of those dead bodies in the Blood Parlor being human. Hope confirmed it."

"And you believe her?"

"Yeah," Paige replied solemnly. "I saw one of them myself. She also said they were cops."

"Jesus," Rico sighed.

"One problem at a time. Cole? What was that thing in the cell the Nymar broke into? Cole!" Paige shouted. "What was stolen from Lancroft's house?"

"Something was ripped from an old Nymar's chest," he replied. "And some shapeshifters set loose whatever was in that end cell."

"You were reading Lancroft's journals. Did he mention what was so special about that dead Nymar?"

Closing his eyes only brought Cole closer to what was happening inside, so he forced them open and stared out the window. "I can't remember. Some of them are on my hard drive, though. The rest are in the trunk of the Cav."

"The Cav's at Pinups. You're sure those journals are in the trunk?"

Blinking some of the murkiness from his eyes, Cole wished he had the strength to hit the button to lower the window. "Yeah. They're one of the things I grabbed when Raza Hill was on fire. Threw 'em in the trunk. E-mailed the recent ones to myself a while ago."

"You said she was a twofer," Rico pointed out.

"A what?"

"A twofer," Paige said as she looked over her shoulder. "Two spore in one Nymar. Two 'fer one. On the rare times when that actually works, it makes them stronger and hungrier. There's no difference with the spore themselves. Any seeds they may produce should be the same as one from any other."

"But the one that seeded Cole wasn't just a twofer," Rico said. "She was one of them stripes as well. The one we questioned brought up evolution. You think they're really forcing some sort of change in the whole Nymar species?"

Paige shook her head and calmly avoided a collision by less than an inch. "I suppose they're about due. Last one I ever read about was . . . damn, I don't even know. Ninety years ago? More? How long do you think that Nymar was sitting in that cell in Lancroft's basement before his chest was ripped open?"

Rico looked straight ahead but didn't see the highway or the other cars Paige was narrowly avoiding. Either that or he was unaffected by such common threats to his life. "You think the old man had that Nymar trapped as a way to keep the species from changing?"

"That's not a bad idea."

"It sure isn't. And Lancroft would wanna keep that carrier alive to study it." The way Rico snapped his fingers and sat up, all he was missing was the oversized lightbulb above his head. "He mighta used that sucker to develop the Mud Flu! I'll be damned!"

"Since I'm already damned," Cole grunted, "would you mind focusing on me until this thing stops burrowing inside of my goddamn chest?"

"Don't be such a drama queen," Paige said. "As soon as I get us somewhere safe, you'll be the center of attention. How's that sound?"

"Where are we going?"

She answered the question, but her voice was drowned out by a groan that emanated from Cole's gut and filled his entire body. His jaw was clenched shut so tightly that he didn't even know if any sound was able to leak out. The spore had found a new place to dig and was exploring freely between his lungs. Alternating between not being able to breathe and not wanting to nudge the burrower inside of him, he gripped the bench seat and stomped his foot so hard against the floorboard that he thought he might stop the car Flintstones style.

Rico turned around and lunged over the passenger seat to grab him, but Cole didn't even feel the big man take hold. He was falling into the abyss that he'd been trying so hard to avoid. What he felt next didn't hurt as bad as the last wave, but only because it sent him into unconsciousness.

"Hang on!" Rico shouted. "Just a little longer!"

Cole might have been able to cling to the waking world, but at that moment he just didn't want to.

His senses returned as if they were attached to a dimmer switch, slowly filling him up before becoming harsh. The pressure he felt on his chest was warm and not too heavy. It shifted slightly, reminding him of a pleasant series of dreams he'd been having ever since he grew closer to Paige. The pain inside him had stopped moving. A sharp pinch jabbed inside his chest. Nothing new. It helped that there was still enough fog in his head for him to view the discomfort from a distance.

"He's waking up."

That was Rico's voice.

Or maybe not.

It was definitely a male. Now that his vision was clearing, Cole could tell the weight on his chest was a figure and the figure was definitely not male. If not for the shorter hair, he might have thought it was Paige. The curves were the same. Just letting his eyes wander along the swell of her breasts and the tight musculature of her arms and shoulders made him think of so many things. Then he remembered Paige's hair. She'd cut it.

"Oh," Cole sighed. "It is you."

"Yeah," Paige said. "It's me."

"What are you doing?"

She reached for something over her head. Maybe she'd gotten him somewhere like a hospital or some sort of safe house that had the equipment needed to remove the spore. He hadn't heard about any equipment like that, but that didn't mean Skinners didn't have it. They had a lot of cool things he didn't know about.

Paige was straddling his chest.

She was looking down at him.

She wasn't about to let anything happen to him.

It felt nice.

"Cole," She said.

"Yes?"

"I'm sorry."

The piece of equipment in her hand extended to a point while giving off a low creaking sound. When he focused on it, he realized it was the stake she'd taken from Lancroft's place to replace the sickle she'd lost in her fight with him. The weapon only had a few coats of varnish worked into the grain, and the thorns were still freshly cut to bond with her. It would take a while for her to craft it into anything nearly as versatile as her old baton, but her will was strong enough to narrow the whittled-down point into something sharp enough to punch a hole through him as well as the floor beneath him. Judging by the way she poised her arm above him, that's exactly what she intended to do.

Cole forced his eyes open and fought to see through them. It took him long enough to wake up under normal circumstances, but his current state only added more layers of muck to slog through before he finally could see clearly. The surge of adrenaline snapped him to the point where he made out every carved line on the stake in Paige's hand as well as every glistening tear running down her cheeks.

"Whoa!" he said. "What the . . . *what*?"

A pair of thick hands pushed his shoulders to the floor and held him there. "Damn it, Paige. I told you we shoulda done this when he was still out."

"I know what you told me," she said.

"You want me to do it?"

Her face took on a ferocity that Cole had only seen directed at an attacker. Even being on the periphery of that wasn't the most comfortable place. "No!" she snarled. "If it's gotta be done, I'm the one that's going to do it." As she shifted her eyes back to Cole, the fiery quality melted away and was replaced by a soft, chocolaty color he'd admired so many times before.

"The spore is attaching to your heart, sweetie," she said. "We gave you all the antidote we can give you. We injected you with enough serum to put you on cloud nine for a week. None of it's doing any good. That Nymar was right. There's something different about this one."

"But if I had a sample," someone squawked from another part of the room, "there are tests to be done and maybe—"

"Can you run the tests before this thing takes root?" Rico asked.

A rounded face looked down at Cole. It scrunched up in a contemplative scowl, allowing his mouth to hang open and one of his top fangs to slide lazily from his gums. A few strands of hair hung down, which he swiped back with one hand to plaster it onto a scalp already marked by black tendrils crossing from one side to another like a tattoo of a bad comb-over.

"Daniels?" Cole muttered.

The Nymar had worked with the Skinners on several occasions, trading his services as a scientist and status as a vampire for protection from the Chicago bloodsuckers who already had it out for him due to several matters that Daniels never wanted to talk about. Normally, the Nymar was one of the more pleasant of his species. Today, however, he looked at Cole as if he was a sample, and couldn't do so for more than a second. "Don't know," he said. "How long has it been since he was seeded?"

"Maybe an hour," Rico said.

"There's no markings showing up yet," Daniels replied hopefully. "That's a good sign."

Paige hadn't taken her eyes off of him. "Check his chest."

Daniels's hands were soft and squishy compared to the ones that had been dragging or pushing him around. Since Cole's coat was already off and his shirt open, all Daniels needed to do was pull aside a few flaps of material to get a look at the skin underneath. He set a pair of glasses on the end of his nose and studied him for a second. "Ahhhh. There they are."

"How bad is it?" When nobody acknowledged the question, Cole struggled to get out from under the weight that held him in place. "I'm the one with the thing in his chest so tell me how fucking bad it is!"

Daniels's eyes flicked up to look at him before darting down again. "Hold on," was all he said before disappearing from sight.

Any other time, Cole wouldn't have complained about Paige's face and upper body being the only things he could see. The stake in her hand took some of the fun out of it, however. "What the hell did I miss?"

"You know what happened, Cole. We've been doing everything we can."

"I thought you got seeded too."

"I did. I even thought this might be a good learning experience for you. Nymar sometimes try to seed us just to slow us down or sometimes just to give us that extra little kick when they can. Our healing serum will heal wounds, but the spore are concentrated Nymar. They're small but tough. A shot or two of the antidote is usually enough to kill it as long as it gets done within ten minutes or so. After that the spore takes root and starts to change you. Your organs, your circulation, everything. That's why our Resurrection Vial comes with a shot of antidote to go along with it. Turning into a Nymar will heal damn near anything, but there's no way to heal the Nymar part. Any Skinner that gets turned has to be hunted and put down before—"

Gritting his teeth against what now felt like a constant gnawing in the middle of his chest, Cole said, "I know that. What about me? This thing is ripping me up and there's nothing you can do?"

"That's just the spore doing its thing. It won't kill you, but it will burrow and move around to where it needs to go. It feeds on blood, so it's got more than enough for it to grow as it moves. Normally, it's not so long before it finds its way to your heart."

"Kind of like Yogi Bear being called to the big pic-i-nic basket," Cole said, and chuckled.

A smile cracked across Paige's face, which also unleashed a short stream of fresh tears. "Yeah. A stupid way to put it, but that's kind of it."

"I'm good with stupid."

"Yes you are."

Paige allowed her arm to drop. Pulling in another breath, she raised it high again and stared down at him with renewed intensity. "The antidote doesn't work on the Nymar with those stripes. It doesn't work on their spore either. I can't let you turn into one of them. I just . . . can't."

"Here we go," Daniels said as he once again stumbled into Cole's sight. Now that the Nymar had something to do, he seemed more like his usual preoccupied self. There was a square plastic plate in his hands, and when he turned it around, he revealed the other side to be a mirror.

The first thing Cole noticed was how bad he looked. His face was never something he fawned over, but it was disconcerting to see just how far it had strayed from his mental self-image. His eyes were sunken and dim. Not bloodshot. Not watery. They simply didn't have the clarity that one would find in eyes that were connected to a living thing. His skin was pale and clammy, which wasn't a surprise. Daniels mercifully angled the mirror down so he could now see the base of his own neck and the upper portion of his chest.

"There," Daniels said while tapping his stubby sausage fingers against Cole's sternum. "See?"

Thin black markings writhed beneath his skin as if someone had dipped a needle into living ink and traced a sparse road map beneath his skin. They weren't as noticeable as the markings of most Nymar but were definitely there, shifting and stretching. If he concentrated, Cole could feel every one of them scraping against the inside of his body like arms from a daddy longlegs reaching for the surface.

"You've been turned, Cole," Daniels said as if talking about a friend of his that had recently died. "If we could have gotten to you before it took hold, we might have—"

"Might have nothing," Paige said in a voice that had been forced from the back of her throat using every bit of strength she had. "He's a Skinner, for Christ's sake. This shouldn't even be happening to him! You saw what happened to me, Cole?"

The memory of Paige doubled over and punching the ground back in the tunnels seemed like one he'd picked up a decade ago, but it was there. He must have nodded because Paige nodded back and continued.

"Hope may have seeded me to slow me down or she may have just wanted to pay me back for old times," she said. "This was different. That other Nymar could have killed you. Instead, she held on so she could do this. We're going to find out why."

Cole had become transfixed with the reflected image of

the wriggling tendrils in his chest. Even though he could feel them, the sensations moved in a different pattern than what he saw. There were overlapping intrusions, fibers pushing his organs aside while wrapping around others. The lump in his chest slid along the side of his heart to cup it like a smooth, confident hand while stretching ever outward, digging deeper.

"I might be able to find out something if I ask some people," Daniels offered.

"It'll be too late by then," Paige said. "It'll be too late an hour from now."

"But I'm not dying," Cole said. "I'll just . . ."

"You'll just grow three sets of fangs and start craving blood," Paige stated without any visible trace of emotion. "You'll become one of the things we hunt."

"I can still be a Skinner."

"You mean like the Nymar that work with those Toronto assholes?" she asked. "They betrayed us. They betrayed all of us. They may have driven every Skinner in this country underground. No Skinner in their right mind will trust a Nymar to join their ranks again."

The mirror being held above Cole's chest wavered as the man behind it nervously cleared his throat.

"You too, Daniels," she said. "I don't suspect you had anything to do with this, but we'll have to watch our backs."

"Even more than I do now?"

"Yes."

The mirror was pulled away and Daniels looked down at Cole to show him a vaguely apologetic shrug. Suddenly, his eyes widened. "Maybe I could get it out of him!"

"Yeah!" Cole said. "Maybe he can get it out of me!"

Although he couldn't see Rico, Cole could feel thick hands tightening on his shoulders as if they couldn't decide whether they were comforting him or making sure he didn't squirm his way off the chopping block. "Once the tendrils start to show, it's too late. That means it's found its spot and is making itself at home."

"I've seen it happen, Cole," Paige said quietly. "And I won't see it happen to you." Without another word or even another breath, Paige dropped the hammer that she'd been holding over him.

Cole knew what she was capable of. He knew what kind of woman Paige was. He'd seen her throw herself into battles that would have made anyone else run for cover. Even with all of that in mind, knowing as much as he did about what crawled around the dark corners of the world and how much else could be out there, he was shocked to see that weapon come toward his chest.

There was no hesitation in Paige's movement.

There was no trace of anything clouding her judgment.

There was no pity in her eyes.

Sorrow, but no pity.

Perhaps she wanted him to see as much because she kept her eyes open for every, eternally long fraction of a second it took for her to stab him with the crude weapon. He also saw the angry surprise that twisted her features when he managed to grab her wrist with both hands before she could drive the stake home.

When he strained to hold her back, Cole felt a jolt of strength delivered to the muscles in his arms. Even with that, he wasn't able to stop her before the tip of the stake punctured his torso. Stopped well short of her goal, Paige closed her eyes and leaned in to put even more of her weight behind the stake.

"What are you doing?" he shouted.

Rather than answer him, she clenched her eyes shut even tighter and turned away.

"Give me a chance," Daniels pleaded.

"We've been talking about this for almost half an hour and you haven't come up with a chance to save him," she said. "I'm not letting him turn. Even if he would become a regular Nymar, it wouldn't be worth it."

"What's wrong with being a regular Nymar? I function as one! I'm trustworthy. Maybe it's just the seeding process that's altered. You don't have to—"

"Don't tell me what I have to do!"

It was all Cole could do to keep the stake from going in any farther. More strength was coming from somewhere, but he knew it was more than his body could offer. He could barely even feel his arms anymore. His muscles were ready to snap off the bone and roll up like cheap window shades.

The spore had stopped moving.

It had stopped digging.

It was part of him.

Paige was right. He'd been seeded for a purpose, and now he knew what it was. The Nymar had a weapon to use against the Skinners that was almost as good as the antidote used against them.

Although he now had the strength to push her back even farther, he resisted the urge to use it. The very thought of becoming what he'd seen prowling the alleys and spitting from the shadows sickened him. If he was going to have to be put down, then at least Paige would be the one to—

"Tell me once more what time he was seeded and maybe I can extrapolate how far along the process is," Daniels mumbled.

When Paige ran down the facts again, she did so as if rattling off diagnostic statistics for a car repair. Her weapon remained partially embedded in Cole's chest. He held onto her and didn't want to let go.

"If it's been as long as you say and he still hasn't developed the first gum pocket yet . . . Umm, has he developed the first gum pocket?"

"Check him, Rico."

The rough hands pinning Cole's shoulders lifted, only to be immediately shoved into his mouth. Cole's jaw was pried open and he was given a real good taste of everything Rico had touched in the last few hours as the big man's fingers roughly felt beneath his upper and lower lips near each set of canine teeth. When the fingers were yanked out again, the hands slapped back down against Cole's shoulders.

"Nope," Rico said. "Don't feel anything yet."

Straining to look up far enough to see Rico, Cole said, "I would've opened my mouth on my own, you know!"

The rough hands slapped Cole's shoulder reassuringly.

Finally, Paige let go of her weapon with one hand so she could gently pull it up and out of Cole's grasp. "Right before your guts get melted down and turned into insect paste—"

"That's far from accurate," Daniels said. "It's more of a process whereby—"

Since Paige hadn't looked away from him, Cole could only imagine Rico was the one giving Daniels the death stare to shut him up.

"Right before that happens," she continued, "a space in your jaws for the fangs will be hollowed out. Once the spore changes too much of you, even if we can find a way to get it out, you won't be able to use what's left. Understand?"

"I'm infected and stabbed," Cole told her. "Not deaf."

"What can you do for him, Daniels?"

"Ummm . . . *do* for him?"

"You said he had more time," she snapped. "So what do we do? Can you get this thing out of him or not?"

"I've never attempted it. I've thought about it a few times." Daniels's face reappeared on the periphery of Cole's vision. He had seen the balding Nymar work through enough difficult propositions to recognize the various stages of expression that accompanied his thought processes. At the moment, Daniels appeared to be somewhere between Stumped and Curious.

"I suppose I could make an incision to try and extract the spore," Daniels said.

"It's on his heart," Rico said. "Wouldn't you have to cut through a lot of bone?"

"Not if I go in between the ribs."

Cole shifted even more. "Wait a second! Are you a surgeon?"

Daniels rubbed his chin and held his hand beneath his nose as if smelling the side of it helped him think. "I can guesstimate where the spore would be by now with some degree of accuracy and go in with some tools that wouldn't require much of an incision."

"Guesstimate?" Cole bellowed. "That's something my high school shop teacher used to say, not a heart surgeon!"

The reassuring pat once more slapped against Cole's shoulder. "Relax, Champ. It ain't like he can put you in any worse condition than you already are."

"But he doesn't know what he's doing!"

"True," Paige said as she held her stake just high enough to catch Cole's attention. "But I know exactly what I'm doing. Want me to continue or him?" Since she didn't get much from Cole, she said, "Good. Daniels, what if we can get the spore to come out to us?"

"How do you propose we do that?" the Nymar asked with a laugh that was equal parts chuckle and snort. "Give it something it really wants?"

Paige slowly smiled and eased the stake back into the holster stitched into her boot. "Pack up what you need to get this done. You're coming with us."

Chapter Twenty-Five

The drive from Schaumberg to West Chicago felt a lot longer to Cole than the one that had brought them to Schaumberg from Rush Street. That was mostly attributed to the fact that he was conscious this time around. Also, every bump in the Veteran's Memorial Tollway was marked by a jab from the needle that Rico used to stitch the wound in his chest.

"Son of a bitch!" Cole yelped as Paige bounced across another pothole. "Can't you just leave it alone? The serum in my system should close that up, shouldn't it?"

"The serum was all used up by keeping the spore from attaching to your heart," Rico pointed out. "And this wound was made by one of our weapons. They're not something a Full Blood can bounce back from right away, so how fast do you think you're gonna heal up from it?"

"Can you at least wait until we stop for a minute?"

Rico pressed one hand down onto Cole's chest to keep him still while giving the needle a few quick tugs. "I could," he said evenly. "But I won't." As if to prove he was a man of his word, Rico continued stitching even as Paige ran onto the bumpy shoulder of the road while passing a red sports car.

"We're on our way now," she said into her cell phone. "I need at least one of you there, and then we'll have to travel afterward." Shaking off Daniels's insistent tapping from the passenger seat, she said, "I'm not sure where we're going yet. I need to make another phone call. Oh, and I'm going to have to ask a favor of one of you girls. I need Dryad blood . . . No, it doesn't matter who donates it. I may need a lot, though."

Cole had heard the bare bones of the plan while being taken from Daniels's apartment. It had to do with an incident a while ago, when Tristan—one of the hottest women he'd ever seen—revealed that she was not only a nymph, but a Dryad, which apparently ranked higher on the "mythological hottie" scale. She also claimed that Nymar spore preferred infecting human hosts as opposed to any other creature with a beating heart because Dryad blood was the most magically delicious treat there was. Considering the package in which it was wrapped, Cole didn't have trouble believing it. And considering that he only had a few hours before his entire existence was to be written off as a lost cause, he was willing to take another frantic drive out to Pinups.

"No, I don't know exactly how much we'll need!" Paige said. Turning toward Daniels, she asked, "How much will we need?"

"I've never done this. How should I know?"

Glaring at the Nymar hard enough to make him press back against his door, Paige said, "Better have a couple of donors ready . . . Yes, it's important, and you *owe* us. In fact, call Tristan and tell her Cole's life depends on this." After that, she hung up as forcefully as her thumb on a button could manage and stuffed the phone into her pocket.

"There," Rico said as he pulled the last stitch taut and hastily tied it off. "That'll hold for as long as you need."

Now that he was able to sit up without leaking, Cole flopped into the corner between the backseat and the door. He looked down at the stitches and said, "I've seen sock puppets sewn together better than this."

"If this don't work, you won't be alive to see tomorrow," Rico said with complete certainty. "Those stitches'll hold that long at least. Maybe even a little longer. I'd like to see you do a better job in the back of a moving car."

"You feeling all right, Cole?" Paige asked.

Normally, the sight of her eyes reflected back at him from the rearview mirror would have been enough to give him some comfort. This time, not so much. Rather than get into that, he replied, "No."

"Tough. Call Prophet and see what he knows about those Nymar in Denver. You were right about them being our next stop. If they've been making trouble this long, it makes sense they'd be hooked into what's going on now."

"Why can't you call him?"

"Because I'm busy figuring out a way to keep you alive. What the hell's your problem?"

"You tried to kill me!"

"I'd expect you to do the same for me."

"I'm thinking about it." Rico tried to pull him back by the shoulder, but Cole shoved the big man away. "After all we've been through, I've got to lump you in with all the other things out there trying to rip me apart?"

"If it's between that or letting you turn into a Nymar? You bet your ass." Shooting a quick glance over to Daniels, she added, "No offense."

Daniels was a smart guy, which meant he waved off the comment without a word.

Apparently, Rico had a similar idea. "You two go on ahead," he said. "I'll call Prophet."

"I won't let you turn, Cole," Paige told him. "Why would you ever think I'd let something like that happen to you?"

"What about what we're doing right now?" Cole asked. "If I hadn't stopped you, we never would have gotten this far. You would've just killed me, wrapped me up in some plastic bags, and then what? Salvaged me for parts? Dumped me in a hole like you do with the leftovers you can't use from all those Half Breed carcasses?"

"You're upset, Cole. I get it. Just calm down and try not to make things worse."

"Worse?"

"The spore is exerting a lot of energy right now," Daniels explained. "It's feeding where it can, and if you get all worked up or excited, it'll make your heart beat faster and add adrenaline to the mix. Feeding all of that to—"

"Yeah, yeah. I get it," Cole grunted as he dropped back into his seat.

Accustomed to being cut off in mid-sentence, Daniels shrugged and looked out the window to let the Skinners settle things among themselves.

Apart from Rico's conversation with Prophet, it wound up being a quiet ride across town.

When they arrived at Pinups, Daniels, Paige, and Rico carried Cole, along with various supplies bundled beneath coats and tucked under arms to keep them out of sight. The security guys at the door wouldn't stop Skinners if they were carrying tactical nukes under their jackets, but there were still customers to worry about, so they moved as discreetly as possible to a large supply room.

The space was smaller than a bedroom but larger than a closet, and partially filled with boxes of paper towels, plastic cups, and stacks of chairs. Rico grabbed one of the chairs, set it down in the middle of the floor, and dropped Cole onto it. "You all right?" he asked.

Cole winced and grabbed his chest with both hands. "I think you just shook something loose."

"Does it pinch inside or do you just wanna puke?"

"Feels like I got hit in the lungs with a baseball bat. And now that you mention it, I may actually have to puke."

"As long as it's not pinching yet, you're good."

Next to come through the door were Daniels, Paige, and two dancers dressed in their work clothes. One wore a mini-skirt that could have been made from a few strips of black tape wrapped around her hips, the other clad in the same shade of purple she'd worn almost every other time Cole had seen her. It brought out the glimmer in her eyes and the luscious texture of her lips. It was Tristan, and unlike those other times, she did not seem pleased to see him.

"What's this I hear about you wanting our blood?" the Dryad asked. "Isn't it enough that we send you and all the other Skinners back and forth across the country with no questions asked? Do you have any idea how long it takes us to collect the amount of energy we've been using for that?"

"Cole's in trouble," Paige said. "The rest can wait."

Tristan looked at him through narrowed eyes. "Are those Nymar tendrils?"

"Yep. Hence the whole trouble and rushing over here thing."

"What can I do for him?"

"Remember what you said about Dryad blood being the sweetest thing any Nymar's ever tasted?" Paige asked.

"Yes."

"Was that true?"

Tristan drifted close enough to Cole for him to smell the intoxicating blend of aromas in her hair. He tended to close his eyes when pulling in a breath like that, almost as if sniffing a pan of hot brownies. The thought of sinking his teeth into Tristan had always been at the front of his mind, but in a sociable context. This time he felt an urge that snapped his eyes open and nearly brought him to his feet with his teeth bared.

"Whoa there, cowboy!" Rico said as he shoved him back down again. "You're gonna get us thrown out of here."

The Dryad's clothes were loose fitting, secured with a dark ribbon wrapped around her waist like the final touch of the greatest Christmas present ever conceived. Even as she hopped away from Cole's seat, the filmy material somehow managed to cover her breasts and hips. "He's not fully changed," she said. "No fangs."

Paige stepped between Tristan and Cole while saying, "I know. The process is slow, but we can't stop it. We want to get that spore out of him."

"Is that even possible?"

Since Cole was still restless, Paige drew her machete and held it flat against his chest, more as a restraint than a cutting tool. "That's what we came to find out. Daniels thinks he can extract the spore if he can get it away from Cole's heart. And the best chance of getting it away from his heart is to make it come out on its own. We're hoping we might be able to get it to poke its ugly little face into the open for the chance to get something every growin' boy wants."

"You," Daniels said as he unrolled one of the kits he kept

wrapped in canvas and leather so it was always ready to travel. "She means you. Can we please hurry?"

"Yes," Tristan said while wrapping her flimsy outfit around her a little tighter. "Have you ever tried anything like this before?"

Daniels removed a scalpel from his kit and scraped his thumb against the blade to test its edge. Rubbing away the blood that swelled up from the little cut he'd made, he replied, "There's normally not enough time to try anything like this. Under regular circumstances, the spore would have either been too small to notice any external stimulus or too entrenched to detach without killing the host. This is a special case."

"It's a case that shouldn't have happened," Rico snarled. "Do you feel that?"

Paige shifted her attention to the door leading out to the main room. "Yeah. Either that spore is growing real quickly or there are more Nymar close by. The old-fashioned kind."

Letting out a quick, impatient breath, Tristan looked to the other Dryad that had accompanied her into the storage room and said, "Get the rest of our sisters back here and send one of the regular girls to see if there are any Nymar in the club."

"What about him?" the other Dryad asked.

"I'll do what I can for Cole. If my blood's not enough to get the job done, yours won't make any difference." To Paige, she added, "I'm willing to do my part, but you people better not get used to storming in here and demanding us to sacrifice ourselves this way."

"Fair enough," Paige said. "You ready?"

"What do you need me to do?"

Daniels approached her with a hypodermic needle. "I'll start by collecting a sample and we'll go from there. If I need more, I'll let you know."

Extending an arm and nodding resolutely, Tristan said, "Do it before I change my mind."

He took the blood quickly and handed it to Paige.

Cole removed his shirt, turned around so his chest was against the back of the chair, and stretched his arms out. After twisting Cole's shirt into a thick strap, Rico used it to tie his wrists together. He then pulled up another chair so he could face Cole and get a firm grip on his arms. "You ready for this?"

"Does it matter?" Cole asked.

"Suppose not. Get to it."

"I brought anesthetic," Daniels said.

"Is there a chance it may slow down the spore?" Rico asked.

"Perhaps, but I can't be certain."

"Then skip it," Paige said. "He can take the pain."

Cole looked over to her, unsure whether he should be flattered or angry at the cavalier way she sentenced him to the agony of his torso being sliced open. Since there was already enough fire in his gut without adding any more, he settled on flattery.

In movies this would have been the part where he was given a bullet to bite, a wallet to chew, or maybe a shot of whiskey to throw down. Instead, he got a jolt of cold from the gel Daniels smeared on his ribs followed by a deep cut from a very sharp piece of steel. Cole's eyes widened, and when he started to move, Rico pulled his arms so his chest was mashed against the chair's back rest.

"Does that—"

Cutting Daniels off sharply, Paige said, "Shut up and keep going."

Cole didn't hear anything specific from then on. Every noise blended together until voices from within the room, music from the oversized sound system, and everything else became a singular entity filling his ears. Pain spread like a fire from his left side, and spread in every direction.

"Give me the syringe," Daniels said.

Cole heard movement, felt something warm spray against his skin, and then felt the cut in his side widen with a few more slices at either end. There was more warmth, which seeped onto his wound and somehow made it feel cooler. He started to wobble and almost passed out before realizing he hadn't drawn a full breath since his hands had been bound. Taking too deep a breath proved to be a mistake, however, and strained his incision.

"Shorter huffs, Cole," Rico said. "Like this."

Cole's arms were pulled taut and the big man demonstrated breathing in short, controlled bursts. "What's next?" he asked through the pain that chewed through him all the way down to his spine. "You're going to tell me to push until the baby crowns?"

"How about I tell you to do this on yer own? You'd like that better?"

"No."

"Then bear down!"

Both of them laughed at that, which was the only thing distracting Cole from the sincere wish that he were dead.

"Cut it open wider, Daniels," Paige said. "It's trying to close it."

"No," Cole wheezed. "It isn't. I can . . . feel . . ."

"It's moving," Daniels said.

"Yeah. That's what I feel. Jesus, I don't know if I'm gonna make it through this." When Cole looked over at Paige, he saw her squatting like a baseball catcher and holding her machete sideways so the flat of the blade was under his ribs like a shelf.

She squirted the last of the syringe's contents onto the side of her machete and waggled it beneath a set of oily black tendrils that oozed out from the incision Daniels was widening. The balding Nymar had his sleeves rolled up and was now using both hands to pry apart the thick sections of fleshy meat between Cole's ribs. Seeing that, combined with feeling it, Cole's most recent breath leaked out in a wavering current.

"Come on, Cole, don't pass out on me." Rico then leaned over and asked, "Is there a problem if Cole passes out?"

Daniels didn't look away from the incision even as he reached to his kit for different pieces of equipment. "As long as he stays still, there's no problem."

"Okay, then," Rico said to Cole. "Switching gears. Go ahead and pass out. Just think about a better place."

When the thing inside him moved, Cole felt as though his vital organs had suddenly gotten a desire to look for a more fulfilling existence in another part of the country. "This *is* the kind of better place I would imagine," he snapped. "Thanks to you assholes, the whole strip bar thing is ruined for me now!"

"Can you get ahold of that thing yet?" Tristan asked.

Daniels shook his head and continued working.

Reaching over to the kit, Tristan grabbed a scalpel and placed it against her forearm. "Get ready to do whatever you need to do because you're not going to get a better shot than this." With that, she made a diagonal slice across her forearm that opened a long, bloody gash that was shallow enough to avoid slicing a major artery. Pulling in a deep breath, she closed her eyes, turned her head away and held her arm down to Cole's side.

Almost immediately, the tendrils reached out for her. They caressed her arm and encircled it, leaving a trail of slime that came from its own body as well as Cole's. As gentle as a lover's touch, the tendrils slid beneath her skin.

"Whatever you're going to do," Tristan said, "do it quickly. It's feeding on me."

Cole was awake, but just barely. He'd almost lost the strength necessary to keep his head up and eyes open.

"Pull your arm back," Paige said. "Can you do that?"

"I . . . don't know," Tristan replied.

Rather than make her answer another question, Paige handed the machete to Daniels and rushed to get behind her. With one hand gripping Tristan's arm and the other wrapped around the Dryad's upper body, Paige leaned back to ease her away from Cole.

"There's a lot of tendril here," Daniels said squeamishly. "I don't know how long it may be before— Oh, shit!"

That might have been the first time Cole had heard Daniels swear. In his current state of mind, it struck him as amusing.

"It's leaving him," Daniels said.

Rico maintained a steady pressure on Cole's arms, keeping them taut so there was no slack or space between his chest and the chair. "You're sure it's the spore and not just tendrils?"

"I think it's the spore."

"You think?"

"I've never seen one alive in this condition. It's . . . yes . . . it's got to be the spore. It's looking at me."

When Cole heard that, his mind filled with all the possible faces a creature like that could have. He'd seen spore when they were dead and decaying. He'd seen them getting pulled out of a living Nymar. Not once had he thought about a spore seeing him. Having designed gross little creatures for any number of video games during his normal life in Seattle, he couldn't stop thinking of what this one might look like. Soon, he was drowning in his own creative juices and slouching forward against the chair.

"It's feeding off you?" Paige asked.

Tristan nodded fiercely. The color was draining from her face and she struggled to keep the corners of her mouth from trembling as she formed her words. "I can feel it. The tendrils are inside. They're pulling me open."

The spore had no teeth but was able to saw into her flesh the way a single piece of paper could break the skin. Tiny slits formed along its surface, opening in what could have been eyes or even mouths filled with a dark, viscous gel.

"Daniels, is it drinking the blood off of my weapon?"

He handled the spore with shaking, fumbling hands. Trying to grab hold of it that way was like trying to serve Jell-O with chopsticks. "Yes," he said. "It's absorbing it."

"Then it's holding onto it, right?"

"I suppose so." Then the proper synapses within his head fired. "Yes! Give me something else to use. Something about the same shape as this weapon."

Rico reached under his jacket and pulled out a hunting knife with a blade that was nearly a foot long. "How about this?"

Daniels took the knife and wiped it across Tristan's bleeding arm. "That should do." Before he could prepare any more, tendrils wrapped around the blade of the knife, and slid against the Dryad blood, then quickly pulled away before being cut open. "Okay," he said. "Ease her back. Just try not to let it get away."

"I don't think that's going to be a problem," Tristan said

through a strained breath. The muscles in her face twitched and the ones in her arm jumped, but she refrained from pulling away. Just to be sure, Paige remained to help keep her arm steady.

Daniels worked with both arms now. As tendrils continued to reach out of Cole, he wound them around both the machete and the knife. Slowly, the larger mass of the spore extended its body out through the incision in Cole's side. Daniels looked down at it without really trying to ingest the sight. Its inky black body was pressed into an almost flat shape so it could get to the source of the Dryad blood. Whatever features it had were only dark and light spots corresponding to dents and welts along its surface. When a wet, sucking sound turned into something close to a squeal, Daniels trapped the thing between the two weapons just to shut it up.

"Here it is!" he said. "Help me!"

Taking hold of the machete so the thorns impaled her palm, Paige summoned every bit of willpower she had to raise several barbs of wood along the side of the weapon. When she pulled the machete away from Cole, the barbs snagged the spore like so many fishing hooks.

"Careful!" Daniels said. "If you shred its skin, it'll only pull back and heal. There's more than enough blood for it to reform."

Cole knew his senses might not have been fully alert, but he could feel it when that much of the spore was ripped out of him. He was able to lean forward, allow his back to slump, and to take a full breath without it hurting, all of which had been difficult to do before. When the pain and discomfort eased, he almost wanted it back just so he could experience the rapture of it stopping again.

"Quick," Daniels said as he fumbled with his kit. "I may not be able to do any more than this."

Paige pulled until the thickest black mass was out of Cole's side. Rico stood up and stuck his fingers through the webbing of tendrils extending into Cole's body and forced the spore out even farther. Once she had it trapped, Paige squeezed the weapons together like she was cracking a lobster's shell.

The spore let out a squeal that tore through Cole's ears and chest at the same time. It lingered like a squawk of feedback from one of the club's speakers, making it difficult for him to decide if he was actually hearing it or if the sound was somehow being projected into his mind. With Nymar, it was never safe to assume either one.

As Daniels continued to spool the tendrils out of him, Cole felt queasy. It reminded him of blowing his nose, only to discover that one string of snot went all the way down his sinuses to his throat. It had to be removed, but part of him wished he could just put it back and forget about it.

"Got it!" Paige announced. "Stand back, Daniels." When the Nymar didn't move fast enough, she shoved him away and pulled the machete until the tendrils became taut.

"There's too much left inside," Daniels insisted. "You'll need to sever it!"

"I heard that," Rico grunted as he used his free hand to draw the same blade that had recently been in a vampire's eye socket. While moving the spore's jellyfish body away, he cut through most of the oily mesh in one swipe.

The spore was breaking apart in the middle. Only one or two strands remained before part of its body would snap back into Cole, where it could disappear into his warmth. Rico swung the knife in a sharp upward slash, twisted it around and brought it down again. Once the remaining tendrils were severed, half the mass of oily black flesh splattered onto the floor, while the remainder dangled from Paige's hand.

She squashed it between the weapons in her hands and dropped it to the floor so Rico could slam his boot down onto both halves with almost enough force to drive them into the foundation of the club.

"All right," he said. "I need a drink. Who wants to join me?"

Chapter Twenty-Six

Rico had his drink, and didn't have it alone. Paige sat with him in another back room at Pinups, a utility room where the strobe lights couldn't obscure their vision, the stages were out of sight, and the music wasn't loud enough to rattle the ice in their glasses. Daniels paced near a wall of pipes and gauges that fed into the building's water and gas supply. The scent of grease overpowered the fragrances of the girls in the nearby dressing rooms, making the club feel like it was in another part of town.

"They're still here, aren't they?"

Ignoring the question, Rico sipped from his scotch and let it trickle down his throat with a strained breath.

Swirling her vodka on the rocks before downing the rest of it, Paige said, "Yeah. They're still here."

"What are they doing?" Daniels asked. "How did they know we were even here?"

"Just relax," Rico snapped. "Tristan's checking on it right now. In fact," he added as someone rapped lightly on the door, "that's probably her now."

The door was pushed open and Tristan stepped inside, conveniently accompanied by Aerosmith's "Walk This Way." The practiced smile on her face was quickly dropped when she said, "There's two Nymar in the club. I don't know if they know you're here or not, but they don't want to leave."

"Have you tried kicking them out?" Paige asked. "Maybe say one of them touched you or something? That worked well enough to get him tossed on his ass." She hooked a thumb toward Cole, who sat on the floor in the corner, nestled among a tangle of old pipes wrapped in insulation and duct tape. His head hung down and his arms were perched upon his bended knees, making him look more like a robot that had been unplugged and shoved there for easy storage.

"They're not approaching any of the girls," Tristan said. "I doubt they even know there are Dryads here. The perfumes usually mask our scent well enough to hold up until one of them actually sees us. They're ordering drinks, keeping to themselves and not moving. One of the regular girls tried to see what they wanted, but she was sent packing."

Rico grunted. "Then they know we're here. Probably followed us, or maybe they have someone working at the club."

"If they had someone planted here, we'd know about it," Tristan assured them. "They would have already come for me or any other Dryad, just like the Nymar that hunted our sisters in St. Louis. I can get you out of here, but it'll have to be quick. This will also have to be the last time you use our bridges for a while. With everything that's happened tonight, we can't afford to have you seen here."

"It'll blow over," Paige said.

"Blow over?" Tristan's eyelashes fluttered nervously, which was still appealing on a face as beautiful as hers. "Haven't you seen the news? How could you think that would just blow over?"

"We know people were killed," Rico said. "We'll find a way to make that right. I'm waiting for a call that should help us get ahead of the next ones that are being set up."

Tristan placed her hand on the door behind her. She leaned forward and dropped her voice to a whisper like a conspiracy nut who'd gotten a glimpse of an unmarked van with a satellite dish parked outside. "Those people that were killed weren't just people. They weren't Nymar either."

"I know that," Paige said.

"They were cops."

The silence that filled the room was thick enough to block out the music, screaming customers, and the rattle of pipes all around them.

Cole's head snapped up, which made him want to drop it right back down again. The incision in his side was closed, but there was still plenty of pain to remind him it had been there. His strength was returning at a steady pace, which allowed him to croak, "How do you know they were cops?"

"It's all over the news," Tristan told him. "They're saying three police officers were killed when you stormed into a bar on Rush Street and murdered everyone inside before setting it on fire! Is that true?"

The Skinners looked back and forth at each other, as if trying to draw enough strength from one another to deny the claim. Unfortunately, their silence did nothing to help their cause.

Paige's phone rang, causing everyone to jump. She answered it, headed for the door and left the utility room so she could stand in the access hall for some privacy. Ironically, her voice echoed more there than in the room she'd left.

"You killed those people, didn't you?" Tristan asked.

Rico stood up and crossed his arms imposingly. "We kill a lot of people, darlin'. Every one of them Nymar used to be a person. Every Half Breed runnin' around out there used to be a person."

"I'm not asking about them and you damn well know it. Dryads have been worshipped for centuries. The only thing we worship is life. That's why we tried to steer clear of you hunters for so long. Skinners, Amriany, even the outlaws from both sides are all killers. I thought I could trust Paige, Cole, and anyone they would vouch for. This changes everything."

"I know," Rico sighed. "We got set up. The bitch who did it mentioned cops being planted there, but that could have been a line of bullshit meant to shake us up. We don't even know what the fuck any cops were doing in a Blood Parlor.

If they were on a Nymar payroll, then that makes them just as bad as the bloodsuckers."

"They weren't," Daniels said from where he sat on an upside down bucket. Holding Cole's phone in both hands, he shook his head while tapping the touch screen with frenetic thumbs. "I've just checked through the first few stories to pop up on a search, and they all say the same thing: undercover police officers slain in the line of duty."

"Son of a bitch."

"And that's not all. I tried looking up other recent reports of dead undercover officers and got stories from Philadelphia, Toronto, New Orleans, and plenty of other cities big and small. It's so widespread, there's been speculation of terrorist involvement."

"Holy shit," Rico grunted as he pressed his hands against his forehead and ran them all the way to the top of his scalp. "Holy mother-lovin' shit. That means the Feds will get involved. Was there anything else about those other attacks?"

After a bit of backtracking, Daniels found a report from one of the national news agencies and skimmed down to the body of the story. "Looks like there were fires in a few massage parlors, some shoot-outs at private nightclubs, botched raids at some escort agencies . . ."

"All the sort of shit Nymar have their fingers into. Give that phone to Cole. Let him see what else he can find."

Cole was conscious, but not happy about it. A thick layer of sweat glistened on his pasty face. Each exhalation caused his shoulders to sag and his chest to deflate. Every move he made brought another stabbing pain. Although his insides seemed to be working well enough, they had all been pushed around by a parasitic slug. That just wasn't easy to bounce back from.

"You want to take a look, Cole?" Daniels asked.

Still weak, but grateful for something to take his mind off what had happened inside his chest, Cole nodded and accepted the phone from Daniels. Tapping the screen and sifting through the familiar Web pages was a comfortable bit of normalcy no matter how bad the results on those pages might have been.

"Kansas City was hit again," Paige said as she stormed in from the hall.

Tristan stepped aside but watched the Skinners with the closest thing to an angry glare as her perfectly sculpted features could manage.

"More cops killed?" Rico asked grudgingly.

"Cops, civilians, construction workers, firefighters, you name it. Twenty-nine in all."

"Jesus Christ. Tell me those bloodsuckers didn't lure any of us there to do that."

"I don't think the Nymar had anything to do with this. If they did, we're completely screwed."

"What are you talking about?"

When Cole looked up at her, Paige seemed almost as drained as he felt.

She held her phone out and said, "That was MEG who just called. After Liam's siege on Kansas City, all the little paranormal watchdog groups and damn near anyone else has been scouring that place. Kayla's Mongrel pack have been staying underground, but—"

"Just spill it, Paige," Cole said. "We don't have a lot of time here."

"A pack of Full Bloods tore through KC."

"A *pack*?" Rico asked. "As in, more than one?"

"That's what MEG said."

"Sure it wasn't just one and some Half Breeds again?"

"There are pictures," Paige replied. "Lots of pictures. They're spreading."

Cole sighed. "Where were they headed when they left?" When no answer was forthcoming, he asked, "They're still there?"

She shook her head. "One of them got away. Looks like it was Liam. He was missing an eye. There were two others. MEG put together the reports and sent them all to me, but I got the play-by-play. Kayla's pack herded them away from the city, led the Full Bloods out past the airport, tripped them up and tore them apart. The cops are sifting through it now."

"Cops? As in the KC cops?" Cole asked as he suddenly

found enough energy to get to his feet. "What about Officer Stanze?"

"I talked to him. It was only for a second, but he told me it's over and the emergency crews are cleaning up. After Liam's first siege, Stanze's been getting preferred treatment on all the freaky cases. He saw the bodies. Here," Paige said as she held her phone out so Cole and Rico could see the screen. "See for yourself."

Rico took the phone first, examined the screen and scowled. After holding it up close enough for the illumination to reflect off the rough features of his face, he raised his eyebrows and nodded approvingly. "I'll be damned." Tossing the phone to Cole, he added, "The Mongrels have been giving the Full Bloods hell for centuries, and supposedly took down one or two here and there, but this is the first time I actually seen it with my own eyes."

The picture on the screen was tough for Cole to make out at first. After letting his tired eyes adjust to the seemingly random carnage, he eventually pieced together the carcass lying on a dirty street or sidewalk. Its skin and musculature were obviously not that of a Half Breed. The teeth were much larger and had even ripped through the thing's face in much the same way as Mr. Burkis's fangs shredded his when he was in full upright form. A man stood close enough to the body to provide a sense of scale. While Half Breeds were generally as large as when they'd been human, this creature was even bigger. It could have simply been a larger human, but he didn't think so. He'd killed enough Half Breeds to recognize them when they were sleeping, running, in the shadows, or in pieces. Whatever was in the picture was no Half Breed.

"So, what?" he asked while tossing the phone back to Paige.

"So," she replied, "this means there's one less Full Blood in the world. As far as we know, there may only be half a dozen of them on the planet at any given time. Losing one of them will throw the others into a tizzy as they readjust."

"They'll probably start a war with the Mongrels," Rico said, as if mentioning the possibility of getting free tickets to the Super Bowl. "Kayla's pack took one Full Blood down, so they'll have the taste of blood on their tongues. They may already be out hunting them down as we speak. Either way, we won't need to worry about those shaggy sons of bitches for a while. Considering how busy the Nymar are keepin' us, that's a goddamn blessing. We may even be able to get some pointers from Kayla in dropping the big boys."

Paige looked at her phone again as though seeing the picture for the first time. "You don't know how huge this is, Cole. This may even be Mr. Burkis we're looking at. The coloring on the coat is right. There haven't been any other Full Bloods spotted in these parts that I know of other than him and Liam. Kayla may have just cleared out an entire territory."

"And what if it isn't Burkis?"

"Then Rico's still right. The shapeshifter community will be in ten kinds of upheaval, and we can scratch them off the list for a while. We don't get to scratch many things off our list, Cole. You should learn to enjoy it when it happens."

"So what's next on the list?"

"That Nymar from the tunnels said Hope and the rest of them were headed out to Denver, Boston, Miami, and . . . somewhere else."

"San Antonio," Rico said.

"That's right." Cole's thumbs flew over his phone's screen as he tapped through several different Web pages. "And as far as I can tell, none of those cities have been hit in this crime wave."

"So that could mean Hope was heading out there to get the ball rolling." For the first time in what seemed like a decade, Paige grinned. "Sounds like a good prospect for 'Next on the List.'" Slipping into the kung fu master voice she'd used for a good portion of their weapons training, she added, "I see the pupil is finally worthy of his teacher."

Cole barely looked at her before dryly replying, "Yeah. Sure." When he arrived at the right note in his phone's planner, he sat up a little straighter and turned it around in case anyone else wanted to examine the screen. "Prophet's boss, Stan Velasco, already knows about these Denver Nymar and will *pay* us to bring them in. Not only does he have information we don't already have, but his men aren't Skinners, so they probably flew under their radar."

"Screw that," the big man snarled. "Last thing I wanna do is bring a Nymar in. It was too much fun gouging that striped bitch's eye out. After tonight, I'm comin' around to Lancroft's thinking. Only good bloodsucker is a dead one. No offense, Daniels."

The balding Nymar tossed an offhanded wave at the Skinners and said, "I've learned to stop taking offense to what you guys say a long time ago. Keeps my nose from being permanently out of joint."

"But some Skinner somewhere would have put a red flag on Hope by now if they knew she was gathering this sort of a following, right?" Cole asked hopefully.

Unfortunately, Rico could only grunt, "Not necessarily."

"Do we at least know something about the Denver Nymar?" Cole asked.

"I've done a little checking since Prophet's been talking them up and found out they're into a lot of different things," Paige told him, "but nothing worth the trip to put them all down. They are organized enough to be ready for an attack."

"How can you be sure about that?"

"Because there used to be a Skinner who worked in the Rockies," Rico said. "Went missing some time ago—and before you ask, yeah, that is pretty common. Also before you ask, yeah, it mighta been the Denver Nymar who did it."

Cole tapped his phone some more as he said, "So they've been busy and have still managed to keep from being taken out by Skinners. Sounds to me like they're more organized than you think."

"What do you mean by that?" Paige asked.

"Well, we've got MEG. What's keeping the Nymar from using some sort of hub for their communications?"

"They're all over the Internet," she reminded him.

"But those are just the sites we know about. If anyone's going to put a system like that to use, it's going to be someone with plenty of reason to want to stay hidden." Jabbing a thick finger at Cole, Rico said, "I like the way this boy thinks."

"And not only that," Cole continued, "Denver was mentioned as a stopping point for Hope, and she obviously hasn't set off whatever's about to pop there. If it's anything like what's already happened, there's bound to be more innocent humans there to take a fall. Possibly more cops. And if we're right about any of what they're doing, the Nymar are going to want to make this public."

"Or," Paige said, "it's a trap."

"They fucked us good," Rico sighed. "Got us to stop looking for markings, jammed the place with bloodsuckers so we couldn't tell who was who, even got us riled up enough to go in guns blazing. Not that that's tough to do, right, Bloodhound?"

"Yeah, you got me there," she snapped. "What was it you got arrested for again?"

Dancing around that particular land mine, Rico said, "We fell into a trap, so Denver's probably a trap that just ain't been sprung yet."

"We deal with plenty of traps," Cole said. "We set them up. We set them off. We stumble into them like idiots. What's one more if it could mean saving some cops' lives?"

"Those cops could be crooked," Paige said.

"Does that mean we should let them be executed?"

Visibly shaken by the sharp, accusatory tone in Cole's voice, Paige blinked and said, "Of course it doesn't. I'm just saying they may be ready to kill us the moment we walk in the door. Who knows what the Nymar told them?"

"I can tell you there's a reason those four places were saved for last," Cole said.

Rico studied him with a critical eye. The other was pinched shut in a grimace of pain as he reached under his jacket to examine a wound he'd picked up somewhere during the night. "How do you know that?"

"Because otherwise the thing Hope was setting up would have happened by now. It would have been lumped in with all the smaller incidents instead of being saved for the next act, whatever that may be. I know what you're thinking, and yes, this is coming from the part of my brain that plots video games. It still makes sense, doesn't it?"

Although he obviously hated to admit as much, Rico nodded.

"We might be able to defuse some of this, though," Cole continued. "Paige happens to be friends with a cop in Kansas City. Maybe even real good friends."

"Not that good, Cole," she replied sternly. "I told you that already. Besides, Stanze's just a city police officer. And in case you need me to remind you, it's the wrong city."

"Stanze's a smart guy. Plus, he's got to be in someone's sights since he's the one other departments have been going to regarding all the wild dog attacks, right?"

Although Paige's nod started off like Rico's, it was soon accented by a crooked little smile. "Right."

"You're the one who's so close to Stanze, so why don't you have a chat with him and see what he can tell us. At the very least, he might know how to get a message to any undercover cops in those four cities to let them know what they might be in for."

"What do you want her to do?" Rico asked. "Have her cop buddy type up a memo in regards to Skinners and any Skinnerlike activities?"

"He could figure out something and get it to the right people. If anyone's got a shot," Cole added, "Stanze would do better than one of us."

"He's right," Paige said. "I'll try to get to him right away. In fact, it might be better if I saw him in person. Tristan, can you get me to KC?"

The Dryad closed her eyes and swayed ever so slightly in perfect harmony with what had seemed like so much random background noise. Before long she stood up and said, "We should be able to send all of you out of here, but only once, whether it's together or separate. After that you'll have to take your chances with the temples wherever you may wind up."

Sifting through the contact list on her phone, Paige said, "Might as well get me out to KC now. Catching up to Stanze shouldn't be too tough, whether he's on the clock or off."

Tristan opened the door to show a stunningly beautiful brown-haired dancer wearing a tight pinstripe suit from the Naughty Secretary collection. "Elle, make sure Paige gets to Kansas City as soon as possible. What about the rest of you?"

"I'm not going anywhere except by car," Daniels said as he hopped to his feet. "If you want me to examine these spore remains, then I'll need to do it at my apartment."

"Fine," Paige said. "Go ahead."

"You might not want to go out there," Elle warned. "Those Nymar are trying to get to the back rooms. I think they know you guys are here."

"Lead them here," Cole said. "Make sure nobody follows and give us some privacy."

"You sure you're up for that?" Paige asked.

"We want to see why they're here, right? Rico and I should be able to take two Nymar."

"Actually," Elle said, "there's three of them now."

"Three. Fine. Whatever. Just go on to KC and get the ball rolling."

Either Paige didn't know what to make of the sharpness to Cole's voice or didn't want to get into it at that point, because she agreed to the proposition despite whatever else was bothering her. Even though Elle didn't follow her, she couldn't leave the utility room fast enough.

"Is everything all right with you?" Tristan asked Cole when Paige had left.

"I'm fine," he assured her quickly. "Just . . ." After taking a moment to soften his demeanor with a deep breath and a strained, vaguely confident smile, he said, "Could you just get the Nymar back here before they call for reinforcements?"

Daniels was happy to leave the utility room with his kit and plastic Baggies full of samples taken from the spore removed from Cole's chest. Since he was still of the male persuasion, he was even happier to be escorted by Tristan to the back exit of the club as she sent a human dancer to fetch the club's vampire guests.

Now that he was alone with Cole, Rico slammed the door shut and wheeled around to face him. "Whatever's going on between you and Paige has gotta be set to the damn side. You hear me, boy?"

"You know I don't like being called that."

"Yeah? And I don't like having to rely on a partner that's got his head somewhere other than where it needs to be. So you two got some bump 'n' grind time in. That's abundantly clear. Now you're worried about her goin' off and letting some cop crawl down the front of her pants?"

"That's not what—"

"The hell it isn't," Rico snarled in a voice quiet enough to remain inside the room, but powerful enough to shake Cole down to the soles of his feet. "You gotta straighten that shit out one way or another. Paige ain't the kind to get too close to just anyone, and she sure as hell ain't the slut you're thinking she is."

Cole jumped up so quickly that it reminded him how weak his system still was. Even so, he kept his back straight and his chin up when he stood toe-to-toe with the bigger man. "Nobody calls her that. Not you. Not a Full Blood. Not even God himself. You hear me?"

Scowling as he took stock of Cole all over again, Rico said, "Yeah. Then you think she's got something for this cop?"

"He can have her. Maybe she'll try to get him killed for a change."

"She's keeping you alive, asshole. But if you got infected by a Half Breed, she'd put you down even quicker than when it looked like you were gonna turn into a bloodsucker. Just because she did you in the nice way, don't think that puts you above the rules of the game."

"There's more to it than that."

"Really? Is there? You wanna share? You wanna curl up with some hot cocoa and tell me all about your fucking feelings? Tough. You hear them voices? That'd be those Nymar headed back this way. How about we take care of business here and then continue the therapy later?"

From the instant he found himself alone with Rico in that

room, Cole had known the conversation would head this way. The only problem was, his mouth didn't come equipped with one of those huge, red, plastic-encased Abort buttons that were next to every guided missile panel in James Bond movies. Damn, his mouth needed one of those buttons sometimes.

Chapter Twenty-Seven

The three Nymar were feeling cocky when a redhead in high heels and a nightie led them to the club's back rooms. More than likely it was a combination of the human dancer's charms and the high that all Chicago Nymar were running on that night. No matter how confident they felt, the vampires didn't have a prayer when they stepped into the utility room. One of them was still wearing the self-satisfied look on his face when Cole's spear pierced his heart. Rico kept the second one quiet by knocking him down and stepping on his mouth.

When the third one started hissing in a threatening manner, Cole flipped his spear around so the Nymar's chin was wedged in the forked end. He was a greasy looking idiot with a gold T hanging from a chain around his neck that must have been forged somewhere in the darkest fashion days of the eighties. "What's your name?" Cole asked.

"M-My name?"

Rather than repeat himself, Cole tightened his grip on the weapon so the thorns sank deeper into his palms. It took only a thought for him to cause the forked ends to extend, curl slightly around the Nymar's throat and tighten.

As soon as he felt the pressure, the Nymar sputtered, "Dave . . . David! It's David, okay? My name's David!"

Tightening the wooden snare a bit more, Cole twisted the

spear to angle the Nymar's face toward the floor. "Take a look at your friends there, David. What do you think they'd tell you if you asked how patient we are tonight?"

"How'd you know where to find us, Dave?" Rico asked. When he didn't respond, Rico flipped out the blade he'd sunk into the eye socket of the Nymar at the tunnels. "I already tortured one of you today," he said while holding the knife close enough to Dave's face for him to smell the oily blood that remained on the sharpened steel. "One more'd just be a bonus."

"Steph and Ace've been recruiting for weeks. She kept most of the newbies around the Blood Parlor and they were all out looking for you. One of them saw you drive away from the parlor, and another saw that same car driving here. Hope wanted us to make sure the seeding took root. Then we'd get our Shadow Spore." His eyes darted toward Cole and his nostrils flared with a quick inhalation. "What happened with that, anyway?"

"Still want to file your report?" Cole asked as he angled the spear so the forked end grew sharper than a pair of scissors and fit snugly under Dave's chin. "What about now?"

"So Steph knew we were coming?" Rico asked.

Dave nodded as best he could. "We didn't know the exact time, but Steph knew you'd show up at the parlor eventually. So did Hope. She said she knew Paige real well."

"What about those cops? Were they on Steph's payroll?"

"They were just cops." Dave squirmed and made the mistake of moving his hands more than an inch. He paid for it by getting Rico's fist buried in his gut. "Some of us approached them as informants," the Nymar wheezed. "I got a card in my pocket."

Rico flipped Dave's jacket open and dug around in the pockets. He came up empty, but found something when he patted down the heavy cotton shirt the Nymar wore over a dark red T-shirt. After nearly ripping the pocket off completely, Rico was satisfied that the card was the only thing in there. Only then did he finally take a look at what was printed on the muted white paper. He showed it to Cole, then tucked it away inside his own shirt pocket. "That's from one of the cops at the parlor tonight?" he asked.

"That's the one who sent the cops," Dave replied. "Some lieutenant or captain, I don't know. Whoever Ace and Steph were talking to."

"Sounds like this has been in the works for a while," Cole pointed out.

"Maybe a month or two," Dave said.

"But it's only been a little while since Lancroft's place in Philly was raided. There's no way you could get all of this *and* the cops on board in that amount of time."

Dave was getting nervous. The sweat trickling from his brow was tainted by the same oily substance found in their blood. It allowed him to maneuver within the spear's grip, but it also caused a reaction with the weapon's varnish that made the forked end twitch against his jugular. "We've been stringing the cops along for months. Some of them got hooked on the girls. Some stayed out in their cars or tried to act casual in Astin's bar. Others just swung by to give Steph and Ace some shit. All we had to do was keep them interested so when the time came it was easy to convince him to send some badges down to wait for you guys. When they started to lose interest, all we needed to do was feed them bits and pieces here and there. Drop a few anonymous tips. Let a few of the scared customers go instead of reining them in. It ain't hard to keep cops looking at you."

"And when the shooting started, you camouflaged them using that striped shit?" Rico asked.

For a second the Nymar seemed confused. "You mean the Shadow Spore. Yeah. We only just got that. We were all supposed to get altered, but there wasn't enough time for everyone to get a taste. With everything that's been happening between us and you Skinners, Hope and Cobb decided to use the Shadow Spore to put everything into motion."

"Who's Cobb?" Rico asked. The Nymar that had been under his foot was coming around and glaring up at the Skinners. Rico wiped the snarl off the vampire's face by stomping his head against the floor hard enough to put his lights out for a good long while. From there, he clamped a hand against Dave's face and slammed him against the closest wall.

"I don't mind doing the legwork for an important job, but I'm getting bored with slapping you fuckholes around," he said. "It's been a long night, so tell me the rest before I decide to spice this up by carving my name into your face. How are the Nymar coordinating these attacks?"

"There'sh a webshite," Dave said, his lips crushed and pursed together by Rico's hand. "It'sh run by Cov Thirty-eigsh."

"What was that?" Cole asked. "Did you say a website?"

Once Rico gave his mouth a chance to move, Dave said, "Y-Yes. It's a message board run by a guy named Cobb. Cobb38. That's his screen name."

"Who the fuck is that?" Rico snarled.

"I don't know. All I know is a screen name." Dave brightened as if he'd found his lifeline. "I can show you how to get to him. Just take me to—"

"You're not going anywhere," Rico snapped.

Cole dug the phone from his pocket and pulled up the Web browser. Between the hell his body had been through and the sense of panic that came from being wanted for killing several police officers, it was a true struggle to keep his hands steady. "Don't give me any shit about needing to be on a certain computer. Just tell me how to find Cobb."

"If I tell you . . . you'll let me go?"

Rico raised his knife and showed the blade to Dave. "How about for every bit of good info you give us, I cut off one less piece from your bloodsucking carcass?"

Dave talked.

Maybe he thought he could walk away from Pinups.

Maybe he already knew he was never going to leave that utility room. The stench of dead Nymar was thick enough to clog Cole's senses, and he was still nauseous from the stink of oily tendrils reaching up through his sinuses while hugging him from the inside out.

When Dave was finished talking about Cobb's website, Rico held him in place and asked, "You got any more antidote, Cole?"

"No. Most of it's in me."

"Then finish him off the hard way."

Cole knew it was useless to tell the big man to do the deed himself, and there was no reason to ask why the job had been given to him. Skinners did what needed to be done, no matter how dirty the job was. When he picked up his spear and drove it through Dave's chest, he figured he was being taught that Paige had simply been doing her duty as well.

"Damn," Rico said as Cole wiped off his spearhead on the clothes wrapped around Dave's lifeless body. "That was cold."

"Sorry. Did you intend on bringing him along so he could screw with us, or let him go so he could warn the others and tell Cobb to change everything on his entire network?"

"I just thought you'd need a little more convincing. Give Paige a call and see where she's at with her cop buddy."

Cole wasn't certain that Rico even had a phone. They were pretty much standard issue for anyone in the modern world, but Rico wasn't always modern. Rather than question the big man on his views of technology, he took out his own cell phone, hit Paige's speed dial number, and tossed it to him while it rang.

Poking his nose into the hall, Cole found Tristan standing watch just outside the door. Several dancers hurried back and forth between the stage entrance and dressing rooms, but deferred to the Dryad's Queen Bee status with a quick nod as they passed her by.

"Any more assholes out there?" he asked.

Without batting a perfectly formed eyelash, Tristan replied, "Just the regular ones. Are you boys through yet?"

"Yeah."

"Did you leave a mess?"

"Nothing a broom, dustpan, and some trash bags can't handle. We'll take the unconscious one with us and dump him somewhere far from here. That is, unless you want us to make sure he doesn't come back?"

Tristan considered the Skinner's offer for all of two seconds before shaking her head. "No. They didn't see me or my sisters here. No need for any more death tonight."

"Whatever. Think we could get a ride to Denver?"

"I can arrange that." Tristan moved even closer to Cole and placed a hand on his forearm. Since he was a human male and she was a member of a species that served as the template for the ultimate ethereal female, that simple touch was enough to separate him from the world as well as his reality. "Please tell me you're done with this kind of bloodshed."

"We've got what we need from the ones we already questioned. I don't think any of us are in the mood to talk to another one."

"Good. I need you to tell me one thing, Cole."

"Name it," he replied before he could think any better of the decision.

She smiled, deflecting the knee-jerk appeasement with grace. "I need you to tell me you're innocent of what they're accusing you of on TV."

Even though Tristan didn't make a threat or even hint at anything along those lines, Cole somehow felt that a lie would be detected instantly by those softly contoured ears or those deep, colorful eyes. Before his baser instincts dragged him any further down into that sweetly scented trap, he told her, "It was a setup. Those cops were set up as targets and we were set up to knock them down. If we didn't do it, I'm guessing the Nymar would have made it look like we did and then fed the same shit to the press."

After taking a moment to size him up the old-fashioned way, the Dryad nodded and said, "I believe you. What I said before about not using our bridges still goes. Until this legal mess gets straightened out, we'll only be able to transport Skinners when it's absolutely necessary. You and Paige are different, though. I owe you two more than I can repay, which means you can come and go through our temples as often as I can."

"What about Prophet?"

Tristan smiled with so much warmth that it cheapened her previous attempts. "He's a cutie," she said. "He had plenty of chances to make things tough for me, but worked to smooth them out instead. He's got a free pass too." Placing her hand on Cole's arm, she quickly added, "But don't tell him I said that. Just tell him he can come and check with us if he needs to."

"I'll do that."

"Should I get things set up for Denver? I'll need to make a few calls but should be able to get you there."

"Yeah, do that. I really appreciate it, Tristan."

"I know you do. That's why you still get the VIP treatment, and the rest of those cocky, stick-wielding jerks have to go to the back of the line."

Watching a Dryad walk away was an event unto itself. No matter what was going on with the rest of the world, Cole felt his muscles loosen as his eyes followed the mesmerizing sway of her hips. Well, some of his muscles loosened. It was definitely easy to see how a shipload of sailors from centuries past could be drawn off course by catching sight of similar creatures frolicking topless in the waves.

"Paige already talked to Stanze," Rico announced as he stomped down the hall from the opposite direction. "She's meeting up with him now." He slapped the phone against Cole's chest and said, "Here. You call Prophet and I'll tidy up the back room. I'll convince that other one what a bad idea it would be to bring any of his buddies back here. There's an art to these things," he declared with a grin.

No matter how badly Rico obviously wanted to discuss his art, Cole wasn't in the mood. He let the big man go and then dialed Prophet's number. The bounty hunter answered on the third ring.

Completely stepping past any hellos or how-are-yous, Prophet said, "Tell me you guys ain't involved with this cop shooting business."

"I could tell you that, but . . ."

"Aww, Jesus Christ. How bad is it?"

"It's a setup. I can tell you the rest later. How about we meet in Denver?"

"Only if we go after those Nymar that Stanley's been on my ass about."

"You talked me into it," Cole said. "What can you tell us about those guys?"

"I've got a whole damn file. They're more of a gang than

anything else. Maybe even like a crime family. No, that's giving them too much credit. I'll go with gang. Not just some street gang, but more like—"

"It's so much easier when you just have some crazy dream and give us a warning," Cole grumbled. "Remember that? I miss those days."

Prophet's tone shifted into something that allowed him to scowl across a digital phone line. "Funny thing about those dreams. I need to sleep in order for them to hit. Ever since you asked me to watch your back in some creepy-as-hell basement in Philadelphia so we could steal a prized possession from a bunch of armed and dangerous, lunatic monster hunters, my sleep schedule ain't been too great. Oh, and finding out that the possession we were taking was the mutilated chunks of a werewolf, any dreams I might have had after that ain't exactly the ones I want either."

"Point taken. What did you mean before when you said 'wait for *us* to get there'?"

After a short pause, Prophet continued without the gruff tone in his voice. "Me and the Amriany."

"You're still following them?"

"Actually, they're following me. From a real close distance."

"They caught you, didn't they?"

"Caught sounds so sinister. They're after the same thing you are, anyway."

"Really? What might that be?"

"They want to recover some of that Lancroft crap, but they also caught wind of some Nymar taking their business overseas. One of them named Hope is traveling with a group that's been putting together some sort of organization. They already got their communications set up. They've been collecting weapons. They got plenty of intelligence on Skinners and now they're looking to take you out."

"So if they're getting so comfortable here, why would they want to leave the U.S.?" Cole asked.

"That's what these Amriany want to find out. Drina, she's the blonde, she thinks one of the Nymar groups that are definitely involved in this uprising will have a computer with some good intel on it or numbers on their phones they can use. I've been trying to steer them to Denver, but they got a line on a group down in Texas."

"San Antonio?"

"Yeah," Prophet said in a voice that made it easy for Cole to picture the surprised look on his face. "How'd you know about that?"

"Never mind. How'd the Amriany get out of Philly?"

"Drove, then flew. They got a real nice setup, Cole. Kind of puts you guys to shame. Not that it's too hard to put a shit-box Chevy to shame, but I'm talking charter planes and the works. These Gypsies have some serious funding."

"You might not want to let them hear you call them that. They're a bit sensitive about the G word."

"Believe me, I understand that kind of aggravation. I still need to check the African-American box on more official forms than I can count. My dad's Jamaican and Mom's from Cuba. How the hell does that make me African American? You're rolling your eyes now, right?"

"Yeah, Prophet. Big-time."

"I'll see about getting us to Denver."

"Tell them we're planning on hitting them hard. The last thing those Nymar will be expecting is another team sneaking in while the fireworks are going. Even below that on the list would be a team of Amriany. As long as your new buddies are willing to cooperate and share what they find, we don't have any problem with letting them in on this."

"You've got the pull to guarantee that?" Prophet asked cautiously.

"There's just me and Rico here, so yeah. I've got the pull."

"What about Paige?"

"I'm sure she'll find a way to get there."

"You don't sound thrilled about that."

"Can you get to Denver or not?" Cole quickly asked.

"Considering everything they've been saying about you guys, that shouldn't be too difficult."

"What have they been saying?"

"'Bye."

Cole looked at the phone as if Prophet might somehow be looking back at him. All he saw was a reflection of his face and a red message telling him his call had come to an end.

"You done out here?" Rico asked as he stepped into the hall.

The latest round of dance mixes had come to an end, which meant the dancers were starting to hustle backstage again. A few of the Dryads were among them. They stood out like finely cut crystal goblets scattered among a collection of free cups collected from fast-food movie tie-ins. Considering how attractive Pinups' human dancers were, that was saying a lot. Elle whispered something to the ladies in her group, which kept the whole procession moving right past the Skinners.

"Yeah," Cole said as he tucked his phone away. "I'm done."

They tagged along with the trio of girls heading for the main stages, savoring the mixed scents of body sprays and female skin. All three were human, and drinking them in was like a welcome bit of familiar cooking. Hooray for the home team.

The procession stopped at a door that would have blended in perfectly with the black wall if not for the handle outlined in white tape. The girls opened it without having to look at what they were doing, and Cole stopped in his tracks when he saw Tristan in the main room. She leaned against a table in a pose that wasn't quite the same as the one she struck when prowling for lap dances. Shifting her eyes toward the door at the back of the room, she looked straight past the three dancers and locked eyes with Cole.

Something was wrong.

His fingers curled in to brush against his palms. Whoever those guys at Tristan's table were, they weren't Nymar or shapeshifters. They sat away from the glare of lights without being coated in black stripes, so they weren't carrying a Shadow Spore. Both of the men were dressed in simple, inexpensive clothes resembling the ensembles of every other paying customer in the place. One of them was in his late twenties or early thirties. He angrily said something to make Tristan look at him, while the older man followed her previous line of sight to the stage door. Even though Cole had pulled back enough to hide within the shadows filling the doorway, he knew he might have already been spotted.

Heavy steps sounded behind him, but Cole didn't need to turn around. The rustle of Rico's leather jacket was more than enough to give him away. Thanks to the cold weather, the leather had hardened into something closer to a shell than the smoother material of the Full Blood coat.

"Never thought I'd get sick of hangin' out in strip bars," Rico muttered. "Tristan out there?"

"She's talking to someone. Doesn't look like it's for official dancer business either."

Placing a hand on Cole's shoulder to keep him in place, Rico leaned forward to get a look for himself. He almost immediately leaned back again and snarled, "Shit. Cops."

"How can you tell?"

"Well, they ain't Nymar. There's two of them, and they ain't buddies out to see some bare ass, because they ain't grinnin' from ear to ear with Tristan being so close. Look at the way they're talkin' to her. One's asking questions and the other's scanning the room. Keeps looking over here. Did you poke your nose out too far?"

"Maybe a little."

"They're cops. I've had enough of them sniffing around after me that I can damn near smell the doughnut frosting on their fingers."

Cole shook his head and eased the door shut. There was a narrow slot filled with tinted plastic just wide enough for a dancer to get a look out to see if an unwanted admirer was waiting for her next set. Although he couldn't see as much as before, Cole could make out the shapes at Tristan's table if he squinted just right.

"Come with me."

Those three words drifted through the air without the slightest bit of warning. Both Skinners wheeled around with their hands headed for their weapons before they caught sight of Elle standing behind them.

"You'd better go now," she said. "Those policemen were asking about you, and it's not like we can refuse if they insist on searching."

"Sure you can," Rico chided.

If Elle had been even slightly intimidated by the Skinners, she didn't show it as she grabbed hold of Rico's jacket and dragged him away from the stage door.

Allowing himself to be pulled down the hall, he looked over his shoulder and said, "See? Told you they were cops."

She led them all the way around the back of the club to the room that had been made into the Dryad temple. The first time Cole had seen the flowing script covering the smooth walls of a similar temple, he was fascinated. Now, it hit him on the same nerve as watching his bus pull up to the curb.

"Will this take us to Denver?" he asked.

Another Dryad was near the edge of the curtain, swaying slowly and humming in time to the thumping beat that filled the club. "No," Elle said. "It's to a club in Boulder, but it's the best we could do. There seems to be some trouble at the Denver clubs."

"Nymar?"

"No. More police. All of our sisters are staying out of sight in case more Nymar are following all the Skinners going back and forth. I don't need to tell you what sort of trouble it would be if they found us."

After having that thing inside him, Cole could still feel a pang of hunger at the very notion of opening one of those beautiful women's veins and drawing their precious fluid into his stomach. He was still fuzzy on the difference between a Dryad and a nymph, other than a Dryad was supposedly much older and more experienced. Sort of the supernatural equivalent of a MILF. All he knew was that the longer he stood among them, the harder it was to resist. Before his resolve was tested further, he was shoved through the beaded curtain and sent toppling through the breezy in-between that smelled of freshly cut timber and felt like an autumn breeze.

Something was different this time. The trips had always

seemed instantaneous before, but this was a bizarre nightmare where the room around him melted away, leaving only
phantom glimpses of things he could hold on to. His stomach dropped. Voices screamed in his mind. Music raked
against his inner ear. Heartbeats pounded against him like
invisible fists, and when he tried to fight them off, his fingers
became entangled in what felt like a blanket of cobwebs so
thick he could hear it tearing.

Upon reaching the other side of the bridge, Cole flopped
onto his side and hit a floor identical to the one he'd left
behind. The music was different, however, as was the scent
of the body spray worn by the dancer who helped him up.

"Oh my God," she said. "Are you all right?"

When Cole grabbed onto the hand being offered to him,
he nearly pulled the slender dancer down on top of him. She
had the ethereal beauty of a nymph and smelled like heaven
drizzled in vanilla. As he struggled to get his bearings, he
spotted another woman standing with her back pressed
against the wall. Her arms were crossed and she glared at
him in a way that said she either didn't like ferrying Skinners through the club or just didn't like him messing up her
floor. Then the beads rattled again and a large boot thumped
solidly against his back.

"What the hell?" Rico grunted.

"He tripped when he came out," the dancer against the
wall explained. The imperfections around her eyes were
subtle, but marked her as human. "Was he drinking?"

The big man pulled Cole to his feet and shoved him toward
the door. "You got a car we can use?"

"Wha . . . ?"

"Not you, Cole."

Cole's feet were moving but the voices and queasiness still
filled his head.

The human woman fell into step behind them, keeping her
arms crossed and her eyes locked on the Skinners. "There's
a blue Civic parked out back. Here are the keys. Just because
I was told to let you borrow it doesn't mean you get to trash
it. Bring it back by tomorrow, or else."

Rico took the keys and rattled them as if purposely trying

to jangle whatever was left of Cole's brains. "We're taking it to Denver and may need it for a few days. That okay?"

"Sure," the nymph replied. Seeing the increased unhappiness on the other one's face, she added, "There's a few out there given to us by the same customer. He's a real nice guy. Very generous."

"Generous to you, maybe," the stern woman scoffed. "The rest of us gotta earn the hard way."

"Gary paid two months of your rent over the summer. What are you complaining about?"

The banter between the dancers went on for the duration of the walk through the back rooms of the club. It was decidedly smaller and quieter than Pinups, but Cole's head was pounding and he still felt as if he'd been dragged a noisy mile before he could walk on his own.

"Blue Civic. Gotchya." Judging by the sharp tone in Rico's voice, he wasn't enjoying the chatter either.

"So you guys are friends of Tristan's?" the nymph asked. She slipped a key into the alarm bar of a steel exit door and turned it so she could push it open. "What are your names?"

"Never mind that," the other dancer snapped while propping open the door with the side of her foot. "The car's right there. You guys need anything else before you go? Some water? Something to eat? Tristan told us to ask."

"No thanks, girls," Rico said. "You've been perfect hostesses. We'll be on our way."

The moment the Skinners were outside, the door was pulled shut, a key was turned, and that was that.

Rico unlocked the Civic and dropped himself onto the seat behind the wheel. After unlocking the passenger door, he started the engine and waited for Cole to lower himself in. "I don't think she liked you."

"She gave me a new car," Cole said. "That puts her one up on my dad."

"I don't think I ever heard about your dad. Wanna regale me with stories of Young Cole Warnecki during the drive into Denver?"

"No."

The little car's engine revved a few times. When it started whining, Rico pulled away from the club. "You know where we're going?"

Cole checked the GPS he'd recently added to his phone's laundry list of services, but wasn't able to get his results before Rico stumbled upon a sign pointing him toward southbound Highway 36.

After Cole stuffed his phone back into his pocket and started fighting with the lever for his seat's backrest, Rico asked, "So what's the deal with you and Paige?"

"I thought you already had that figured out."

"And I thought you weren't such a prissy little bitch."

Cole rolled down the window and closed his eyes to feign complete relaxation as the cold air tore into his cheeks. "If this is building into another 'she did what she had to do' speeches, you can save it."

"Well," Rico grumbled. "She did."

"Maybe."

"But?"

"But she didn't have to make it seem so easy," Cole replied.

"Easy? Are you fucking blind?"

Cole shook his head. "I'm not talking about what was going through her head or whatever was on her face. I'm talking about the weapon in her hands being stuck in my chest. I felt her trying to push it in, and wouldn't have been able to stop her if it wasn't for that . . . that thing giving me the strength. Spare me all the talk about duty or mercy or whatever else you were going to use to justify it. She was going to kill me and I couldn't have done that to her. Even if it was the right thing to do, it would have been nice if she'd taken a moment before letting me go to . . ."

The highway was covered with a layer of snow that crunched under the Civic's tires, and the wind coming in through the window smelled clean. It was late enough for there to be relatively few other cars on the road with them, but even if they were in the middle of a traffic jam with police helicopters closing in from all sides, Cole would have felt like a solitary figure in the middle of a frozen field.

"To what?" Rico asked.

In the time it took Cole to blink, he thought back to the first time he'd been dropped off in front of Raza Hill. The sting of Gerald and Brad's deaths was still as fresh as the injuries he'd sustained after getting knocked around by a Full Blood. The Blood Blade was just a weird knife tucked away in his luggage, and vampires were just sexy fairy tales. When Paige walked out to meet him that first time, his entire world had kicked into overdrive. When she told him about Skinners, Nymar, and Full Bloods, he believed her. When she asked him to come along with her to help with the Blood Blade, he followed. When she told him about a warrior's spirit and offered to train him, he accepted. At the time, no matter how much of it he might or might not have truly understood, he still would have gone along with her. There just wasn't any other place for him to be.

"To *what*?" Rico asked again. "Say a proper goodbye?"

There was a reason Cole hadn't wanted to say that part out loud. Even hearing it from someone else hurt worse than the lingering pains and incessant tightening within his chest.

"She didn't get a chance to tell you the rest of what happened back in Urbana," Rico explained.

"I heard enough. Her friend Tara was seeded and killed a bunch of doctors and nurses. Ned found her before, so he probably found them again. Paige probably did what she needed to do and now she's a Skinner. Can we just flip on the radio and drive?"

"You don't wanna hear the rest?"

"You're telling me you memorized those Shampoo Banana journals?" Cole scoffed. "I know she's your friend and everything, but that's a little stalkeresque, don't you think?"

"You want to hear what happened or not?"

"Do I have a choice?" Cole grunted.

"Sure. You could listen or you could plug your ears like a little—"

"*Don't* call me that."

When Rico spoke again, the edge was gone from his voice. "You need to hear this, Cole."

Chapter Twenty-Eight

Thomasboro, Illinois
The past

Things were a little too hot for Rico to stay in New Mexico. It wasn't the only spot where he'd had legal problems, but it was the most nagging pain at the moment. Fortunately, it was a pain that could be alleviated by some time spent away from the authorities who might arrest him on sight. Ned didn't like hearing about such things, and Rico was more than happy to keep them to himself. In that aspect and a few others, it was a good partnership. More recently, Ned had set his sights on a Nymar group that staked their claim on the nearby college town of Urbana. No longer content to hang back and watch the bloodsuckers come and go, Ned shifted into a more proactive gear. Rico enjoyed that aspect of the partnership even more.

It would have been ideal for them to set up some sort of home base within reach of the university, but the Nymar had Urbana scoped out so well that whenever Rico drove around on a scouting run, Hope and Evan would drive by and wave at him and Ned within minutes. So they chose Thomasboro instead, a short drive away from the university and secluded, which made it easy for them to slip back and forth undetected. Ned was renting a little house on South Church

Street that had a prime view of Highway 45. It wasn't exactly scenic, but allowed them to watch the main route in and out of town. If the cops or any fanged visitors showed up, the Skinners could easily bolt for that same highway and put their evasive driving skills to the test.

The attack at the residence hall party had come and gone without much more than a few mentions on the local news. If Hope was anything at all, she was careful and tidy. No bodies were found, one girl was presumed missing, but nobody had filed a report until well after the party. Wes was popular enough among his buddies to convince them to back his story about Amy and Tara leaving together and heading back to their dorm. By the time anything more suspicious than that had surfaced, the bodies at the hospital were found. Once the press got hold of that story, anything as mundane as a wild party was left in the dust.

Bending a few slats of the plastic blinds covering the front window with one finger, Rico watched the highway while Jason Banks of Champaign's *Local News at Five* informed the late night audience of the latest developments. Rico heard the story when it was first broadcast, but he listened to the repeat just to make sure he hadn't missed anything. Also, the sitcom rerun playing on the other channel would have only distracted him.

Jason Banks was cut from Grade A newscaster cloth. Lantern jaw. Dark, closely cut hair. Stern eyes and the occasional genuine smile. He was so good at his job that when he said the doctor and nurses killed at Carle Foundation Hospital had been victims of a mental patient who was corralled within minutes after the slaying, Rico almost believed him.

"Although authorities believe Gracen was responsible for at least two of the slayings," Banks said, referring to the mental patient by name, "the short time in which the attacks were carried out led investigators to believe that more than one assailant was needed to commit the murders. Gracen is in police custody and hasn't denied killing one of the nurses. As of this time, however, he hasn't given any useful information regarding the identity of a possible accomplice."

Rico smirked and watched a familiar car speed down the

highway: Ned's battered, light blue four-door. He knew it would only take another few minutes to turn off and backtrack to the driveway, and he continued watching through the bent plastic blinds. When he saw the second familiar car streak past on the highway, he grunted under his breath and leaned forward enough for his nose to press the blinds against the window.

By the time Ned pulled up, Rico had already eased into his shoulder holster and was checking to make sure his Army model Colt .45 was ready for use. After he heard the car door slam, Rico counted down the appropriate number of seconds required for someone to make the walk around the house and kept his finger on the trigger. After an acceptable amount of time had passed, Ned stomped in.

"You were followed again," Rico announced.

"I know. Whoever's doing it is getting sloppy."

"Did they track you to the house?"

The older man's steps brought him into the living room, where he threw his light jacket onto the festering couch that had come with the place and watched the TV long enough to spot the already expired weather forecast. "Yeah," he grunted. "I even slowed down when taking the corners. Thought we could all go out for pizza."

"Who is it?"

"Not Hope or any of her bunch. Haven't felt any of them bastards within spitting distance of the hospital since them folks were killed. What about the university?"

Still watching the roads in front of the house, Rico said, "Wes is supposed to be out of town. I poked around, but all I got was a phone number to some Motel 6 in Florida from some jerkwad at that dorm. When I walked the grounds, I got more of an itch from lookin' at all them college girls than from anything a Nymar might give me."

"That's real nice, kid. We got a job to do out here. I know you're used to running loose on your own, but this ain't the time to start sniffin' around the locals."

Just as Rico was about to calm the older man down, he felt a twitch in one of the deepest layers of flesh on his palm that made him feel as if he'd suddenly developed an allergy to the bones inside his hand. According to the look on Ned's face, he was feeling the same thing.

The older Skinner pointed toward the back door and then at the short hallway leading to the two bedrooms. Rico nodded and hurried down the hall in steps that were quick and light enough to carry him to the first bedroom without making more than a few subtle squeaks on the floorboards. As his itch intensified, Ned went to the couch and stuck his hands in between the cushions. Pushing past some loose change and a few stale Cheetos, he found a .38 that had been sandwiched out of sight.

The bedroom Rico chose had a small window looking out to a backyard only slightly bigger than a postage stamp. He couldn't see anything moving in the shadows, but the itch in his palms became more intense. Rather than take his chances on alerting multiple Nymar as well as the neighbors with gunfire, he tucked the .45 away and reached under the red flannel hanging over his plain T-shirt to unclip a wooden oval that hung from his belt by a D-ring. It had points extending from each end and was studded with thorns that punctured his palm as he grabbed hold of it like an oversized set of brass knuckles. Once the thorns sank in, the points grew into short thick blades that were somewhere between stilettos and hunting knives. The knuckle guard tightened around his fingers, spread out and sprouted half-inch spikes that curled into hooks before straightening out again as if they were flexing to limber up.

There was movement at the front of the house. Whoever it was, they weren't trying to sneak along the wall beneath the windows or through the bushes, because no living creature could walk on the ground too close to the house without setting off one of the traps the Skinners had set. Footsteps echoed outside and occasionally scratched against the sidewalk until the visitor got to the front door and knocked.

Ned waited long enough for his partner to get situated and then stomped toward the front door while bellowing, "Who the hell is it?"

"I need to talk to you," the visitor replied.

Instead of blinds, the windows of the front bedroom were

covered with a thick set of drapes that were yellowed by
the sun and stained by rainwater that had gotten in through
cheap insulation. Rico eased the edge of one curtain aside
just enough to place the girl who stood on the front step as
one of the students attacked at that party. She'd made herself scarce after those people turned up dead at the hospital.
Paige, he suddenly recalled. That was her name.

The Nymar were still out there as well, but too far away to
be on the front stoop. Ned was probably thinking the same
thing when he pulled the door open and asked, "Where the
hell have you been?"

"Following you," she replied.

"I gave you my damn card. You could've just called."

"I did call. Remember those messages about the sightings
of that missing girl?"

"Yeah."

"That was me," she explained. "I told you to show up at
those places and waited for you to show up and you did."

"I also got some strange messages from cops," Ned told
her. "Was that you too?"

"Anonymous tip along with your phone number. All I
needed was for you to show up to meet one of them and I
was able to follow you all the way here."

"When I gave you that card, it was 'cause I wanted to work
with you. No need for all this other bullshit."

"Would you have invited me back to your house?"

"No," Ned reluctantly told her. The older man didn't like
being the one steered through a conversation, and it showed.
Rico had to smirk at the sound of that.

"What if I told you I knew where to find Wes?" she offered.

"Do you?"

Now it was the girl's turn to pause. Rico had seen her tail-
ing Ned at least three different times, but getting all the way
to the house was impressive. At least, for a beginner.

She shifted on her feet, but not out of nervousness. There
was something else, and it was tough for Rico to pin it down
given only his partial view through the hairline slit he'd created between the window frame and curtain. Before he could
study her any further, he caught a hint of movement to his

left along the next door neighbor's roofline. A figure hung from the gutters of that house; too slim to pull the rusted metal down and too fast to send more than a metallic creak through the air.

"Let me in and I'll tell you where Wes is," Paige said.

The figure was no longer hanging from the gutter, and Rico was unable to figure out where the hell it had gone. As he pulled the curtains aside to get a better look, he knew he might be spotted by the girl on his doorstep. But some things were more important than trying to get the drop on a single, albeit crafty, college girl.

"Why do you want to get inside so damn bad?" Ned asked in a tone that made Rico certain the older man was reaching for his weapon. Always one for practicality, and hiding in plain sight, Ned's club was about the size and shape of a stickball bat or possibly a broken broom handle. More than likely he was just prepping the bat for use and making sure the girl saw he was ready for trouble. It would be a while before the spikes came out.

The dark figure launched itself from the neighbor's gutters, to land softly on the lawn directly in front of Rico's window. At that moment, Paige took her hand from her pocket to point a little .32 revolver at Ned's face. "Tara told me all about you guys. Step back before I shoot you."

As that simple threat drifted through the air, the figure on the lawn stood up and drove her hand straight through the pane of glass in front of Rico's face. He knew it was Tara because Ned had made a point of describing her to him in detail. Tara's dirty blond hair may have been a little stringy and dirty, but went along with the wear and tear on her slightly rounded face. What Ned hadn't told him about was the Nymar tendrils that traced paths up along both of her cheeks like skinny black fingers reaching up to massage her temples. When Tara bared all three sets of her fangs, it seemed more like an inexperienced gunner pulling all of her triggers at once simply because she hadn't figured out which weapon in her arsenal was best for the job. Despite her lack of finesse, Rico was barely fast enough to jump away from the window before getting his head torn off.

Tara jumped straight through the broken glass head first, hit the floor and crumpled into an awkward, off-balance roll. Her hands were scratched from hanging onto the gutters and left smears of oily blood on the floor as she rushed to stand back up. Venom dripped from her fangs and dribbled down her chin while trickling into her throat, where she quickly coughed it up again.

Rico had never seen so many markings on what was obviously a freshly turned Nymar. That, however, didn't stop him from throwing himself at her with just as much enthusiasm as he would show to any other bloodsucker out there.

Ned backed away from the door, allowing Paige to step inside and kick it shut behind her. She was obviously nervous, but not enough to make her hands shake. Neither of them seemed concerned about anyone else seeing what was going. If the neighbors were that friendly, Ned wouldn't have rented the house in the first place.

"What are you doing here, girl?" he asked.

"Keeping you away from me and my friends."

"I take it that's your friend who just busted into my place and attacked my partner?"

The sounds of struggle rattled down the hallway from the bedroom. Neither of the two in the front room so much as glanced in that direction.

"You and your partner are killers," Paige said. "I've seen it. I saw what you did to Hector."

"What did you see?"

"It was the night after Tara and I left the hospital."

Ned was quick to point out, "You mean the night Tara killed those four good folks who worked at that hospital? Those folks who I knew, by the way."

"The night we got out," Paige continued as her eyes twitched with the effort of holding back all the emotions broiling beneath her surface, "we went to a safe place and that psycho came after us."

Just then something heavy slammed against another wall in the house. That was followed by a distinctly male grunt and an animal snarl. When Ned took a look toward the bedroom, Paige said, "Not that psycho. The one who killed Amy. Hector followed us, so I made sure Karen got away."

"She's the short one with the glasses?"

"Yes. After she went home, I helped Tara get what she needed."

"She shouldn't have needed anything after all the feeding she did in that hospital room." Watching her carefully to measure her reaction to every word, Ned told her, "The only thing she left of those doctors was what was splattered on the walls. I got a look before the cops showed up. There was a spot in a corner where she was either licking up more blood or slopping it up with her fingers."

"Tara's sick," Paige said.

"You're damn right she is. So was that vicious little creep Hector. You should be thankin' us for putting that one down." When he didn't get a response to that, Ned added, "Sounds like your sick friend is still hungry."

"Once you and him are out of here, Wes and Hope will leave town. They'll pack up and move along so we can do the same."

"And then what? If you're looking for a clinic to help folks like Tara, you ain't gonna find any. All you'll find is more vampires who will either turn you into one of them or eat you." Since the fight in the bedroom was amping up, Ned jumped on the first sign that he'd hit a sensitive spot with Paige. "That's right," he snapped. "I said vampires. That's what they are, girl. By helping them, you ain't nothing more than a ghoul. Or if you'd rather put it in legal terms, you'd be an accessory."

"Better that than a murderer," Paige replied while holding out the .32 in a stiff firing pose.

Ned lowered the bat so the end touched the floor and the rest of it dropped across his foot when he let go. Holding out his hands to show his bloodied palms, he winced as if those wounds still registered. "So what now?" he asked. "What was your big plan? You shoot me while Tara feeds?"

She shook her head but was too rattled to say a word. It was then that Ned knew she didn't have any intention of pulling the trigger. All she'd wanted was to find the Skinners and keep them occupied until backup came.

"They're coming, aren't they?" he asked.

Paige blinked, took half a step to one side and turned to glance at the front door. That was all the opening Ned needed to lean to one side while snapping up his foot to pop the wooden bat up to his waist level. The .32 went off once, sending its round past his face and into the cheap plaster behind him. Ned snatched the bat from the air and drove the handle's thorns into his palm. Although Paige was surprised that she'd been able to pull the trigger, she was doubly shocked when the side of the bat caught her just below the knee.

With one of her feet swept completely out from under her, she fell over and twisted around to try and keep Ned in her sight. Her shoulder hit the floor hard, driving the wind from her lungs and causing her finger to tighten desperately around the revolver's trigger. The gun jerked in her hand, to blast a hole into the ceiling and send a dirty, chunky rain of plaster down on them both. None of that debris had a chance to settle before Ned was standing directly over her with his bat poised for a strong, chopping blow.

Chapter Twenty-Nine

The bedroom looked as if it had been rammed by a small car. Glass from the window lay scattered among broken pieces of the frame on a scuffed floor. What little furniture there was had been destroyed, and blood from both combatants stained the walls like streaks of cast-off paint.

Rico had tagged her several times with the wooden weapon wrapped around his fist. The spikes on either end were slick with Nymar blood, but the wounds they'd created had already closed. What bothered him even more was Tara's speed. Despite the fact that her movements were clumsy and poorly timed, she could still get at least three blows in before he could follow through with one. He slashed at her with the weapon's top spike, catching nothing but air. Swinging that hand back along the same path, he watched her pull her head away before the weapon got anywhere close to her. Rather than try for a third swing, he waited until his knuckles were in position and then snapped his fist straight into her mouth.

That one stung.

Thin black filaments spewed from her lip. No matter how quickly the tendrils moved to repair the damage, they weren't able to save the fangs that Rico's powerful jab had just knocked out. Within seconds after reeling from that, she came at him again.

The .45 had been knocked from his grasp early in the fight. Tara's initial flurry was so fast and powerful that Rico didn't know how the gun had been taken from him or where it had gone. He just knew he had to find it again. She'd already buried her remaining fangs into his chest and was frantically drawing whatever blood she could from the meat under his shirt.

He grabbed a handful of her hair and pulled. All that did was convince Tara to wrap her arms around his torso and mash her face against him even harder. From there his only option was to snake an arm between his body and hers, hoping the weapon on that fist tore into her more than it did him. He realized how bad a plan that was when his fist became wedged in place between their two bodies, harmless as a dried flower pressed between the pages of an old book.

"Son of a bitch," he snarled.

It was the first time he'd ever felt a Nymar's heartbeat. To the Nymar spore, the human heart was barely more than a piece of hijacked equipment. It squeezed the muscles, manually circulating fluids to speed the process of conversion and churning blood however it saw fit. The older ones even knew how to play it like an instrument to mimic a human rhythm. With just a bit of attention focused in the right direction, he should have been able to pinpoint which side of the heart the spore was on. This time he felt two separate and distinct patterns.

Suddenly, he understood.

Even for a Nymar that had recently fed, Tara was too fast and too strong. More than that, she showed no signs of letting up.

The markings on her face were too symmetrical compared to the random patterns formed by a creature stretching out wherever it liked within its human shell.

She healed too quickly and was too hungry.

Tara had been multiseeded.

It was a rare thing for a very good reason: Nymar spore were hungry and selfish. They preferred to be the sole inhabitants of their feeding grounds and didn't play well with others. On those rare occasions when two did latch onto the same heart, they turned their carrier into a genuine nightmare. Nearly every physical attribute was doubled, but they burned out in a quarter of the time. Some say the Nymar could have stayed hidden forever if not for the actions of a few multiseeded members of the species who created a mess that was too big to ignore. If he didn't turn this fight around real quick, he was in danger of finding himself in the middle of one such mess.

Once Tara saw the error in trying to draw blood from solid muscle, she pulled her teeth out and tried to sink them into his jugular. Rico's grip on her hair was the only thing preventing her from accomplishing that goal. Her face wound up less than an inch from his neck, giving the moment a somewhat intimate flavor as her quickening breaths created a warm spot on his skin. If he could get his trapped arm loose and turn it even a few degrees, he could open her up like a garment bag. It would be a messy way to end the fight, but very effective.

He managed to pull his hand up an inch or so before the sound of another gunshot from the living room caused her to twitch. Every one of Rico's muscles strained to keep her fangs away from him. That wouldn't help for much longer since Tara was now pulling hard enough to rip her own hair out at the roots.

"What'd they do to you, kid?" he asked once he'd dragged enough breath into his lungs.

Her eyes were disappearing beneath the thin tendrils that competed for every millimeter of space within her slight frame. She pushed her body down while twisting her head so she could clamp a hand around his neck to hold him steady as she fed.

The moment he had some wiggle room, Rico pulled his arm free and drove the weapon's bottom spike between her ribs. He diverted its mass to grow inside toward her heart. Through the connection between him and that weapon, he could feel when he hit pay dirt. The spore was softer than bone, more fluid than muscle, and too mobile to be an organ. Once he found one of them in her, Rico punctured the spore and did his best to tear it apart. Then Tara got really angry.

That was one of the many problems with multiseeded Nymar. They were tougher than hell and close to impossible to put down. Even if one spore was damaged, the other would carry on until the first was healed. Tara straightened up as if she'd completely forgotten about the hunger gnawing at her insides. She looked down at the source of her pain, grabbed Rico's hand and let out a throaty snarl while forcing him to pull the spike out of her.

He did his best to fight her, but simply wasn't strong enough. Half a second after the notion crossed his mind to let go of the wooden weapon so he could get to his gun, Tara shifted tactics. Once both hands were clamped around his fist and the spikes were sawing into Rico's flesh, she squeezed them even tighter. "Looks like this hurts you as much as it hurts me," she said while eyeing the blood that trickled from between his fingers.

Since she seemed content to try and crush his fingers around the weapon, Rico let her maintain her grip so he could roll onto his back and stretch his other arm out toward the .45.

Her eyes had gone completely black. Rico knew it was the spore looking out at him without allowing the human host to see. "Hope told me that Skinners live to hurt us," she said. "I'd like to make you hurt."

"Why's that?" Rico grunted while straining to get to his pistol. "I'm not the one that killed a bunch of innocent people."

"No. You're the ones that made Hope recruit new members. If you hadn't forced Evan's hand in this, I could have spent that party fucking and sucking like every other party." Smiling luridly, she added, "You like hearing me talk like that?"

When Rico's fingertips brushed against the worn grip of his .45, he curled them until his nails caught in the grooves etched into the handle. "Don't flatter yourself, girl. I've heard dirty talk before and I seen plenty of skinny little bitches like you. It'll take more than whatever tricks you use on the frat boys to wrap me around any one of your bony little fingers."

"Really?" she said as she slipped her fingers on top of Rico's. In one powerful clench, she crushed his hand between hers and the barbed, varnished wooden handle of his weapon. She then grabbed onto the section of the weapon encircling his knuckles and started grinding the weapon against the hand that held it.

Skin tore.

Tendons were shredded.

Sharpened wood scraped against narrow bones.

Rico forgot about the .45 as he kicked his heels against the floorboards and let out a pained, howling wail.

Ned had missed his chance to end the fight before it got any further. He'd gotten the drop on Paige, managed to lift his bat over her skull, but wasn't able to follow through. There was something in Paige's eyes that connected with him. She had a spark, familiar to all Skinners, that allowed them to survive and flourish where most people would give in to the insanity of their new world. Some of Ned's attention was diverted when Rico's agonized voice exploded from the bedroom. Even for someone with Ned's experience, hearing a sound like that from a man like Rico was jarring.

Paige put her spark to use and took aim for another shot at him. Ned didn't hesitate this time and swung the bat like a golf club to knock her .38 aside as it went off. The bullet hissed past his head and she was already rolling away while splinters fell from the hole that had been punched into the ceiling. Somehow, she hung on to her pistol.

In Ned's opinion, this one definitely had promise.

"Whatever they told you, it's a lie," he said.

"You already killed one of them," Paige said through teeth gritted by pain. "You'll come after the rest! Including Tara. I can't allow that. Not after all that's already happened to her."

The house's back entrance was a thick sliding patio door held in place by a latch and steel bar that lay wedged between the door and the other side of the frame. It was pulled open amid the sound of metal being snapped and wood being crushed as the bar was driven into the frame like an oversized nail. Footsteps flooded through the kitchen and living room like a flood of rats that had only been held back by a single rotten barricade. The three Nymar making all that noise wasted no time in swarming the bat-wielding Skinner.

Hope was first to arrive. She wrapped both arms around Ned from behind before he had a chance to turn and face her. "Where's the other one?" she hissed.

Wes and Evan ran into the living room but were reluctant to make a move against the man that Hope had claimed for herself. Their eyes fixed upon Paige, who'd taken the last few seconds to switch her .38 from her bleeding right hand to her left.

Rico let out another grunt, which was followed by a heavy impact. A second later Tara was the one to cry out. Evan pointed down the hall and snarled, "Kill him." When Wes bolted down the hall, Evan crossed the room, making certain to give Hope and Ned their space. "You did good, Paige."

"You're here. They're here. Let me and Tara go!"

Ned struggled with Hope, grabbing onto the arm that had snaked around his neck to try and give himself some breathing room. Even Hope seemed surprised when she was unable to choke the life out of him right then and there.

"We'll see how this pans out before we let anyone go," Evan said. He held out one hand, palm up, and beckoned to Paige. "Now hand me that gun."

"Let Tara go first."

More screams ripped through the house, unrecognizable apart from the fact that they were female. Rico then unleashed a torrent of profanity as solid impacts thumped from one bedroom to another. Paige caught a glimpse of the big man throwing Wes into a wall before the Skinner was slashed across the face by the Nymar's claws and shoved into the next room.

Evan bent down to reach for Paige's trembling hands. "Give me that g—"

She cut his threat short by pulling her trigger twice, catching Evan in the stomach, up high near his solar plexus. The Nymar staggered backward while letting out a breath that sounded as if he'd sprung a leak. Several black fibers stretched out of the bullet wound to grip its edges, widening the wound into a single, surprised eye before a chunk of lead was pushed out. By the time the bullet hit the floor, the wound was closing.

Tears emerged at the corners of Paige's eyes as she bared her teeth and pulled her trigger again and again. Her shots hit Evan in the chest and hip, respectively, sending the Nymar back a few steps without dropping him to the floor. He leered at her hungrily, making fists with both hands as the tendrils patched him up enough to move forward again. He managed to take half a step toward Paige before arching his back and throwing both arms out to either side. His mouth opened and all three sets of fangs extended far enough from the sockets in his gums that the tender, whiter portions of each one stretched down from the pink line of flesh.

A muffled tearing sound bubbled up from the back of Evan's throat and his fingers trembled like frayed sections of a live wire. The middle portion of his light brown shirt became dark and wet. There was no hole in the material, but it was obvious that one of Paige's bullets had found its mark. That theory was disproved the moment something arose beneath his shirt, strained the fabric, and finally poked through. The wooden stake was coated in the Nymar's blood and was sharp enough to cut Evan's hands when he tried to grab hold of the object that had impaled him.

Evan's struggle was over in a matter of seconds. He slumped forward to hang off the stake as his bodily fluids flowed out of him. When he finally did drop to his knees, he cleared the way for Paige to see Ned behind him. Somehow, his bat had shifted into a thinner weapon that drove all the way through Evan's back and out the other side. Ned looked up from the dying Nymar, saw Paige, and croaked, "Run."

Rico's hand felt like a mess of chopped meat hanging from his wrist. It was too bloody for him to see how much damage had been done, so he focused on the hand he could actually use. When he renewed his attempts to get to his .45, he heard the commotion from the other side of the house. All of his senses were dulled by the strain of fighting Tara and the blood he'd lost to her. Despite the fact that she was stronger than any Nymar he had faced thus far in his career, Tara hopped away like a scolded pup when Wes stormed into the bedroom, grabbed him and stood him up.

No matter how torn up Rico's fingers were, they remained locked around his weapon. He could barely feel the varnished wood in his hand when he slashed Wes's throat with the upper spike. Rico didn't know how long his grip would hold, so he turned and swung at Tara while he could. The wooden spike ripped across her upper chest, tearing a section of Tara's shirt and digging a messy gorge a few inches above the slope of her breasts. She screamed, pressed both hands against the ugly wound and staggered away.

Although it would take longer to heal a wound from the Skinner's weapon, Wes pushed through enough of the pain to grab Rico and throw him into the hallway. Rico's free hand closed around Wes's shirt, locking the two of them together as the momentum of their struggle carried them into the adjacent room.

There was next to nothing in there apart from two chairs facing each other and a single box bearing the label of a moving company. Wes staggered backward into the box, clutching the neck wound that was already closing. He kicked over one of the chairs and got his legs entangled with the other. When the Nymar shifted his weight to compensate for the slip, Rico shouted directly into his face. It wasn't so much of a threat or statement, but an obscene roar that made him sound even more like a wounded animal.

Apart from the strain of his leg muscles, Rico's entire body was numb. When he grabbed Wes's shoulder with his left hand, he didn't even feel it enough to know if he'd trapped anything within his grasp. And when he unleashed a series of straight gut punches using the wooden weapon in his right hand, he felt more like he was clumsily moving a rusty tool instead of anything that grew from his shoulder. Even so, the weapon in Rico's bloody rasp managed to hack away at the Nymar's torso.

Wes grabbed Rico's neck amid the punches and began to squeeze. His grip remained strong and his fingernails dug into the skin covering Rico's throat, straining it to the point of tearing it open. One more punch from Rico forced the Nymar's grip to slacken.

With all the blood coming from Rico's flayed palms and fingers, his weapon was covered with a layer of gore thick enough to make it look like something that had truly formed from his own flesh. The hole he'd dug into Wes's stomach was massive. Rico jammed the weapon in as deep as it would go and showed the Nymar an ugly, blocky smile as he willed the charmed wood to stretch up toward an infected heart. Since the weapons were bound to their Skinners by blood, Rico's responded quicker than his own fingers. The wooden spike snapped up, out, and then diverted as much of its mass as possible to form a series of branches that punctured and tore just about everything within Wes's chest cavity. In moments the spore was reduced to pulp. Rico drank in the sight of Wes's vacant stare as he lost the last bit of strength he had.

Paige turned toward the front door and shouted, "Tara! We're leaving!"

Tara emerged from one of the rear bedrooms, glancing back and forth between Paige and the wounds that her tendrils were slowly knitting back together.

Hacking up a strained breath, Ned was unable to utter a single word. Hope had shifted her hands to grab his chest and rake through his shirt using black claws that had emerged from the tips of her fingers. When those claws sank in, his eyes widened and the bat slipped from his hand.

A steely calm drifted onto Paige's face, settling in beneath the tears and dirt that covered her like a cheap mask. "Tara," she said. "Get out of here. Now." The moment Tara backed away, Paige shifted her attention to Ned. Hope was taking her time with him, slowly peeling him open while feeding through the holes her fangs had drilled into the base of his neck. Paige picked up the bat, which had been frozen into a long, gnarled stake. Shifting it around to grab the handle, she winced as its thorns bit into her palm. After adjusting her grip so her fingers fit around the thorns as best they could, she held the stake out in a trembling, two-handed grip. "You too, Hope," she said. "Out."

The Nymar's eyes wandered up to her, and the corners of her mouth curled into a grin without allowing her fangs to come away from Ned's flesh.

"Out!"

When Hope tightened her hold, she looked as if she was hugging Ned from behind. She even let out a soft, throaty moan while pulling another drink from his veins.

Paige stuck the Nymar's arm using the stake that was still coated in Evan's blood. "I said get the fuck *out*!"

Hope glared angrily at Paige and tore her arm out from the stake without seeming to notice the damage it caused. Paige's response was to pull the weapon back and drive it in again. Hope's face twisted with pain and she looked up to speak. Before she could say a word, Paige angled the sharpened end of the weapon to drive it in farther and twist.

The rage that surged into the Nymar's face was the first truly demonic thing Paige had ever seen. Stark terror mixed with wonder on her young features, but she maintained her grip on the stake and continued to grind it within the widening wound. Hope couldn't take much more of that before pulling away from Ned.

"I'll kill you!" Paige swore.

Clutching her arm to her chest, Hope surveyed her surroundings to find nobody else in the room to come to her aid. She scurried down the hall and glared at Paige with solid black eyes. "You've got to sleep sometime, Paige. I don't." Holding up both arms to show them to her and Ned, the Nymar trembled as the gaping wounds began to slowly seal. "I'll come for you."

Those were Hope's last words before she was overpowered by the slender woman who charged at her from the bedroom. Despite the veil of dirty blond hair covering her face, Tara's broken fangs and crazed expression could be seen as clearly as if they were illuminated by a searchlight. Thanks to the multiple spore attached to both of their hearts, Hope and Tara moved like streaks of frenetic energy. Tara wrapped her arms around Hope's midsection and forced her into the kitchen, where both Nymar exploded through the hole left by the broken patio door. Once outside, they were not heard again.

"Give me that weapon," Ned grunted at Paige.

"Only if you promise to leave me and Tara alone!"

"That ain't gonna happen," Rico said as he staggered from the bedroom. The syringe was still in his arm when he walked down the hall. After emptying the healing serum into himself, he tossed the syringe toward the spot where it had been stashed and braced himself against a wall while it took effect. "After what happened tonight, there ain't any deals we're gonna strike with you."

Ned's wobbly steps carried him to the cheap stand used to hold the television set. Kicking open a little cabinet intended for videos or possibly a game console, he stooped down to retrieve a small leather manicure pouch. "Hope had me dead to rights," he said while opening the pouch, then taking one of the syringes that had been slipped through a loop meant to hold a nail file. He popped the cap off, injected himself, and sighed, "Until this one here got her offa me."

"Fine," Rico said. "She can go. But them bloodsuckers out back are dead meat." At the sound of a single inhuman wail from outside, he added, "Or whichever one is left, that is."

Tightening her grip on the gnarled wooden bat, Paige set her feet shoulder width apart, pulled in a shaky breath and said, "You're letting both of us go."

Ned held a silencing hand out to Rico before the big man could respond. That visibly perturbed Rico, but he let it go with a muttered curse.

"Your friend's sick, girl," Ned said.

"I know. I can help her."

"Can you?"

The skin around Paige's left eye twitched. Whatever was trying to get out of her at that moment, she fought to keep it buried.

Ned stared her down as he asked, "What's happening outside, Rico?"

The big man hauled his aching body into the kitchen and took a quick look through a small rectangular window situated above a cheap, stained vinyl countertop. "Shit! Hope's gone."

"What about Tara?" Paige asked.

"She's gettin' up. Oh wait. Damn it to hell! She's gone now too. Damn, those bitches can jump!"

Paige nodded. "Now it's my turn. I'm out of here, and neither of you are following us. The first time I see either one of you assholes anywhere near me or Tara, I'm calling the cops and telling them about you."

"Telling them what?" Ned asked. "That we killed a bunch of vampires?"

"You guys can't tell me this is your first time doing this sort of thing," she replied. "You want me to believe the cops won't dig up something rotten on you if they look for more than a few seconds?"

Ned kept his composure, but Rico was too tired to prevent the worry from showing on his battered face.

"That's what I thought," she said smugly. "Those vampires or whatever the hell they are got what was coming to them. They were about to kill all of us, but you kept that from happening. I appreciate it, but don't think I'll let you near me again. All I ask is for a head start so me and Tara can get the hell out of here."

"Hope's still out there," Ned pointed out. "And there are more to help her do what she wants or attack whoever she pleases. If she can't find any friends, she'll turn the next batch of people she can find just like she turned your friend."

"Whatever. This is the first bunch of vampires I've ever seen, so I'll just head back to any other place I've ever been that was vampire-free."

"Nymar. They're called Nymar."

"Again. Whatever. I'm leaving now. Don't try to follow me."

Ned took a tentative step toward her. "What are you going to do when they come after you, Paige? How are you going to help your friend? Do you think you'll even find her again?"

"She's a multiseed," Rico said. "Even among the Nymar,

they're freaks. Wild, strong, and tough to control. If they don't got the smarts to rise to the top of the heap like Hope did, they're hunted down and ripped apart."

Paige remained silent, but her arms suddenly seemed too tired to hold the weapon she'd grabbed.

"You wanted to protect Tara from them and us?" Ned asked. "That's why you struck this deal to give them what they wanted."

"And we ain't about to forget that," Rico said.

Jabbing a finger over to the big man, Ned wheeled around and barked, "Shut up!" When he spoke to Paige again, it was in a tempered but commanding voice. "We don't have much time before we have to worry about police coming to check on all the noise over here, so listen up. Hope will come after you, Paige. If not her, it'll be one of the others as soon as they find out what you know about us."

"Then I'll tell them everything," she said. "It's not like you did jackshit when I needed you or when Tara needed you. Even Karen . . . she's probably . . ."

"Karen's fine," Ned told her.

"Are you sure?"

He nodded. "She came by the hospital a few times after you and Tara ran away. She may have been trying to be sneaky, acting like she didn't know what happened, but she asked too many of the wrong questions and I caught up with her on the way out. Someone was there to pick her up. She left. I made sure she got away safely and haven't seen her since."

It seemed that was the last thing holding Paige up. Once that had been taken away from her, every ounce of fear, fatigue, and confusion sank in like a weight pressing her down. Without the strength to lift her arms, the weapon in her hands tapped against the floor.

"So," Ned said as he tentatively approached her, "what now?"

Paige shook her head, her head still lowered. "I don't know. I guess they'll come after me. Hope's gone. Tara will be gone too."

"How do you know that?" Rico asked. "You weren't gonna meet up with her somewhere?"

"No. The only plan was finding you guys before you killed her. Hope found us first, and when they told me you'd killed the one who killed Amy that night at the party, I thought you'd come after us next. To be honest, I didn't think I'd make it out of here before one of you or one of them finished me off." She started to look up at Ned but quickly clenched her eyes shut. No matter how hard she tried, she couldn't keep the tears from flowing. When that happened, she dropped down to sit with her arms propped on her knees her hands pressed against her face, leaving crimson smears on her skin. "I mean . . . what the hell am I supposed to do against this? I can't fight you. I can't fight *them*. I don't even know what *they* are!"

Ned stopped just outside of her reach and lowered himself to one knee. "Nymar," he told her. "They're Nymar."

"Great. You've told me that already. Mind telling me whose blood is this?" she asked after looking down at her hands and using the back of one to try and clean her face. "How did this stick change shape? How many more days do I have until someone pops out from somewhere to tear me apart?"

"They may find you again or they may not."

"Is that supposed to make me feel better?"

"No," Ned replied. "But you may feel better once you learn how to defend yourself."

Paige's arms dangled along the top of her knees as she looked up at the older man with bloodshot eyes. "You're going to teach me how to swing a stick?"

"That's the plan."

"Come on, Ned," Rico said from the kitchen. "Think about this."

"What do I need to think about? She's a fighter. She's got the spark in her eye. Besides, she's already seen enough to be useful to us. With a little bit of training, she can—"

"She can what?" Rico snapped. "Kill us in our sleep? Find out even more about us and then turn that shit over to some multiseeded Nymar bitch?"

"It won't happen that way," Ned insisted. "We'll keep an eye on her."

Paige might have needed the elongated stake to help get up again, but she didn't need it to remain standing. Once she had her balance, she threw the weapon down so it clattered against the floor near its owner's feet. "None of us will have to worry about any of this bullshit. I'm out of here."

"You won't be able to shake this, Paige," Ned said as he scooped up his weapon and stood up. "You're not one of those people who can convince yourself this didn't happen or that what you saw can be explained away. Your eyes are open. I know, because I looked straight into them."

"What do you want from me?"

"I want you to become a Skinner." Despite the look that got from both her and Rico, Ned continued unabated. "I want you to keep that fire inside you alive. It's the same drive that got you out of that hospital in one piece and out on the street until you tracked us down. Do you know that nobody—not the cops or the Nymar—have found us here until now?"

Reluctantly, Paige said, "Well, you did give me a card."

"Now I want to give you the means to put that fire of yours to use. There aren't a lot of us around and we need all the good fighters we can possibly get. Hope and Evan were members of a small group in a small town. There are larger groups out there, doing much worse things in bigger cities. You don't even know about the other creatures out there, Paige. There are things preying on people like your friends that make the Nymar look like insects. Your instinct is to fight them. That's something that can't be taught. What *can* be taught is the means to win the fight. We can teach you that."

"Fuck that," Rico snarled. "That girl walked in here tryin' to kill us! Have you forgotten that already?"

Ned grinned as the weapon in his hands re-formed into its unassuming broom handle shape. "And she got closer than the cult in Topeka. That says a lot."

"Yeah," Rico scoffed. "She's a real bloodhound. I ain't letting those freak jobs in Topeka get away with what they did and I ain't about to forget about this. You wanna train this one? It's on your head. Keep her the hell away from me."

"Are you forgetting what kind of things hang over your

head, Rico? Can you seriously look at her and say you're so much better than her?"

"Don't flip that 'he who is without sin' crap at me," Rico grunted. "I'm not talking about who gets to cast the first stone. I'm talkin' about who can be trusted. I proved myself a long time ago. That one there," he said while jabbing a gnarled, bloody finger at Paige, "has proved that she'll jump sides at the first line of sweet talk whispered into her ear. You want your first lesson, girl? Bloodsuckers are real good at sweet talk. If yer too stupid to have figured that out after dealing with assholes like Wes, then you ain't gonna be any use to us!"

"So if you train me, does that mean I get to spar with him?" Paige asked.

"More than likely," Ned replied.

"Then sign me up," she said with a tired, halfhearted grin. "It'd be worth it just to kick his ass a few times."

Rico's cold scowl was all he needed to let them know what he thought of that.

"There may be a better fit for your initial training," Ned told her. "I need to get back to those sightings in the Everglades, but Gerald is free. I think you two should get along just fine."

Chapter Thirty

"So," Cole said once he finally got a chance to speak, "that means Hope's been chasing Paige for over ten years? I suppose that was a long way to go for that information. She could have just told me there was a history there."

Rico sat in the driver's seat with his elbow propped against the steering wheel. The car was parked, so he devoted his attention to picking at a stubborn strand of beef jerky with a toothpick as he replied, "That ain't the whole reason she wanted to tell you that story, and it ain't why you needed to hear it."

They sat along East Fiftieth Avenue, a stretch of road in a section of the city filled with industrial parks and fenced lots of building supplies behind large, two-level storage units. It was just past two in the morning and the air was cold enough to grate against Cole's eyeballs as it leaked in through the poorly insulated car windows. As much as he wanted to stop being angry with Paige, he simply couldn't bring himself to that point.

The few other cars that passed them after Rico had first come to a stop were just as anxious to remain unseen as the Skinners keeping watch on the second building within the closest fenced-in lot. According to the latest word he'd gotten from the local news sites, the Denver PD was being kept occupied by a string of fires set in random spots around the city well away from Fiftieth Avenue.

Rolling down the window, Rico said, "Love that mountain air."

"Yeah. Joining the Skinners has really given me a chance to travel and see the sights. Too bad I get to see every damn city in the middle of the night."

"And you wonder why Paige didn't have any trouble jamming a blade through your chest? The more you gripe, the more I get behind that idea myself."

The car that rolled up to them was easy enough to miss. It was just battered enough to blend in with the others on the road, slow enough to flow with the rest of the sparse traffic, and turned sharply enough to get close before Rico could do much about it. The big man did already have his Sig Sauer resting on his lap and ready to fire up through his window. Fortunately for the passenger of the other car, the Skinners weren't so easily spooked.

"Stanley's not gonna believe you guys are really here," Prophet said as he leaned his elbow out the other car's window. "He actually giggled when I told him we were closing in on these guys tonight. The man's got scars from a war and two different street fights, but he giggled."

"What's he think?" Rico asked indignantly. "That we weren't gonna hold up our end of the bargain? Your boss bailed me and Cole here out of that cell in St. Louis and we said we'd do this. What made him think it would go any other way?"

"Well, there was that voice mail you left where you told him he could stick his favor up his ass."

"That don't count," Rico replied without missing a beat.

"Who's with you?"

"It's just me and Cole."

"Where's Paige?" Prophet asked.

"Warning the cops that they're being set up by these informants they think they got."

Prophet's comfort level dropped quicker than a phone

call in the middle of a cement tunnel. "She's warning them? What happens if the Nymar get wind of that?"

Leaning over to make his presence known, Cole said, "Then things might get a little crazy. Oh, wait. That already happened. Are we doing this tonight or what?"

"Yeah, we are. Best pick up the pace too."

"My thoughts exactly. Who's driving that car?"

"Gunari. We got the whole Czech crew in here. We've gotten pretty tight over the last day or so."

"Hey, Drina. Haven't seen you since Philly," Rico said. "Keepin' busy?"

The rear passenger window came down and the green-eyed blond woman acknowledged him with a curt upward nod.

Showing her an ugly smile, Rico asked, "Walter getting on your nerves yet?"

"It's been a long trip," she said before leaning back and rolling her window up.

"Check your e-mail, Cole," Prophet said. "Stan should have sent you the rest of our files on these guys we're after."

"There's more than what he already sent?"

"Sure. That shit's confidential. We're not just gonna spread it all over the place until we need to. You know how it goes."

After refreshing his e-mail in-box on his phone's Web browser, Cole found the newest arrival from S.Velasco@ LibertyBailBonds.com. "Is there anything more than where to find them?"

"There's a whole history in there. Prior arrests. Suspected involvements in—"

"Anything that can help us *tonight*?" Cole cut in.

Wincing, Prophet said, "There's the location. Only thing is, that information's a little old. Last time one of our bondsmen checked, that address had gone through two other owners."

If not for the hit he'd taken to his credit card and the two year service plan he'd already signed, Cole would have thrown his phone out the window.

"There's something else we need to talk about."

Rico's eyes narrowed as he asked, "What might that be?"

"It's about why we're here in your country," Tobar said from Cole's side of the car.

Not only hadn't Cole heard the other man approach, but he hadn't seen a single shadow to announce the Amriany's presence. Rico snapped his arm up to point the Sig Sauer across Cole's face toward the window, proving he'd been just as surprised.

"I wouldn't advise you sneakin' up on me like that again, Gypsy boy," Rico said.

Tobar's stocky build filled a good portion of Cole's window. He grinned to display his missing section of teeth as he replied, "It speaks a lot that it was so easy to sneak up on you. And if you speak the word Gypsy as if it was a curse again, I will shoot you both through this door."

Cole leaned over just enough to see the .357 in Tobar's hand. "He's got us there," he said while settling back into his seat.

Despite the gun in Rico's hand, Tobar kept talking as if he was ordering lunch from a familiar menu. "Your country has been exporting Kintalaphi and we have traced them here."

"At first we thought they had come from your *prala* Lancroft," Gunari said from the driver's seat. "But there are too many of them and they are too old for this to be the case."

"I thought you only came here to steal from Lancroft," Rico said. "What's with all the jet setting?"

The rear window of the other car came down again so Drina could say, "Our stolen belongings have been scattered to every corner of this country. And you call us thieves?"

"No. I called you Gypsies."

Tobar's expression remained unchanged as the menacing tap of a gun barrel against the outside of the car filled Cole's ears.

Compared to Tobar's movements a few seconds ago, Nadya practically announced her exit from the car with a marching band. She slammed her door, stomped around the rear of the vehicle and marched straight over to the Amriany that wielded the .357. "You know better than this," she said to Tobar. "The Americans always goad us. It's what they do."

Rico shrugged in a comically apologetic fashion.

"And you," Nadya continued while bending down to glare through Cole's window, "should have better things to do than pick a fight. We came here because you asked us, remember? We had plenty to do in Texas when your friend here convinced us to come to the mountains instead. Tell us why we should help you or we'll drive away and continue doing our own work."

"First of all," Cole said, "if you guys are gonna shoot each other, could you at least wait for me to switch seats?" When Rico laid the Sig Sauer back on his lap, Cole could only assume the nod from Tobar meant the .357 had also found its home. "And second, what's a kin-talapia?"

"Kintalaphi," Tobar said in an accent that had been lifted from every Frankenstein movie to come out of Universal Studios' golden age. "It's—"

"It's their word for a multiseeded Nymar," Rico cut in. "You know, like Tara and Hope?" Running his fingers in straight lines along both sides of his face, he looked out to the Amriany on Cole's side of the car and asked, "Ain't that right?"

Tobar nodded. "We have many reasons to come to your country. Many possessions to reclaim. Until now we were willing to let you squabble over our trinkets while the Nymar picked you apart. Now that the Kintalaphi are spreading, we must come to make sure it goes no further."

"Ain't that nice, Cole?" Rico asked. "They're here to lend us a hand."

"It is not our concern if all Skinners will probably be killed in the war to come. We are only here to make sure the blood does not spill too far beyond your own shores."

Sitting up straight, Cole asked, "What war?"

"The one that has already started," Nadya replied. "The weapons have been collected for generations by killers like Jonah Lancroft, put to use by demons like the Kintalaphi. To make matters worse we—like your common people and your police—are being manipulated by the Nymar. This must end."

Tobar nodded solemnly. "Before long we may become as blind and ignorant as you."

Rico wasn't about to bite on the worm being dangled in front of him. "So you guys got anything to share?" he asked. "Sounds like you may know some things to make this easier."

The look on Tobar's face wasn't giving much away.

Prophet hadn't opened his mouth in a while and sat in the Amriany's car as if there was a gun stuck into his ribs.

Cole could only assume the other European hunters were in the car as well, but they weren't talking either.

Finally, Nadya said, "We have friends who watch the Nymar in your country. They are the ones who pointed us toward Texas. We were ready to close in on a group in Austin, but the Nymar all left that place to go somewhere else before our plane could land."

"Where did they go?"

"We don't know. Since you seem to have more current information, we came here. If this place turns out to be empty or a trap, then we'll know who had something to do with it."

When Cole met Prophet's eye, he got the distinct impression that the bounty hunter wasn't as willing a passenger as he might have been letting on. Either that or Walter was going along with the Amriany without tipping off the Skinners for some other reason. Neither of those possibilities sat very well with him.

"Who are these friends of yours?" Rico asked. Upon seeing the glares coming from every Amriany in sight, he added, "For all you know, they could be the ones that are misinformed. Hell, they could be the ones tipping off the bloodsuckers."

"They are friends," Tobar said. "We trust them much more than we can trust you."

"Look here, asshole. You can call them whatever you want. Hell, you can call me your papa, but that don't mean I screwed your—"

"He gets it," Cole said before Rico sparked something that would involve way too much gunfire crossing in front of him. "We're not doing ourselves any favors by having a convention out here in the street where we can be spotted by any Nymar out for a smoke break. They do take smoke breaks, right?"

"He's got a point," Rico grudgingly admitted. "If those Austin bloodsuckers got access to the Internet, we may know who tipped them off."

"Who?" Tobar asked. "Is it someone we can look up now?"

"Probably," Rico told him. "But you can look it up the same time Cole has a look at whatever computer setup they got in there or wherever they moved to since then."

"They're about a mile from here on Oneida Street," Prophet said.

Rico's face turned even uglier than usual. "How long were you gonna wait before telling us that little tidbit?"

"That was our doing," she said. "After we caught him trying to follow us out of Philadelphia, we brought him along with us and convinced him it would be easier to work with us. As for meeting you here, we thought it might serve us better to work out our differences before attacking the Nymar."

"That actually makes sense to me," Cole said. "How screwed up is that?"

Although Rico seemed ready to bust someone's head open, he nodded and grudgingly sighed.

The Amriany were happy with the development and got back to their car. Prophet watched through his window, seeming genuinely shaken as he was driven away.

"What?" Rico grunted as he turned his deathly glare in Cole's direction. "You feel sorry for poor little Walter?"

"Hell no! Son of a bitch is riding with the Gypsies now, right?"

Rico slapped the car into Drive and pulled away with a lurch.

Bracing his feet against the floor and making sure his seat belt was fastened, Cole did his best to appear relaxed as Rico followed the other car. "Besides," he added, "what did Prophet ever do for us, right? Saved me and Paige in Wisconsin. Oh, and he did lay the groundwork for our arrangement with the nymphs. Guess that's something."

"Free strip club buffets don't make up for switchin' sides," Rico snapped.

"He didn't switch sides."

"Yeah? We'll just have to wait and see about that."

Chapter Thirty-One

They drove east through the industrial district. It was a part of town defined by abandoned cars, flat buildings made of cement and metal siding, open fields of dying grass, and businesses that might or might not have been empty shells. The brighter part of the city could be sensed more than felt. Its glow smeared the stars overhead, but its voice was too distant to be heard.

Cole took advantage of the short travel time to dial Paige's cell. Just when it started to ring, he spotted a familiar face on the side of the road. As they drove closer, the figure waved its arms to flag him down. Cole hung up the phone, stuffed it into his pocket, and swatted Rico's arm. "Pull over!"

"Huh? Why?"

"Just do it. Look!"

As Cole pointed to the side of the road, Rico spotted the figure. "I'll be damned!" he said as he hit the brakes and steered toward the shoulder. "That you, Bloodhound?"

"What the hell are you doing out here?" Cole asked.

"Just got in town and I thought I'd try to catch up to you," Paige replied. "Mind if I get in?"

As Cole's phone rang, he reached back to unlock the door directly behind him. "Go ahead."

"Is that your phone ringing?" she asked while climbing in.

"Yeah."

"Give it to me. I'm expecting a call."

"What?"

"I lost my phone and knew you'd be here, so I gave them your number."

When Paige shot her right arm over Cole's shoulder and impatiently snapped her fingers, he gave her the chirping phone before it was taken from him by force. She tapped the screen a few times, muttered to herself, then slumped back against the overly worn seat cushions. "Too late," she huffed. "They hung up. I'll just wait for them to call back."

"So how'd you get back in town?" Rico asked.

"Same way you did, only I had to get a cab to get this far."

Before they could get into any more explanation than that, the brake lights on the Amriany car lit up. Cole's phone chirped again, so Paige took it from her pocket and answered it. After a few quick sentences and an even quicker explanation as to why Cole hadn't answered, she hung up and pointed to a white building surrounded by chain-link fence. There was no sign to be found, but the place was too utilitarian to be a residence. The stark cement walls without the first attempt at decoration reminded Cole of a large storage unit or an even larger garage.

"That's the place," she said.

The other car killed its lights and rolled to a stop in a lot adjacent to the white building at the corner of Fiftieth and Oneida Street behind a small cluster of tractor-trailer trucks. All four doors of the car opened, allowing Prophet and the Amriany to file out and disperse into the shadows. The bounty hunter and Drina stayed close to the darkened trucks as they hurried to the corner.

Rico parked farther up along Fiftieth, which meant a somewhat longer walk to the white building. A small Nymar presence could be felt within Cole's scars as well as throughout his entire body, but he knew that meant nothing where Shadow Spore were concerned. His muscles tensed and a jab shot through his heart like a phantom pain caused by the body compensating for a vital piece that had been cut away. He did his best to forget about it.

By the time the Skinners had gotten out and circled around the car, Prophet and Drina were close enough to speak without shouting.

"The others are scouting ahead," Drina told them. Tapping her ear, she added, "I will keep in touch with them with this."

Rico removed a small pouch from his pocket and said, "Yeah, we got electronics stores over here too." After dumping similar earpieces into his hand from the pouch, he handed them out to Cole and Paige before taking one for himself.

"Where are the others headed?" Paige asked.

"The Nymar must be preparing something," Drina said. "If they are watching the street, Gunari will give them something to see other than us."

"Paige was checking on some things too," Cole said as he turned to her. "What did you find out?"

Using her left hand to flip her hair back, Paige fit the earpiece in place with the other in a series of short, practiced movements. "Now's not the time for that. Let's get off the street and I'll fill you in as we go."

"Sounds like a plan," Rico said enthusiastically.

The five of them crossed the street and headed for cover provided by the semis parked in the nearby lot. From there they wove between the darkened hulks until Cole signaled for them to stop. "Camera," he whispered while pointing to a single black box mounted under the building's gutter.

Drina's hand drifted to her earpiece. She tapped it twice, paused for a moment and then tapped it again. About a second later Cole heard the distinct sound of a metal door on the other side of the building being kicked in. Hurried footsteps scraped from different sections of the lot as well as on the building's roof, quickly followed by angry voices.

"You have your distraction," Drina said.

Rico smirked, picked up a rock that he'd trapped beneath his foot and said, "Good. Then nobody should take much notice of this." With that, he threw the rock at the camera. It didn't hit hard enough to smash the device, but cracked the lens while also turning it toward the street and away from the lot. Making certain to walk in the newly created blind spot, he led the way toward a side door that wasn't marked by anything more than a small handle set into a thick steel surface.

Before Rico could touch that handle, he was pushed aside by Drina. "There's another alarm. Step away before you set it off."

He raised his hands and did as he was told.

She fished some tools from her jacket pocket and put them to use in the short amount of time it took the others to settle in around her. Though Cole had a vague idea of what was involved in deactivating an alarm system, she might as well have been performing brain surgery. The last time he'd seen anything like it was when Paige had snuck into the back entrance of Steph's Blood Parlor the first time they visited the place.

He looked over to his partner, and when Paige noticed that she was being watched, she flashed him a quick smile.

"Get ready," Drina said. The next tool she used was a little plastic gun that looked better suited for attaching price tags to shoes. After a few pumps on the long trigger and a couple twists of the gun itself, something clicked and the door came open. She held it in place so the others could file in.

Rico entered first, stepped to one side and drew the Sig Sauer from the holster under his shoulder. "Where are the cops supposed to be, Paige?"

Stepping inside next, Cole said, "Forget about that. Let's find the computer terminals. They'll probably be close to their own power source since this place doesn't look like it's wired too well. Also, if the Nymar are waiting for trouble, I doubt they'd keep their system up front where it was easy to get to."

While following Cole down the left side of a T junction leading away from the door, Rico asked, "How can you be sure?"

"Because there were no lights on in the other corner of the building and there are over here. This Cobb38 guy is supposed to be coordinating things, right?"

"Yeah."

"Then the computers are probably still on. You got any better guess, then feel free to tell us." Directly in front of Cole was a narrow hallway lit by a set of fluorescent bulbs along the entire ceiling. Evenly spaced doors ran on both sides of the hall. Suddenly, the second door on the right swung open and a man stepped out. As luck would have it, he turned his back to them and started walking without so much as a glance at the Skinners or their escort. Cole took advantage of the distraction provided by the Amriany up front by rushing toward the man.

He was a good old-fashioned Nymar. Black markings stretched up from beneath the collar of a thin cable-knit sweater, and the grease in his veins sent a familiar itch through Cole's scars. When he drew his pistol, the Spetznaz holster moved the slide back and chambered the first round. It was a smooth, metallic sound that caught the Nymar's ear and spun him around just in time to look down the business end of Cole's .45.

"Any more in there with you?" he asked.

The Nymar was only an inch shorter than Cole, but glared at him as if he was the one with the cards stacked in his favor. It was plain to see that he wasn't about to start talking, but that didn't bother Cole half as much as the other warning that rippled beneath his hands to send a heat up through both arms.

Without taking his eyes off of the Nymar, Cole asked, "Any of you guys feel that?"

"Yeah," Rico replied. "There's a shapeshifter around here."

Grabbing the Nymar by the throat, Cole shoved him back into the room he'd just left and knocked the barrel of his .45 against the guy's head loud enough to make a dull *crack*. "Where's your computer room?"

"What computer room?" the Nymar asked.

"The room where you keep your fucking computer! Where *is it*?"

The Nymar lost his confident grin as well as a good portion of the color in his face. "Down the hall on the left. I was just headed there."

Rico stepped up to send a quick jab into the Nymar's ribs. "You expectin' any Half Breeds?"

"What?"

"We know they're here. Them or a Full Blood, and since they ain't tearing this place apart, that means you must already know about 'em. What's going on? You keeping them locked up somewhere like those assholes in Tijuana who thought they could train 'em as guard dogs?"

"My partners will find them," Drina said. "Let's just do our part so we can help them quicker."

"Computer," Cole snarled. "Take us to it."

The Nymar led the way across the hall as gunfire erupted from the front section of the building. After one of the longest walks he'd ever taken, Cole found himself across in a room that smelled like stale coffee, new plastic, and air that had been blown through a hot processor. If two-day-old pizza and spilled, overcaffeinated soda was added to the mix, he might have thought he'd been transported back to the offices of Digital Dreamers, Inc.

"Right over there," the Nymar said while pointing to the wall on the far side of the room.

Cole tightened his grip on the guy's collar and pushed him forward. "Prophet, sit at the keyboard. Type what I tell you to type and do it slowly so I can see everything that happens." Dropping his voice to a snarl that surprised even himself, he added, "I know every sort of red flag you can send, Trojan you can unleash, signal you can give, or any other thing you might be able to do here. I can also hack into this terminal and get what I want on my own, but if you save me that time and trouble we'll thank you by giving you a head start before we put down every last one of you fuckers. Got me?"

The Nymar nodded, accidentally bumped his head against the barrel of Cole's gun and stammered, "Y-Yes. I understand."

"How do we reach Cobb38?"

The Nymar started rattling off Internet addresses and passwords. Prophet sat at the keyboard until Cole gave him the okay before touching so much as one smooth plastic square. It turned out that the Nymar communication network operated through a ring of websites and e-mail accounts that were only connected by a few members who passed information from source to source. Once Cole had committed some of the details to memory, he wanted to try to get a member of the inner ring of the network to send something to him. Every e-mail came with tags and source codes that could point him in the right direction when looking for the source, and hopefully a flesh-and-blood Cobb38. With enough time he knew he might even be able to send something to Cobb that would truly mess up his day, as well as his entire system. That dream was quashed when Rico shouted at him from his post at the doorway.

"Looks like Gunari is pushing them toward us!"

"Pull up another e-mail, Walter," Cole said quickly. "One of the ones addressed to Cobb's whole system. Add my e-mail address to the list of senders and send out a generic reply so it's placed into the circulation. Drina, you and Rico buy us a minute and then head back out."

"What about Paige?" Rico asked.

"Me, her, and Walter will stay here to wrap this up. Just go!"

Either Rico was surprised by the forceful tone in Cole's voice or he truly did respect him more as a partner, because the big man nodded once and motioned for Drina to help him carry out the orders they'd been given.

"Done," Prophet said as he tapped the last key.

Cole didn't need to do much more than shift his eyes to get a look at Paige. She stood in the middle of the room, between two cheap folding tables that looked like those professional wrestlers used as landing pads when jumping from the top ropes. Apart from the computer setup and tables, there wasn't much of anything else within the room. Paige met his glance with an intensity that made it seem they were secluded from the rest of the world. Unfortunately, it wasn't the good kind of intensity, and it sure as hell wasn't a good kind of seclusion.

"What do you want to do from here?" he asked.

"You seem to be doing pretty well," Paige replied. "I'll follow your lead."

"Prophet, take this."

The bounty hunter stood up and had to act fast in order to catch the Nymar prisoner that was shoved toward him. Old instincts combined with job skills nicely enough for him to take control of the prisoner by twisting one arm behind the Nymar's back and shoving him face first against the computer desk. "What should I do with him?"

"Find out whatever you or your boss needs to know about these Denver assholes," Cole said. "Right after you find out where the cops are that're being set up for a fall. If he acts like he doesn't know about any cops, kill him." Shifting to look down at the squirming Nymar, he added, "Use those antidote rounds I gave you. They should do the trick."

"What's next, Cole?" Paige asked.

Releasing the .45's slide so he could safely holster the pistol, he snapped it back into the holster on his belt and drew the spear from where it had been strapped to his back. "Next, you tell me who the fuck you are, because you're sure as hell not my partner."

Chapter Thirty-Two

An angry twitch drifted across Paige's face as she backed away. Although the fierceness in her eyes seemed like the woman Cole knew, their color was off by a few shades of brown and they were just a little too vivid to be natural. They shifted to a more sedated hue as she said, "Of course. You have feelings for this one. That would explain the inconsistencies."

"Who are you?" Cole demanded.

Instead of the muted crackle of broken bones or the internal ripping of muscle and sinew that went along with other shapeshifters' transformation, Paige's change sounded more like a breath pulled in through a constricted throat. Familiar features dissolved and her skin pressed in around a narrowing frame. Even as her body's curves faded like a dream and her clothes turned into rags, her eyes remained the same.

The figure that stood in front of Cole was vaguely familiar to him. Thinking back to the drive from where they'd met up with the Amriany, he realized it was the figure he'd first mistaken for Paige on the side of the road. Tightening his grip on the spear, he took comfort from the trickle of warm blood between his fingers. The bite of the thorns into his palms gave a much needed burst of adrenaline through his veins. "You're a Full Blood?"

"My name is Kawosa and I am no Full Blood. No more than a king is merely a citizen."

"Why can't you guys just talk like everyone else?"

"And why can't humans ever ask the first question on their minds without trying to dress it up with a lot of chatter and threatening gestures?"

"Where's Paige?"

"Where did you last see her?"

"You must have known what she looked like or you wouldn't have been able to change into her. It's gotta be something like that, right?"

More gunshots ripped through the building, followed by Amriany voices calling back and forth. Somewhere within the building, doors were thrown open and different voices were added to the mix. Cole's earpiece chirped once and Rico's voice followed.

"This place is crawlin' with those goddamn striped bloodsuckers. Someone else is coming and my money's on them bein' cops. What the hell happened, Paige? Didn't you call these guys off?"

Kawosa's eyes rolled around in their sockets as if he was following a pattern of lights dancing in front of his eyes. After they settled in the direction of his right ear, he pulled the device out, tossed the earpiece to the floor and smashed it under his foot as if it was a tick that had been lodged in his flesh.

Looking at his own hands, just to make sure the weapon was still in them, Cole said, "You're a shapeshifter, so I know this weapon will hurt you. Tell me what happened to Paige."

"I took her from your thoughts when you first laid eyes on me."

"Shit. Another Mind Singer?"

"Oh, no. I can only read what lies on your surface, but that's all I ever need. It's rare your species ever uses much of anything deeper than that. Tell me, when did you know I wasn't your Paige?"

"The moment you got in the car."

"I doubt that very much."

The expression on the shapeshifter's face was so confident and so extremely arrogant that Cole wanted nothing more than to knock it off of him. With the firefight outside and no sign from the real Paige, he figured it couldn't hurt to buy himself a few more seconds for reinforcements to arrive. "Her arm was wounded in Kansas City," he said. "Yours wasn't scarred. It wasn't even stiff."

Kawosa absently rubbed that arm. "And the eyes, right?" Despite the fact that Cole didn't respond, Kawosa nodded serenely. "It's always the eyes when it comes down to someone a human cares about. You'd think I would know that by now, wouldn't you? The fact of the matter is that you care deeply for this woman. That's why you envision her in such pristine condition."

"Pristine, huh?" Cole chuckled. "You seriously need to do more research on someone before you try to mimic them."

"And perhaps you should think harder about what you feel for her," Kawosa said with a cruel, confident smile. "You may not have a lot of time left to enjoy each other. As for the Full Blood claim, I do share certain traits with them. Skinners have rarely been able to detect me, however. Your forefather Lancroft worked for years on end just to catch my scent. That itch in your hands probably came from them." Kawosa nodded toward the back of the room in a corner near the computer desk.

Cole knew better than to turn around and look. If there was anything worth seeing, Prophet would have spoken up by now.

"Uhhh," Prophet said. "You better get over here."

Heavy footsteps scraped against the floor, sounding like sandbags being dragged across the linoleum. The breaths drifting through the air were the low rasp of wind snagging upon ravaged throats. A pair of werewolves stalked across the room, leaving a juicy trail of saliva that fell from their mouths. They moved with a purpose that was nowhere to be found in any of the beasts that had ripped through Kansas City or the wild things that slept in filthy pits after tearing apart any man, woman, or child that crossed their path. They were bigger than Half Breeds and walked without lifting their paws fully from the floor. Their heads swung easily back and forth and their lips curled up to reveal a set of elongated fangs marked by two pairs of curved tusks sprouting from top and bottom jaws.

Watching the bulky creatures, Cole shifted his stance so neither they nor Kawosa were behind him. Unable to come up with a better guess, he asked, "Burkis? Is that you?"

The moment the werewolves got within striking distance of the computer desk, they snarled at Prophet, but shifted their eyes back to Kawosa before doing anything else.

"You have one chance for me to call them off," Kawosa said. "Tell me all you know about the Skinners, how they communicate, and what else they've gleaned from Jonah Lancroft, and I'll give you a chance to escape before I set these two loose. Make your decision now."

Cole didn't want to fight an unknown creature, but knew there was no possible way he would ever tell the shapeshifter a damn thing.

"Fine," Kawosa said. "If you don't talk, I know there are others here who will."

"I hate mind readers," Cole grunted as one of the bulkier Half Breeds came straight at him.

The other one lunged at Prophet. Until now he and the Nymar had been watching Kawosa and Cole without knowing how to insert themselves into the situation. When they finally saw a chance to do something, both of them sprang into motion. The Nymar lunged for the computer desk, reached beneath the cheap printer setup and hit a button that sent a piercing shriek through the room. A second too late to prevent the alarm from going off, Prophet grabbed the Nymar and shoved him toward the closest werewolf.

The Nymar was lifted off his feet and shaken from side to side when the werewolf's tusks were driven up under his rib cage. It disemboweled the Nymar and then tossed him onto the computer desk so it could feast. Oily blood ran down its face as it opened its mouth to let out a howling snarl. Prophet fired his pistol at the creature the moment it set its sights on him.

Those shots echoed like a distant, bass-heavy stereo in

Cole's ears as he planted his feet and willed his spear to shift into something that would hit the other creature before it could get to him. Although the metallic spearhead was too rigid to change shape, the rest of the weapon responded to Cole's mental command without hesitation. It was still shifting when he drove the spear into the Half Breed's chest using a motion similar to digging a hole with a shovel. The gleaming spearhead, infused with pieces of the Blood Blade, ripped through the Half Breed's upper body even easier than bullets from Prophet's gun. All it took from there was an exertion of muscle for Cole to divert the Half Breed's glistening fangs away from him and toward the third shapeshifter in the room.

Kawosa dropped to all fours. By the time his hands touched the floor, they were neither hands nor paws. He was a being completely different than anything Cole had seen thus far and shifted from one form to another with as much effort as someone else might use to change an open hand into a fist. Kawosa's animal form was lean and wiry. Pointed ears rested high upon his head to point straight up at the ceiling. His snout was long and gnarled, filled with unevenly spaced fangs that angled down and back like teeth found on a hacksaw blade. As the Half Breed sailed over him, Kawosa kept his smoky gray eyes fixed upon Cole.

Suddenly, Cole wanted to set his spear down and have a quiet chat with the thing staring up at him.

If not for all the previous beings that had tried to manipulate his thoughts, he might have done just that. But with the Mind Singer's presence still fresh in his memory, he wasn't about to roll over so easily for another trickster. It took every bit of his willpower to lower his spear, pretending to behave like a good little zombie. When Kawosa took a less defensive stance, Cole slashed the forked end of the spear across his eyes. The shapeshifter recoiled to avoid getting his face torn off, but the weapon's points snagged in the clothes that hung off his spindly frame.

Cole had barely even noticed Kawosa was still wearing clothes. The creature's fur had a coarse, greasy texture that allowed it to lay flat against his body in a manner very similar to the rags he wore. When Cole pulled the spear free, he ripped a section of the fabric, allowing something to come loose and hit the floor. It was the cell phone Kawosa had taken after hitching a ride with the Skinners. Also, the phone was ringing.

Prophet fired his remaining bullets at the werewolf in front of him. Even after its skull was busted open like a piñata to spill its gory candies all over the floor, its legs still drove it forward. After ejecting his magazine with a quick snap of a lever and downward motion of his hand, he dug a fresh one from his pocket, reloaded and chambered a round so he could empty half of it into the stubborn creature. Whatever hold Kawosa had, it was powerful enough to keep the creature plodding forward no matter how badly it wanted to use its speed to choose another angle. At such close range, Prophet was able to put his next several rounds into the wet pulpy matter within the creature's head.

Cole's Half Breed was having trouble getting back to its feet. After hitting the floor and skidding to turn itself around, a good portion of its blood and some even more vital pieces had spilled out through the opening made by the specially modified spear. The werewolf lifted its head, let out a bellowing roar and leapt at Cole. He braced to defend himself, but the creature didn't even manage to get off the ground before its strength gave out and its body hit the floor with a wet thump. Both front legs were trapped beneath its opened chest, which scraped against the floor.

Kawosa flowed back into a mostly human form and regarded the eviscerated Half Breed with morbid curiosity. "Such simple creatures," he said. The moment he averted his eyes from it, the Half Breed let out a pained whine and gave up the ghost. "They have evolved into such useful tools."

Keeping his spear in front of him, Cole inched his way toward the ringing cell phone. By the time he stretched a leg out to kick it toward him, it stopped ringing. It only took a moment for him to scoop up the phone, but it felt like hours before he was able to regain a solid grip on his weapon. "You're working with the Nymar?"

"No more than I work with any deceiver," Kawosa replied.

"What's that supposed to mean? Who the hell are you?"

"I am smoke and mirrors. I am the encouraging hand that prods a child to tell his first lie. Some have written legends about me, but the rest prefer to worship my gifts in secret so their supposed loved ones will not know what untruths are about to be cast at them."

Tapping his earpiece, Cole said, "Rico, I've got some nut job here who was passing himself off as Paige. Says his name's Kawosa. That ring any bells?"

The gunfire that crackled through the digital connection simultaneously echoed through another section of the building. "Little busy here! You finished dicking around with the computer so you can help us with the real work?"

"How many Nymar are left?"

"Oh, you want me to count? Let's see . . ." The gunfire erupting from that side of the building intensified and was still blasting away when the earpiece chirped again. "Still a fucking lot of them! Get over here!"

When Cole looked back to Kawosa, he found the skinny figure reaching out to touch the metallic spearhead with a set of sticklike fingers. "Where did you come from?" Cole asked. "And give me the short version before I drop you and call it a day."

Kawosa raised an eyebrow that looked more like something hastily glued to his face before he shifted into another form with enough speed to make his bones snap. Every inch of his flesh was pulled and stretched. His muscles tore and squashed in on themselves. His entire structure crumpled into something else in less time than it took Cole's heart to beat. When he dropped down to all four of his newly re-formed legs, Kawosa was covered in dark fur and brandishing teeth that looked strong enough to chew through the side of an Abrams tank.

The creature wasn't quite Full Blood and was definitely not a Half Breed. Cole might have put his money on a Mongrel, if not for what his scars were telling him. He didn't have to think long, however, before remembering where he'd seen that dark, snarling monster before.

When he and Paige had faced Lancroft for the final time

in the dungeon beneath that Philadelphia house, he'd caught a glimpse of Kawosa in his present form. Every instinct in Cole's body had told him to stay away from that cage and be thankful that Jonah Lancroft knew how to keep those bars from breaking. When he'd seen the empty cage during his last visit to the Lancroft house, Cole had wanted to forget about what had been set loose. Somehow, after this simple introduction, the situation had the potential to be much worse than he'd feared.

"Tell me you're afraid, Skinner," Kawosa snarled through a mouth that shifted just enough to form the words. "And don't lie to me. I'll know."

Cole used every bit of training Paige had given him. He watched Kawosa's movements, from the subtle shift of his weight, all the way down to the bob of his head. When the moment was right, he feinted with a quick stab to Kawosa's face and then followed up as soon as the shapeshifter moved to avoid the blow. Dropping to one knee, Cole swung his spear out and around in a wide arc that caught three of Kawosa's legs. Although he was going for a simple takedown, the thorns in the weapon tore away the shapeshifter's flesh as he fell heavily onto his side. The creature had barely hit the floor when Cole drove the metal-encrusted spearhead into Kawosa's chest. He twisted the weapon and pulled it back out as his phone started to ring.

Since Kawosa wasn't moving and the Half Breeds were down, Cole checked the phone's screen. Paige had been trying to reach him. More than likely that was why Kawosa had kept the phone in the first place. "Hello?" Cole said after establishing the connection.

"Where the hell have you been? Why the hell would you pick *this* of all times to start ignoring that piece of shit phone of yours?"

"There's my girl," Cole said with relief.

Prophet had reloaded his pistol and was shifting his aim between all three of the creatures lying on the floor. "Is that Paige?"

Cole nodded.

"You sure about that?"

"Ohhh, yeah," Cole replied.

"I hear gunshots," she said. "What's happening over there? Did you start the raid without me?"

"Had to," Cole said.

"But I just got into Denver!"

"Did the nymphs charge up again?"

"No, Bob got me on a chartered jet. It's a long story."

Even though there was more than enough going on in the immediate vicinity, Cole felt his hackles raise when he heard that name. "Bob Stanze? Officer Bob Stanze from Kansas City?"

"That's him. He knows some people. I'm not sure if they're Feds or what, but he says they're from police departments all over the country." She paused to take a breath, and no matter what else was going on at that moment, Cole waited for her to finish. "They know about us," she said. "They know about Skinners and what we do. From what he's been telling me, they've known for a while now."

"So on top of everything else, we've got to deal with some kind of conspiracy?"

"That's why I've been sticking with them," Paige hissed. Her voice had become louder and scratchier, making Cole certain she was cupping her hand over her phone when she said, "Just tell me you're getting to those cops the Nymar set up. I don't know how big this thing is yet, but the last thing we need is more bad blood on our hands where the police are concerned."

"I'm getting to it."

"Good. Call when you've got something. I'll be there as fast as I can."

When the connection was cut, Cole felt as if he'd been severed from damn near everything in his world. He wasn't alone in that stark white building, but he no longer had the guiding force that had gotten him this far. Knowing what needed to be done was one thing. Doing it, no matter what might happen to him along the way, was another.

Prophet grit his teeth and kept his back to a wall as hell spilled into the hallway on the other side of the door in front of him. "All right," he said. "What's next?"

"You're gonna stay here and hack that computer."

"I don't know anything about hacking a damn computer!"

"It's already unlocked," Cole explained as he waved at the bloodstained terminal. "The screen's a little gross, but the pass codes have already been put in. Do you know how to go through PC files?"

"Yeah."

"Then go through as much as you can and look for anything that might be useful. If you find something, print it up or e-mail it to yourself."

"Won't that be dangerous?" Prophet asked.

The gunfire had moved into another part of the building. In the time it took for Cole to place his spear into the harness strapped to his back, several voices boomed from the front and back rooms. He couldn't make out exactly what they were saying but they had the cadence of authority mixed in with several choppy syllables that could either be "freeze" or "on your knees."

"I doubt there'll be anyone left around here to follow up with viruses or backward traces," Cole explained. "Cobb38 must have security measures in place, so he'll probably figure out something's up and send you something to corrupt your system. Just don't open anything until I can do a sweep of whatever computer you send it to."

"I meant safe as in me being safe screwing with computer shit while everyone's trying to kill us!"

"Sounds like cops out there," Cole said, "Since they're probably going to be more careful than any of us, you should have enough time to get what you need and get out. There's gotta be something in there we can use. Addresses, phone numbers, a contact list. A contact list would be great!"

Another eruption of official-sounding voices was washed away in the roar of shotguns. Prophet reflexively covered his head as he approached the computer but stopped short of ducking under the desk. Cole, on the other hand, kept walking toward the hall.

"At least we took out these . . . whatever the hell they

are," Cole said. Just to make sure, he checked the bodies on the floor. Both of the werewolves were still lying in their pools of blood, but Kawosa was nowhere to be found. He left behind no blood, tracks, or anything more substantial than the memory that he'd been in that room. "Of course," Cole grunted. "Things aren't ever that easy."

Chapter Thirty-Three

The building had a simple floor plan with one ring of rooms surrounding a block of larger ones. One large hallway wrapped all the way around, connecting two main entrances, one in front and the other in the back. Rico guessed there was at least one side door but had been too busy getting shot at to find it. The other Amriany came in through the front and fought their way inside, guns blazing to make the biggest spectacle possible. Somewhere along the line Nadya had caught a bullet. Gunari dragged her down the hall by her collar so her legs were splayed out behind them and she was able to keep firing her semiautomatic in controlled bursts.

After regrouping with them, Rico tapped his earpiece and asked, "Cole, where the hell are you?"

"Right behind you." Sure enough, Cole rounded a corner to find Rico and Drina on opposite sides of the hall with their backs pressed against a soda and snack machine, respectively. Before he could get to Rico's side, the rest of the Amriany came along to meet them.

"The Nymar retreated into the east side of the building." Knowing Cole's lack of an internal compass, Rico pointed down the hall past the vending machines and added, "That way. They drove us back here after we took a few of them down then fell back into that room at the end of the hall. I'm guessing it's an open space because they'd be crammed in like clowns in a Volkswagen if it was just another closet.

"Did you hit anyone other than Nymar?" Cole asked.

"Nope. Barely slowed down the ones I did hit. Only a few of them twitched at the antidote rounds. The rest've been scampering around like rats. Probably just holding us here until their backup arrives."

Drina pressed a finger to her earpiece and frowned. "Tobar was taken by the police."

"And that'd be their backup," Rico grunted.

"Let's just clean this place out," Cole said. "I've got the best armor, so I'll draw the aggro."

"What is he talking about?" Gunari asked as he tightened a length of torn fabric around one of Nadya's knees. Her leg was soaked in blood that oozed out through her jeans, but she barely acknowledged it with anything more than a sharp breath.

Rico shook his head and chanced a look around the soda machine. "I barely ever know what he's talkin' about."

"Aggro," Cole said impatiently. "One guy goes in to draw fire and the others circle around to flank the bad guys. Don't any of you guys ever do *any* gaming? For the love of God, it's the twenty-first century!"

The screaming from the front half of the building died down, followed by the occasional crash of a door being kicked in.

"By the way," Cole said as he gripped his .45 and closed his coat by threading one of the thick wooden slivers that passed for buttons through a rough slit Rico had cut into the leather, "there's some other shapeshifter running around here. Not a werewolf. Mind controller. Be on the lookout for him." With that, he set his sights on the doors at the end of the hall and rushed toward them.

There was plenty of noise within the building to mask his footsteps as he jogged toward the door. Although he could wrap his mind around any number of inhuman terrors that might be waiting for him in the next room, he still didn't know how he was going to deal with the police. Apart from not shooting them, his choices seemed pretty limited. A hu-

morless grin drifted onto his face as he brought his gun up
to eye level and extended his other hand toward the door.
The way the odds were stacked, he probably wouldn't need
to worry about much of anything beyond the next half hour,
so it didn't make sense to plan much further than that. The
pain within his chest tightened as though a length of dental
floss was being drawn taut after being wrapped around all
of his major organs. The muscles he was about to use all
flushed with heat as his throat became drier than the floor of
an old kiln. A tickling sensation sprang up near the base of
his spine, and he was hungrier than he'd ever been.

Cole meant to shove the door open but wound up knocking it off one of its hinges and leaving it askew in its frame.
Compared to the stark lighting of the hallway, the space directly in front of him was a single shadowy mass. Several
bare bulbs hung from the ceiling to reveal a loading dock
or some sort of industrial storage space. Pallets covered in
dusty tarps formed a wall to his left. Two vans were parked
to his right with their noses pointed toward a pair of large
garage doors covered by steel shutters. The lights hung from
the ceiling amid a thick webbing of girders and beams,
topped by the slanted roof of the building itself. He took
all of this in within his first few steps. That was more than
enough time to notice the Nymar that swarmed in on him
from all sides like a colony of centipedes.

Since police departments didn't generally hire from the
superhuman wall-crawling labor pool, Cole fired at every
overhead Nymar he spotted. One slender figure wrapped
its arms around a beam and looked down at him with wide
unblinking eyes. Cole aimed carefully and fired again. His
shot sparked against the beam but got close enough to shake
the Nymar loose. The vampire hit the floor on its back. Now
that he was beneath the lights, the solid black hue of its skin
melted into thick stripes. Cole meant to hold the Nymar beneath his foot long enough to get to his spear, but his heel
dropped heavily onto the Nymar's upper chest to snap its
collarbone with a solid wet crunch.

While he shifted his aim to the shape dropping down to
get behind him, he pulled his coat open and reached for the

weapon harness. One shot punched through the Nymar's ribs, the next clipped its ear, and the one after that was a clean miss. The vampire wore only a pair of black pants, keeping as much of its shadowy skin exposed as possible. His bare feet slapped against the concrete floor, putting an extra kick behind the breath he used to spit a wad of venom at Cole's face.

The toxic substance hit his hand and neck, cooling them on impact and forcing him to look away when the next wave of gunfire erupted. Most of those shots erupted from a Sig Sauer and a FAMAS submachine gun.

"How many times I gotta tell you to stop goin' for those head shots?" Rico snarled as he moved to Cole's side. With a few more pulls of his trigger, the big man carved a large and very messy hole through the spitting Nymar's chest. It fell straight back with cracks forming in its flesh before it hit the floor.

As Rico and Cole moved forward, Drina and Gunari fanned out to either side. Even while hobbling on a wounded leg, Nadya joined her fellow Amriany by finding the first piece of solid cover and running behind it.

"Goddamn Gypsies," Rico growled as he fired at a shot-gun-wielding Nymar that stepped out from behind one of the stacks of pallets. "First chance to hide and they run for it."

Overhead, electricity crackled through the uppermost fixtures nestled above the beams to bring several rows of fluorescent bulbs to life. A few seconds later the other half of the room was illuminated, exposing the Nymar that were sneaking down from where they'd been hidden.

"I think you can thank the Gypsies for that," Cole chided.

Rico squeezed off a few quick rounds to put down one long-haired Nymar that stuck her head around the corner. "Don't call them Gypsies," he said. "They don't like that."

Cole emptied his last few rounds into a group of Nymar gathering near large doors that must have opened onto one of the truck-filled lots outside the building. Even though he could see the reaction of the antidote infused into the bullets on two of the Nymar that were hit, the ones with the Shadow Spore barely flinched. The standard issue vampires staggered away, allowing their enhanced partners to close the distance between themselves and the Skinners.

"Cops are headed your way," Prophet said through the earpiece.

"Shit," Cole grunted.

Rico reloaded his Sig Sauer with practiced efficiency, but had given up on trying to take deliberate shots. "I know. I heard."

"Not that. My phone's ringing." After digging out the cell, Cole glanced at the screen. "It's Paige."

"Better take it. She's been known to get snippy if you ignore her calls."

Even in the middle of a war zone, Cole had to chuckle at that one.

"We're only about fifteen minutes away," Paige said. Her voice was straining to be heard over the roar of several loud engines.

"Are you on a helicopter?"

"Yeah. I'm telling you, these guys are serious."

"Well so are the Nymar," Cole said as three of the vampires coordinated their efforts to form a quick firing line and unleash a salvo in his direction.

"When I get there, you're gonna have to trust me," Paige said.

"What's the plan?"

"Just follow my lead and trust me. Please, Cole."

When his .45 ran dry, he holstered the gun and gripped his spear in both hands. "Someone was here impersonating you. Called himself Kawosa or something like that. Ring any bells?"

"Great. Another thing coming after us. Never heard of him."

"How long before you get here?"

"Shouldn't be long," she replied. "Are you going to be okay?"

"As good as always."

"Just hang in there and—"

"Follow your lead," Cole interrupted as a pair of Nymar leapt from their positions behind a parked van to bounce off the walls and launch themselves at him. "Got it." The last syllable was still in his mouth when he held the spear up to block the first incoming Nymar. The vampire's hair streamed over her shoulders and she bared two sets of fangs at him. Apparently, she wasn't worried about poisoning him, so she left the curved pair sheathed beneath her gums.

His spear caught her across the chest. Cole took advantage of her momentum by pivoting to send her flailing into a stack of pallets. Still hesitant to use anything without a trigger, Rico blasted another airborne Nymar with a torrent of .45 caliber slugs that sent it bouncing off a cement pillar and to the floor. "Get to the garage doors," he said while running to finish off the Nymar he'd taken down. "Spread the word to the Amriany."

Gunarl and Drina had moved their fight through the open section of the room. They held their own well enough to force the Nymar to form a small cluster there. Every few seconds the Nymar sent a few out at a time, like larger versions of the tendrils that crept through their own bodies.

Cole rushed at the Nymar he'd bounced off a post, snarling viciously as he impaled the creature at the end of his spear. This wasn't one of the Nymar infected with the Shadow Spore, which made it easier to find a soft spot with the metal tip of his spear. "Where are the cops?" he asked.

"They're already here," she replied. "Are you deaf?"

"I mean the cops you were going to frame us for killing. Where are they?"

"Are you going to . . . let me go?" she grunted.

"If you tell me quickly, yes."

"There's two in one of the offices and more in one of the vans," she told him. "But you're too late to do anything about them. They're dead and one of your weapons is still sticking out of a body. I don't know what kind of shit you smear all over those sticks, but I bet it's real distinctive on any tests the cops might run on the wounds."

"Where'd you get one of our weapons?"

The Nymar showed Cole a tired smirk as the light in her

eyes faded. Black tendrils crept out from the spot where she'd been impaled to grip the spear like several weak little fingers trying unsuccessfully to coax the weapon from where it was lodged. Suddenly, a rage swept through Cole's entire body and he pushed the spear down until the metallic tip scraped against the cement beneath her.

"Answer me!"

She gripped the spear and was able to lift it up an inch or so while snarling savagely at him.

If not for the thorns in the handle, the spear might very well have slipped between his fingers or been taken away from him altogether. The Nymar's burst of strength was not only fueled by the thing inside her, but from a final act of self preservation. She became stronger than any Nymar he had ever faced. Paige had warned him about jolts where a vampire could flush all of their blood-fueled power into a single attack. He was taught to either do as much damage to such a Nymar as quickly as possible or get the hell away until it faded. With his spear already trapped, both of those choices were blocked.

It was then that he felt a surge of his own.

His hands closed around the spear with the sole intent of preventing the weapon from being taken from him. As his grip became tighter, the thorns were driven in deep enough to hit nerves that hadn't been deadened by previous contact or protected by scar tissue. They dug all the way through, growing longer due to the desperate commands rushing through his mind, until they formed little bumps on the tops of his hands. Letting out a primal scream, he straightened his legs and used both hands to scoop the Nymar up off the floor. She still grabbed the spear, if only to keep from sliding all the way down the length of the weapon like a hunk of meat that was too heavy for its kebob.

"Where'd you get one of our weapons?" Cole roared.

The Nymar's legs flopped uselessly and her mouth hung open as she struggled painfully against the laws of gravity. "Hope . . . brought it . . . from Miami."

"Are any more cops going to die?"

"Most of the ones that tried to get close to us . . . are already . . ." All of her grievous wounds caught up to her and the color drained from her face.

Rico's voice echoed through the room, tainted by rage, pain, or both. A small group of Nymar rushed around the stack of pallets, only to be stopped cold by the sight of Cole holding the impaled Nymar several inches off the floor.

". . . already dead," the Nymar croaked. "Killed by Skinners . . . all over the country." The fight was quickly draining out of her, and the effort of holding onto the spear dimmed the spark of life in her eyes even more. The only thing she had left was a tired, resigned smile.

Since the Nymar seemed content to fade at her own pace, Cole shook his spear to rattle the body attached to it.

Her eyes snapped open and she looked around as if she were taking in the sights for the first time. Fresh waves of gunfire erupted in the vicinity, but since he wasn't getting pelted with live rounds, he figured Rico and the Amriany were dealing with it. "Tell me the rest, God damn you!" he demanded.

"Every cop in this building will be executed," the Nymar announced. Baring her fangs in a spiteful glare, she added, "You being here will be enough to brand every one of you as cop killers. You're fucked! Every Skinner everywhere is fucked!"

Cole could no longer contain his anger. He didn't even want to. He twisted his entire body around to fling the Nymar at the pallets without a single thought about the strength required to toss her that far. Ignoring the fiery pain that incinerated his insides, he tapped his earpiece while racing to the door that led to the hallway.

"Something's happening to those cops that busted in here," Cole said.

Rico's voice was the first to come back to him. "Whatever it is, I hope it lasts long enough for us to get the hell outta here!"

"I'm with him," Prophet chimed in. "By the way, I got all I'm gonna get from this computer."

"Prophet, just go. Rico, we need to get to those cops. They're going to be torn apart."

"They probably got bigger guns than us and—" Something snarled into his earpiece but was just as quickly silenced by a muffled gunshot. "And we got our hands full in here as it is."

"Fine," Cole snapped as he bolted into the hallway with a few stray rounds thumping against the back of his coat. "I'll handle this on my own. Come find me when you can."

Following the sound of shouting, gunshots, and squawking radios, Cole jogged down the hallway to retrace the steps that had brought him to the loading dock. The doors behind him were thrown open and someone charged through them. Driving his shoulder into the same soda machine Rico had used for cover a while ago, he allowed his body to slide along it while turning around to point his spear at his pursuer.

Nadya hobbled down the hall carrying Drina's FAMAS with the stock pressed against her shoulder and the muzzle pointed downward. "Where are you going?"

"Those cops are going to be killed."

"I know. I heard what that Nymar said as you lifted her. How did you do that?"

Cole had already turned back around and was heading toward the branch of the hall that led to the front of the building. "I don't know. Adrenaline, I guess."

"Where are you going?"

"I didn't sign up for this Skinner crap just to let innocent people get killed while I run away."

"Then I want to help you."

"But you're injured."

Shifting the submachine gun against her shoulder, she nodded at him and said, "So are you."

When Cole looked down, he saw no fewer than five deep gouges across his chest and a few holes in his jeans that were ringed with blood. Although he could recall being scratched a few times, he didn't know where the holes in his jeans had come from. The healing serum in his system must have been doing its job because the wounds weren't anywhere close to slowing him down. Most of the commotion he heard was confined to the rooms closest to the building's front entrance, so that's where he went. Since he didn't feel like arguing with Nadya, he tucked the spear under his arm and reloaded the .45 before jamming it back into its holster.

"What will we do when we get there?" she asked.

"Will your partners back us up?"

"There were many Nymar back there, including Shadow Spore and a Kintalaphi. My partners will be lucky to get out alive."

"Then maybe you should go help them."

"We came to do a job and we'll do it," she said. "They do not need me getting underfoot and you should not go on alone."

"All right, then," Cole sighed as he placed his hand on the long metal bar of the door separating the hallway from the front of the building. "Sounds like those cops are fighting for their lives, so let's help them out. Hopefully that'll be enough to convince them which side we're on."

"And what about the police that have already been killed? Aren't you and your friend wanted for that?"

"We'll wait for a lull in the fight and slip away."

"What is your plan for slipping away?"

"Ask me when the shooting stops," Cole said as he shoved the door open. "Hopefully I'll come up with something by then."

Chapter Thirty-Four

The door opened into a room that stretched out for about ten feet on either side. Less than six feet in front of him was the back of a counter and a window that looked out to a larger room that had the appearance of a lobby or display area. At the moment every square inch of that tiled floor was covered by cops, overturned furniture, broken glass, Nymar, or spilled blood. It was impressive, considering the room on the other side of the window was large enough to hold several cars and a few desks with plenty of space for customers to wander freely and peruse whatever the front company was supposed to sell. The front windows were blacked out, but powerful searchlight beams still managed to get in through narrow gaps in the paint around the edges of the glass.

Cole picked out half a dozen Nymar, based solely on markings he could see on exposed skin or wounds that were too serious to be on a human being without putting them permanently out of a fight. What disturbed him the most was all the officers clustered at the front door. The armed figures in bulky gear were backlit by headlights and watching what happened inside. They all seemed to be held back by a solitary man standing at the doorway wearing raggedy clothes over a wiry frame.

"There you are," Cole snarled as he set his sights on Kawosa's back. Jabbing a finger at him, he told Nadya, "Stay here and cover that skinny bastard. If he makes any sudden moves or starts to change into something, shoot him."

"My bullets won't do much to a shapeshifter."

"Then aim for the head. Maybe you'll knock him out long enough for me to get to him."

She wasn't happy about it, but took a position in the doorway and sighted along the top of the FAMAS.

The Nymar in that room were increasingly easy to spot, wearing their affliction on their sleeves by baring their fangs and hissing like animals. Clawed hands were wrapped around pistols taken from the dead, and when the cops put a bullet into them, they straightened up to allow the mashed hunk of lead to be ejected from their bodies by greasy black tendrils.

Cole gripped his spear, hopped over the counter and into the battle. When he was targeted by the closest vampires, he tucked his chin against his chest and twisted his body around so the shots fired at him thumped against his coat. The impacts hurt like hell, but mundane rounds couldn't even scratch the hardened Full Blood leather. A second later something larger than a bullet slammed into his right side.

Hope tackled Cole as if she'd been launched by a catapult. Her shoulder pounded against his ribs and her arms wrapped around him like a pair of steel bands. If he hadn't been fast enough to get his spear around to buy himself an inch or two of breathing room, the life would have been squeezed out of him in a matter of seconds.

"There's more Skinners here," Hope shouted. "Find them!"

A few Nymar separated from the group. One of them clung to the ceiling, so it got to Nadya first. Although Cole couldn't check on the Amriany, he heard the FAMAS chattering and saw the muzzle flash from the corner of his eye.

Once again, strength rushed through his body. It was enough to pry Hope off, but left him too unsteady to stay upright. He dropped to one knee, using the spear as a crutch to prevent him from keeling over.

"Don't worry about the police," Hope sneered while popping lightly to her feet. "The ones that aren't under our control are dead on their feet."

Cole turned to take a better look at the cops. Sure enough, many of them had a slick coating of venom on their faces. If any of that crap had gotten into their eyes, they were susceptible to suggestion as well as disoriented and groggy. Cole reached up to feel his own face, hoping to explain some of the strangeness going on inside of him. The only thing he found was some blood and a whole lot of sweat.

Approaching him while craning her neck to look at the rest of the room, Hope took in the carnage as if she was enjoying a movie. "I'm torn on what to do with you," she said. "Our coordinated efforts have come together nicely to either put your kind into the ground or in the sights of your own authorities. It's tempting to let them have you. Still, I do enjoy the taste of Skinner blood. You all have such a nice blend running through your veins."

She crouched down slowly as chaos closed in around her.

Nadya emptied her last few rounds into whatever was attacking her.

Cops who'd expended their ammunition swung blindly at anything that moved, while others fired at their partners because of the temporary mind control forced on them by the venom. Nymar exploded from the shadows, dropped from the ceiling, or struggled with the few officers who'd managed to keep their wits about them. The only calm within the storm were Cole and Kawosa. The shapeshifter stood in the doorway, quietly talking to the anxious officers waiting to barge in while occasionally motioning to the room behind him as if the bedlam was just another busy day at the office.

Cole remained still because he was too weak to waste what energy he had left. He'd had enough training and been through enough hell to recognize the anticipation in Hope's eyes as a ruse meant to lull him into committing to a wild attack. When she switched direction like a cobra swaying back and forth, the hunger in her eyes spiked. He knew what came after that.

The markings on her face pulsed in a way he'd never seen on a Nymar. They covered the sides of her head like a pair of hands gripping her between them. Her attack came so quickly that Hope didn't even seem to move. She simply flickered from one spot to another, confirming that the two spore attached to her heart could truly work in lethal concert. Somehow, Cole was able to move fast enough to intercept her.

His muscles felt as if they were being shredded from his bones, but they pulled his body down and brought his arms up in short, powerful motions that allowed him to jab the spear into her chest. He knew he'd missed her heart, but when she landed, the metallic spearhead was completely buried inside her torso.

Hope gripped the spear and snarled at him. Unlike the previous Nymar to be caught that way, she had the power to wrench it out and shove him back. "You can't kill me with your weapons," she said. "No Skinner can."

Her mouth continued to move, but Cole wasn't listening to what she said. His strength was fading so quickly that he barely had enough juice in his batteries to process the sights flooding into his eyes or the sounds filling his ears. Something pounded against the floor just enough for him to feel the impacts. A fast, chopping rhythm washed through the building, which soon distinguished itself as the roar of helicopter blades. Paige had arrived, but every fiber in Cole's body told him that he couldn't hold out until she got to him.

He needed to fend for himself.

He needed to feed.

As Hope began to recover from being impaled, Cole swung his spear at her throat. She leaned away from that with ease but underestimated how quickly he could follow it up. The forked end of the spear twirled around almost as fast as the blades of the helicopter outside the building, and she ducked under it before her head was taken from her shoulders. A deep gash was torn across her jugular, and before she could place her hand to the wound, Cole was on her.

What his leap lacked in finesse, it made up for with sheer power. Every joint in his legs felt as if it had snapped loose. His groin muscles strained to the point of tearing. As soon as he got his hand on Hope's neck, however, all of that discomfort went away. He rode her down until her back hit the floor, slipping his hand up under Hope's chin and driving the back of her skull against cement and tile. The thumping impact resounded through his ears as he clamped his mouth upon the open wound on her neck.

He didn't know what he was doing.

The rational part of his brain had been shoved too far back into his subconscious to be heard.

His teeth scraped uselessly against the torn flaps of Hope's skin, so he jammed his face in closer and probed the wound with his tongue. A tremble moved through her body as he licked and sucked, adding another layer of disgust to the many that were already heaped on top of him. Hope's blood trickled into his mouth at first. Once his tongue found a stronger flow coming from one of her severed arteries and directed the fluid into his mouth, the pain in his muscles lessened. All of the tearing he'd felt before simply faded as if the twine cinched around his innards had been loosened or cut.

Then the tastes hit him.

The coppery sweetness of blood mingled with something bitter and pungent. Each gulp was sweet and then sour. Something in him pushed through the latter just to get more of the former.

"What are you doing?" Hope groaned. "Are you feeding from me?" She tried to squirm away, but Cole's entire body reacted to hold her in place. Despite his best efforts, she was able to draw enough strength from both of her Nymar spore for her to gain some purchase on the floor. "This is even more interesting than I'd anticipated."

Nadya may have had a chance to reload the FAMAS, but that wouldn't explain the multiple bursts of gunfire erupting from different angles. Other voices came from the hallway, speaking in some sort of European dialect Cole couldn't place. Someone yelled for the damn Gypsies to speak English. He didn't need more than one guess to figure out who that was. At the same time, voices chattered through his earpiece, trying to get his attention, asking where he was and what he was doing.

Even though she seemed capable of getting away, Hope

remained within Cole's grasp. "So you were unable to prevent the seeding, even after somehow ridding yourself of the spore," she said in a breathy voice that was the only one Cole cared to hear. "This alone was worth the trouble of making sure I saw you and your partners again. This changes everything."

Her body swelled against him as she writhed on the floor. Her chin brushed against Cole's face as he dug his mouth in deeper. Finally, when his throat was all but filled with the oily Nymar blood, he tore himself away and struggled to stand up. Hope lay beneath him, looking up at him longingly while her fingers trailed along the dripping wound. "Now you have another reason why you can't kill us," she said. "Soon, every Skinner will have that same reason."

"Cole!" Rico shouted from the back of the room. "Are you all right?"

The big man was finishing off one of the Nymar that had charged over the counter to greet him and the remaining Amriany. Of the policemen and -women who had been in the room, only a few very confused cops were still standing. They'd finished off the couple Nymar that had stayed behind, then checked with each other, radioed to the ones outside, and started screaming at the solitary figure that stood between them and backup.

Kawosa raised his hands in compliance to the orders being barked at him and dove away from the door. Gunshots rang out, punching holes into the wall and thumping against Kawosa's hide. The gunfire intensified, causing the shapeshifter to stumble and fall forward. That small victory was taken away as his body flowed into a lean, four-legged canine form and darted toward the back of the room. He raced past Cole, cleared the counter in one jump and scampered away like a fleeting thought.

Gunari had a gun in each hand but was unable to pull either trigger. Instead, he watched the shaggy blur streak past him and gasped, "Ktseena."

Cole absorbed all of this as if his senses had been extended in every direction. Perhaps it was the blood that gave him that gift because Hope surely didn't have it. Otherwise, she would have seen Drina come up behind her with what looked to be a thick metal arrow in each hand. The Amriany bared her teeth and dropped both arms to drive an arrowhead into each of Hope's shoulders.

The way the Nymar rose to her feet meant that she had either pulled herself up by bending the laws of physics or was dragged up by the objects in Drina's hands. When Hope twisted around to slash as Drina with her claws, she remained attached to the arrows by thin silver chains.

"You bitch!" she snarled. "Whatever this is, I'll shove it down your throat and pull it out through your fucking ass!"

Without reacting to the vulgar torrent spewing from Hope's mouth, Drina stepped back and allowed her partners to swarm in around her.

Nadya fired a few rounds at Hope's feet, taking them out from under her.

Gunari grabbed Hope's wrists and wrestled her to the ground, forcing the rest of the chain to spool out and be pulled taut from where it was housed within the shafts of Drina's arrows. She stood over Hope, lowering her arms as more of the chains were pulled into Hope's torso.

"What the hell?" Rico grunted.

"It's an old Amriany method for extracting the spores," Gunari explained. "Keep those police away so she can work."

But the cops were already backing out of the building through the front door. They kept their weapons drawn but weren't about to interfere with the procedure. Outside, there were enough people walking back and forth between the chopper and the building to cast a shadow play on the windows.

"What's happening to her?" Rico asked.

Hope had grabbed onto the chains, only to have her hands burnt by something within the metal. Without enough strength to pull the intrusive implements from her body, all she could do was pound her fists against the ground and continue to spit insults at the hunters surrounding her.

"The metal is treated to become . . . like a magnet," Gunari said. His English was fine in conversation, but the specifics of this particular exchange were testing the limits of his syntax. "It is forged specially for the Nymar."

"Like a Blood Blade for vampires?"

"Yes. The arrowheads are attracted to the Nymar spore. Once inside, they will go to it, cut through everything and not stop until they have found it."

"Then what?"

"Then," Drina said, "this." She tightened her grip on the tools and lifted them straight up. All but a few links of the chains had been swallowed up by Hope's upper torso and resisted the Amriany's efforts to extract them. With sustained effort, Drina pulled them loose. She turned both hands in small circles, wrapping the bloody chains around her knuckles until the arrowheads snagged on the upper levels of Hope's skin.

"Why didn't you do that to all those other bloodsuckers?" Rico asked.

Gunari scowled. "It is not a method we use very often. Too messy."

Hope was no longer even a humanlike shell anymore. All she could do was scream and hit the floor until the tiles cracked and bits of broken concrete became wedged in the bloody gashes covering her fists. Her flesh strained like thick rubber as the arrowheads came to the surface. One more pull was all Drina needed to remove them completely, along with the spore that each one had found.

Normally, when Nymar spore were in jeopardy, they tried to nourish themselves on whatever they could find. Something in the Amriany tools held an even greater temptation because the spore latched on to them to wrap tendril after tendril around the charmed shafts as well as the hands that held them.

"This is another reason we do not use them so often," Gunari said as he reached over to help his partner pull free of the clinging parasite.

Cole couldn't bear to look at Rico. He couldn't even bring himself to look at the Amriany. Even with Hope reduced to a flailing, wounded animal, he wasn't able to look at her. That didn't leave him with any other option than to turn his back on everyone and stagger toward the front door. "Paige?"

She pushed through the cops that had clustered around the building's main entrance, her hands empty and concern written across her face. The moment she spotted him in the shadows at the back of the room, she smiled with relief. "Cole! Thank God!"

The look in her eyes and the way she favored her right arm told Cole it was truly her. Spinning around, he used his sleeve to wipe the oily blood from his face. Both spore entangled around Drina's hands like so much rotten seafood were crumbling into dried ash. When he grabbed one of the silver tools, he had more than enough strength to tear it away from her.

"What are you doing?" Gunari demanded.

"Does this need to recharge or something?" Cole asked. "I need to use it."

Rico and Nadya straightened up and raised their weapons as the cops at the front of the building moved in.

"It's all over!" one of the men in tactical black uniforms barked. "Drop your weapons and put your hands over your head!"

"What is it, Cole?" Rico asked.

Locking his eyes on Gunari, Cole said, "Answer my question. Can I use this?"

"Pull the handle at the other end."

The chain was locked into the silver tube with a bar that passed through the last link to keep it from being pulled out completely. Cole pulled the bar, drew the chain all the way back through the handle until the arrowhead was locked, and then drove the pointed end into his chest. He was barely able to break the skin. Whatever had powered him before either wore off or sapped his strength, staying his hand.

Rico charged forward without lowering his Sig Sauer. "What the fuck are you doing?"

"Put the guns down!" the SWAT team member shouted.

All three Amriany focused their attention on the police and spoke to each other quietly through their earpieces. There were more Nymar in the building. The itch in Cole's scars which told him that much. But Nymar were no longer the problem. No matter what language they spoke, he knew that the Amriany had to be discussing their chances of getting Tobar away from the authorities so the group could make a clean escape. "Get out of here," he told them.

Drina approached him cautiously.

"I told you to go!" Cole said. "We came here to keep cops alive, goddamn it."

"Give me the Talon," she said calmly.

Paige had yet to get into the building. There were enough cops at the door to hold her back, but she wasn't making it easy for them.

Rico stood his ground, paying no attention whatsoever to the cops, the guns in their hands, or anything other than his partner.

Cole pushed the sharp instrument in deeper, grinding it through the meat beneath his skin and scraping against the bone. "I don't feel anything happening," he grunted through the pain. Within his body, the tension in his muscles shifted away from the front of his chest and inched down to his feet. "It's in me," he said. "I know it is."

"Was in you," Rico said as he stepped forward. "We got it out. Remember?"

"No. I can feel it. I even . . ." But he couldn't bring himself to say what he'd done. Since Rico and all of the Amriany were also covered in spilled Nymar blood, the stains on Cole's face didn't stand out enough for the others to draw conclusions.

All except for Nadya.

She'd stormed that room with him. She'd been there when Hope first jumped him. She was still there now. The only question remaining was just how much she'd seen while the Nymar stragglers swarmed in for their last push and he'd had Hope pinned to the floor. She looked at him with cautious pity and a hint of fear as she told him, "If there was a spore in you, the tip of that stake would have been drawn to it. The spore would have been drawn to it as well. Do you feel that?"

"No."

"Then you have no spore." When she reached for the tool in Cole's hand, she didn't have to fight to take it away from him. He relinquished it along with a heavy breath as several standard-issue police flashlights threw their beams across the top of the counter.

Once the arrowhead was out of him, Cole looked down to the wound in his chest. It was a clean, deep cut. The ends pinched together a bit, but that could have been the work of the Skinner healing serum in his system. No tendrils emerged to close the gap. He could, however, feel the bands cinching back into place around his muscles. "Paige is with these guys," he said to Drina. "She's your best chance of getting Tobar out. Trying to break him out now is just a good way to get us all killed."

"He's right," Rico said. "I don't know what's holding these SWAT guys back, but it won't last forever. Can you get out?"

"Yes," Gunari said. "Only if we go now."

Recognizing the commanding tone in his voice, Drina helped Nadya toward the door that led back into the hall.

"Freeze!" the cops said as they cut loose and rushed inside like guard dogs that had finally broken from their leash.

Cole stood up to face Rico and the retreating Amriany. Raising his hands caused his coat to hang like a leather curtain between him and the main entrance. He handed over his weapon and said, "Take this and—"

Shots were fired that hit Cole in both shoulders. Something scraped against his back amid the crackle of electricity. He assumed those were leads of a stun gun, but they were unable to snag within the tough material of his coat.

"On the floor! *Now!*"

"Get out, Rico!" Cole shouted. "Paige is with them. We'll handle this."

Rico's swearing filled the air and then Cole's earpiece as his footsteps echoed down the hall. A few of the cops screamed at him and struggled to climb over or around the counter to engage in a pursuit. Before they could get through the door Rico had just used, Cole jumped in front of the cops to absorb the next rounds that were fired.

"I won't forget that," Rico said. "Call me as soon as you can. Prophet?"

"Right here."

"Can you get out without being spotted by the cops?"

"Are you kidding me?" the bounty hunter replied. "I've been watching the police swarm that building from half a block away."

"Good. Wha—"

As the cops rushed at him, Cole ripped out his earpiece and crushed it beneath his boot heel.

"What was that?" A heavy hand dropped onto Cole's shoulder and spun him around. The cop was a stocky man in his late thirties with a clean-shaven face that looked as if it had been sand-blasted from a hunk of solid rock. He was dressed in head-to-toe tactical gear including a vest that resembled the harness Paige had modified to hold werewolf hides. "What did you crush on the floor?" he asked. "Answer me!"

Three more cops in matching gear encircled Cole while several more passed through the doorway into the hall. Cole could only hope that he'd given the others enough time to put their escape plans to use.

"You got any weapons?"

As much as Cole wanted to lie, he sighed, "Yeah. Under the coat. I wasn't going to shoot any of you. I just needed to protect myself."

The coat was pulled off him with so much force that Cole wouldn't have been surprised if his arms were still in the sleeves when it was taken away. "Got a few guns and what looks like some sort of drug kit. Syringes."

"I can explain those."

"Shut your mouth and stand still."

Cole did as he was told as the holster and harness was taken from him. After that, the muzzle of the cop's assault rifle was jammed into the small of his back.

"Make one wrong move and you're dead," the cop promised.

From the front of the room one of the officers shouted, "This looks like Hendricks!"

"What?" the cop behind Cole asked.

"Hendricks from Vice. He's dead."

The muzzle of the assault rifle gouged into Cole's back as a thick arm wrapped around his throat to put him in an uncompromising lock. He was surprised by the lack of panic he felt as he thought about which method he could use to escape the hold. Paige had taught him several over the last few months, and her grip wasn't much different than the one choking the life out of him now.

Attached to the cop's vest was a radio that crackled with a voice that reported, "There's more dead at the loading dock. Looks like a bunch of the dealers and Anderson's unit."

"All of Anderson's unit?"

"Haven't found them all yet, sir, but there's two of them in the back of a van. The dealers are toast. Anderson and two of his men are hurt pretty bad. They say the others are somewhere on the premises."

Cole's head hung low. "Try the offices."

"What?" the cop snarled a few inches from his ear. "Is that where you're holding them?"

"No, I—"

"Shut up!" Keying the radio, he said, "Sweep all the offices."

The cop nearly pulled Cole's arms out of their sockets while securing his wrists behind his back. From there Cole was moved toward the front door at the behest of an occasional prod from an assault rifle pounding against his spine. Considering all the dead cops discovered in that room alone, he considered himself lucky to be breathing at all. He felt even luckier when he got close enough to the front door to hold Paige's eye for more than a second.

She nodded and showed him a shaky smile while the cops jostled past her in their haste to get him out of the building.

Gunshots crackled down the street and tires squealed. By now Cole had heard the FAMAS and Rico's Sig Sauer enough times to know neither of those guns were being fired. Somehow that didn't make him feel much better. The parking lot directly outside the building was filled with police cars and two large black SWAT vans. He couldn't help but shake his head at just how far away he was from the guy who'd researched tactical teams just like this one for use in a video game.

"Top o' the world, Ma." Cole sighed.

"Shut your damn mouth," another man said as he was roughly thrown against a van, where he was searched again. There was an exchange of words and some more scuffling. When Cole was roughly turned around, a pair of new faces stared back at him.

Paige stood beside a man who looked to have spent thirty out of his forty or so years being dragged behind a truck. His pockmarked skin and bristly hair were coarse enough to scrape the paint off the SWAT van in one pass. The eyes he fixed upon Cole were light enough to be either green or gray. His stern expression, illuminated by flashing police lights and headlights trained on the parking lot, made it clear the guy had no qualms about pulling the trigger of the M-16 in his hands.

When Paige reached out for Cole, she was held back by the SWAT guy who'd taken him into custody. "I don't give a shit what kind of pull you have," he snapped. "This one's in our custody now."

The man with the M-16 and pockmarked face replied, "He's all yours. We're willing to cooperate."

"If you would've been so generous before, maybe the rest of these assholes wouldn't have gotten away!"

The man with the pockmarks kept his mouth shut and stepped back.

"You need to go with them, Cole," Paige said.

Suddenly, the sight of her wasn't so comforting. "What? That's how you fixed this?"

"Just trust me. Go with them."

"Go where?" Cole asked.

"If I had my way, you'd be goin' into a fuckin' box and buried under six feet of dirt for all those cops you killed," the SWAT officer said. In a harsh whisper he added, "And if it weren't for them news crews, I'd do the job myself without losing a damn bit of sleep over it."

Cole was pulled away from the van and shoved toward another one parked ten feet away. He nearly fell on his face after two steps, finding out only then that someone had locked shackles around his ankles while he'd been looking at Paige. He looked at her again, still waiting for her to step in and play whatever card she'd been saving for him.

"You set this up!" Cole said once he realized that card wasn't coming. "What happens now? Huh?"

Catching up to him, she explained, "I didn't have a choice, Cole. We all got set up too well for me to do anything else. There's another one in town somewhere."

"Another what?"

"One like Hope. If things didn't turn out like this, more would have died. I'm sorry."

Cole was turned away from her and forced into the van. His stomach flipped and it became increasingly difficult to maintain his balance. Cars and vans filled the street beyond a perimeter the cops had set up. He didn't recognize all the letters painted on those vehicles, but they had to have represented most or all of the local news stations. In the time it took for him to figure out that much, lights from a dozen different cameras were pointed his way.

Muscles strained against the metal restraints as well as the hands that shoved Cole into the back of the van. His senses were overloaded with everything from camera lights and venomous words to the scents of recent gunfire and exhaust fumes from the vans that were about to take him into a cell or possibly a shallow grave on the way to the police station.

"She would have killed you, Cole," Paige shouted to him. "If it wasn't Hope, it would have been the other one. I couldn't let that happen to someone else that I . . ." She had trouble getting her next few words out but was also being jostled by the police officers taking over the scene, as well as the soldiers who'd been with her in that helicopter. When Cole was seated in the van and getting his shackles bolted through a steel ring between his feet, she spoke again. All he could hear was, "It was Tara! I won't let her—"

The helicopter's rotors powered up, washing out Paige's voice in an all-encompassing roar.

Cole could still taste oily blood in the back of his throat. When he moved his arms, he felt certain he could pull the chains apart in a few good tries and there was enough healing serum in his system to absorb some punishment from the cops along the way.

He could get out of that van if he wanted.

At that moment, knowing what Paige had done, he just didn't want to.

As the van doors slammed shut, scaling him in a steel box full of chains, shotguns, and an angry SWAT team mourning friends they thought he'd killed, Cole found solace in words from another man who'd become an enemy to his own people.

Is it too much to ask to receive a little gratitude? Jonah Lancroft had written in one of the journal entries that had stuck with Cole long after he'd read them. *I've purged villages of evil, only to be chased out by the same frightened simpletons who'd begged for help from a deity that in all likelihood doesn't exist. If God does exist, why wouldn't He be far from here, creating new miracles while his former ones eke out a life of their own? If there is a God, I believe we are not forgotten by Him. We are simply allowed to live on our own and enjoy the gifts we have been given. Why, then, must so many choose to be blind to the evils that so obviously exist and can be seen, felt, and heard every day and night?*

I have withdrawn into a life of quiet research, founding my reformatory as a place to keep monstrosities away from those they may harm. I have spent years studying ways to improve my fellow Skinners and give them a fighting chance against demons that have proven to be more resilient and adaptable than those who kid themselves into thinking they are the favored ones on this earth.

If we are made in God's image, then I do not want to pray. Those words would only be seen as weakness and turned against me, just as my pleas and confessions have been thrown into my face by the select few with whom I'd mistakenly aligned myself.

And still, because I am a Skinner and know of no other way, I continue to fight. Is it wrong for me to desire a word of thanks or gesture of gratitude? Is it wrong to want the solace given to any common soldier who bleeds for home and country?

I suppose it is too much to ask. And so, from this day hence, I will never ask again.

Cole set his jaw in a firm line, clenched his fists and allowed his strength to bleed into his grip upon nothing instead of using it to make a break for it. Freedom didn't do him any good if there was nowhere left to run.

Chapter Thirty-Five

Byers Peak, Colorado

Kawosa crouched at the edge of a sharp drop-off separating the narrow path behind him from the side of a mountain. His bony knees were splayed to either side, one of which poked out through a tear in his ragged pants. Narrow arms reached down between them and gripped the ground a few inches in front of his stubby toes. When a cold wind scratched along the Rockies, it set Kawosa's stringy black hair into motion without flushing cheeks that were more weathered than the mound of ancient stone. Denver was a glowing collection of light and movement sixty miles to the east, and Kawosa gazed at it as if tracing every last glimmer back to its source.

A burly figure bounded through the National Forest below, appearing between the pines and leaping over sections of ground that were too densely wooded to cross on foot. If the creature had been inclined to take a more deliberate pace, its black fur would have allowed it to blend in with its surroundings. As intolerant of the terrain as he was with most everything crawling on or beneath it, he shouldered past an old tree with enough force to knock a piece of its trunk away before launching himself into the air.

In a matter of minutes the Full Blood had emerged from the forest and was crawling up the side of the mountain.

Taking the narrow trail forced him to shift into the human body he'd all but cast aside over the last few days.

"Where are your Mongrel friends?" Kawosa asked.

"Having a word with the packs in Montana and Wyoming," Liam said in his thick, vaguely antiquated, cockney accent. "From there they'll head south into New Mexico and out into the desert. Plenty of lost souls out there."

"Do you think they will come around to our way of thinking?"

"After what we showed Max and Lyssa? They'd be insane to stay on their own."

One of Kawosa's eyebrows shifted upward so slightly that even a Full Blood's senses might have missed the gesture. "Perhaps I should have a word with them just to be certain."

Liam crouched so his legs could offer the rest of his body some protection against the wind's chill. "Like you had a word with Randolph?" When Kawosa glanced over, he added, "He was sticking real close to you until now. I assume you must have done something to escape from his watchful eye."

"He has business of his own."

"You're referring to the two Full Bloods that came over from across the pond?"

Smirking, Kawosa said, "He thinks there is only one new arrival."

"Sandoval?"

Kawosa nodded and shifted his gaze back to the city.

"That Spaniard always did carry a stronger scent than most. Randolph never met him, but how'd you get him to overlook Minh?" Liam drew his legs in a little tighter and passed his tongue over a dry bottom lip when he said, "She's not the sort any man would overlook. Even on four legs, she's a vision. Lyin' to humans is one thing. Lyin' to us is another."

"Perhaps the stench of this paved-over land had washed her from his memory. Or Randolph merely could have grown tired of our company."

Liam drew a breath and let it out as a huff of steam from

his nostrils. "I know the legends about you, Kawosa. Or Kt-seena or whatever the hell the humans call you. Older than the deepest dirt and teller of the very first lie. The Trick-ster Coyote that's been roaming the New World when there wasn't nothin' here but herds of buffalo and teepees."

"My, my. You are very knowledgeable."

"Why the hell do you think we busted you out of that dungeon?"

"There are more reasons than you know," Kawosa said.

As he stood up, Liam shifted into his hulking two-legged form. His feet scraped upon the narrow path but he hung onto the rock as though his paws had been nailed in place. Stooping down so his single eye level was with Kawosa's face, he snarled, "Randolph's head has always been full of smoke and foolish notions. He gets sentimental and thinks too much about the past. He's also restless. I know he wants to leave here, and I ain't of a mind to stop him. You got a job to do here, though, Coyote. Don't you forget that."

Despite the fact that the Full Blood loomed over him while casually stripping away layers of rock with sicklelike claws, Kawosa regarded him with the same amount of concern he might show to a posturing eight-year-old boy. "The Half Breeds are my children. Guiding them, shaping them, giving them a purpose is no chore."

"And the Mongrels?"

"They are a thorn in both our sides."

Only another Full Blood could have recognized the glimmer of a smirk that flicked across Liam's gaping, hellish mouth. "Speaking of thorns," he said with a simple nod toward a section of the city that was alive with circling helicopters and flashing red and blue lights.

Whether he noticed Liam's grin or not, Kawosa did nothing to hide his own. "The humans were a simple matter. I told the police their dead comrades were winning the fight against the Nymar and they believed. It has always been so. And no matter what the Skinners know, what they concoct, or what they do, they are humans as well. Playing with them has always been one of the greatest pleasures of my very long life."

"So, sitting cooped up in Lancroft's basement. That was a pleasure?"

When Kawosa sneered, it gave Liam a glimpse at a hatred that ran down to the bottom of a black, soulless pit. The Full Blood moved away and adjusted his grip upon the mountain accordingly.

"Lancroft was exceptional," Kawosa admitted. "He taught me the danger of my own arrogance. Although I would have enjoyed waiting for him to choke on his own confidence and wander close enough to the bars of that cell so I could tear his head from his shoulders, it was even sweeter to see him killed by the very Skinners he cherished so dearly. Now, with everything that has been set into motion, the fruit of Lancroft's efforts will unleash discord the likes of which I have only dreamed."

"Ohhhh yes," Liam sighed. "The times, they are a'changin'."

Chapter Thirty-Six

The Nymar had worked out several different escape routes from the cement building, but most of them were cut off by the police or were in the process of being severed. It had only been twenty minutes since the authorities took over the area, which was more than enough time for the vampires to gather in a parking lot within spitting distance of I-70 used by semitrailers and other large transport vehicles.

The van that rolled to a stop next to the others that had just arrived was still spattered with blood it had picked up from the loading dock where it was parked half an hour ago. Its driver's window came down so a woman bearing symmetrical black markings along both sides of her face could look out. "Where was she? You told me she was going to be there!"

Two Nymar, men in their early twenties, approached the van. Although they had markings of Shadow Spore that swelled in size as they left the pool of light cast from atop a nearby post, neither of them were anxious to get any closer to the Kintalaphi inside the van. "Hope told you she'd be there," the bigger of the two said. "All we knew was that Skinners were coming."

"Where's Hope?"

"Dead. I don't know if they were Skinners, but the ones who killed her used some kind of metal thing with chains that I ain't ever seen before."

"You watched her die?"

Both of the Nymar looked at each other and stepped away from the van. When the driver kicked the door open, she exploded from behind the wheel as if she'd been launched from an ejector seat. Black claws snaked out from her fingertips to sink into the bigger Nymar's chest like a set of fishing hooks. He didn't even have a chance to try and free himself before he was on his back.

"You watched the Skinners kill her and did nothing?" she hissed.

"That room was full of Skinners when Hope was killed. And I already told you, I don't know what the hell was used to kill her." He blinked, but had trouble opening his eyes again as the claws embedded in his flesh took their toll. "I didn't even know they could kill one like you."

"The purpose of this was to kill *them*."

When she pulled her claws out of him, the Nymar shot back with, "Then why'd you cut and run, Tara?"

Apart from longer hair, paler skin, a greater concentration of tendrils and hardened eyes, Tara looked much as she had when she'd been a student at the University of Illinois eleven years ago. "Hope told us to fall back and that's what we did," she replied. "Your orders were to find Paige and bring her to me."

Seeing the clueless expression on the other Nymar's face, Tara grabbed the front of his shirt along with several layers of skin beneath it. "The Skinner with the black hair and the wounded arm!"

"One of the chicks had a wounded leg."

"Not her!"

"Why don't you ask that shapeshifter? If there was anyone there that we missed, he probably would've smelled them."

"Are you talking about the shapeshifter that held the cops back?" Tara asked.

The Nymar on the floor nodded. "I saw him when I was

on my way out. He said he'd keep the cops busy so we could get away and that he'd be in touch. Said he had something important to talk about."

"So Paige was never there?"

"I . . . I don't . . ."

Another Nymar stepped forward when the one under Tara had become too flustered to talk. He was a smaller man, with a large grommet fitted into his right earlobe. "I think I know the one you mean," he said. "There was a Skinner talking to the one that got dragged away by the cops. She came in a helicopter. Dark hair, short, wearing some kind of body armor like a bulletproof vest. Her arm looked stiff and scarred."

"Where did she go?"

"I don't know. The cops were spreading out, searching the whole place and sending teams after the Skinners who got away."

"They got away?" Tara asked.

"When the cops were busy arresting the guy in the coat, I saw four or five of the Skinners run out the back door. Thought they were coming after us, but they scattered. One guy had a biker jacket on. He was picked up by some black dude in a run-down four-door. I lost track of the others when we came here."

Slapping the chest of the Nymar pinned beneath her, Tara asked, "Did you tell this one what you saw?"

"Started to, but he had to keep driving."

"You had one thing you *had to* do," Tara snapped. Before the Nymar beneath her could say a word in his defense, she tore into his throat with every fang she had. The wound was messy and uneven, so she dug the claws of her right hand in and pulled it open wide enough for her to bury her mouth in the gore. A few seconds later she stood up and let the body drop.

Another of the Shadow Spore who'd remained silent until now stepped forward. "We need to stay together, like Cobb said. We can't start infeeding just because things go a little wrong!"

"You're right," Tara said. "We knew tonight would be hard. How many cops did you kill?"

"All but the ones in the van. One of those bitches who came here with the Skinners cut them loose before we could do anything about it."

"So that means the other two are dead?"

All of the Shadow Spore around Tara nodded. The pierced Nymar said, "I did the ones in that back office myself, and we got plenty more of the ones that kicked in the front door."

"You used the Skinner weapon and left it where it could be found?"

"Oh yeah," he said while holding up his hands to display a palm covered in shredded flesh that wasn't healing. "Ripped the hell out of me, but it did an even better job on those cops."

Tara offered her hand to the Nymar below her. The bigger man took it and was all but thrown to his feet. The wound on his neck was no longer bleeding, but the light gray tint of the tendrils beneath his skin meant he'd lost an unhealthy amount of blood. Turning toward the van, she said, "All of you get out of Colorado. I don't care where you go, just hide and stay put until you hear from me. If I can't call you directly, I'll send word through the usual sites."

"What happens now?"

"Now, I call Cobb." Tara pulled the door shut and looked at each of the other Nymar in turn. Her skin was several shades lighter than it had been a few moments ago and her eyes burned with the intensity of someone who hadn't tasted a decent meal for years. Her muscles nearly twitched out of her skin as she faced front and turned the key in the van's ignition as though she meant to snap it off. "Things may happen quickly or we all may have to lay low and wait. The Skinners that haven't joined us will be primed for a fight. Be careful."

The big Nymar rubbed his torn throat, massaging the wound while holding it shut so his spore could knit the flesh back together. "Who's that Skinner bitch with the dark hair? Why was she so important?"

Letting out a deep breath, Tara closed her eyes until the markings on either side of her face stopped trembling. "She's an old friend that I haven't seen in a long time. Now that I've finally flushed her out, it won't be any trouble at all to catch her up on what she's missed over the last ten years. Did you stay out of any cops' sights tonight, Seth?"

One of the Shadow Spore who'd just arrived at the meeting replied, "None of them saw my face."

"Can you still call in any favors?"

"The vice guy I know in the Denver PD thinks I handed him the information leading to the cop killers they found tonight. He'll set me up with free doughnuts for years."

"Find out where they took the Skinners that were captured. As soon as you know where they're being held, get word to any of us that are locked up in the same place. If it's a prison with no Nymar inmates, seed some of them. The nastiest ones."

Seth nodded sharply and ran away. By the time he crossed beneath I-70, Tara was headed for the on-ramp and the others had dispersed to opposite ends of the city.

Epilogue

The Half Breeds had taken Randolph on a circular trail through Louisiana, Arkansas, and down into eastern Texas over the course of several days. Dawn was only a few hours away when the beasts pointed their noses toward Oklahoma and bolted in the straightest line they'd taken since Kawosa had first set them loose.

If Half Breeds were good for anything besides killing and eating, it was tracking. They could pick up a scent, follow it for hundreds of miles, rest for an entire day and pick it up again later. Randolph could do the same over a much wider expanse and without rest, but there was one scent his nose simply wouldn't allow him to catch. Once Kawosa had convinced the Half Breeds to forgo their natural tendency to either attack or avoid a Full Blood, the wretches had caught that scent for him.

It was a region of the country inhabited by creatures that thrived in harsh terrain and knew how to live without catching the eye of predators equipped to challenge them. Mongrels unassociated with any pack, savage felines that had completely abandoned their human form—even reptilian tribes that rarely stuck their leathery noses above the waters of their home swamps—were commonplace this close to the southern coastline. The humans didn't know much about them, but they didn't know much about anything. That's what made them such good company to the man that had taken the name Randolph Standing Bear almost two centuries ago. Even that was about to change.

The leeches had been entrenched for too long, and the Skinners had proven too weak or lazy to prevent it.

Mongrels were clawing their way into civilization from the ground up.

A few of the modified Half Breeds had already been discovered by Skinners, but the hunters would be too preoccupied to see through the deception Kawosa had put in place. They would think they'd killed a Full Blood or two, which should keep them chasing their tails for a while.

Liam's call to arms in Kansas City had been answered by not one, but two Full Bloods. When Randolph figured that out, it had been difficult to keep it from Kawosa long enough to strike out on his own. The First of the Deceivers was conceited enough to think anyone who knew his true nature would trust a word that came out of his mouth. To Randolph, the fact that Kawosa's brethren were converging on his territory only made his own task more important.

The moon hung midway in the sky and was nearly full. Every shapeshifter would feel its pull, but the reddish hue on its face meant tonight would be the night he would get what he came for. It wouldn't be a true Blood Moon, but the shadow passing over the lunar face was deep enough to sharpen the younger werewolves' yearning to shed their human skins. Randolph could only imagine the hell being endured by Mongrels that had survived Liam's attentions.

Both of the Half Breeds had already started cocking their heads and casting accusing looks up at the moon with glazed eyes. When they arrived at a run-down little house on the outskirts of the little town of Atoka, Randolph was certain Kawosa's wretches had done their job properly. If the old Coyote could be trusted that far, Randolph thought, perhaps he could be trusted with the other task that weighed heavily on his own mind. One thing at a time, however. This night's business was much more pressing.

The house was constructed of wood that could barely hold onto the nails that held it together. Warped walls leaned in on each other beneath a slanted roof that sagged in too many places. Chipped white paint flaked off every plank and hissed when the wind caught it just right. The sturdiest thing on the tiny patch of land was a brick chimney that stood tall and straight even as the rest of the house clung to it for support.

Randolph approached the house on all fours, creeping with his chest less than an inch off the ground. As he passed the Half Breeds, they snarled at him and bared their teeth. The Full Blood dismissed them with a growl that rumbled up from his chest and caused saliva to flow along teeth that had grown long enough to scrape against each other. Lowering their heads, the wretches scampered away.

Randolph circled the house, peering in through cracked panes of dusty glass held shut by latches that were only intact because there was nothing inside worth stealing. The Full Blood wasn't interested in theft, however. On this night, he wanted to watch and witness something that his kind rarely got to see.

The time was drawing closer.

The moon had reached its zenith, the reddish tint approaching its deepest hue.

Pushing past the dead bolt on the front door with a nudge of his head, Randolph padded through a sparsely furnished living room and down a short hallway leading to a pair of bedrooms. One was occupied by a solitary man sleeping soundly beneath a patchwork quilt. Randolph was sure not to let his eyes remain on him for too long. Even in their sleep, humans could sense when they were being watched by something as deadly as a full-blooded werewolf.

In the next room two twin beds were set up on either side of a cluttered space. The floor creaked beneath Randolph's weight as he stalked forward while shifting into something that spread his bulky mass out a bit more. The bed on his right was occupied by a girl in her late teens. On the left was a boy of approximately the same age. Both of them had dark hair that reflected the moon's rusty glow like an oiled raven's wing. Their skin was almost the same color as the rich clay found on a desert floor, and their wide, rounded features marked them as descendants of the only humans who had any right to challenge Randolph's claim to this land.

The boy shifted in a restless sleep, kicking at his covers and pounding his mattress with sweaty fists.

Randolph nodded and cursed silently at the fact that he still couldn't detect the scent belonging to the only one that interested him. This fault was by design, he knew. A natural way to prevent greedy Full Bloods from thinning out the small number of beings they might consider competition.

When the boy allowed his head to slump and his chest to resume its normal pace, the girl on the opposite side of the room sat bolt upright and sucked a haggard breath into a tightening throat.

She picked out the intruder immediately and stared at Randolph with wide, crystalline eyes. Before she could question his presence there, she grabbed her face, rolled out of bed and hit the floor on arms and legs that creaked and stretched with the first of what could be an eternity of transformations. Her back arched beneath a short nightgown decorated with faded yellow daisies, sprouting up like a ridge of stone pushed from previously unbroken soil. Claws tore through her fingers, and when she tried to scream, her voice was stifled by the agony of daggerlike fangs cutting through her gums.

The boy in the room stirred but was too frightened to move any more than that.

"When one falls, another shall rise," Randolph growled. "Hopefully you will serve us better than poor, misguided Henry."

The girl watched him intently, recognizing Randolph but unsure why. Shifting into a taller, unsteady two-legged form, she stretched her arms up to claw at the ceiling and let out a prolonged, wailing howl.

MARCUS PELEGRIMAS's
SKINNERS
HUMANKIND'S LAST DEFENSE AGAINST THE DARKNESS

BLOOD BLADE
978-0-06-146305-1

There is a world inhabited by supernatural creatures of the darkness—all manner of savage, impossible beasts that live for terror and slaughter and blood. They are all around us but you cannot see them, and for centuries a special breed of hunter called Skinners has kept the monsters at bay, preventing them from breaking through the increasingly fragile barriers protecting our mortal realm. But beware…for there are very few of them left.

HOWLING LEGION
978-0-06-146306-8

Cole was designing video games in Chicago when he learned the truth about the foul creatures of the night who lust for our blood. Now he's a Skinner, entrusted with keeping humankind safe. No one knows what's coming—but Cole and his seductive partner, Paige, will be the first to dive into the meat grinder.

TEETH OF BEASTS
978-0-06-146307-5

Cole and Paige race across the Midwest to uncover the shocking secret of the "Mud Flu." For a nightmare of destruction and blood sacrifice is looming—one born of an unholy meeting nearly two centuries ago—that will pit man against beast, and Skinner against Skinner.

Visit www.AuthorTracker.com for exclusive information on your favorite HarperCollins authors.

MP 0510

Available wherever books are sold or please call 1-800-331-3761 to order.